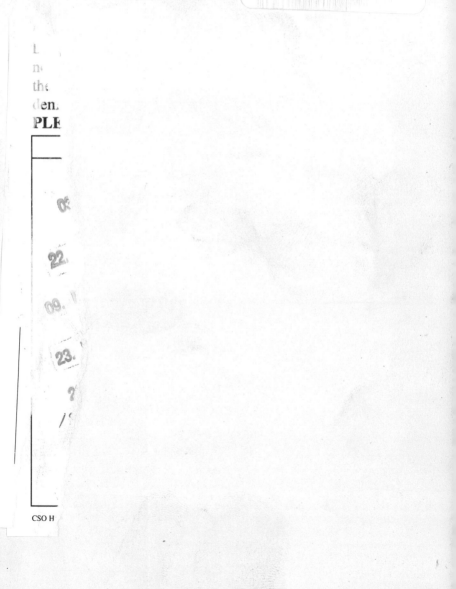

L
n
the
den
PLE

03

22.

09.

23.

CSO H

FINAL
DIVE

FINAL DIVE

Alexander Fullerton

LITTLE, BROWN AND COMPANY

A *Little, Brown* Book

First published in Great Britain in 1998
by Little, Brown and Company

A CIP catalogue record for this book
is available from the British Library.

ISBN 0 316 64467 6

Typeset in Palatino by
Palimpsest Book Production Limited,
Polmont, Stirlingshire
Printed and bound in Great Britain by
Creative Print and Design (Wales), Ebbw Vale.

Little, Brown and Company (UK)
Brettenham House
Lancaster Place
London WC2E 7EN

1

---◆◆◆◆---

He was on the ship's high, railed bow, watching the flying-fish and thinking about Lucy. Holding on hard – knees bent and feet spread, hands grasping the curve of guardrail for stability against the heavy, rhythmic pitching. Thinking of other things besides Lucy, but most of them linked back to her, and pervading it all was the fact he was distinctly nervous.

Didn't have to be, at all. Could have told them he'd changed his mind, or she'd dissuaded him. Re-hearing her voice as it had come to him over the radio-telephone last night: 'It's no way your job, Mark! For God's sake!'

The only reason it *was* his job was that he was making it so.

Just about full daylight now. Wind still cold and there'd been spray in it now and then. The fish broke out sporadically, sometimes just one or two and often with longish intervals between appearances, then a whole scattering over a wide area, breaking out of the dark-blue planes of the Atlantic swell in sudden flurries and trails of salt-white, gliding on spread pectoral fins over distances that varied from a few feet to a hundred yards or so. Not many stayed airborne that long: he'd pick one out with his eye and follow it, backing it as a potential champ then as often as not seeing it splash in, as a swell lifted close ahead of it and that was that. They swam only just below the surface, he'd been told; so you might guess there'd be no cognizance in their tiny brains of the huge mass of ocean under them. Ocean more than three miles deep, at this point. The wreck was lying at eighteen thousand four hundred feet, on a sloping bed of silt, in pitch darkness and an ambient pressure of four tons to the square inch.

Where he'd be, in a few hours' time.

When you let yourself think about it, bloody terrifying.

He'd answered Lucy, 'Want the stuff up, don't we?'

Avoiding the use of the word 'gold'. There was a lot of outside interest in what was going on here. Not that substituting the word 'stuff' for 'gold' would fool anyone who'd been tuned-in to that conversation; it was a manner of speech one had adopted in the course of recent weeks, the intention being to avoid words that might trigger special interest in an otherwise casual eavesdropper.

She'd demanded, 'Why *you*, Mark? Why are they letting you, what do you *know* about it?'

'Operating the grabs? More than anyone else here except Bairan. And Emile Huard. They taught me in Odessa – for amusement. Remember, I told you? And I'll have Huard to lean on – or breathing down my neck – won't be doing it alone, you know!'

'Doesn't the fact the other one's refusing to go down tell you anything at all?'

'Certainly. Tells me *I* have to.'

'But – Mark, you're home and dry, you don't *need*—'

'Nothing to do with it. Look, I can't talk on this thing, anyway. If you don't mind—'

'If the Ukrainian's so sure something's wrong – I mean, he wouldn't back out if he wasn't, would he?'

He hadn't argued with her, only stone-walled. He had a

whole set of reasons, but he wasn't sure they'd have made sense to her. There was an old man dead, for one thing. Fine old man, who'd deserved a *happy* ending. That on its own was reason enough to see this business through.

On the *Norsk Eventyrer's* stern deck, he saw, technicians, probably including the two pilots, Bairan and the Frenchman Huard, were still at work on the submersible. At any rate they still had the floodlights on, despite the arrival of daylight. They'd been at it all night, those two and the diving-control team's Norwegian engineers, checking every inch of the ultra-deep-dive vehicle's anatomy for faults or potential weaknesses of the kind that had shown up in earlier dives and were the reason the Ukrainian had refused to go down again. A factor of course was that he – Bairan – was on straight salary – and at that, paid in Odessa, in roubles, by the submersible's Ukrainian owners – so that failure or partial failure of the salvage operation needn't affect him at all; while Emile Huard was in for a small percentage of profits, stood to take home a fattish pay-packet if they got enough of the stuff up to *show* an adequate profit, but a lot less or even damn-all if they didn't. You could bet *he* wouldn't be backing out.

Mark was looking aft now – holding on one-handed – seeing the brilliance from those floods surrounding the after end of the ship like a giant halo in the salt-damp early morning air, and throwing a polish on the long blue-black ridges of the swell. How far might those ridges stretch, he wondered. The swell was an aftermath of a three-day storm they'd recently endured – diving had not been possible – and the disturbance would have covered a wide area. The southwestern extremities of those great undulations might, he guessed, be washing over the rocks outside Ponta Delgada in the Azores, five or six hundred miles away; and northeastward, pluming white against Cape Finisterre. According to last night's forecast it should have gone down a lot more than it had, by now. It wasn't going to be too easy or comfortable launching the submersible – not until you were well under, getting down towards the dark – but there was more bad weather predicted, the charter of this support ship had only about a week to run, and there was an opposition team, Franco-German, reportedly waiting in Brest, all geared-up and ready to horn in.

Knowing the wreck's precise location now, too. Not all the aircraft that had overflown or circled at low altitude in the past fortnight would have been Press.

He started aft. Using the support of the guardrail to start with, then making a quick dash to the fo'c'sl ladder and down its short slant to the welldeck. Realizing as he went that the ship's rise and fall was more or less vertical now, as the swells ran under her, and guessing at what he hadn't appreciated before, that she was back in station above the wreck, was therefore making no headway through the water, only her screws and side-thrusters holding her in place. They called it Dynamic Positioning. The ship's screws and thrusters would have been switched to computer-control, and the computer would be taking its orders from GPS, the satellite navigation system. Another black-magic angle was that on their first dive, about ten days ago, Bairan and Huard had put a sonar pinger on the wreck, and it would be showing up as a small bright triangle on one of the numerous monitors in the control van – back aft, from where the ship would be controlled now, watchkeepers on the bridge left there only as lookouts.

To him it *was* all black magic. He'd absorbed the bare facts of it – more or less – but couldn't have pretended to understand it. When any of the technicians or the ship's officers took explanations a step or two too far, he tended to glaze over and switch off. Apologizing for his dim wits . . . But that pinger on the wreck, for instance – 'pinger' incidentally being a colloquialism for 'transponder', he'd picked up a bit of the jargon – well, the submersible had its own sonar beacon, there was something called a transducer on this support ship – or under it – and when the peculiar little craft landed on the ocean floor – having free-fallen for three miles and then not knowing with any exactitude where it was – which on its own was a frightening thought, in conjunction with the fact that one would be inside it, for Christ's sake – its position would show up as a little 'o' on a screen in the control van, and they could guide it to the wreck, guide the 'o' to the triangle, by passing instructions to the pilots over their underwater telephone.

But for 'pilots', now, read 'pilot', singular – namely Emile Huard. Mark would be with him, but only to control the manipulators – the submersible's robot arms. Oleg Bairan had taught him how to do it – in Odessa – Bairan's Ukrainian boss having seen it as being in his own best interests to humour the potential customer.

He was making his way down the ship's port side, passing the control van – a rectangular steel compartment about twenty paces long by ten wide, welded or riveted or whatever to the ship's deck – then the workshop, under the raised helicopter pad – and arriving in the floodlights' glare further aft, where the submersible sat in its cradle like some outsize, futuristic-looking toy. Big toy bug, brightly coloured, red and yellow, with its name in yellow lettering on the red sail – Russian lettering, Cyrillic capitals КРАИ, Russian for 'crab'. So named on account of its claws, the Ukrainians in Odessa had explained – the three 'manipulators', or robot arms, two forward and another aft. No other submersible in existence, apparently, had more than two.

He stopped, holding on to a stanchion for support against the ship's motion, staring up at it. Inside the cradle – two big arms curving up each side, imprisoning it – the Crab stood on the wide skids on which it would glide over the soft sea-bed. The manipulator gear was between and above the

skids, close under the gleaming yellow hull. The forward
lower bulge – might be the bug's pot-belly – was part of
the pressure-tight sphere in which the two-man crew could
live and work. It was made of a titanium alloy encased in
fibreglass, had an internal diameter of just under seven
feet, access hatch at the top and two circular viewports –
windows – low down in this frontal bulge. When you were
using the rear manipulator, you could only see what you
were doing in a small TV monitor inside there; the camera
for it was set centrally in the after assembly of hydraulics
and geared to the movements of that manipulator. There
was a forward-facing camera too, for video recordings – as
had been made by Bairan and Huard of the earlier dives.
Propulsion – mainly over the sea-bed – was by electric
motors: one each side, each with its propeller enclosed in a
protective cage. And what might be seen as the Crab's shell
– the free-flood body-frame – protruded forward above the
crew-sphere's viewports with, centrally above them, the
sonar dome and suchlike, and a horizontal bar carrying
two big underwater lights. Like eyes, bulging malignantly,
and the manipulators below might be the bug's antennae,
folded under it.

Other external gear too. He couldn't have identified it all,
not by any means. But on top, what they called the 'sail'
– conning-tower, it might have been called in an earlier
age, but it served only as a weather-screening approach to
the crew-sphere's entry hatch – formed the highest part of
the scarlet upperworks. You got to it by means of a ladder
which was part of the cradle in which the Crab was held
secure against the ship's roll and pitch.

Overall length, nearly thirty feet. Sphere diameter six feet
ten inches. Height on its skids ten feet six inches. Weight in
air forty-five thousand pounds.

Emile Huard might have seen Mark through one of
the two viewports: he was climbing out of the sail now,

squeezing out past a Norwegian in engineer's white overalls and coming slowly down the ladder on this side.
Smallish, muscular, hatchet-faced, narrow-headed man of
about thirty, with dark hair already thinning and receding.
Dark-faced too: dark complexion made more so by the fact
he hadn't shaved for a day or so.

'Ça va, Emile?'

Mark's French wasn't bad – by English standards – but
it wasn't good, either. Vocabulary particularly limited.
Luckily Huard could get by in English – with roughly
the same limitations, and American-accented, but mostly
comprehensible. Good enough for communication over the
underwater telephone, anyway.

From three miles down, for Christ's sake.

The Frenchman nodded. 'Ça va – bien sûr. You – OK?'

'Fine.'

'Still you come?'

'Of course. Everything OK, is it?'

'Coming now, Oleg.' Glancing back over his shoulder to
where the Ukrainian was clambering down to join them.
Another black-haired man, but taller and scraggier. About
Mark's height – half an inch under six foot, say – and
long-faced, pale, moustached – whereas Mark was clean-
shaven and summer-tanned, his light-brown hair at this
time of year almost blond. Emile Huard looked more like
the sort of character you'd see vaulting on and off horses in
a circus ring. Except his legs might have been a bit short for
that. Mark grinned to himself, thinking: well, *small* horses;
and tried another question: 'You fit for this? Worked all
night?'

'Not for *all* night. Also sleep now, a little.' He spat over
the side, down-wind. 'Maybe two hour. Capitain say wait,
sea go down.'

'Right . . .'

He'd expected to be starting almost right away. The delay

came as a relief: to which he would not have admitted. But it made sense too, if the sea-state *was* improving. He called to Bairan as the Ukrainian stepped off the ladder, 'All right, Oleg?' Aiming to seem unruffled and non-censorious of him for letting them down. They did at least still have his technical assistance here on the surface. He asked him again, 'Crab OK?'

Turning, all three of them, to glance up at the alien creature crouching over them. There *was* a malevolent look about it – if you allowed your imagination that much rein. Better not to, he supposed. These professionals wouldn't anyway. To them it was only a work vehicle, part of their working lives. Even if it wasn't exactly routine to be going to such a depth. Bairan stroking his long jaw thoughtfully; turning away then, avoiding the others' eyes, patting his pockets in search of a cigarette. A glance at Mark – sidelong glance and then away again, looking down at the squashed pack of Marlboros as he found it and thumbed it open and on an afterthought offered one to Huard – not looking at him, only extending the pack in his direction. He knew Mark didn't smoke. He answered that question, finally: 'Most be OK.' Thin-voiced, with the cigarette between his lips; Mark interpreting 'most' as 'must' . . .

'*Most* be – uh?'

2

————⟫•◦•⟪————

Might snatch an hour's sleep himself, he thought – or try to. But on the way to his cabin he called in at the control van, to check that intentions – the delaying of the dive – were as Huard had said. It was so. Mark had been right, too, in his guess that they were in position above the wreck, holding themselves there. Klaus Eriksen, the *Norsk Eventyrer's* first officer, was in charge of the watch and at the driver's console in the van's port forward corner: he had a computer key-board, twin joysticks and a row of other knobs and switches; above him, a bank of monitor screens, digital read-outs with brilliant red and green figures rippling. Turning on his swivel-seat: bulky, curly-headed, in an open-necked denim shirt with his first officer's three stripes on the shoulders. The ship's officers were all specialists, experienced in the support of diving operations. Others on duty were – mentioning this one first because she was the most noticeable – Frieda Stenberg, assistant navigator, at the central plotting-table; Andy Baird, a gum-chewing Canadian/Scottish electronics genius, close to her with a mug of coffee or somesuch in his fist; a sonar man at those sonar monitors and the console below them – port side, halfway along; and one of the diving team's engineers, name of . . .

Jens something. Johannessen? He still didn't know all of them all that well. Some – like Eriksen – he'd made friends with, and they all spoke good English, but (a) he was still an outsider, neither seaman nor technician, and (b) at an earlier stage he'd made himself quite universally unpopular. He'd had no choice – and it was all over now – but a lot of them still viewed him with suspicion.

More so – now he'd volunteered for these next dives – or less?

Flickering monitors, hum of machines, clicking chatter of the sonar. Sonar didn't send out pings and get pinging echoes back the way it did in films of WWII, just sort of chuntered to itself and drew pictures. Literally drew pictures, on out-rolling sheets of computer print-out. At least it had when they'd been searching for the wreck: and it had drawn the wreck's picture when they'd found it. Now, there were changes and pauses in vibration as the screws and/or thrusters were started or stopped or their revs varied, all by computer. The satellite navigation system and the computer did the work, Eriksen only supervised. Sound-effects were muted; nobody wore headphones. Frieda Stenberg had smiled and wiggled her fingers at Mark, and the Canadian had raised his mug as if drinking his health; the girl had returned to her paperwork. This wasn't what you might call the action team; when the time came for the dive there'd be eight technicians on the job, in direct support of it, as well as either the *Eventyrer*'s captain – Skaug – or his chief officer – this Eriksen – and a couple of others handling the ship herself.

Mark pulled the door shut behind him: Eriksen called from the driver's seat, 'Can't sleep, Mark?'

'Thought we'd have been starting down about now. Emile Huard says not for an hour or two – is that right?'

'Best to wait a little for the weather. Swell's high for launching, you wouldn't like it much, I think. Soon, much better.'

'Right. Fine . . .'

'We have a thirty-six-hour fair-weather spell coming.'
Frieda told him this; she was moving from the L-shaped
plotting-table in the centre to her own nav. station on the
starboard side. There was another bank of monitors there,
most of them lit. Screens everywhere, some sections covering the whole bulkhead. What they called the flyer's console
was to this side of the nav. position – starboard side – and
sonar controls and monitors took up most of the port-side
space. Two more computers filled the port side after corner,
and ranged along the short after bulkhead were TV and
video monitors, the terminal of the underwater telephone,
other radio gear, and – well, God knew what else. The
only way Mark could have made himself useful in this
setup would have been making coffee or changing tapes
in the stereo.

Thinking now, though, of Frieda's promise of good
weather for only thirty-six hours. The earlier estimate
had been of minimally forty-eight hours. He mentioned
this to Eriksen, who agreed that any further worsening of
the outlook would certainly pose new problems. But as it
was, he pointed out, two dives of say ten or even twelve
hours would allow for an adequate rest and maintenance
period in between. It had been agreed that two ought to
finish the job off. But a dive to eighteen thousand feet could
hardly take less than ten hours. Getting down there took
three, coming back up another five, so a total of ten allowed
for only two hours actually at work.

Challenging Mark: 'Better be real smart with the manipulators, eh?'

As with many of them – as well as the Frenchman, Huard
– his English was American-accented. Mark shrugged. 'Pity
Bairan's arm couldn't have been twisted.'

'Twist it right off, had my way.' Shaking his head: with
one finger poised above the keyboard and his eyes on the

screen. The girl navigator asked Mark, 'Doesn't scare you, you're doing this?'

'Oh.' Turning, looking back at her through the flickering, multi-coloured light. She had a wide, pale face, close-cropped dark hair and rather small, round eyes. Also near-fluent English. He suggested, 'Could be advantages being pig-ignorant, Frieda.'

'I suppose.' A nod – taking it seriously. A lot of these people didn't laugh too easily, he'd noticed. She told him, 'And Huard's a good guy, knows what he's doing. Rely on him, eh?'

As one could not rely on Bairan, was the inference. They all felt badly about the Ukrainian.

That renewed clicking was from the sonar. As he'd been given to understand – or semi-understand – this ship's transducer as it were challenged the transponder that was on the wreck three miles down, and triggered that response, the transponder's own signature, self-identification. In very deep water the sound was magnified and fish could be near-deafened and seriously annoyed, porpoises and whales sometimes screaming protests while high-tailing it to more peaceful areas of ocean – so one of the sonar men had told him.

'Klaus—'

'Huh?' Eriksen kept his eyes on what he was doing: Mark asked him, 'Pete Lofthouse in the sack, I suppose – d'you know?'

'I think. Was here, was asking for you – half-hour ago, maybe. Been talking to Mr Kinsman – Kinsman joining us soon, he said, maybe before you start your dive.'

And Lucy would be with him. She'd flown out from London to Vigo, bringing Kinsman's young daughter to join Daddy on his yacht. It was from the yacht she'd called last night, having had the news from Kinsman about this dive, about Mark taking Bairan's place. Robert Kinsman was her boss. He owned an insurance company, newspapers – God knew what else – and had interests in Canada and Australia. *The* Robert Kinsman, head of the Kinsman Group: he'd financed all this.

He was Lucy's boss for sure. What else – well, that was speculative, had been painfully so for quite a while. And he had her with him on the yacht now.

With any luck, they'd be sick as dogs.

He asked Eriksen, 'Skipper doesn't intend waiting for them – does he?'

'Far as I know, waiting only for the weather.' The chief officer did a double-take: 'For *them*?'

'Kinsman and his PA. Miss Greenstreet. She'll be with him.'

He unlocked his cabin door, pushed in and hung the key on the hook inside. For as long as the charter ran this was Kinsman Group territory, entry forbidden to all others. In a small safe bolted to the deck in one corner he had copies of the charter agreements for both the *Norsk Eventyrer* and the Crab, and other papers such as employment contracts, a certain amount of currency – British, Norwegian, French, Spanish and Portuguese – allowing for unscheduled calls at any of those countries' ports – and other items, including the keys of the strong-room, in which just over three-quarters of a ton of gold so far reposed. When they'd sailed from Dundee the safe had been supposed also to have contained a note of the latitude and longitude of the wreck: in fact it hadn't, because Mark, who at the time had been the sole possessor of that vital information – which was the reason he was here at all – had preferred to have it in a less obvious place, a crumpled envelope containing a letter from Lucy when she'd been in Devon visiting her parents, and dating from a time when things between them had been good. Had been bloody marvellous, in fact. A time when his preoccupation

with her had made the fact that his business was going to
pot seem practically inconsequential.

Wrong word. For 'inconsequential' read 'bearable'. There'd
been a lot of sleepless nights.

Sleep, now. At least, get head down, rest. One or maybe
two hours, they'd said. A bit less, maybe, because they'd
wake him in time to have a few gulps of coffee and maybe
a sandwich before the dive. You didn't eat or drink more
than you needed before going down, since there were no
lavatorial facilities in the sphere other than a bottle and a
plastic bag. He sat down on the chair on the back of which
he'd slung his padded anorak, and pulled his yellow rubber
boots off. Change underpants now for thermal long-johns –
to save time when turning out. He'd sleep, or try to, in those
and a thermal vest, would then have only to pull on outer
clothing including two sweaters – two thin ones being better
than one thick one. So he'd been advised. And take a spare
one down loose. The free-fall descent to eighteen thousand
five hundred feet would take about three hours, and he'd
been warned that at that depth it would be very, very cold.

OK – take also the wool ski-hat. He'd brought it along
as protection against Atlantic *surface* weather. Not much
one could do about cold *feet*, unfortunately – the ailment
he was suffering from already. The one steadying thought
to which he was clinging was that although Bairan was
chickening-out, Huard, who was just about as experienced
and knowledgeable, wasn't. And *he* wasn't stupid.

Committed, anyway. Couldn't possibly back out now. In
any case one *needed* to go through with it. Not for financial
reasons either. That was what they'd all be assuming was
his motivation, but the great universal profit-motive didn't
actually come into it. Not now, anyway: as Lucy had mentioned last night, he'd *made* his million.

When he'd laid the gear out ready on the other bunk,
he'd used up about five minutes of snooze time. If there

was to be any. Brain rather too full of stuff, he suspected: and jittery, at that . . . He got up on the bunk – it was high, with drawers under it – swung his legs up, lay back, pulled the blanket over.

Didn't need it. Threw it off. Telling himself to think about Lucy. Not of the problems now, but of when it started.

When this treasure-hunt started?

No. First sight of Lucy: of Lucy as she had been. Maybe still was, and might be again. Maybe when you come out of this, if you give her time to come out of whatever had *her* locked in . . . Better chance of falling asleep on the happier memories, anyway. Clock back a year, therefore: year and a half, in fact, it was in that spring, had been a beautiful spring day and in the evening was turning cool under a still clear sky. He'd been in London for business meetings, and had gone to his club – the Lansdowne, in Fitzmaurice Place at the bottom of Berkeley Square – to pay his bill, collect his suitcase and then high-tail it to Victoria and the Brighton line; but having scribbled out a cheque at the reception desk he was on his way across the hall when the sight of her, that first sight ever, stopped him in his tracks.

Not easy to describe her. Medium-small, with a very eye-catching figure, hair such a dark brown that in some lights it looked more like black. Delicate bone-structure, creamy skin – which a few months later he was to discover tanned easily, almost instantly – and large blue eyes contrasting wonderfully with that hair. *Lovely* mouth. Words couldn't do her justice: maybe not even a camera could. Unless it was only some very special reaction that the sight of her elicited from *him*. That smile of hers, for instance: especially the quiet, inward one when she was thinking of love. But that evening, his first sight of her, the truth was that he hadn't exactly stopped in his tracks, only faltered in them: and maybe caught his breath. Like being shot: and she'd seen it.

Seen the same before, maybe? Recognized it?

She'd slowed, sort of hesitated, smiling at him. The first time he'd seen her smile. He'd muttered – in the British fashion, as if he'd somehow impeded her although he hadn't – 'Sorry . . .'

'What for?'

Nice laugh. They'd passed each other, but she'd stopped, turned to look back at him. She was wearing a short black dress that fitted her like an outer skin and left her arms and shoulders bare.

'Couldn't you stand it either?'

'I'm sorry?'

'Oh. I thought perhaps you'd been at the party upstairs.'

'Party?'

'Now *I'm* sorry. You weren't. It's the Under-35s do. Up there. I came down for a breather.'

'Bad as that, is it?'

'Not really. I was just sort of casing this joint. Not having been here before, and—'

'Regrettably I don't qualify for the Under-35s. But – look, the bar's just through there – if you're on your own, I don't suppose you'd save me from having to drink alone?'

'Why wouldn't I?'

'Well. That's – terrific.' Looking down at her, confirming to himself that this was probably the most attractive girl he'd ever met. In no disloyalty to the memory of Sally, his wife, who'd died several years earlier and whom he'd loved and cherished, as she had him: no disrespect to her, whom he still thought of in loving memory as enormously attractive, the plain fact was that this girl was absolutely stunning.

Indescribable.

'I'm Mark Jaeger.'

'Lucy Greenstreet.' They shook hands. Her hand felt very small in his: small-boned like the rest of her. She added, 'Before you ask – no, no relation to Sidney.'

The actor, she meant. He told her, 'I'm no connection of the knitwear lot, either. That's a smashing dress.'

'Thank you.'

'I suppose I mean it's great on you. Referring to its contents, in fact – I don't mean it that crudely, I mean it's—'

'Mr Jaeger, this is so sudden!'

'I mean the whole package, whole effect . . . What would you like?'

'Upstairs I had a vodka and tonic.'

'OK. Let's sit here? Not much room at the bar, now they've shortened it. Used to be all along that wall. D'you live in London? No – hang on, I'll get the drinks.'

She sat down laughing. Her eyes laughed, or seemed to: at least, they smiled before her lips did. He *thought* that was it . . . He brought the drinks back to the table, and she told him, 'Yes, I live in London, but I work in Brighton.'

Gazing at her: 'I don't believe it!'

'Don't tell me. Your great-grandmother used to live in Brighton.'

'No, she didn't. I *don't* believe it.'

'All right. Why not? Cheers.'

'Cheers. You aren't real, for one thing—'

'I am, I promise. What else?'

'I both live and work in Brighton.'

The smile again as she put her glass down. 'You just made that up.'

'No. Honestly. I have a flat at the seafront end of Brunswick Square and offices just off Church Street. Where's *your* place of work?'

'Montpelier Place? Between it and Western Road. I'm not sure *I* believe this, now.'

'What d'you do?'

'I'm a head-hunter. Come up and see my skulls some time. And you – offices off Church Street?'

'Estate agency – boring and depressed – but we've

recently moved into property development. Less boring, currently more frightening.'

'Do you manage it? Own it?'

'Sort of. Both. I'm a partner. Took it over, with some chums. Well – colleagues. Anyway—'

'Things are supposed to be picking up – aren't they? Depends who you talk to, I know, but—'

'It's a bad time to have picked, for the plans we had. Government policies – which perhaps one might have foreseen. But you're right, we'll get there . . .' He touched the wood of the table. 'And things *are* picking up – as of about ten minutes ago. Look – is someone waiting for you up there – some other juvenile?'

A nod: 'My flatmate and her boyfriend. I was at a loose end, she wanted me to come along. She's not a member, he is. He mentioned there's a swimming-pool – in the basement? I thought I'd take a look. That's—'

'Where you were going when I kidnapped you. I'll show you the pool – we can go out that way. How about telling them you've run into an old friend who's asked you out to supper?'

He left his suitcase in the porter's care, and after the guided tour took her around the corner to the Italian restaurant in Curzon Street, where they ordered melon with Parma ham, scallopini with spinach, and Chianti. She asked him even before the melon came, 'You don't qualify for the Under-35s, you said. Can't be by much?'

'Nasty question, that. I'm forty-two, coming up forty-three. Hardly dare ask how far behind that leaves you.'

'Not so *very* far.'

'Come on. You're – twenty-four, twenty-five?'

'Pushing twenty-eight.'

'Meaning you're twenty-seven. So I'm more than half your age again.'

'That's making it sound worse than it is. The age business bothers you, does it?'

'Over forty, and you're under thirty?'

'It's not going to spoil *my* appetite.'

'Good. Although I was thinking a bit farther ahead – *hoping* to see more of you than just this once.'

'Well – if we *were* to – and it's a nice idea – there's one much more important question, Mark.'

He nodded. 'The answer's no. I *was* – and now I'm not. She died – of cancer, five years ago. Her name was Sally. I have a son who's at prep school. Timothy – he's ten.'

'Christ.'

'Yes. Well . . .'

'I'm so sorry. Really, truly. It must have been – no, there aren't words, are there? How old was she?'

'Then, she was thirty. Yes, it was a nightmare. Over very quickly – the thing itself – a matter of days, really, nobody'd had any idea. Left one – stunned, almost literally. As well as – well, all the obvious . . . Anyway – that's what you were going to ask – right?'

A nod. 'How have you managed with Timothy?'

'Sally's mother takes him sometimes. Whenever she can, in fact. And I have a sister – married – who rallied round, and still does. They have two of their own, and he spends a lot of time with them. In Yorkshire. Also I have a fairly ancient uncle and aunt who have him – have *us*, as often as not – for short holidays et cetera. That's down in the New Forest – Hampshire.'

'Would he and I get on, d'you think?'

'I like that question.' He nodded. 'Yes, of course you will. That's a *great* question, Lucy . . . Answer *me* one – while we're at it?'

'As long as it's not incriminating.'

'Why were you on your own tonight? There *must* be boyfriends – I'd guess dozens?'

'There've been some. But one in particular rather took over, some while ago. Became the one and only, you might say. And now that's – at an end. Has been for some time.'

'Chucked the poor devil out, did you?'

'He went back to his wife. Accounts for the question I asked *you*, you see. I mean – never again.' Studying his face for the effect of that: then looking down at her hands folded on the table's edge. 'But there. Whole truth and nothing but. *Is* somewhat incriminating, I suppose.'

He didn't think he'd slept yet. Could have been part-dozing, part-dreaming, some of the time. He was resting, anyway. Remembering that night and the days and nights that had followed: and his own belief at the time that he was being cautious, cannily *not* rushing his fences. Although he had been, of course – as hard as she'd let him. And when he wasn't with her, thinking about her – day and night.

Since Sally's death there'd been a girl or two, but nothing serious, nothing that had meant anything beyond the moment. Lucy was – had been – something else entirely. And what got to him wasn't just her looks, shape. All right – *initially* it was: and the sexual attraction and tension certainly didn't fade, if anything had intensified. It was Lucy herself, then – who *happened* to be decorative and sexy enough to make even a plaster saint's toes curl.

At the Italian restaurant he'd suggested that after the meal he'd take her home to her flat in Bayswater. She'd mentioned earlier that the flatmate, known as Dizzie, wouldn't be back until the small hours, that she and her boyfriend had been planning on dinner and then a nightclub; and she'd added – this had been over coffee – 'I wouldn't have gone, even if you hadn't made your surprise appearance. I start early-ish in the mornings, I try to avoid late nights, during the week . . . You'll pick up your bag at the club, then drop me and go on to Victoria, will you?'

He shook his head. 'I think I'll drop you and then come back. Stay at the club, go down in the morning first thing.'

'What – about nine o'clock?'

'Something like that.'

'Nothing like being the boss, huh?'

He frowned. 'I work quite hard actually.'

'Oh, I'm sure. I didn't mean—'

'And this is a *very* special occasion.'

'It's a *lovely* occasion . . . Have you always been – I mean, always had this business in Brighton?'

'Lord, no. After school I went to agricultural college and then farming.'

'*Really?*'

'That surprise you?'

'Certainly never have guessed—'

'Long time ago now. Wasn't all bad – in some ways I loved it. The farm wasn't big enough, was the main thing, it wasn't viable. I couldn't afford help, and – well, minimal return for slave labour, really. I was damn lucky to be able to sell out when I did. As it happened my mother died about then – father had some while before that – so I'd inherited a few bob, which later on I put into the estate agency business. D'you *want* this boring story?'

'Yes, please.'

'Well, I just worked in it, to start with. The owner was the stepfather of a man I'd known at college, and eventually he and I and another guy took it over. The old boy wanted to retire, and – seemed a good bet at the time. And I wanted to marry Sally, which wouldn't have been possible, farming.'

'Why did you go for it in the first place?'

'Well – I'd still *like* to farm. On an entirely different basis, that's all.' He put his hand on hers again. 'You're beautiful, Lucy. Really sensationally beautiful.'

'Must be the Chianti. And since I do have to work in the morning – if you don't mind—'

'Of course not.' He'd caught their waiter's eye, signalled for the bill. Turning back to her . . . 'Sometimes I think the best things that happen are accidental, unexpected. Tonight's a prime example of it – for me, *the* prime example . . . You wouldn't like a liqueur?'

'Ugh. *Hate* liqueurs!'

'Talking about trains to Brighton, what time do *you* start?'

'Train just after eight. I'm at my computer by nine.'

'That how you head-hunt?'

'That and a telephone, yes. Mostly . . . Are you sure the club will have a room for you?'

He nodded. 'Place is half-empty.'

'Because – Mark – in case you had any other ideas about it, I won't be asking you into the flat when you drop me. Perhaps I needn't be saying this, but – just in case it *was* lurking in your mind . . .'

Looking into the blue eyes – which were quizzical, assessing his reaction. It was taking him a few seconds to get *some* sort of response together.

'You're very – forthright.'

'That a bad thing?'

'Oh – no, not in the least . . .'

It hadn't come as all that much of a disappointment either. He'd have expected her to hold him off to start with: in the long run it might have spoilt things if she hadn't. There'd have been a doubt that it meant anything much to her – any more than those others had to him. She made much the same observation herself, about three weeks later. They'd been out dining and dancing et cetera a dozen times by then; it was a Sunday morning, and she was sitting up in his bed in the flat in Brunswick Square. First morning together, first night they'd spent together: his general feeling was of having stumbled into paradise. She'd exclaimed, with an expansive wave of one hand, 'And a sea view too!'

'Nuts to sea views. Mine's *far* better.'

View of *her* – her naked upper body in silhouette against that brightness. Reaching to her: 'Most stupendous view ever. Or anywhere. You're *exquisite* – you know that?'

'I ought to, if I took notice of your blarney. You kept telling me last night.' Holding his wrist, smiling down at him. 'We're visiting Timothy today, remember?'

'Of course I remember. Lucy, I love you. I'd forgotten it was possible to feel like this – *be* like this—'

'Just as well I didn't let you in the flat that first night, isn't it?'

'Is it?'

'Wouldn't you have thought: oh, she does this with any-one?'

Exactly what he *would* have thought . . . He'd denied it flatly.

'No. I would not have. In any case we hardly knew each other, there was never any *question*—'

That gurgly laugh. 'Never entered your mind?'

'Well—'

'Entered mine, all right . . .'

About a month later she moved in with him, and the London flatmate found a replacement for her. She and Timothy got on well, seemed genuinely to like each other. Mark had been worried that the boy might have resented her, but they were careful not to present her as a substitute for his mother, and he made sure that he and Timothy spent no less time together than they had before.

It was fine. Everything was – except business – until she landed the job with Kinsman.

Wait. Clock back again, a little. He'd wanted her to marry him, and her answer had been yes, but not right away. She wanted to be certain it was what they both wanted and that formalizing the relationship wouldn't wreck it. It would be bad for Timothy, too, for his father to acquire a new wife who mightn't last. Marriage was pointless unless it was permanent: she wanted to be sure it would be.

He *was* sure. He could see her expression now as it had been when he'd been trying to convince her too. The way her eyes softened – the loving look, bedroom look with a curtain half-drawn to shut out the sun's dazzle on a summer afternoon: then the harder focus as she reverted to her defence of the *status quo*. They felt like this about each other now, but they couldn't be certain it would be the same in a couple of years' time. Look around you, see how often it goes like that. And all the perfectly happy *un*married couples . . . And listen – here's another thing . . .

His business: *it* was resisting all efforts to improve it, and there'd been a second débâcle on the property-development front. She'd criticized his own attitude to this, what she saw as his virtual acceptance of Messrs Swanton, Jaeger and Brooks perhaps never doing much more than tick over, yielding a modest return, however much effort he and his partners put into it.

She'd argued, 'It's a tough world, Mark, isn't it? Competition's ferocious whatever line you're in. To survive, it's no good just treading water, you've got to go out and *win*. Means being ruthless – single-minded, no holds barred. Obviously I'm not telling you anything you don't know already—'

'Teaching Grandpa to suck eggs.'

'*Down*, Grandpa . . . But – OK, you *know* it, but do you put it into practice? You see, in this job of mine – well, I'm dealing with all sorts, all the trades – or rackets – and mostly at quite a high level, and there *is* a lot of throat-cutting.'

'Which you'd like me to go in for – that it?'

For quite a while, as it happened, what had struck him most about the business scene was the prevailing atmosphere of greed; and the ethos that if you'd got it you were OK; if you hadn't you might as well piss off. The subject had come up more than once: this particular exchange, in fact, as

recorded in Mark's memory, might have been an amalgam
or example of several, from that period in their relationship.
Mark, for instance, challenging Lucy with 'Money's the one
and only yardstick – isn't it? And not only in business
– everyday life – everyone money-grubbing, demanding
"compensation" for practically everything that happens?'

'Hasn't it always been like that?'

'Money's always been important, but I'd say it used not to be
everything. Now, a man can be a total shit but if he's somehow
got rich he's OK, you can respect him. Right? No –' holding
up a hand to ward off an interruption – 'this is *not* sour grapes
because SJ and B aren't exactly coining it at the moment. I don't
think that's got anything to do with it. The answer to *that*, I
think, is I'm simply not a very good businessman.'

'Perhaps you're too "nice". Could be half the problem.
What about your partners, anyway?'

'Tony Brooks is the only one who pulls his weight.'

'So get rid of Swanton.'

'How?'

'Oh, Christ . . .' Both hands to her head, and wide-eyed as
if he was driving her frantic. '*Buy* him out. Try your bank—'

'I'm in hock enough already. Believe me . . .'

He'd put every penny he'd been able to scrape up into
the takeover of the business. OK, so the business *was* ticking
over, and he could reasonably and legitimately take enough
out of it to live on in reasonable comfort, but he had no
reserves whatever. Timothy's school fees came out of that
income, too.

Lucy had asked him, 'This flat?'

'Hefty mortgage on it.'

She rode that one. Nodding slowly, as if thinking to
herself: *Might have known* . . . Then: 'So what it comes down
to is that SJ and B is the only card in your hand. You've
got to make it work. No reason you shouldn't, either. It's
potentially a money-making vehicle, like any other. You've

got to become less decent, Mark, more ruthless, go for the chances when you see them, not let anything else get in the way. Whether or not you want to make a lot of money – which you *do*, whatever you say, *everybody* does. Includes me, incidentally!'

That was how she saw it – a philosophy perhaps dinned into her by the management consultants who employed her. And it came into the marriage plans. The deal they settled on – provisionally, subject to both of them feeling the same way when the time came – this incidentally being *her* reservation, he'd had no doubt at all – was that they'd aim to do it before her thirtieth birthday; this gave them two years, by which time by hook or by crook he'd have the business up and running and – touch wood again – have bought out the useless partner. She wouldn't necessarily give up her job then, but if it all came off as planned she'd have the option of doing so, then might either join him in the by then thriving property company, or they'd move from the flat to a house and start a family.

'Or both.'

'No babies before that, though.'

'Please God, no!'

'*I'm* not leaving it to God . . .'

Six months later she told him, over supper at Wheeler's, 'Going up to Town tomorrow, Mark.'

'Oh?'

'Interview.'

'Client company, or another scalp?'

'Neither. Interview for a job.'

'A job for *you*, you mean? But you've got one!' He'd chuckled slightly: not taking this seriously, yet. 'A damn good one, and you're brilliant at it!'

'This'd pay twice as much, and the scope's – unlimited. At least – from as much as they've told me so far – it's staggering.'

'Who are "they"?'

'The Kinsman Group. Actually –' she'd crossed her fingers – 'Robert Kinsman himself. Haven't met him yet, I've been working through lesser fry. Didn't dare tell you before because – well, tempting Fate, never thought I'd get this far.' Shrugging, with a short laugh: 'The head-hunter got head-hunted, would you believe it?'

'If you get it, you'll be working in London?'

'Afraid so. But I lived there and worked here, didn't I. I can just as easily live here and work there. OK?'

He gulped some wine, shook his head. With – for the moment – nothing to say.

'Mark – there's nothing definite about it.' That resolute look – holding his own startled, don't-want-to-believe-this gaze. She'd have known he'd hate it. 'I'm only telling you because – well, if by some miracle it *did* come up—'

'Yes. Where would it leave *us*? I admit, I hadn't thought of you – moving away.'

'I *wouldn't* be. Just moving my *job*, for God's sake.' The blue eyes shifted away momentarily. A small shrug: 'All right, we'd see less of each other, obviously—'

'What would the job be?'

She took a swallow, put the glass down, touched the napkin to her lips.

'Robert Kinsman's personal assistant.' She went on quickly, 'Well, I *won't* get it. They'll have seen maybe a hundred and there'll be a short-list of – a short-list, anyway. Bound to be high-powered competition. Probably some who are in that sort of work already. I know how these people operate – I've sent my own candidates to them, several times.'

'But you haven't met *him* yet, you say.'

'Not yet. Tomorrow.' She reached for his hand across the table: it was a movement as quick as reaching for a lifeline. 'Mark, darling – wish me luck?'

3

She got the job, of course. As he'd guessed she would. He'd realized in the minute she'd told him about it over their Dover soles that if she hadn't been fairly sure of getting it she wouldn't have mentioned it at all. Why break bad news before it's a certainty?

She'd have known *he'd* see it as bad news. But grabbing the chance when it had been offered – as she herself had propounded her career philosophy to him, he remembered – 'To survive it's no good playing nice-guy and may the best man win, *you've* got to go out and win!' All that stuff – wherever she'd got it from. And if she'd foreseen the extent to which the move might disrupt their relationship – no 'if' about it, she would have – well, she'd have seen the risks and accepted them, no doubt felt confident that she could handle it.

Whether he could have stopped her – if he'd made a big issue of it . . . He rolled over on the bunk, deciding for the umpteenth time that he could not have. Because (a) it was what she'd wanted to do, (b) she wasn't a girl to be easily pushed off-course, (c) to have tried to might have been *more* disruptive, in the long run, and (d) in his own business situation he'd hardly been in a position to begrudge her what she regarded as a startling success. And later on he'd effectively jumped on the same wagon himself, by using her to approach Kinsman for financial backing for this treasure-hunt: even though it had been her suggestion and to start with he'd been dead against it.

Lucy's mouth and eyes and scent. In fading summer-evening light her voice a murmur, breath warm on his chest. 'Seriously, Mark. Why not at least talk to him about it?'

'Why are you so keen I should?'

'Because it might answer your problem, of course! Why else?'

Eyes shut: telling her in his mind but not uttering any of it, *Because I still think you're screwing the bastard* . . .

They'd rowed on that very subject earlier in the afternoon, and resolved it – or rather left it *un*resolved – by tearing their clothes off as if they'd been on fire and falling into bed. In his own case because he was in love with her, *wanted* to believe he was wrong, and in hers because—

Well. How it had been, that was all. How *they'd* been, together.

A double knock on the cabin door broke into growing drowsiness. In the same moment he realized that the ship's motion seemed easier than it had been. The swell might have subsided, he guessed. At least to some extent.

'Yup?'

Must have slept, he thought. Blinking as the light came on.

'Sorry to bust in, Mark.'

Pete Lofthouse. Pale, with a ginger crewcut, and wearing the white submarine sweater and denim trousers he seemed more or less to live in. He'd been sonar officer in a nuke, at one time, and since leaving the Navy had become a self-employed marine surveyor. Lucy had head-hunted him, on Kinsman's instructions – somewhat triumphantly, as he even had a smattering of Norwegian, the result of having worked with them on oilfield business. Effectively, he and Arne Skaug, the *Eventyrer*'s captain, were directing the salvage operation as a whole, while Carl Qvist, diving superintendent, controlled the dives, launchings and recoveries.

Lofthouse pushed the door shut. 'Aiming to launch you in about half an hour, Mark. Fit for it, are you?'

'Better be, hadn't I?'

'Still happy to be volunteering?'

Sitting up, in his vest and long-johns, and feeling his unshaven jawline. Wondering – not for the first time – whether he wasn't being bloody daft. He yawned. 'Unless Bairan's changed his mind?'

'That arsehole.' A shrug. 'Fat chance . . . You – er – spoke to Lucy Greenstreet, did you?' Mark nodded: Lucy had made her call last night after Lofthouse had reported to Kinsman – as he'd been bound to do. Kinsman was after all his employer. 'So you know she's dead against you doing this. Whereas the boss—'

'Wants his gold. Naturally enough.'

'*I'd* do it – if I had the least idea—'

'That's rather the point, isn't it. Ridiculous as it may seem.'

The submariner nodded. It *was* ridiculous. A ship full of seamen and technicians, and the only man capable of operating the Crab's claws an estate agent from Brighton, Sussex. He said, 'Should have waited for the back-up team, shouldn't we. My fault, I suppose. If I'd insisted—'

'The boss, as you call him, would have over-ruled you. Anyway, it's going to work out. Bairan may be technically OK but in other respects he's peasant-like, I'd say just plain superstitious. Could be the start and finish of his problem?'

'Well – *could* be . . .' Lofthouse looked and sounded

surprised: then pleased. *'Yes* . . . Explain why he's not
explaining anything – wouldn't it? Simply because he *can't*?
Hell, why didn't *I* see that?'

'Don't know your Ukrainians well enough, perhaps.'

'Maybe I don't. But if that's all – well, feel a lot easier,
can't we . . . Look, are you going to have some breakfast?'

'Cup of coffee, perhaps, piece of toast. I'm – er – advised
it's best to go easy.'

Because of the potential embarrassment of the bottle and
the plastic bag. A fleeting thought, trifling in comparison
with what was really filling his mind now – the three-hour
descent, like space-travel in reverse, killing pressure in
place of killing vacuum, black darkness instead of starlight,
moonlight, earthlight: and Bairan, the one who knew it all,
who'd been in and around the Crab throughout its refit and
knew it inside-out, declining to take part.

Comforting, therefore, to write it off as superstition.

Lofthouse had obviously found comfort in it. So *he'd* been
more worried than he'd allowed to show. Despite all the
reassurances he'd been offering about everything having
been checked over and put right, all systems 'go' now . . .

He said – on his way out, as Mark slid down from the
bunk – 'See you in the saloon. Ten minutes? Boss'll be on
his way soon. La Greenstreet too, eh?'

He didn't know about Mark's relationship with Lucy. As
far as Mark knew, he didn't. In fact, if he hadn't known of it
before they'd left England, there was no way he could have.
Mark asked him: 'The yacht with us now, is it?'

'Five or six miles off. Won't want to get their bums wet,
they'll transfer by chopper.'

Getting dressed – no point shaving – he found himself
thinking of young Timothy, who was in Yorkshire with his
cousins. Might give him a call tomorrow night, he thought
– after the second dive. There were to be two, each of about

ten hours' duration. Ring Timothy when it was all over and he didn't have to pretend he was on a cruising jaunt with Lucy and her boss. For as long as possible they'd tried to keep this business secret.

It was Mark's uncle Jack who'd set this whole business going, with a telephone call to the Brighton flat on a Saturday morning when Lucy had happened to be there. Captain Jack Jaeger, DSO, DSC, RN (Retired), was in his eighties and lived in Hampshire with his wife Edith, who was suffering from the early symptoms of Alzheimer's disease – confusion and loss of memory. Mark was well aware his uncle worried, fearing for the future and daunted by the costs of full-time care. Jack himself had respiratory problems and was lame as the result of a hip-replacement operation that had gone wrong; his concern was all for Edith, since she was virtually certain to outlive him and couldn't be expected to manage on her own.

By this time, the weekend when he telephoned, Lucy had been working for Robert Kinsman for six months, and Mark had been seeing even less of her than he'd expected. She worked long and unpredictable hours with Kinsman, working late in the evenings so often that it was easier to stay in London, and as Dizzie's new flatmate hadn't lasted, she'd re-installed herself there, in Battersea. On the salary Kinsman was paying she could easily afford to pay her full share of the rent even when – as at first – she was only making use of the flat two or three nights a week. Now, she was up there five nights a week and not infrequently at weekends too.

One notable weekend, though, she hadn't been there when she should have been. Mark had gone up to surprise *her* with a visit, as a change from trying to get her down to Brighton. Kinsman had been on one of his trips to the USA, she'd explained, and an Australian entrepreneur and his wife had been arriving by Qantas that Saturday; Kinsman had phoned asking her to meet them at Heathrow, take them to their hotel and give them any other help they needed. He'd asked Lucy herself to do it – 'not one of the office boys' – because these were what he called 'special' people and he wanted them to know that he regarded them as such, although unfortunately there was no way he could get back until early the following week, et cetera . . .

Whatever the Qantas arrival time had been that afternoon, she'd expected to get back to Battersea by about eight in the evening, when she'd said she'd give him a ring, and he'd decided on impulse to be there instead and take her out for supper. Surprise, surprise – however tired she might be. It was another gambit in his current effort to keep things going – and not the way it was beginning to seem they *might* be going.

At the flat, Dizzie had opened the door to him. It was about seven – autumn, already dark, with a wintry chill in the air outside. Inside, Dizzie was in a thin house-coat with all that streaky-blonde hair loose on her shoulders.

'Mark! *What* a surprise! Come on in . . .'

She'd noticed his overnight bag then. As well as a toothbrush and shaver he had a couple of bottles of champagne in it – two rather than just one, as he'd known Dizzie might have been here, perhaps a boyfriend too.

'Lucy not back yet?'

'Back?'

'She was meeting some Australians, wasn't she?'

'Yesterday, that was. She took off this morning quite early.'

Untidy sitting-room: coming from outside, it seemed rather over-warm. Hair-dryer on the sofa. Hence the warmth, he supposed – or some of it. Dizzie's hands smoothing the house-coat over her hips. It was ivory with green dragons on it. She was decidedly curvaceous.

'You thought the Australians were *today*?'

'Thought I'd surprise her – take her out somewhere. You say she – took off?'

'Well – *rushed* off . . . Mark, your coat—'

'Yes. Thanks.' He'd put the bag down, and it clinked. Pulling his coat off then, dropping it across a chair. 'Rushed off where, Dizzie?'

'I – honestly don't know . . .'

'Kinsman's in the States – right?'

'He was.' Hand to her mouth again. 'He was getting back this morning. Why Lucy had to meet the Aussies yesterday. I *think* – he'd have gone straight to the Savoy to pick them up – the Aussies – and take them down to Wiltshire with him. So it's *possible*—'

'She's gone there too?'

'It's – possible. I don't know, Mark. Mind you, Bob does have a housekeeper – but I suppose with VIP guests to entertain—'

'How d'you know he has a housekeeper?'

'Well – from Lucy!'

'Often been down there, has she?'

'I suppose – I don't *know*, but—'

'Dizzie, you *would* know. Hell, living with her – and neither of you into vows of silence exactly?'

A laugh: eyes on his. She stretched, and a dragon squirmed across her breasts. She had nothing under the house-coat, he'd already guessed. Well – already noticed. Trying not to notice too obviously, in fact: but noticing too that Dizzie was loving it. Smiling: 'I'm being interrogated, aren't I. What comes next – third degree?'

'I take it you're saying yes, she's often in Wiltshire.'

'Darling – a PA *would* be, on occasion. Isn't social life often a part of business – and vice versa?'

'Especially since his wife's buzzed off—'

'Oh, I wouldn't know about that—'

'– and he'd be lacking a hostess?'

'Perhaps. But honestly, I don't – I mean, one doesn't actually discuss—'

'That amazes me!'

'Anyway.' Body-movement. 'She'd have to be crazy.'

'I take *that* as a "yes", finally – Wiltshire's where she is?'

'You might take it as a compliment . . . By the way – changing the subject *slightly* – did I hear bottles rattling, in that portmanteau?'

'Yes.' Glancing down at it. 'You did. Although there's a damp towel in there, so you shouldn't have. They were cold when I left Brighton, anyway.' Looking up again: into wide hazel eyes holding his at point-blank range. *Everything* at close range and somehow edging closer. Thoughts meanwhile on such lines as 'sauce for the gander' and 'cut your losses': inspired less by logic than by anger – as well of course as by Dizzie's manner and proximity. He suggested, 'How about we open one, stick the other in the cooler?'

Right from the start, Lucy had been tremendously impressed by Kinsman. The tycoon was younger than Mark – thirty-eight now, only ten years older than she was. She'd come back from her interview with him bubbling with excitement.

'He started it all from scratch, you know. Hadn't a bean. That word "dynamic" – he really *is*.'

And since then he'd separated from his wife. Quite a while ago now; the tabloids had splashed the news on their front pages only a few weeks after Lucy had started working for him. Amanda, Mark's secretary in the Brighton office, had brought the *Mail* in with her that morning when she'd come through to take letters, and without comment put it in front of him on his desk. There'd been a photograph of Kinsman with his boyish grin and slightly hooded eyes and an arm round the blonde and glamorous Paula, both of them in skiing gear; the picture had been taken in Gstaad the previous winter, linked then to a report of his having taken over a group of periodicals in Australia. This time the caption had been BOB AND PAULA SPLIT.

Mark had shrugged, managed not to show much interest. 'So it's public now.'

Amanda had looked disappointed. 'You knew . . .'

She was a nice girl, and very efficient, had become to all intents and purposes his office manager. Overweight, unfortunately – not getting any smaller either, and with a penchant for inappropriately short skirts and those ghastly leggings.

After that weekend – 'the Australian weekend' as Mark had it labelled in his memory – Lucy had telephoned him at his office, Amanda putting the call through, telling him, 'It's Lucy, Mark – I mean, Miss Greenstreet?'

He'd picked it up. 'Hi.'

'*Quick* call, Mark. Just to say I'm sorry I wasn't there – when you went to all that trouble. The Australians came in a day early – I hadn't thought of telling you, it didn't seem to make all that much difference – well, wouldn't have – and you see, Bob had another meeting coming up – well, *today* – so I had to get them from their hotel and drive them down that night—'

'I thought it was Sunday they were going down.'

'You had a great time with Dizzie, anyway.'

'Well – we drank the bubbly I'd brought for *us*—'

'And?'

'And I took her out to supper. Chinese, actually.'

'*And?*'

'And that was that. Why, what—'

'Dizzie isn't a great one for not making the most of her little triumphs, Mark.'

'I dare say not. Anyway—'

'Quite. Anyway.'

'Will I see you this coming weekend?'

As far as he remembered, neither of them had ever mentioned the 'Australian' weekend again. 'Australian', or 'Dizzie' weekend: 'Australian' was safer. He'd stayed clear of the pad in Battersea since then – for one reason and another, and despite a few calls from Dizzie – and Lucy came down to Brighton on average about one weekend in three. And she was there – unexpectedly, a surprise visit, much as his would have been to her that other time – on the morning when his uncle telephoned. Three months ago now, roughly. She'd come down on the Friday evening and was going to stay until Sunday night – which was marvellous. One had to keep Kinsman out of one's thoughts, that was all. When the phone rang, not long after breakfast on the Saturday, she was in a navy silk wrap with her legs up on the sofa and a magazine in her lap; she didn't look up as he crossed the room to answer it. He was hoping it wouldn't be Amanda: he'd told her he wouldn't be coming in, that she should cope with any emergencies herself.

'Hello?'

Uncle Jack. Mark was extremely fond of the old boy, who'd always treated him as much like a son as a nephew. He and Edith had had two of their own – twin boys, who'd died in infancy. Whether it had been on medical advice or as a result of Edith's traumatic reaction – or both – one didn't know, but there'd been no more children.

'Good to hear from you, Uncle. How are you both?'

Listening. Frowning slightly, then. Half-turning to look at Lucy: looking worried.

'If I came down for an evening during the week, say—'

Listening again. Then a shrug. 'All right . . . Well, I don't know – yes, she's here, but whether she'll come—'

Lucy said quietly, 'No, she won't.'

'She's got a lot on, this weekend. Oh – well, *yes*, of course, but—'

She'd muttered, 'Really, it's the bloody limit!'

'– I could get back here this evening, then . . . What?'

A longer pause. Eyes on Lucy. Cutting in, then: 'Look, Uncle, I honestly don't think I can. What if—'

She could hear the old man's voice grinding on. Neither he nor Edith was exactly mad about her, she realized. She'd been there twice for meals but hadn't ever been asked to stay the night or for a weekend when Mark and Timothy went down.

Mark said, 'All right. I'll be there between six and seven, stay the night and leave after breakfast – that all right?'

Lucy had tossed her magazine away: glaring at him as he hung up. 'Bang goes our weekend. You fuss when I *can't* get down—'

'I'm sorry. Truly. But there's something he's het-up about – no idea what, he said he couldn't discuss it on the telephone . . . Hell, he's eighty-seven, semi-crippled, poor old bugger . . .'

Jack Jaeger had shrunk, with age, was quite a small man now, but no-one could have failed to see the family resemblance. The same short, strong jawline and blunt nose – what Lucy had referred to as Mark's 'bruiser's' face, which he'd pointed out only showed how misleading appearances could be. There were other similarities too – in their manner of speech at times, and certain mannerisms. Mark had often been told, in days gone by, that he was more like his uncle than his father. Although they'd been very close – father and uncle – all their lives.

Aunt Edith by comparison was quite tall, slim and still straight-backed. Still in a faded way quite pretty. Very English colouring: blue eyes, floppy grey hair that still had darkish streaks in it.

Forty years ago, when Mark had been a babe-in-arms, Edith had been a beauty. There were photographs around to prove it.

'What a pity you couldn't bring Sally with you, Mark.'

He couldn't have agreed more. He nodded. 'Rotten shame.'

Sally had been dead for the past six years, but Aunt E. didn't always remember it, although she *knew* it perfectly well. Her lapses of memory seemed to be concentrated in particular areas, and that was one of them. She and Jack had adored Sally, and it was evident, though never stated, that in their estimation Lucy didn't come up to scratch. In fact the old boy had murmured to him once, '*Awfully* pretty. Clever too – isn't she? But you know, lad –' shake of the thin white tonsure – 'it's a stayer you want. Sally was a stayer – eh?'

'Wasn't she, just.'

He'd defended Lucy, of course, pointing out that the comparison wasn't fair, considering how well they'd known Sally and how little they knew Lucy: and that if he had anything to do with it, Lucy was going to be a stayer too.

'We'll go outside.' Edith had gone off to prepare vegetables. 'Glorious evening – talk out there, eh?'

'Fine. I've been wondering what this is all about.'

'Bet you have. But you'll understand my – reserve, over the telephone, when you do hear it.' He bawled in the direction of the kitchen. 'Edith – we'll be out by the pond!'

'Try not to fall in!'

'What she *always* tells me . . . Want to top up that whisky first?'

'Well—'

'Get me a refill too. You know where everything is. I'll see you out there.'

There was a timber seat under a big willow on the far

side of the pond, which had had ducks on it once – until
foxes had got them – and was said to have fish in it now,
if herons hadn't got *them*. The old boy had limped out and
settled himself down by the time Mark joined him, handing
him his gin and water and taking a sip of his own Scotch as
he sat down beside him.

'What a smashing place this is.'

'Should never have given up smoking, though. A pipe's
the only sure way to keep these damn midges off.'

The cottage stood end-on, up a grass slope with stone
flags in it as stepping-stones; it was roughish grass because
he didn't cut it more often than he had to. He still insisted
on doing it all himself, despite the hip problem. Sniffing at
his drink: 'Put a great whack of gin in this, didn't you?'

'I'll get some water.'

'No – don't bother.' He'd tasted it. 'Not all that lethal.
Fault on the right side, anyway. Now here we go. D'you
remember me telling you – donkey's years ago, probably
– that I once sank a Japanese submarine?'

'Got your DSO for it, didn't you?'

'Yes. That's so.' A sidelong glance. 'You're now saying
to yourself, "My God, the old bugger's dragged me all the
way down here just to shoot *that* old line" – eh?'

'Not at all. I'm enjoying these surroundings and your
company. Also agog to hear whatever this is.'

'But you're not expecting to remain agog for long, I dare
say.' A shrug. 'Why should you – suddenly now, out of the
blue. But – you'll realize, presently . . .'

Realize what, Mark wondered? It had tailed off, that
little speech. His uncle was sitting back with the gammy
leg stuck out in front of him, slapping at midges with his
free hand and watching what might either have been fish
rising or air-bubbles surfacing from the mud.

'I'd better start by filling in a little potted history, Mark.
Subject – German blockade-running during '39–45. There

were certain raw materials they could only get from the Far East – materials essential to their war production and home consumption – and initially they used surface blockade-runners, fast merchantmen bringing this stuff from Japan, Singapore, and such places, detouring around danger-spots – or aiming to – and docking in the Biscay ports – *when* they got through – with cargoes of tin, wolfram ores, molybdenum, rubber and various odd things such as quinine, opium – even bismuth I saw listed. I've been into this, you see, researched it – well, a few years ago.'

'Researched it where?'

'Public Record Office, for one source. Remember a chum of mine by name of Donald Macintyre?'

'No.'

'Three DSOs, all for sinking U-boats, and he wrote several books of naval history. Worked in Naval Historical Branch – after he retired, of course. He helped me a great deal. Well, it fascinated me, of course, and it was very much his line of country. Very nice fellow, and a good friend.'

'I do remember now. You gave me one of his books to read once.'

'Dare say I would have. Anyway – the surface blockade-runners took a hammering. The German Ministry of Food and Economics demanded an annual inflow of several hundred thousand tons of these materials, but they never got more than a quarter of their needs. I think I'm right in saying that in the course of 1943 out of thirty-five ships that sailed from East Asia, only fifteen or sixteen reached Europe. And in the winter of '43–44, out of five fast ships, *one* got through. So, they turned to the idea of using cargo-carrying submarines. They'd been thinking of it since '42, as it happened. They were even experimenting with submarines towing underwater barges – would you believe it? That didn't work, largely because – if you can understand this – the minimum towing speed to keep the barge at a given depth and under control proved to be four knots, and their U-boats didn't have the battery capacity to maintain that speed, dived, throughout daylight hours. That comprehensible to you?'

'Of course.'

'Hm. As an old submariner it's obvious to *me*, but one can't assume it would be to others. Anyway – what it boiled down to was that after January '44 there was no surface blockade-running, only cargoes carried in ordinary U-boats which happened to be on passage to and from the East. Taking mercury and lead *to* Japan, by the way. They also took over some large Italian submarines, which they manned with German crews and put to work on the same run, but that didn't work too well, in fact most of them were lost. And in the later stages – 1944, anyway – a few large Japanese submarines joined in. One was the I.52 – of which you may have seen mention recently, efforts to salvage gold she was carrying? We're getting close to the point of all this, now – to the one *I* sank. The I.67. I might mention that there's a somewhat confusing element in some records, through the Japs' re-numbering of their submarines. The Yanks sank I.52, for instance – aircraft from an anti-submarine carrier group did it – but that was a modern boat, almost brand-new, whereas the *original* I.52, 1920s' vintage, had been re-numbered I.152 earlier in the war. Doesn't matter much, for present purposes, I only mention it because there's a similar possible confusion in the case of the I.67 – the original of that number was lost on her trials in 1940, and the number must have been re-allocated to the boat I sank. She was of recent construction, and effectively a one-off – laid down as one of what are categorized as the "I.15" class – biggest submarines the Japs ever built, incidentally – but taken over halfway through construction and completed as a cargo-carrier. Being different from the others would account for their having given her an out-of-series pendant number.'

'Pendant?'

'The "I" number. Equivalent of the German "U".'

'Right.'

'I don't want to burden you with superfluous detail. Only enough to understand the background. And I should explain, we knew about the cargo-carriers – that they were coming, and their route – from Kure via Singapore and Penang, across the Indian Ocean, round the Cape and up past the Cape Verde islands and the Azores into Biscay and usually Lorient – and, as it so happened, that both I.52 and I.67 were carrying gold bullion as well as other cargo. Repayment to the Nazis of some war debt, no doubt – and the eggs in two baskets rather than all in one. We knew as much as we did because our cryptographers at Bletchley Park – the "Ultra" operation – were deciphering signals that U-boats and the U-boat Command were coding-up on their Enigma machines. In I.52's case, a U-boat was going to rendezvous with her off the Cape Verde islands to transfer to her a Gerry liaison officer and signal staff. And as I said, the Yanks got her, an acoustic torpedo from a carrier-borne aircraft. And in my case – well, it was quite soon after D-Day that the I.52 was sunk. June '44. At just about that same time one of our own submarines, *Telemachus*, sank the I.166 off Penang in the Malacca Strait. Penang being their first port of call after Singapore, and I *imagine* where they'd load the rubber. *Telemachus* was from the flotilla based in Trincomalee, Ceylon – as we called Sri Lanka then – working down those straits and along the Burma coast and islands such as the Nicobars and Andamans. And as it happened I was taking a boat of that same class – *Tigress* – out to join that flotilla. This was about a month later.'

'You were her captain.'

'Yes. Aged thirty-three, a lieutenant-commander then.

We'd done our work-up based on Holy Loch in the Clyde, and we sailed in July for Gibraltar and thence Trinco via Suez and Aden. But when we were on our way south through the Irish Sea the backroom boys and girls in Bletchley intercepted signals to and from I.67: she was on her way to the same kind of rendezvous as had been intended for I.52, but this was to be a lot closer to home – a couple of hundred miles off Cape Finisterre. Know where that is?'

'Top left corner of Spain.'

'Precisely. I.67 was routed to pass midway between the Azores and the Portuguese coast near Lisbon. Thence to that R/V position off Finisterre. So we knew the spot she was coming to and the course she'd be steering to get there: all I had to do was R/V with her myself a little further south. Not too far south, in case she'd gone adrift in her navigation and had to approach the R/V from a different angle. They gave me the job, you see – I'd have been taking *Tigress* within spitting distance of that position anyway. Cutting a long story short – or short-ish – we hung around for three foul days and nights – awful weather, despite being mid-summer, mark you. It was the time gales were hitting the Normandy beachheads, smashing up our Mulberry harbours, making things damned awkward there – but near dawn on my third day on the billet we heard the Jap on asdics.'

He'd paused. 'This could get complicated, if I were to explain it in much detail. Submarines had to spend the dark hours on the surface, you see, to charge their batteries, and as it happened I'd just dived although it wasn't fully light. I was alert to the fact that this was supposed to be a rendezvous, so we'd probably have a U-boat in the vicinity as well as the Jap coming from a southerly direction. Anyway, my asdic chap heard him – asdics were what nowadays they call sonar, by the way –

and he was still running on his diesels – i.e. on the surface. I suppose for the purposes of the rendezvous, so that he and the Kraut would see each other. The sea-state certainly wasn't ideal for asdics. In fact it was so rough that when we got in close I had practically to surface to see him above the waves – periscope right up, and a hell of a job maintaining trim – in other words *not* surfacing, involuntarily. If he'd spotted me he'd have turned away, I'd have lost him – and there wouldn't have been a *second* chance . . . But I got four fish away at him and hit with one – just about amidships and just as he was diving – I actually saw the plumes of his main ballast blowing, then *whumpf*, and that was that!'

'Fish, meaning—'

'Torpedoes.'

'Plumes?'

'Air rushing out with spray in it, when he'd opened his main vents to dive. But now here's what this is all about. I wasn't hanging around: there was supposed to be this U-boat coming to hobnob with the late lamented, and who could be sure *I* mightn't get unlucky. Anyway, no *point* hanging around: my brief had been to sink the Jap, nothing else, and we were all keen to be on our way, get to our new flotilla and – justify our existence, you might say. First thing, anyway, the immediate thing after we'd got well clear of what we'd reckoned was the rendezvous position, and then surfaced, was to bang out a signal reporting the Jap's destruction. Incidentally, there was no doubt it had been the I.67. Darned great thing – biggest submarine I'd ever seen, *and* a distinctive shape. Well, I told my navigator – a young sub-lieutenant – to fill in the position, latitude and longitude, which of course he did, then it was cyphered up and the PO telegraphist tapped it out. And in due course we received congratulations from all and sundry. But my navigator had given the position as the lat. and long. of the German-Japanese R/V position – whereas the truth was that the sinking had been miles and miles away from there. In fact I think the Jap must have been ten or twelve hours astern of schedule – due to the weather, no doubt – which meant I'd been even luckier than I'd thought. I only saw all this afterwards, when I was writing my own report of proceedings, and I left it uncorrected, let the erroneous version stand. Well – why not? We'd sunk the thing in two or three miles' depth of water, it wasn't going to be any navigational hazard – which was the only thing that might have warranted a correction. No question of salvage ever entered one's mind. At *that* sort of depth? Only a complete ignoramus or a raving lunatic – or Jules Verne – would have given it a moment's thought . . . Anyway the position we'd given was wrong by the best part of a hundred miles. We'd had very bad weather, not a glimpse of stars, sun or moon – no fixes at all. Retrospectively though, purely for my own satisfaction, I worked out what had been the true position – by working back from the first accurate fix we were able to get, a day or so later when the sky cleared enough for me to use a sextant. We were not far short of Gib. by then, of course. And I've got it still – in my own navigational notebook – the whole navigational picture, but *notably* the latitude and longitude of where that wreck must still be lying today.'

'And no-one else knows it.'

'Nobody at all. Never went into any record. Why would it? In those days – even say a dozen or fifteen years ago – as I say, nobody in his right mind could have envisaged a salvage operation at that depth. They were breaking all known records in – oh, 1981, I think it was – when they got the Russian gold up from the cruiser *Edinburgh* – and that was from only about nine hundred feet!'

'What depth exactly – your I.67—'

'Between eighteen and twenty thousand feet. Can't be more accurate than that, soundings vary a lot in those waters: going by the figures on the chart, the bottom must be all ups and downs. And when a ship's sunk in such a depth it doesn't necessarily go straight down, all neat and tidy. There are currents, for one thing: and the ship breaks up. If my torpedo had left any of that submarine's compartments intact, that's to say watertight, at the kind of depths it was designed to operate at – about five hundred feet maximum, that would have been, possibly less – well, when it sank any deeper, the pressure would have crushed it. Any watertight compartment would have imploded. And there'd probably have been a scattering of wreckage.'

'So the gold—'

'Yes. *Could* have been shed all over the ocean floor. In which case –' he shrugged – 'too bad. It could have been scattered over a wide area and the bars would have buried themselves in the sludge. By this time there'd be no possibility of finding them, I should imagine, let alone recovering them. I *think* –' he'd raised crossed fingers – 'it's more likely to have been contained inside the wreck's hull. I'll explain why, before we finish. Incidentally, there's a lot about sinking ships' debris trails in the book by that American professor – name of Ballard – chap who found the *Titanic*. Did you read it?'

'I saw something about it on telly, I think.'

'I've got it here, you can take it with you. Give you a few pointers. But salvage teams *have* looked for I.67. One effort was – year before last, I think. And there was something else – on TV – on the subject of some Yank having located the I.52, it must have been. I *think* there was another expedition being mounted – to salvage its gold, of course. But you see – looking for *mine*, they'll always start their search in the wrong place, won't they? Get the point, Mark? I know where it is – or as near as damnit where – and no-one else does, not a blithering soul! And d'you know I never thought about it seriously until these last few days? What's the knowledge worth, would you guess?'

'D'you know how much gold she was carrying?'

'Yes. Intelligence direct from Kure, Japan – where she was built and where they loaded her.' The old man's narrowed eyes glinted almost orange in the sunset's glow. 'Five tons, Mark. Value today not far short of fifty million pounds.'

Edith had made them a delicious supper, with which they drank the wine Mark had brought with him. She was bright and bubbly, full of stories about personalities and events in their local village. They were mostly stories she'd told before, but that didn't matter. Then suddenly: 'How's Lucy?'

'She's well – very fit. Up to her eyes in work, though. Her job with Robert Kinsman, you know?'

'Kinsman.' She'd narrowed her eyes. 'Now where have I heard *that* name?'

'Probably on television and/or radio and newspapers. He's always in the news.'

'What they call –' Uncle Jack helped himself to more peas – 'a whizzkid. Money pouring out of every orifice.'

'You're so vulgar, Jack.' She'd turned back to Mark. 'So she's working for *him*. Does she enjoy it?'

'Yes. *Very* well paid, too. And – very much involved. Consequently – well, just at the moment – I'm not seeing as much of her as I did.'

'Really.' His uncle's eyes were on him questioningly – even hopefully. 'You mean—'

'That she's finding it a very full-time job. Long hours and often weekends too.'

'And where –' Edith's faded eyes on his – 'does this person live?'

'Kinsman? Well – if it matters – he has a house in Wiltshire, and did have a flat in Eaton Place, or Square

– but he and his wife are separating, she's living there and he's taken a suite in – I think the Dorchester.'

'Well.' Chuckle from old Jack. 'How the other half lives!'

Later Mark was to remember this conversation: the fact that with the Japanese gold in their minds they'd discussed Kinsman and his business without the slightest notion that within a matter of weeks the two were to be very closely connected.

He'd asked the old man, after Edith had gone to bed, 'So – back to the main topic – what are you proposing?'

'Really I'd only thought of putting our heads together and seeing what came up. But it seems to me the two obvious alternatives; broadly speaking, might be either to sell the information to whoever'll pay for it, or get together with such people – form a syndicate, and go after it. After the gold, I mean. Then again, since neither you nor I have the least idea of what's involved – *or* any capital, even if one were prepared to risk it – at least *I* haven't—'

'Ditto.'

'In fact as you know – you *do* know, I've bored you before this with my anxieties concerning the future, in particular for Edith – eh?'

'A windfall would come in handy.'

'Wouldn't it, just.' Wagging his white head. They were in the sitting-room, with its windows and doors open to the garden; the evening was still warm. '*Wouldn't* it. Take all the strain off. She'll outlive me – bound to. Women seem to go on for ever. But *how* – in what circumstances? She couldn't live on her own, not here anyway.'

'No. So on the face of it, the best thing might be a fairly quick deal, sell the information to – whomever, salvage company or treasure-hunter, maybe whoever it was you said tried before. I'd have to sniff around: as you say, knowing damn-all . . .'

'Two points there. One, I *would* be grateful if you'd take it off my hands. Being something of a wreck myself—'

'Getting around might be a problem. And with Aunt Edith—'

'Exactly. The *other* point, though – I'd guess that if you did get on to some potentially interested party – perhaps, yes, whoever tried and couldn't find it – rather than an outright purchase of the information, they might push for a percentage deal – paying us a percentage according to results. After all, we'd want a *lot* of money, and they'd only have my word for it. I could be a con-man, for all they'd know!'

'Yes.' Nodding at him. 'You do have a criminal look about you, Uncle.'

'Confidence tricksters *don't* look like crooks. Successful ones don't, anyway. But alternatively they might put me down as a dotty old fool suffering from delusions. Why didn't I ever do anything about it before, they'd ask.'

'I can answer that. It's because you aren't by nature or instinct money-orientated. Your mind never ran that way. We've talked about this before, haven't we? This age of greed – the fat-cat syndrome, claiming compensation for being farted at—'

'Need counselling, for that!'

'Oh, certainly. I've aired it all to Lucy, once or twice. But she's closer to the whizzkid mentality, I'm afraid.'

'Reading between the lines – just about all over, is it?'

'No.' He touched wood. 'At least, I hope it's not. I'm in love with her – have been from the start. Only – crazy as it may seem – it's as if there were two of her, and I'm in love with her as she *was* – might get to be again, once she's got the Kinsman thing out of her system. One aspect of it, incidentally, is that money *is* all-important – that's the key-note, in fact.'

'And it is to *me*, now. An eye-opener, really.' He'd paused.

A troubled look . . . 'You call it the age of greed, but – when you get a pile of it in your sights, and you happen to really *need* it—'

'Surely less greed than desperation.'

'Well – perhaps. At my age – it's a sense of helplessness. Chances blown – that's the feeling. Whatever might have been done should have been years ago.'

'Then you suddenly realize you're sitting on a gold-mine – or that you could be—'

'Could be. Yes. A lifebelt, as it were.' A small nod. 'But you're right, I suppose I'm *not* greedy – if I was I'd have cottoned on to this before, wouldn't I . . . ? And you can hang on to as much as you like – if there's *anything*, mind you. All I want is to see Edith taken good care of. I've really no other use for it. See what you can do, Mark – will you?'

4

The swell was down a lot, but the dive had been further delayed. Mark was with Lofthouse in an open wing of the *Eventyrer*'s bridge, Lofthouse with binoculars trained on the yacht lying about two miles off – white and sleek, the sort of craft you'd expect to see off places such as Monaco. The dive's postponement now was due to some fault in the winch of the salvage-hoist – cargo-hoist, some called it – the steel basket in which the gold bars were brought up; it had to be sent down before the dive could start, Lofthouse had said.

He was talking about Kinsman now, though.

'Probably still in the bath. Or *their* bath.' He lowered the glasses. 'Jacuzzi, whatever. *Real* gin-palace, isn't it? Brings that kind of thing to mind, uh?'

'If you *have* that kind of mind.'

Staring at him: the submariner holding the glasses a few inches from his eyes. He looked surprised. 'Well – not seriously implying—'

'Good.'

Obviously did *not* know about Lucy and himself. Maybe he'd catch on, when he saw them together. Or maybe not. All Mark foresaw at this stage was a certain awkwardness.

In fact it might save embarrassment as well as further argument if he could be on the way down before she got here.

Lofthouse had muttered, with the glasses focused on the yacht again, 'God knows what it must cost him to run that thing.'

'Costs him nothing. Costs the group's shareholders.'

'Ah. Right . . .'

He didn't think she'd be misbehaving with Kinsman on the yacht. Having the child with them, for one thing. And the yacht's crew – including stewards and/or stewardesses, whatever – and the tabloids with eyes and ears to every keyhole – around a man like Kinsman, anyway.

But his own closeness too, even with a couple of miles of sea between them. The imagination somehow didn't run to it.

Trusting her?

Well. If it hadn't been for the Australian weekend – about which she definitely had lied.

'You'd have thought –' Lofthouse again – 'that having flogged all the way out here – and more than likely brought his supper up last night – you'd think he'd want to see the start of the dive – wish you luck with it, sort of thing?'

'They may know about this hold-up.'

'Oh – yes . . . If he's been on the blower to Skaug.'

'As well as Tokyo, Sydney, wherever. They're open in Docklands by now, of course.' The Kinsman Group's new headquarters were in Docklands. Mark had turned for'ard to look down into the welldeck, where they were working on the winch – twin-drum capstan winch, and two boiler-suited Norwegians working at it, the deck around them strewn with tools and parts. A lot of other gear, much of it brightly coloured, stood or lay around. Drums of cable – although most of it was down below, the huge weight of it *had* to be – and a big Day-Glo-orange buoy, for instance, which crewmen or divers in one of the *Eventyrer's* rubber boats had retrieved earlier on. It was now lashed to the guardrail on this port side, while a silver-tinted wire that had been attached to it had been transferred into the ship and secured to a spring-like contraption maintaining an even tension on it, compensating for the ship's rise and fall. It was lighter than the black hoist-wire, less than half that one's circumference. Its other end was anchored close to the wreck, three miles down, and there was a linking wire which they called a 'messenger' – and so on, and so forth. Lofthouse had explained it all to him in the ship's saloon last night, briefing him for what he'd have to do today; at the time of earlier dives Mark hadn't taken all that close an interest in the details – hadn't had reason to, not as he had now. The basics of it were that the linking wire (or 'messenger') would run up and down the guide-wire, its other end attached to the basket of the salvage-hoist – the salvage basket, Lofthouse called it – which at this stage lay on the deck on the port side, close to the bright orange of the buoy. It was a white-painted metal framework about the size of a single bed – except that it was round – with a curved bottom of steel mesh to contain the gold. It also had fibreglass buoyancy compartments, a mechanism underneath with hooks from which anchor-weights were suspended, and a transponder – sonar device, cylindrical and about three feet long. When activated by a sonar impulse from this support ship, the transponder would electronically trigger the release of the weights – which would be dumped, left on the sea-bed, replaced later by others up here on deck for the next trip down. Because it needed that weight to take it down, did *not* need it when it was lifting nearly a ton of bullion.

Only one man was working on the winch now. The other was talking into a telephone. Problems? Or finished, and that one putting it back together again? Two other Norwegians, deckhands, were reaving the salvage-hoist wire through sheaves on the crane, which eventually would be trained out over the side for the basket to be lowered from it. It would be linked to the guide-wire so as to fetch-up on the sea-bed where it was wanted – close to the wreck, within reach of the Crab's manipulator arms and claws.

Mark asked Lofthouse, 'One thing – you said we can't start our dive until the basket's sent down?'

'Well – you could. But then you'd have a long wait on the bottom. It can start down ahead of you, *or* they'd wait until you were bottomed, and then send it. See – you're free-falling, at a hundred feet a minute – take you three hours. That thing travels twice as fast, and if you happened to drift into its way – we all might wish you hadn't.'

You could imagine it smashing down on the Crab from above. Pictures of that sort did rather spring to mind, being so conscious of the fact that several things had gone wrong already.

He acknowledged, 'Better to have it down there ahead of us, anyway. Can't do much without it, can we?'

'Depends how much work there may be. Getting access – as we were saying, if there's been any silting-up, for instance. Could have been, in this long interval. Hope *not*, but – until you get down there, we're guessing.'

Glasses up again, focusing on the yacht. 'Aren't in any hurry to join us, are they . . . ? Mark, tell me – how did you happen to pick on Dick Monteix?'

'Found him before I ever met Kinsman, actually.'

They were talking like this now, with quite a few gaps to fill in, because until recently they'd hardly exchanged a word, certainly hadn't been inclined to swap confidences. They'd first met on board the *Eventyrer* only a day or two before she'd sailed from Dundee, Mark had been seasick for about the first week, and then when he'd had to dig his heels in – because Kinsman was trying to cheat

on the contract – Lofthouse had been forthright in his
opposition. As Kinsman's direct employee, he'd had no
option. Dick Monteix, though, was the fixer who'd got
all this lot together – the support ship, the Crab, divers,
Carl Qvist the diving superintendent, others who'd had
to be recruited . . . Mark told the submariner, 'My intro
to Kinsman was through Lucy Greenstreet. As it happens,
I knew her before she went to work for him. And I got
on to Monteix through Lloyd's Register – well, indirectly,
through them. A month or so before you came on the scene,
of course. I didn't know anyone in the salvage business,
I'd barely heard of submersibles – and never in my life of
Remotely Operated Vehicles.'

'Such as we ought to have here. As I remember telling
you and Kinsman.'

'Monteix told us the same thing, earlier on. But – starting from scratch – I knew a man in Lloyd's who'd had
something to do with marine insurance, and I telephoned
him, asked did he know of any companies involved in
deep-sea salvage. He didn't, but he told me that Lloyd's
Register produced an annual list entitled *Offshore Units,
Submersibles and Diving Systems*, and he gave me a clue
or two as to what I should be looking for – just sort of
vaguely. So I rang the Register people, and was told I could
see a copy in their information department – in London,
100 Leadenhall Street. I went along, and a very helpful girl
produced the latest edition and allowed me to sit down
with it and make notes. Companies' names, addresses and
telephone numbers. I could narrow it down to just a few,
because the details of submersibles were given, including
the depth at which they could work, and there aren't many
can get down to three miles, are there? Anyway – back to
Brighton, and I made half a dozen calls—'

'I could have put you on to the man you *should* have
rung.'

'Didn't know you at that stage, did I? But what's wrong with Monteix?'

'Alternatively, if your uncle as a former submariner had got on to our submarine headquarters at Gosport—'

'Don't suppose it occurred to him. We were thinking of commercial underwater work – oilfields and so forth.'

'It overlaps. Submarine rescue's now well organized and integrated, internationally. Especially between NATO countries.'

'I'm glad to hear it. But I didn't know – wasn't looking for that anyway. What *have* you got against Monteix?'

'Nothing. Except they say he's a bit of a cowboy. I wondered where you'd dug him up from, that's all. I agree, considering the circumstances, he's done a good job for you.'

'He has, I think. At very short notice too. This Bairan thing's not *his* fault, is it . . . ? Anyway – on my fifth or sixth call to companies whose names and addresses I'd got out of that Lloyd's Register list, I wound up talking to an individual who said I might find Dick Monteix helpful. A rough diamond, but he knows his onions – something of that sort. He gave me Monteix's number in Aberdeen, I rang him, he said he'd help if he could or point me elsewhere if he couldn't – which was exactly what I wanted. So I flew up, stayed at the Station Hotel – because he'd told me it was handy for his office. and it was, easy walking distance – and there we were. Rum character at first sight, I admit. Shook him rather when I mentioned the depth of twenty thousand feet: his mouth did literally drop open – and crikey, those teeth!'

Lofthouse nodded. 'First time I met him I found myself trying to remember when I'd had my last tetanus jab.' He had his glasses on the yacht again. 'Still no signs of life. See the chopper there, on his stern?'

He could, just, with the naked eye. But as the submariner had said, no movement, no-one near it.

'Anyway.' Lowering the binoculars. 'Let's see how we're doing at this end.' He opened the wing door into the *Eventyrer*'s bridge, and asked the young Norwegian on watch in there whether there'd been any progress on the winch yet.

A nod. 'Putting together now, sir, I think.'

'Great. Thanks.' He pulled the door shut. 'Hope springs eternal . . . You were saying – Monteix was alarmed by the working depth?'

'He admitted he'd never been involved in any job this deep. But he knew – knows – everyone, what deep-diving craft exist and who owns or operates them – and as a middle-man—'

'Told *me* he'd been a diver and diving superintendent – and he dived on the *Edinburgh*, he tell you that?'

'Yup.'

'Then after he'd damaged his back he had a stroke of luck with some salvage job that must've been very profitable, really set him up?'

'I'm sure Kinsman must have had all that checked out.'

'How?'

'He checks on everyone. Even on quite junior executives in the companies in his group. I don't know what he's scared of – media informers, commercial rivals – whatever. He retains a firm of private investigators, anyway. They'll have checked *you* out for him, you can bet on it. Christ's sake, he had them visit my uncle – would you believe it?'

'Your *uncle* . . .'

'About Monteix, though, I went up to Aberdeen, and – as you said – dug him out . . .'

Monteix Diving Contractors Ltd occupied a few rooms on the top floor of a granite-faced building near the Victoria dock, only a few hundred yards from the Station Hotel, and Monteix had been expecting him, Mark having telephoned the day before from London. He found himself shaking the hand of a man of about fifty, who would have been about his own height if it hadn't been for the stoop, the result of some underwater accident, it transpired. His thick hair was greying at the edges but was otherwise still reddish blond; he had very large, stained teeth and droopy, sometimes pleasantly humorous eyes crowding a nose that had a flat end, like a bull's.

Pale, as well as flat. His complexion was florid, otherwise.

They'd chatted for a while, getting the measure of each other. Mark expanded a little on what he was after, and admitted his own ignorance of the subject. Monteix blinking at him meanwhile over a Gauloise cigarette – Mark had declined the offer of one – then buzzing through on an intercom that looked as if it might have come out of an aircraft or a ship; this had brought in a stocky, dark-haired girl with mugs of instant coffee.

Mark had commented, 'I'd thought of your name as Monteith, "th" instead of the "x". Especially – being in Scotland.'

'Puzzles a lot of folk.' He shrugged. 'Portuguese, that "x". My dad was a trawler skipper, worked out of Oporto and Figueira da Faz. Little dark feller, he was, I take after my mum's folk. But Jaeger, now – wouldn't be an English name, would it?'

'Originally Dutch. An ancestor was taken prisoner in the First Dutch War, and settled here. I mean, in England. Family legend says he commanded a ship in Admiral Tromp's fleet.'

'Salt in the blood, then!'

'But you know families and their histories. Might have been a ship's cook.'

'Yeah.' Broad smile: he'd liked that . . . 'Look – I'll tell you. I've put salvage teams together often enough, and I've

worked in the business since I was a lad. I was a diver, and
diving superintendent on a few biggish jobs, did my back
in though, so –' shrugging – 'started *this* going.'

'Going well?'

'Well. They *say* we're out of recession, like—'

'Coming out, I hope.'

'If you say so. But listen, now. I could find you the craft,
and the gear, and the guys you'd need – for whatever the
project might be . . . Take it you'd have the money behind
you, the finance?'

'The rewards – profit – would be very considerable.'

'Talking about profit before you've much notion what
your costs might be?'

Mark shook his head. 'That's part of the advice I'd hope
to get from you. In particular I've been wondering whether
it might be possible to set up a consortium on a basis of
percentage shares.'

'You'd still need cash up front, Mr Jaeger. Depending on
the nature of the job, of course, but – you'd need finance.
There's some as might work for a slice of the cake, but for
a start they'd want to be damn sure there's a cake worth
slicing. You sure there is?'

'About fifty million?'

Intake of breath: reaction disguised as a smile, which
amounted to a baring of the teeth. The eyelids had drooped
a little, lifted again now.

'Pounds, or dollars?'

'Pounds. The figure's approximate, but it could be more
than that as easily as less.'

'Sounds like – gold?'

'Right first shot.'

'Sounds like the *Edinburgh* over again. But she was lying
at less than a thousand feet. I know – I dived on her.'

'*Did* you!'

'And that was on a share of profits. "No cure, no pay" is

what we call it. Working out of a diving-bell, breathing a mix of oxygen and helium, in a suit with hot water pumping through it all the time. Barents Sea not being exactly tropical . . . What depth of water are we talking about, this job of yours now?'

'Ready for a shock?'

'I've mostly *lived* on shocks, Mr Jaeger.'

'Not much under twenty thousand feet?'

'Oh. Oh, *well* now . . .'

He'd only just stubbed out that cigarette, but he was fiddling one-handed for another. Shutting his mouth, which had momentarily sagged open. First the mention of fifty million, then the depth of twenty thousand feet, both had rocked him. Eyes on Mark's, and no smile in them. They were slightly pink-rimmed: the left one rather more so than the right.

'Atlantic, would this be?'

'It – might be.'

'Cape Verde islands, maybe?'

'No.' Mark smiled. 'Not that one.'

His uncle had mentioned that the wreck of the I.52 – which some American salvage outfit was said to have located – was in the vicinity of the Cape Verdes.

Monteix evidently knew about it too. Inhaling smoke deeply, and the droopy eyes on Mark's through a haze of it. Removing the Gauloise from his lips now between fingertip and thumb: exhaling. The impression was that he depended on it, might have died without it. Pointing it at Mark now: 'There's a Jap submarine been found, down that way – Cape Verdes. No connection – eh?'

'None I know of.'

'I keep my ear to the ground, Mr Jaeger. Have to. Name of the game, you might say. Did you know there was another bunch fitting out? French salvors, German finance?'

'No – but—'

'It's a fact. Way I heard it, there's this one a Yank team's on to, and another – likewise a Jap, and gold in her too. Deep – like yours, eh? Nothing like the old *Edinburgh*, lads working on her in suits. When you're talking about twenty thousand feet – that's more than three nautical miles deep, Mr Jaeger!'

'I know.'

'A lot deeper 'n anything I ever did, I'll tell you that.' Shake of the head: 'Doesn't mean I couldn't or wouldn't, but – see, you're talking about submersibles or ROVs, and a support ship, you're talking about – hell, five or ten million basic cost!'

'*That* much . . .'

'Shock for you, eh? And the Jap's not your target – the bugger these Frogs are after?'

'Put it this way. The wreck we *do* have interest in—'

'Submarine, of Nipponese origin?'

The nicotine-stained teeth baring themselves again . . .

'What I was saying is the wreck we're after – which does have gold in it – we know exactly where it is. Latitude and longitude. I'm not going to tell you *how* we know it, but the fact is we do, and no-one else does – or *could*. You can take my word for it.'

'Can, can I?'

Mark waited. Holding Monteix's gaze, saying nothing.

'Well.' Another grin: 'Maybe just this once . . . You're certain you're the only ones in the know. OK – and that's very nice, but—'

'It's not on record anywhere, except with a position that's—' he'd caught himself in time, finished with, 'Let's say it's a very long way out.'

'And the position you have is the real McCoy.'

'It's why I'm here, Mr Monteix. For the moment, just accept that?'

'All right. Otherwise why *would* you be here. Right – let's accept *you* believe it.' Slow nodding: droopy, pink-rimmed eyes on Mark's. '*Could* be the sub the Frogs are after?'

'I suppose it could. But if it was, it wouldn't worry us. I repeat, nobody has the information we have.'

'May I ask who's "we"?'

'Me, and one other person. But – going back for a moment – you said submersibles or – ROVs?'

'Remotely Operated Vehicles.'

'Oh, yes, I've read—'

'Three, five years back, Mr Jaeger, it's all manned submersibles, now it's ROVs – unmanned, controlled from a computer keyboard in the support vessel up top. A robot submersible, d'you see – does as much as a manned submersible can, and there's no lives in danger. An ROV can have its own satellite ROV, even – small enough to go *inside* a wreck . . . Eh?'

The toothy grin again, and the saggy eyes gleaming, excited. Mark shook his head. 'Incredible.' He thought it *was*, really. 'Hence the steep costs you mentioned, I suppose.'

'You suppose right, sir. We're talking about gear that's very costly and needs high-paid engineers to run it. And, don't forget, a fully manned ocean-going support vessel – again, special equipment, diving system an' all. I won't try to blind you with science, Mr Jaeger, but what we're talking about here's nothing run-of-the-mill, believe me. *Nor* easy or cheap to come by. Of course, if you did as you say know the exact location—'

'We do.'

'– that'd cut the time you'd need to spend searching. But there again, that's gear I didn't mention yet – sonar gear, what they'd use now would be an item we call a towfish – looks like a big torpedo but it's packed with sonar. Support vessel tows it, you get pictures on a screen – like telly?'

'As in Professor Ballard's book – thing he found the *Titanic* with. Only that was more like a kite than a torpedo.'

'That was a video search, not sonar.' Stubbing out the second Gauloise. 'Mr Jaeger – you're certain of the location of your – of the wreck you're after. Taking your word for that – I've no reason to doubt you, and I can afford to take it, can't I, *I*'m not putting five or ten million on it . . . Thing is, *someone*'d have to – right? So – when there's this much you're not letting on about, how'd you convince *them*?'

Mark frowned, thinking about it. Monteix probed. 'You can see what I mean, I'm sure. OK, like we were saying, you wouldn't be wasting your time on it if you *didn't* believe you had the goods. But – a bank, say. They aren't going to say: oh, he looks straight enough, let's take his fucking word for it . . . I mean, *are* they?'

'What about a well-established salvage company?'

'You got a lead to one?'

'I thought you might have . . . Might there be some such company, with all the know-how and equipment, who'd come in on it on a profit-sharing basis?'

'If you could convince 'em – and they reckoned the odds was right – yeah, why'd they pass it up? Their business, isn't it . . . But they wouldn't jump to it right away, mind. Gear that's costly's not left lying idle, they're either using it or it's out on charter. That's a point, too – if you was in a hurry . . . Well, I don't know. If all you're putting in the kitty is this latitude and longitude—'

'That's what we have – and it's worth fifty million, roughly.'

'Less the cost of recovery, might come down to half that, say?'

'Or – three-quarters? That's thirty-five, forty million?' He nodded, to Monteix's shrug. 'Only going by your own estimate, costs of five or ten million . . . And as to convincing them – if we did have people of that sort positively interested—'

'You'd tell 'em a bit more.'

'The information – and proof of it, of a kind – is my partner's. I'm doing the leg-work because he's – getting on a bit.' Pausing, thinking about it; he couldn't see any reasonably intelligent and perceptive salvage man choosing to disbelieve his uncle's story. Why should he have made it up, where would that get him? And a lot of it could be checked out – in Ministry of Defence records, for instance. He met the equally thoughtful, droopy eyes again. 'I think we could convince such people to take it seriously. They'd have to come down south, or send someone – the old boy's lame, as well as – as I say, getting on a bit.'

'Wartime saga, then, is this?'

He wasn't slow, or stupid. Mark said, 'I'd rather not go into much detail.'

'OK.' The teeth showed again. 'OK.'

'While I'm up here, would it be worth my meeting anyone of that kind? On your introduction, obviously?'

Meaning, *Not cutting you out . . .*

Monteix had slung himself round in his swivel chair, was gazing out of the window at a sea of grey roofs, grey stone and, very distantly, green hills. Slewing back again then: reaching for another cigarette . . . All of this, Mark assumed, covering a pause for thought.

'You don't—'

'No, thanks. Did, but I gave up.'

'Wiser 'n me, I dare say.' The lighter clicked and flared . . . 'I'll put my mind to it. Not wanting to waste your time – or my own, but – I'll give some thought to it . . . Mr Jaeger, you've come up here solely to see me – am I right?'

He nodded. Wondering whether it might not have been

a total waste of time already. But he'd had to start somewhere. From the Lloyd's contact onwards he'd simply
followed his nose. 'I was recommended to you – well, I
explained—'

'Aye. Not that I've heard of this feller that put you on to
me . . . Listen – you'll be staying overnight, back south in
the morning?'

He'd nodded again. Monteix suggested, 'Suppose I was
to call in at your hotel this evening. Might've come to
conclusions of sorts by then. Say six-thirty?'

They'd agreed on that. Why not? He'd had nothing else
to do. Time to kill, in fact. He walked around the town for
an hour or so; not having been to Aberdeen before, he was
impressed by what he saw of it. He'd also been impressed
in some ways – or intrigued, might be a better word for it –
by Monteix. Despite the teeth – and rather less enthusiasm
than he'd hoped for. Monteix was a character, all right. And
obviously knew the diving and salvage business – from
the bottom up, one might say. There were indications of
basic honesty, too: he'd made no effort to present himself
as anything he wasn't – hadn't hesitated to admit his
lack of experience of ultra-deep salvage operations, for
instance.

And he'd shown *very* sharp interest in that figure of fifty
million.

Back at the hotel, Mark had a shower, went down to the
bar at six-thirty and Monteix joined him there ten minutes
later. Looking exactly as he had earlier, even to the detail
of a loosened tie. They both drank Scotch with water, taking
it over to a table reasonably well out of earshot of the
scattering of other customers.

Monteix grimaced slightly, Mark noticed, in the process
of sitting down. The injured back hurting him, he guessed.
The wince would by now be a habitual reflex.

'Had any good thoughts, since I left you?'

Raised eyebrows: a canny, thoughtful look, while extracting a Gauloise and dropping the packet on the table.
'Done some thinking, off and on.' Click of the lighter. 'But
not good, especially. I'll tell you. Cheers.' Mark nodded,
sipped his drink and put the glass down beside his guest's
half-empty one. Monteix saw him glance at it, and briefly
bared his teeth: 'First of the day, and it's been a long one
. . . Look, I'm *Dick* Monteix.'

'Mark.'

'Right then, Mark.' The teeth showed briefly again,
through smoke. 'Here we go. As I see it – far as I can,
from as little as you've told me – right?'

'Wouldn't have expected me to give the whole thing
away, would you?'

Shake of the unkempt head. 'Wouldn't much like it if you
did. Part of the game's a tight mouth – has to be. There'd
come a time, mind – if we was to get together on it, though
God *knows* how . . .'

'Tell me how you see it.'

'I'll do that. Yeah.' He tapped his forehead. 'While this is
still half-clear, eh?' He paused, blinking slowly, getting it
straight – or into words an outsider might understand . . .
'Item one: any salvage company you'd want to do business
with is up to its knackers right through to autumn. If it
wasn't, it'd be in trouble, or no damn good. This time of
year, plenty of summer ahead, like – see, there's not only
salvage, there's pipelines, sea-bed cables, oilfield work –
that's maintenance and exploration – and all the rest of
it. Whoever you was to go to, after you'd got 'em to take
notice, settled the finance and that – it's still odds against
they'd have a slot for you *this* year.'

'In that case—'

'Aye, but hang on.' A drag at the cigarette. 'You say you
can put your finger on this wreck. And it could be the same
one the Frogs are after – right? Why do I guess it is? Because

it's gold, both cases, and there won't be that many wrecks with bullion in 'em at twenty thousand feet.'

'Is the one the French are going for at that depth, then?'

A nod. 'That's what we're hearing. Eastern Atlantic, too. And gold. Three points in common there, right?'

Mark sipped some whisky, put the glass down again. 'Suppose it *is* the same one. Fact remains, we know where it is, and they don't. There *is* no way they could. The position of the sinking – latitude and longitude figures – it's in one man's head, nowhere else.'

'Tell him to keep his mouth shut, then. Else he might get – you know, unwelcome attention. Got to the wrong ears – that's a lotta money to carry round sort of between *his* ears – you know?'

'You seriously think someone might—'

'*One* million, let alone bloody forty . . . Listen. Another way to go about it – you may not have thought about this. Save yourselves a lotta work and hassle, see . . . Just sell your info. Get yourselves a good lawyer, you'd need that – and someone like me, say, as 'd know where to go with it – well, we'd fix a price and have it in a contract, legal and watertight, payment if it's there, no payment if it's not – or within a certain distance, say. *Then* you give 'em the position. Maybe you're still not identified, even – only the lawyer is, and all it costs you is his fee.' A shrug. 'And my percentage.'

'Which you'd have earned, I'm sure.'

'Sarcasm, is that?'

'Not at all!'

'Well . . . Mark, there's sharks in and around every business, isn't there . . . ? But listen, here's more. Suppose it's the same wreck – yours and the French. You reckon you know where it is, and they don't; but they must reckon they've a chance of finding it. What's more, they're good, the Frogs – don't under-estimate 'em, they're experts, been at it a long time. *And* sonar search technology's come a long way, these last years. You were saying about Ballard and finding the *Titanic*, weren't you? His support vessel towed – well, sort of a framework, cameras and that on it, video, monitors on the support ship in what they call the van – right? But that had a narrow field of search – read about it, did you? Yeah – ran their search lines only a mile apart. "Mowing the lawn" he called it. Days and nights, weeks of it maybe, up an' bloody down. But the towfish they'd use today – side-scan sonar, the system's called – you're sweeping as far as nineteen miles each side, getting a picture as good as any video. Fact – if the tow's at eight knots, say, eight or ten – in a twenty-four hour search you'd cover – what, almost eight thousand square miles? Eh? See what I'm telling you? Your Frog friends get out there first – if they got even half an idea like where it is, won't take 'em long – huh?'

Gazing at him. With a sick feeling that this *might* have put the kibosh on it.

'News to you, is that?'

He nodded. Recalling that his uncle had said the officially recorded position and the true one differed by something like a hundred miles. A search-device with the extraordinary advantage of a thirty-six-mile spread might well start at the wrong place and over-run the right one within hours. Might not: might depend on which way the search was extended, he supposed.

Something *else* one didn't know the first thing about. The imagination jumped around, trying to compensate for ignorance. With no way of telling whether it made sense or didn't. But (a) it might *not* be the same wreck the French were targeting, and (b) the search's first swathe drawing blank, mightn't they just as likely extend it in the wrong direction, and therefore *not* find it?

Guesswork, and imagery. And a dread of having to break

it to the old man that his information mightn't be worth much after all. Not enough, anyway, to put Aunt E. into care and comfort when/if her condition deteriorated to the extent it might.

He drew a breath. Twisting in his chair then, putting a hand up to summon a waiter. It was the waitress who saw it, and started towards them. Mark turned back to Monteix. 'What it boils down to – I suppose – is if we're going to do it at all we should get on with it good and quick.'

A gesture . . . 'Only like I said, you won't find anyone'd take it on – not in this next six months, say. Not if the finance was plain sailing, even. If you had it all, was only looking for a charter. And from what you – well, what you *don't* say—'

'*You're* saying it's hopeless.'

'No, not—' He checked: showing his teeth to the waitress. 'Hello, my darling . . .'

She stepped back, as he reached for her: ignored him then, taking Mark's order and – deftly, at arm's length – Monteix's empty glass. Mark smiled at her: there was an apology in it, if she could read that. 'Any chance of peanuts, or—'

'I'll see, sir.'

The trivialities of life, he thought. Peanuts as the topic, for instance, while sitting amongst the wreckage of an old man's hopes for his wife's well-being in her last years. It hadn't been such a hell of a lot to hope for. The money might be, but the principle wasn't, surely . . . Monteix muttering, crushing out the damp-looking stub of cigarette, 'I'm not saying it's hopeless. No. That I'm *not* saying.' He wasn't reading a notice that said *Please, no smoking*, either. 'What I *am* saying is this. Suppose it's the same wreck you and the Frogs is after. I don't know how near ready they are, only there's a team getting put together. Oh, and they'll work out of Brest. *When* – couldn't say. Finance mightn't 've come through yet – Krauts dragging their feet like. Or the hardware – might be having to wait for it, till they wind up some other job, say. There's always hold-ups, one kind and another. Then again, though, could be tomorrow – we'll hear sudden they're on the job. I did hear divers was signed up, but whether they're on that payroll now or working some other place and the French job's next in line, I *don't* know. See – no-one lets on. They talked, they'd be out on their arses, that's how it is, this business. But – well, that's one thing, the next is – like I said, you'll not find any bugger's going to say right, you're on, let's go. Not this year, you won't. And here's another one for you – any way you can be sure the gold's there, is there? In the wreck. I mean?'

'Well.' Mark frowned. '*Reasonably* sure. After all, how—'

'A ship's sunk, see, carrying gold. Doesn't have to be there now. Ships break up, stuff spills out – gold bars being small, heavy, break out easy, and – even in boxes, small enough and heavy with it, any of it falls where there's a soft bottom, odds are it's fucking *gone*. Lot o' places it's yards deep, mud and that. Crevasses too. Cape Verde islands to the Azores, for instance – foothills of the mid-Atlantic Ridge, you might say – crevasses, peaks, cliffs, deep holes—'

'Excuse me . . .'

Their drinks: also a dish of olives and another of little biscuits. Mark paid, tipped and thanked the girl, and she left. She'd stayed on his side of the table, he'd noticed. He looked at Monteix: 'So it's a gamble there too.'

'Say *that* again.' Monteix picked up his glass. 'Here's luck. What she think I was going to do – eat her?'

Mark shook his head, stuck to the subject. 'Your advice to me is forget it – right?'

'No.' Glass in mid-air: staring at Mark over it, lips drawn back . . . 'No – *not* right.' Through the distorting effect of the glass his teeth looked about two inches long. Shaking his head now, putting the drink down carefully. 'Wantin' to give you a clear picture, is all. One – you don't move quick, Frogs 'll be on it first. Two – getting started quick's a problem. Three – find answers to that, it's still a gamble.'

He'd sat back: glared at the no-smoking appeal, then back at Mark. 'Being straight with you, see. Don't want you thinking it's easy when it's bloody *not*. And see here now, the other thing – finance. I'll tell you why that's so vital. I mean, apart from what's obvious . . . See, with these other problems, only way you'd get going is have some bugger like me put it together for you – from whatever. God knows what. . . I mean, what might be available . . . Well – I'd need to nose around a bit before I'd say definite, but I can say here and now that without finance – a lot of it – I couldn't bloody *start!*'

'No chance you'd get people who'd work for a share of the profit?'

'Oh, some would. There's always chancers. You end up paying out more than you would otherwise, mind you. Why else 'd they take the chance of a lot of hard work and no return from it?'

'What would your own angle be?'

'I'd want expenses – might come steep, at that – and a share of profit. Ten per cent, no less.'

'Ten percent – of say forty million—'

'Could be ten percent of say fuck-all too, couldn't it.' He tossed back his whisky. 'Chance we *might* get finance sorted, is there?'

5

He told Lofthouse, 'He was at it in Odessa too. They chartered a tart for him. I mean, on the house. Monteix had made a pass or two at the Ukrainian captain's girl interpreter – who I think might have been the captain's own bit of crumpet, so he had this one laid on as a diversion.'

'Kinsman know about that?'

'How could he?'

'I suppose – if you told him.'

'Last thing I'd do. Monteix and I discussed it – whether the Ukrainian was trying to bribe him – but if that *was* the idea he was wasting his roubles. We knew we wanted the Crab, by then. Monteix's attitude was why look gift whores in the mouth.' Mark shrugged. 'Sort of guy he is, that's all.'

'Yes – I suppose . . .'

Checking the time. One engineer was still working on the winch. Lofthouse looked back at Mark. 'So – having as it were discovered Monteix, you put him and Kinsman together, and – hey presto! Right?'

'Eventually. As I said, up to that point I hadn't even met Kinsman. When I did, I gave him the gist of what Monteix had told me, and Kinsman said, "Let's get him down here."'

That first encounter with Monteix had been on July 4th. Easy to remember because there'd been a party of pub-crawling Americans in the bar later on, celebrating their Independence Day, and one of them had known Monteix, greeted him as a long-lost buddy. So you could peg the rest of the opening moves on that. Back in Brighton late on the 5th, for instance, and a full day's work in the office on the 6th – which was a Saturday; and down to Hampshire the next day, Sunday. He'd thought of updating his uncle by telephone, to save himself that trip – there was a bit of a crisis in the office, a threat to the continuance of a valuable management and letting agency which he'd negotiated a year earlier on a very large block of flats close to the Marina, and he'd had a back-log of work which he'd have liked to have got through during the weekend; but he'd decided against telephoning, partly through having in mind Monteix's warning about security, attracting 'unwelcome attention'.

Later, he was to wish he'd taken it *more* seriously. He'd explained it to the old boy anyway, when he'd got there – why he hadn't used the phone . . . 'May be overdoing it a bit, but better to play safe, don't you agree?'

'I suppose so.' Jack Jaeger had shrugged. His neck was as scrawny as a turkey's. 'Though who'd be agog to pick up anything *I* had to say – eh?'

'*Could* be, that's all. Once we start talking to people – as I have, now. It's an awful lot of money, isn't it? Or we hope it will be . . . Monteix himself's straight enough, I'd guess – on *this*, anyway; if it comes off he's on to a good thing, he's not going to take risks with it, is he!'

'Ten percent of however many million . . .'

'Exactly. *He* won't be talking out of turn. But as soon as he starts asking around – what ships and so forth may be available for charter – well . . .' Mark shrugged. 'Word 'd get round pretty fast, I'm sure, in that business – the oily

world, he called it . . . Uncle, on that subject – more or less
– you've got a note of the wreck's latitude and longitude
in some notebook, I think you said.'

'I'll show you.'

'Thing is, if it's worth so much – and Monteix seemed to
agree it might be—'

'Hang on, lad.' Pushing himself up. 'Get yourself another
drink, if you want one.'

'I won't, thanks.' He was planning to start back to Brighton
after lunch, which Edith had assured them wouldn't be long
now. She'd been with them earlier, with her usual enquiries
about Sally – why did she *never* seem to come down with
him nowadays? Mark couldn't bring himself to remind her,
sadden her all over again. But it was a pleasant aroma
wafting from the kitchen now: roasting beef, and there'd
be Yorkshire pudding with it. He sniffed appreciatively:
watching the old man limp across the room to his desk,
fumble a drawer open and shut it again, try the next one
down and start rummaging.

'Ah. Here we are.' Wagging his white head. 'Cheating,
actually – had it out just the other day.'

Turning with a brown-covered, tattered-looking notebook in one hand: he brought it over, lowered himself
carefully back into the chair, tilting the book for Mark
to see the faded lettering on its cover: *Navigating Officer's
Notebook.*

'Used these all the time. See – HM Stationery Office.
Supplied buckshee. And look how it's lasted – more than
half a century, practically an antique!' He riffled through
discoloured pages of pencilled notes and figures . . . 'Here.
See those figures?'

Mark read out, 'Forty-two degrees fifty north, thirteen
degrees ten west. That it?'

'No. Wouldn't win you tuppence. That's the position
as my signal reported it – the original Japanese-German

rendezvous position.' He flicked over a few more pages. 'Here. Quickness of the 'and deceives the eye. *This,* my boy, is where our gold is!'

Mark saw, marked by his uncle's thumb, *41 degs 39' N, 17 degs 09' W.*

He nodded. 'What about putting that in the bank?'

'No. You take it.' He dog-eared the page, shut the little brown book and gave it to him. 'Put it in *your* bank, if you want to. But you might as well have it, you're doing all the work. Got a safe in your office, have you? But make a separate note of those coordinates elsewhere, perhaps. Or memorize them? Beyond me now, I can tell you, barely memorize my own name. But then when the time comes—'

'When, or if?'

'It will. *Must.*' The old boy had been in an optimistic mood. Probably heartened simply by Mark having started work on the project and Monteix not having dismissed it out of hand as impractical for one reason or another. But in any case he'd always been an enthusiast. 'You'll find a backer, surely. These days, when as we were saying everyone wants to get rich quick? Who do you bank with – Lloyds, like us?'

'No. But a merchant bank might be best. Or – what would be my choice, really – an individual. There's a man I know slightly, a property magnate . . . I'd like to get straight to the chap at the top, you know, not be bogged down among po-faces in dark suits – uh?'

'Absolutely!'

'Might ask – well, his name's Moed—'

'Mowat—'

'Spelt M-O-E-D. My lawyer – darned good one. Funny-looking, but – nice man, dead honest and razor-sharp. Then also of course there's Lucy's boss, Robert Kinsman.'

'Wouldn't want to deal with *him*, would you?'

'No. Not – by choice, you're right.' Jack Jaeger was a discerning old bugger, memory or no memory.

All he'd told Lucy before the trip to Aberdeen was that he'd be away for a day or two on business. He hadn't planned on telling her any more than that. Her business was Kinsman Group business, this was his own: and it had started with that visit to his uncle, which she'd resented, and that, it had seemed to him, made it even less her affair. But she came down to Brighton the following weekend, on the Sunday, just to lunch with him and to go back that evening, and she'd been so keen to find out where he'd been – what property interests he had in Scotland, was one question – that he'd wondered what dark suspicions she might have been entertaining. Maybe Dizzie had been away at the same time? He had guilt-feelings over Dizzie, knew he'd been stupid, that he qualified for whatever kind of suspicions might be in the air now – clearly *were* in the air – and to clear it he'd told her all about it – his uncle's story, Aberdeen, Monteix, the lot.

He'd seen her relief, as well as interest. Her hand in recent minutes had been resting on his thigh. It was a banquette table with a red-checked cloth on it, and they were very close: as they'd always liked to be, and he'd never exactly fought her off.

Sunday the 14th, this must have been. Bastille Day.

'Don't mention it to anyone else, Lucy.'

'Of course not. But you're doing something about it, are you?'

'Decided last Sunday evening, *would* have done something by now, but the guy's away. Potential source of finance, this is, a property tycoon I've had dealings with. I don't much like him, but—'

'Why not talk to my boss?'

'Well.' Glancing round the restaurant. Coffee was on its

way. 'It had crossed my mind – amongst other things. But – anyway, the delay won't make all that much difference. I rang Monteix and he hasn't anything positive yet. In fact I doubt he will have, until I tell him it's on.'

'I'm sure Bob K. would be interested. In very, *very* strict confidence – I really do, Mark. Sooner not talk about it in here, but – well, he'd definitely be worth trying. In fact I could set it up for you – a meeting – if you'd let me tell him what it's about?'

'No. Please. I mean thanks, but—'

'Because he happens to be my boss?'

'Because I don't want anyone knowing about it who doesn't have to, and I'm trying this other guy. As I say, I'm not crazy about him, but – bags of cash, and he *is* a gambler.'

'It is a gamble, is it?'

'Yes. Has to be. My uncle has the location pinpointed, and –' he glanced round, dropped his voice to a murmur – 'he knows there *was* gold in it. But you see—'

'Someone else might have—'

'Might *now*, if we aren't quick, but otherwise no, very unlikely. Work at that depth is – really, state-of-the-art stuff, very new technology. Monteix described it as "space travel in reverse". Primarily, you see, huge external pressure instead of vacuum and weightlessness. The guys who do it call themselves aquanauts. But apparently when a ship sinks – in water that deep, anyway – it breaks up. Pressure can actually implode it. Bits break off and things drop out, you get what's called a debris-trail.'

'Sounds – spooky . . .'

'What I'm saying is the gold could have been scattered.'

'Divers get down there and find nothing.'

'Yes. Could happen.'

A pause: looking into her eyes, and at her small, straight nose, the delicate but firm curve of jawline and the soft swell of her throat. Little pulse beating in there, in that rather long, slim neck where his lips had spent a lot of time.

Quirky smile. Her upper arm and shoulder against his, overlapping, and her hand down there. She asked him, 'Shall I predict the question you're about to ask?'

'No, don't bother – since you know it. I'll take that as an assent.'

'I'll come back to the flat with you, anyway.'

'That's a must.'

'I think so too.'

'And you can tell me what you won't say here – about your boss's propensity to be interested?'

'Tell you that on our way. I want to ask you something too.'

'So let's go.' He signalled to the waiter. Anticipating their walk back along the seafront to Brunswick Square – conveniently close, only a few hundred yards, technically in Hove, not Brighton – and wondering if she'd ask him about Dizzie. Which in fact added up to nothing, but she might think it did. Just as he thought about her and bloody Kinsman. In which it was possible he was being unfair to her. The Australian weekend *might* have been as she'd tried to explain it.

If Dizzie had got her version of it wrong on purpose?

No. He'd thought about it a lot, through many sleepless hours, and it didn't add up. *Still* didn't. He'd have liked it to, but it did not.

'Thanks.' He retrieved the credit card, and left a fiver for the waiter. Sliding out of the banquette seat then, easing the table out for her. 'You're so – *beautiful* . . .'

'Oh – *you* . . .'

'Also just about every other man in this room.'

'Rubbish, Mark. Really, you do exaggerate!'

It was a fact, though. *And* she knew it.

They were on their way out then, and crossing to the sea

side of the road, the long sweep of promenade. Gusty wind, wind-blown streamers of high cloud, sails out there starkly white on the glittering blue.

'So tell me – a particular reason Kinsman might be interested?'

'Well – without saying anything I shouldn't – which in any case I'm only guessing at – if there's a net profit of ten or twenty million just lying there waiting to be scooped up – who in his senses *wouldn't* jump at it?'

'That's it?'

'What more do you want?'

'I don't, really. Only you said something about very, very strict confidence. I was expecting—' he shook his head. 'Doesn't matter, anyway.'

'Because in any case you're not interested – right? In talking to Bob, I mean – for reasons of your own?'

'As I said, this other guy—'

'Whom you dislike, you said. Must be fairly small beer too – isn't he?'

'Worth a good few million.'

'Talking *my* language now?'

'Far from it!'

'Thanks. And you haven't met Bob, so the only thing you can have against him is I work for him. Correct?'

Skirting a family with dogs on expanding leashes. The two of them walking fast – for some reason . . .

'That the question you were going to ask?'

She nodded. 'Near enough. Do I get an answer?'

'Yes. If you insist. You do, do you?' She nodded again, impatiently. He began, 'The easy bit is that what I've read and heard about him I don't much like. As to "small beer" – Kinsman's not exactly a Maxwell or a Branson, is he? Or a – what's his name? Murdoch. Gets a lot of publicity, but—'

'He's going places, Mark. Honestly. Actually a slightly

rough patch at the moment, but – you'd be amazed. Obviously I can't talk about it, but—'

'I'm inclined to take tycoons with a pinch of salt, anyway. And the more personal side of it – yeah, fact he has you around him to the extent he does – including weekends in Wiltshire—'

'I have not spent *any* weekends in Wiltshire!'

She'd tripped, as she'd squawked that, and he'd put out a hand but she'd scorned it. Glaring at him . . .

'When you had to meet the Australians?'

'Not a weekend. One night. Christ almighty. That's enough for you to infer that I slept with him – or *sleep* with him. Right? So in your view I would with anyone I worked with or spent more than ten minutes a day with?'

'Now you're being—'

'If they paid me enough?'

A bunch of youths with ice-cream cornets and one sad-looking girl between the four of them. Then a rotund individual in a Panama hat and a flowered waistcoat, smiling at them both as if he knew them. Mark said, 'Good afternoon': it could have been some past client of the agency.

'Well? *If* not, why the hell—'

'Let's say numerous small indications, followed by obvious discrepancies in the Australian explanation. I tried to convince myself there weren't, that it might hold together—'

'And *I* stopped short of saying "slept with him, *as you did with Dizzie*", because I wouldn't want you to think I was implying that might make it OK. It wouldn't at all, but – something of that kind in *your* thinking?'

'I was angry. Because you'd – I *thought* you'd lied to me. I felt you'd written us off – written yourself and me off, I mean. *And*—' He checked himself. 'No. No other excuses.'

'That's *something*.'

'Is he still slumming it at the Dorchester?'

'He's back in his flat. That was only a temporary arrangement. Paula's moved out.'

'Has, has she? Has – er – anyone else moved *in*?'

'I honestly don't know what I'm doing here, Mark. That we're still talking to each other, even!'

'Listen.' He took her arm: surprisingly, she let him. They'd had to separate, getting past a couple who were also arm-in-arm. He told her, 'I *am* prone to sexual jealousy. Actually I don't know how anyone can be in love and not be. That's one thing. Another is – another thing I can't imagine is any man *not* trying to get you into bed. And Kinsman having you at his beck and call seven days a week – and having no wife now either—'

'That's *my* fault?'

'There was also a high degree of enthusiasm on show. As from Day One. Immediate readiness to work long hours, weekends—'

'And you see that as evidence of depravity?' A laugh, high-pitched with incredulity. 'Moral turpitude?'

Brunswick Square, across there. Regency frontages, ochreous paintwork. Slanting left towards the road, to cross at the intersection and the lights, Lucy's eyes on his while she let him lead her as if it didn't particularly matter to her which way they went – except they were both still hurrying. 'Why don't you ask me point-blank? Come on, Mark – *ask* me!'

He shook his head. People close around them, and anyway he didn't want her answer. If it had been 'yes', that would have been that – finish – and if 'no' he wouldn't necessarily have believed it. Amongst the people bunching here to cross the road, several of the nearest had their eyes on him and Lucy, might well have been straining to hear above the traffic noise. He put his mouth close to her ear, murmured, 'I *am* in love with you.'

'Odd way of showing it!'

'Excuse *me!*'

'I'm so sorry—'

Lucy smiled at the old girl with dyed coal-black hair: 'He is *so* clumsy—'

'Gotta train 'em, ducky.' Cackle of laughter. 'Never mind, no harm done . . .'

In the lift, minutes later, alone and in each other's arms, she began to cry. And it was all right – in the flat then, with the door locked and nothing else in mind – as marvellous as it had ever been, perhaps even more so, wilder than even at the very start, those first sensational releases, revelations. She'd known it too, had been aware of it long after, in the stillness, afternoon light – sun deflected all to one side of the window – and from way down the continuous traffic-hum. Mark rather hazily working out the answers to several questions: whether it was what she'd come down from London for, or just that proximity and contact had had the effect on her that it had certainly had on him. In the restaurant especially. Then the flare-up of fairly savage recrimination virtually as a preliminary to tearing each other's clothes off.

For them both, a break-through to where they should have been all the time, needed to get back to?

Sustainable, he wondered?

And might 'obsessed with' be closer to the truth than 'in love with'?

He'd dropped off, woken to find her still sprawled across him but also stirring. They'd made love again, and in its aftermath and the fading light she'd again brought up the subject of discussing the salvage project with her boss. He'd been less responsive than he might have been, in fact had distrusted her motives in pushing it so hard and in the prevailing, otherwise thrillingly *happy* circumstances hadn't wanted to discuss anything involving Kinsman. But she came back to it yet again later, over an early supper – he'd wanted her to stay overnight and take an early-morning train, but she'd said she couldn't, had to be in her office early and with a clear head – she'd told him that if 'Bob', as she called him, could be convinced there was a good chance of recovering the gold he'd jump at it, as the perfect answer to certain temporary problems that were looming over his group's finances, but which would then never have to come to light.

'*Definitely* in strict confidence, Mark. Not a whisper – please?'

'Of course. And I'll – bear it in mind. But if he's strapped—'

'He is *not*! I said *temporary* problems! Mark – it might save *weeks*. And you should be getting a move on, shouldn't you?'

Because of the threat from the French, she'd meant.

Then on the Tuesday, when he'd had word that the local man had decided to stay on in his house in Tuscany for at least another week, he telephoned her at her office and asked her whether Robert Kinsman would grant him an audience. He'd put it like that, facetiously, out of embarrassment at what had seemed to him like surrender – or worse, in terms of what might be her relationship with Kinsman, like selling out. She'd been unamused, had told him impersonally that she'd call him back, probably within the next day or two. Might have had someone else in the office with her at the time, he'd guessed.

He'd seen the tycoon in his Docklands office at eleven a.m. on July 22nd – Bastille Day plus eight, a Monday. Lucy had telephoned to confirm the appointment on the Thursday, he'd asked her whether he'd be seeing her at the weekend and she'd told him no, she'd be in Wiltshire.

'Wiltshire.'

'Yes, Mark. Working. A conference – very important one.'

Impersonal again: nothing like the 'Sunday' Lucy. He'd considered cancelling the Monday appointment. If he'd had only his own interests to consider he probably would have, but he was conscious of all this being primarily on behalf of his uncle and old Edith, and that time was being wasted. And while his lawyer, Sammy Moed, had told him that he foresaw no great problem in finding a backer or backers, he'd added that at this time of year when so many people were away it was bound to take 'a little while'. Mark's conclusion was that if Kinsman wasn't ready to make an immediate and positive decision, the hell with him, back to the Brighton-based tycoon: if necessary, fly out to Italy to see him.

But on the face of it, especially in the light of Lucy's hint, Kinsman did look like the best bet. Moed had thought so too. He'd offered, apropos the Monday meeting, 'I'll come along with you, shall I?'

'Well – when it comes down to negotiating terms, Sammy—'

'Won't terms come into it? Aren't you both going to want to know how profits'd be split? Kinsman's a tough nut, you know!'

'Meaning I'm soft?'

'Comparatively – perhaps.'

'Lucy'd agree with you.'

'When am I going to meet the wonder-girl?'

'Chez Kinsman, maybe – at some point. But I'll start this off on my own, Sammy. Less formal – break the ice. *Then*, please—'

'As you like.' Moed was about five-five and roughly the same width, with a big, wide head, legs like tree-stumps and eyes that could suddenly become laser-like. He claimed – or admitted to – Austrian-Hungarian ancestry. Nodding the big, mostly bald head now . . . 'Very well, then. But for your general guidance, here's how I see your position. First of all, this information – the wreck's location – is your property and your uncle's. That's your ace-in-the-hole, where the whole thing starts. Once you let that cat out of the bag, you've got nothing, you're dispensible. So you *don't* – under any circumstances whatsoever. If Kinsman wants to take the gamble, OK, you'll accommodate him – you and your uncle naturally taking your own share of the profits – as per contract, to be drawn up by yours truly. But you don't let him into the game for nothing. It's *your* game – if he wants in, he'll have to ante-up. I'd set a fee of – two and a half million.'

'*Plus* share of profits?'

'Of course. We'd ask for – let's say twenty-five percent?'

Docklands, the Kinsman Group headquarters building, the penthouse executive suite. Half or more of the building was let out to other companies, Mark noticed. But downstairs, uniformed reception staff, elaborate security systems, and a lift that shot up like something from Cape Canaveral and was met at the top by Lucy.

Kinsman looked younger than his thirty-eight years. Could have been close to Lucy's age. A smallish man – five-eight, maybe – obviously fit, probably worked-out regularly. He had wavy brown hair, wide-set pale-brown eyes that were slightly hooded, and a nose to match – a beak, with a high bridge to it.

You'd have thought too young to have come as far as he had already. Having started from nothing, too.

Best way to start, maybe?

Firm handshake: eye-contact steady. 'Good of you to have come along.'

'Well. Lucy's idea.'

'You're an old friend of hers, I gather.'

'Oh – not *that* old. Year – eighteen months—'

'Through having had Brighton as your common stamping-ground?'

'We have, yes.' Kinsman had waved him to an armchair, and now slid into its twin, on this same side of the big glass-topped desk. Mark adding. 'Although actually we met in London.'

'At a cocktail party, at the Lansdowne Club.' A small smile as he glanced round at her: Mark wondering if there was anything she *hadn't* told the bastard. She'd pulled a straight-backed chair up beside the desk and had a tape-recorder in front of her: a red light glowed as she switched it on. Kinsman asked him, pointing at it with his head, 'You don't mind that thing?'

'Not at all.'

'Good. Good.' A glance at his watch – gold, with a black strap, looked like a Cartier. 'Lucy's told me about your salvage project. At least as much as she knows of it.'

'I'll elaborate – as far as I can. If you're interested?'

'Of course I am. Whether or not we'd want to involve ourselves in it remains to be seen, but thank you for coming here first with it.'

Whether or not *we'd* want, he'd noticed. Royal 'we', or Kinsman Group as a plurality, or him and Lucy?

Shrugging . . . 'Because of the time-factor, mainly. And as I said, Lucy's instigation. The appeal to me was that she could set up a meeting very quickly. Did she explain to you why we need to move fast now?'

'Competition from some French outfit.'

'Right. How ready they are isn't clear. But we know the wreck's location, and they don't. That's our strength.'

'Because your uncle, who sank it, kept that detail to himself.'

'I wouldn't put it quite that way. Until very recently there'd have been no possibility of any salvage attempt, because of the depth of water. Roughly three miles deep –

Lucy tell you that? So at the time and for years afterwards there'd have been no point in correcting the position which he'd – well, which his navigator had given and was totally erroneous. But since then, having read about new deep-diving techniques – finding the *Titanic*, for instance—'

'Yes. Understood. Coming back to the French, though – what chance do they have, *not* knowing the true location?'

'Hard to say. Especially as I'm as new to this scene as you are. But they'd be starting in the wrong place – a long, long way out – where incidentally I think searches have started before and naturally enough drawn a blank – searchers given up, gone home—'

'So why should they think – as they must – that they've a better chance now?'

'I gather, because of technological advances, especially in sonar. Which apparently is the – the search method, nowadays. But wider search areas now, so as to cover a bigger area in less time, and I suppose they'd hope to strike lucky.'

'And might they? Might they have an even chance with you, despite starting in the wrong place?'

'Very much doubt it. We do know the precise location, so we can go straight to it. Whereas the French – as it were flying blind – maybe in the wrong direction altogether . . . All I know about this sonar stuff, by the way, is what a man by name of Monteix told me recently. Lucy mention him?'

'Yes, I did.' She added quietly, 'Wasn't sure of his name, though.'

'Salvage expert, Aberdeen.' Kinsman hadn't any notes, spoke only from memory of what she'd told him. He'd thrown a smile in her direction, nodded to Mark now. 'You went up to see him just the other day, didn't you? How does he spell that name?'

Mark spelt it out – for the benefit of the recorder – and added, 'He knows it all – the diving business. Although he admitted he's never handled a salvage job as deep as this one. But he was a diver himself, then a diving supervisor – dived for gold on the cruiser *Edinburgh*, incidentally – and now he's a middle-man, sets things up, finds chaps for jobs, et cetera. So he's pretty well what we need. He warned me there'd be problems in getting going at very short notice and in what's apparently the busy season – ships and equipment all at work, out on charter, and so forth, but once I can tell him we have the necessary financial backing—'

'Hold it there, a moment?'

Glancing round at Lucy: she nodded, confirming that she had the recorder running. Kinsman turned back. 'Necessary financial backing. The nitty-gritty, one might say. What sort of investment are we talking about?'

'Monteix guessed at something in the region of five to ten million.'

'Did he, indeed.' Gazing at Mark as if mind-reading, or trying to . . . Then a frown. 'To produce a return of something like *fifty* million?'

'That's the hope.' Mark nodded. 'If it's all there and it can be got at – which we can't know until we get down to it. It's in international waters, by the way, there'd be no nation with any right to interfere . . . On that rather vague estimate of costs, though – can *only* be vague, I suppose, until Monteix's got down to it and knows what's available. *If* we commission him to do so, of course.'

'Better get him down here – d'you think?'

'Well – why not. He'd still have his researches to do, of course. I was going to say, though – that figure of fifty million . . . For the record – thing is, we know five tons of gold bars were loaded into the I.67 in Kure, Japan, and it must have been on board when my uncle sank it. That's roughly fifty million sterling at today's price – or last month's, whatever. No point trying to be too exact, because it may *not* all be there – or accessible. In other words, it's a gamble – high stakes, and a good *chance* of cleaning up, but – no guarantees.'

'Well. That's – clear enough.'

'Monteix 'll tell you the same. As he told *me*.'

'We'll get him down here. Peculiar name, incidentally?'

'Portuguese extraction. But – further warning, before you decide on that. One, you'd have to pay his expenses – air fare, hotel—'

'No problem.'

'– and in the longer term – I asked him this – he'd want substantial expenses while he's getting around and setting it up, *and* a contract entitling him to ten percent of net profits.'

'Well. One might negotiate on that basis, arrive at *a* percentage.'

'He pointed out that it could end up as ten percent of nothing.'

'So *he* accepts the gamble.'

'Oh, yes, unquestionably.'

'There'd be a VAT problem too, when the gold was landed.' A shrug. 'But that's – something else. What I pay accountants for. Tell me, what led you to this fellow?'

'Chance, really. I looked up deep-diving and salvage companies at Lloyd's Register, made some calls then, and one of the people I spoke to put me on to him. There must be others, of course – if you'd sooner find an adviser of your own—'

'No. We'll have a look at him. Lucy—'

Monteix flew down next day, and they met in the Docklands office on the Wednesday. Monteix told Kinsman very much the same as he'd told Mark in Aberdeen, but also that he did now have a couple of possibilities up his sleeve. One was a Norwegian diving support ship currently lying in Hamburg and unexpectedly available for charter: if it was decided to go ahead with the salvage project, he'd go over there himself to look her over and check on her diving control system's adaptability.

'Adaptability to what?'

'Ah, well. This ship has no ROV, d'you see, and no submersible either, so—'

'ROV?'

'Remotely Operated Vehicle.' The yellow teeth flashed a quick smile. 'Sorry. What it is, is – well, an unmanned submersible. For a job such as you're contemplating, it's what we should be going for – if there was one available with the working capability we'd want – which there is not. Four tons to the square inch down there, you don't send men down if you don't have to, see. And an ROV's – well, it's a robot. Controlled from the support ship – computer-controlled – manipulators, the lot.'

He'd had to explain what manipulators were, then. Every second sentence had needed some degree of interpretation, for Kinsman to understand it. But he caught on instantly, nothing had to be explained twice.

'So – there's no ROV – that'd meet your requirements – that'd be available between now and bloody Christmas. That's plain fact. This Norwegian – *Norsk Eventyrer* – she does have a towfish – that's a towed side-scan sonar search vehicle, as we'd need for locating the wreck—'

'I thought we knew exactly where it is?'

'Latitude and longitude in degrees and minutes—' Monteix shot a glance at Mark – 'if I'm guessing right?'

'Yes.'

Wag of the head . . . 'One minute of average latitude's near as buggery one nautical mile. Right? You could send your sub down on that lat. and long. but she'd like as not fetch up on the bottom a mile or more away. Pitch dark, and not a clue which way to go. They don't go down straight, vertical, see – no more 'n ships that've been torpedoed do.

And there's no saying the bottom's flat. Could be hid in a trough, or – anything . . . So you'd locate your wreck first – with sonar, the towfish – then you stick a beacon on it, that's sonar too, and you hold your support ship right over it by means of what's called DP – Dynamic Positioning, that is.'

Back eventually to the Norwegian ship lying in Hamburg: and Monteix's readiness to fly over and inspect her diving control system and talk to her engineers. *'Because . . .'* Grimacing, including a further baring of the fangs, in preparation for yet more explanations: *because* he'd got wind of there being a manned mini-submersible with a depth capability of twenty thousand feet currently in Odessa, Ukraine, where engineers had been fitting it with a third manipulator. An innovation that had been tested and proved successful, and the word was the Ukrainians would be very glad to get a short-notice charter.

'On account there's an ongoing dispute between them and the Russkies, like who owns what ships down there. This one *was* Russki, got shifted to Odessa for fitting the third manipulator. Wouldn't 've been there otherwise, except on shallow-water work – like at the other end, Batum maybe – seeing as there's no such depths to warrant the deep-dive capability. But with three manipulators now, *and* deep-dive, the Ukrainians reckon it could be a money-spinner, and it'd suit 'em to get it out on charter double-quick and for what's left of summer. *Their* charter, see, not a Moscow one. Well, you wouldn't want it *that* long—'

'What would it cost to charter?'

'Well. Seeing as they're keen – might get if for – ten thou' a day?'

'Pounds – ten thousand—'

'Per diem. If they're minded like I heard—'

'And the Norwegian ship?'

'Ah . . . With the towfish – twenty thou', maybe?'

'A day.'

'Yeah. Wouldn't be bad, at that. Fully crewed – except the diving control team's not complete now, or so I heard.'

'Where d'you get this sort of information?'

'Mostly – routine stuff anyway – the *Aquanaut*. That's a news-sheet we all subscribe to. Market intelligence for the underwater industry – what we call the oily world. Then there's the Offshore Intelex wire service. Word o' mouth too – gossip. But – what I'd want to know is how the *Norsk Eventyrer*'s control system 'd adapt for the submersible that's in Odessa.' He'd nodded at Kinsman: 'Owners might send a bloke down too, if they see a charter in prospect. See us and set a price. They been let down, some geezer welshed on a charter that was all fixed up, see. And some of the control team took off like. Well – gotta live, a man goes where the work is, eh? We'd replace 'em – no problem except they'd be on your payroll, extra cost—'

'Norwegian owners might see *us* there, you said?'

'Yeah – they're in Oslo, see. If there's charter terms to settle—'

'I'll send one of my own people – either with you or to join you there – if it gets to that stage.'

'Saying you want me to go, then?'

Kinsman looked at Mark. 'We still need the terms of *our* collaboration settled, don't we?'

He nodded. Thinking that that might be where this express would hit the buffers. Having moved this fast – the way Kinsman always worked, according to Lucy – having got this far in three days, he and Sammy Moed would lock horns and that might well be that. Irresistible force, immovable object: disengage, start again elsewhere.

He agreed, though. 'Whenever you like. I'll need my lawyer here, that's all. I might get on to him from here, save to-ing and fro-ing?'

'Good.' Kinsman swung back to Monteix. 'Can Aberdeen do without you for another day or two? The hotel's on us, of course—'

Lofthouse, in the wing of the *Eventyrer*'s bridge, leant back against the timber-topped rail. 'You had him sold on it *that* quickly.'

'Not really sold. It seemed so, but actually he was still keeping his options open – beyond financing Monteix's frolics around the West End, then the trip to Hamburg. Meanwhile he was up to various tricks of his own. But – yes, he did seem pretty keen.'

Remembering Lucy's obvious satisfaction. She'd fixed this – brought Mark and the great Bob K. together and seen the wheels start turning. Accompanying Mark to the lift that day – after he'd called Moed and they'd agreed to meet the next morning at ten – he'd murmured, 'Like a house on fire. Astonishing!' and she'd whispered back, with that look of extreme complacency – a cat with all the cream it could possibly want – '*Always* like this. What makes it so exciting.' The lift doors sliding open with no more than a gentle sigh: 'Tomorrow at ten, then?'

'Not tonight?'

'Heavens, no. *Hours* of work to catch up on!'

Pecks on cheeks. Mark thinking on the way down, *Can't have it* all *ways . . .*

He told Lofthouse – quite liking the man, now they'd got to understand each other – 'Kinsman did obviously *want* to come in with us – and make himself a packet in the process, of course – and he was letting me see that. But first there had to be a meeting with my lawyer – he wasn't sending Monteix to Hamburg until that was in the bag.'

'Terms easily agreed, were they?'

'Well – we haggled it out, you know. Had to compromise a bit. My lawyer had been talking to City friends and heard a rumour that the Kinsman Group had cash-flow problems looming. As it happened, it matched another hint I'd had – and explained the attraction to Kinsman of a quick, fat profit. Anyway Sammy'd warned me we might have to meet him halfway. Incidentally, Monteix had to lower his sights too, accepted seven and a half percent instead of the ten he'd said he wouldn't budge from. I only heard that afterwards. Kinsman's lever was Monteix refusing to come to sea himself – on the grounds his bad back wouldn't stand it – which was why they had to take *you* on, I imagine.'

'Saved himself some money, then. *I'm* not getting two and a half.'

'Flat fee and a very small percentage as bonus on successful completion – right?'

'Christ – everyone knows *everything*!'

'Well – not quite, I don't think . . .'

In his own negotiations – or Sammy's – he'd settled for fifteen percent of net profit instead of twenty-five, and a non-reclaimable payment in advance of one million, instead of two and a half; with contractual acceptance that the position of the wreck would not be divulged until that payment was received. Contracts would be exchanged when charters had been arranged and the decision taken – by Kinsman – to go ahead. They'd all been very much aware at this stage that the French team might still pip them to the post; in which case he'd put it all on hold, wait for the Frogs to draw a blank – please God – and then start again.

Mark said, 'That fee in advance was what the fuss was about later, of course.'

'Yes. Had the wrong end of the stick, didn't I.' Lofthouse sounded apologetic. 'But he's good for the rest of his debts here, I hope!'

'*Your* cut, you mean.' Mark nodded. 'I'd guess so. As long as he's legally bound – written contract – which you have, eh?'

'Oh, yes—'

'*And* if we get the rest of the gold up.'

'Which thanks to you—'

'Let's hope.'

On the day before the meeting to discuss contractual details – the day Monteix had been there, in fact – Jack and Edith Jaeger had been visited by a tall, smartly dressed redhead, age around thirty, who'd told them she was a television researcher collecting ideas for a programme about WW2 submarine commanders. She'd telephoned the evening before to make an appointment, and whether or not the old boy had smelt a rat at that early stage, he'd tried to call Mark to tell him about it, but failed to contact him. Mark had been spending that night in London, at the club. So the first he heard of it was the following evening when he got back to Brighton and called his uncle to report progress. In effect, simply that progress was being made. He wasn't going into any financial detail, because he didn't want to raise the old man's hopes and then dash them. With nothing certain yet, and the French still an unknown quantity in the wings, the message at this stage could only be that things were looking good but still had a way to go.

Jack Jaeger had received this cheerfully enough, and had obviously very much enjoyed the redhead's visit.

'Charming young woman, I must say. Close on six foot tall, and most attractive. But she asked the wrong questions, didn't seem to know the first thing about the subject she's supposedly researching!'

'Questions such as?'

'Nonsensical, a lot of them. But here's an odd thing, Mark. She knew I sank that Jap, and she wanted me to tell her where. Really made a point of it – didn't I have a note of the latitude and longitude – surely I would have, such a splendid achievement – gush, gush. But that girl wouldn't know a latitude and longitude if it bit her in the neck. And when I said, "Try the Public Record Office", she said she'd heard there was some confusion on the subject. I was probably the only person alive who knew where the thing was, and this would make my contribution to the programme enormously interesting. Didn't seem to know anything else at all, though – for instance, didn't know the name of even *one* other submarine CO. Quite charming, and most attractive – lapped up *three* glasses of gin, I may say – and Edith liked her—'

'What TV company – did she say?'

'No. Told me they were independent researchers, sold ideas to the established programme-makers. Of course *I* wouldn't know . . .'

'Sounds like a load of crap, doesn't it?'

'I'm afraid so. Edith doesn't agree with me, but – yes. Damn shame – good-looking girl like that . . .'

Lucy had told him quite a long time before this that new employees in Kinsman companies had been aware of having their private lives investigated. She'd been asking him whether there'd been anyone around asking questions about *her* – which there hadn't been, as far as he knew. They might have nosed around her previous place of employment, of course.

He asked his uncle, 'Your redhead give a name?'

'Yes. Amelia. Pretty – don't you think? Not many of 'em about, these days.'

'Surname?'

'Odd one. Hutt? Yes, that's it. H-U-T-T.'

'Amelia Hutt. Right.' He'd made a note of it, and confronted Kinsman on the subject a day later, when they met with Sammy Moed present again to check over the contractual agreements which by then Sammy had drafted. Before that Mark had asked Lucy, in the reception area where she'd come to meet him, 'Remember you told me your employer used a firm of private eyes to check on people?'

She'd shushed him, led him over to the big room's far
end, where there was a brightly lit tank of tropical fish to
goof at.

'Well?'

'Is one of them a tall girl with red hair, name of Amelia
something?'

Hand to her mouth, eyes wide: 'Oh, God . . .'

It was all he'd needed. In Kinsman's office – Moed had
arrived and Lucy was apparently to be present at the
meeting – he'd opened with, 'Before we start—'

Kinsman glanced at him, frowning. 'Yes?'

'I think you have an employee by the name of Amelia
Hutt.'

'*Do* I . . .' He shrugged – glancing round at Lucy, then
back at Mark. 'If you say so . . .'

The pale-brown eyes guarded, under their droopy lids.
Behind him, Lucy had glanced up sharply from her perusal
of the contract forms. Mark added, 'May not be her real
name. But she's about six feet tall, a redhead, very attractive.'

'I have quite a large number of employees, Mark, and
sixty-seven percent of them are female. I suppose the odds
are that one might have red hair?'

'This one snoops for you. Visited my uncle – when you
had Monteix here, as it happens – and tried to trick him
into giving her the position of the I.67's wreck. Posing as a
television researcher. Drank three gin-and-tonics and rather
gave herself away. What it comes down to is that if you
want me to sign *any* contract, you'll first have to give me
your assurance that from now on my uncle and his wife
won't be bothered by you or any of your employees.'

'Damn your bloody cheek! Look here, Mark – I very much
dislike your tone and—'

'Quite a bit I dislike, too. But the timing was much too
neat. Before agreeing this, you'd have wanted to know the

old man really does exist – that this isn't some sort of scam
– right?'

'I *would* be justified in having enquiries made – before
agreeing to invest up to ten million—'

'Money which won't be in my uncle's hands or mine. But
all right – to check he exists and he's the man I've told you
he is – and whom incidentally Lucy knows quite well, you
could have asked *her*—'

'A lot of my money would – if this project went ahead,
Mark – pass through Monteix's hands, and he's *your* recruit.
Then again, you and Lucy here have been – close friends,
shall I say—'

'Say lovers, if you like – but our private lives aren't your
business. Or do you have some reason to think they are?'

Blinking . . . 'It *could* be a scam, you see. Could *have* been.
You're right, your uncle might *not* have existed. I'd have
had every right—'

'Sending some snooper to interrogate the old man about
the position of the wreck? Some *right*?'

'As I said, I have no knowledge whatsoever—'

'You could then have gone ahead solo, couldn't you?
Wouldn't have needed this contract. Cut me and my uncle
out, saved yourself paying us anything at all?'

Lucy sitting frozen, watching them both. Sammy treating
Kinsman to his laser-beam stare. Kinsman with his head
back, glaring at Mark down his little beaky nose.

'That allegation is defamatory and insulting!'

'Call the deal off, shall we?'

'Wow.' Lofthouse blew his cheeks out. 'But you – kissed
and made up?'

'Hardly. He gave me the assurance I wanted, though,
and Sammy Moed smoothed things over. Pointed out the
practical advantages of going ahead – the time factor, all
that. It obviously *would* have been curtains, if Kinsman

hadn't been very reluctant to give up his pot of gold. He hated me from that moment on – even if he hadn't before. And of course – as you know – he tried to get even later. He'd have saved himself a million, but also saved face.'

In Lucy's eyes mostly, he suspected. But maybe also in his own.

Lofthouse was rubbing his close-cropped ginger head. '*Does* explain all that. I'll be damned . . .'

'Commander Lofthouse—'

The Norwegian watchkeeper on the bridge: pushing open a sliding-glass window.

'Yes?'

'—and Mr Jaeger. Excuse me . . . Captain Skaug would like very much to speak with you. He is in his cabin.'

6

Arne Skaug, the *Norsk Eventyrer*'s captain, was a huge man
– bigger than Eriksen, his chief officer, but with no fat
on him, just tall, broad and big-boned. And quiet-voiced,
quiet-mannered.

His cabin door was ajar. Lofthouse rapped on it. 'Kaptein?'

'Ah. Thank you both for coming.' He filled the doorway.
Intelligent, friendly face. 'Please come in. How's it going,
Mr Jaeger – Mark, I should say – not sick any more,
I hope?'

His English was near-perfect. And more impressive than
that was his friendly, easy-going manner, the fact that he
seemed not to harbour any animosity from the time when
he'd been kept steaming around in circles, Mark refusing to
give him the wreck's position until Kinsman had paid up, as
per contract. And then two more perhaps even worse days,
with the towfish 'streamed' – as they called it – and not
finding any wreck anywhere near that position . . . Mark
asked him – inside the day-cabin – 'Does anyone ever get
over seasickness for good?'

'Unfortunately not. A spell ashore, or fine weather, then
back into the rough stuff –' shake of the head – 'bad as
ever. Even your Admiral Nelson, he was sick like a cat

every time he put to sea. Now – please, sit down . . . Like
– coffee, or—'

'No, thanks. Nothing.'

'Ah. Yes.' Understanding *why* not: glancing at Lofthouse
as Mark subsided into an armchair. Its floral-patterned
loose cover seemed somehow incongruous. One could more
easily imagine such furnishings in the yacht that was lying
only about two thousand yards away now – still showing
no signs of activity on her decks. Mark paused at the
window; but this was the wrong side, there was nothing
in view except the slant and slide of blue-black ocean.
Skaug saying to Lofthouse meanwhile – about the coffee
he'd offered – 'We do without too, eh, you don't mind?
Sit down, please . . .' Folding his big frame in behind
a stripped-pine desk: beyond it another door led to his
sleeping-cabin and bathroom. He told Mark, 'The winch is
OK, they *hope*. They have to test it out now, going to take
just a little longer. In fact it may have been a good thing,
this further small delay. I'll tell you. I just had Huard up
here, by the way – telling him what I must tell you now.
No – what I must *ask* you. By the way, Mr Kinsman will
be with us very soon – I think – and he knows about this,
I explained it to him.'

The build-up suggested some major problem looming. It
would have been more in character for him to have come
straight to the point without any such preamble. Mark
glanced at Lofthouse, then back enquiringly at the captain.

'So?'

'First – you're OK, huh, to make the dive?'

'Oh, yes—'

'It's my fault, I must say. Not just that Bairan's, *I* take
the blame. To sail from Scotland with only two pilots was
– stupid. I very *much* take the blame.'

'Kinsman's fault primarily though, surely. He was insisting—'

'Mr Jaeger – I'm the boss here. Where the buck stops?'

'Well – if that's how you see it. It's spilt milk anyway. But – what's new?'

'Yes. It's a question of the weather that's coming, mainly. You know we were told we could expect good conditions for forty-eight hours – then thirty-six, only. Now, it's down to twenty-four.'

Lofthouse groaned: 'Bloody hell!'

'The front is moving this way faster than before, evidently. Presents us with a problem. Uh?'

'How to fit in two dives –' Lofthouse explained it to Mark – 'each of no less than ten hours.'

'Yes. Twenty hours' dive time, certainly no less, and—' he was addressing this to Mark, too – 'necessarily some rest *between* dives. But with the interval only four hours – or less, you can't be always so exact, you know – this would mean none for Huard, he'd need every minute, *more*—'

'For maintenance routines.'

Lofthouse had murmured it – keeping Mark in touch. Skaug added, 'And that's putting it at the best. If the dives were each completed in ten hours, *and* no further worsening of weather prospects.' He was looking at Mark. 'What it means is we could proceed now as we have planned – one dive lasting ten hours, one full load being brought up – which would almost certainly be the one and only, because with this bad weather coming we could not send you down again, uh? Or – this is the alternative I'm putting to you – *or*, we decide to go for one much longer dive. One dive, *two* loads up on the hoist.' The big man leant forward, hands flat on the desk-top. 'That way we'd get up – well, about as much gold as seems to be accessible, from as much as the earlier dives and the videos suggest. But it would be a long – immersion. I've estimated it as something like eighteen hours. Therefore it has to be your own decision. If you prefer to make it one ten-hour dive – or twelve-hour if you needed it, in those circumstances you would be less pinched for time – then it's a safe bet we bring up one more load, and the rest would remain where it lies.'

'For the French to pick up.'

'Well.' A shrug. 'In the circumstances—'

Lofthouse put in, 'There's also the complication of our charter-period running out, isn't there?' He shrugged. 'But the weather anyway . . .'

Skaug's pale eyes rested on Mark. 'It has to be your decision. You're the guy who's doing this – if you are still wanting to, that is. But we must have a decision now.'

'Well.' He hesitated. 'Just to be sure I know what we're talking about – the crucial point is that bringing two loads up from one dive would be saving eight hours' travel, as it were. Right?'

The submariner agreed. 'Crab travel – yes.'

'So – three hours to get down, an hour or two hours' work – well, at least two, I suppose, me doing it – getting the hang of it – then a wait of roughly five hours on the bottom while the first load's hauled up and the basket's sent back down to us. That's ten hours gone.' He saw their nods: and Skaug checking it on his fingers. 'Then say another two hours' work – makes twelve – and maybe half an hour's wait on the bottom while you get the load up and on its way?'

Lofthouse said, 'You'd need at least that long to recover the pinger, wouldn't you? Wouldn't care to leave *that* for the French. There's also the hoist's guide-wire to be disconnected: once your second load's on its way up, we could start reeling that wire in. The pinger you'll bring up with you, of course. Right?'

'Well – Huard—'

'Yes. I suppose . . .'

'And five hours to come back up to the surface, then. Altogether seventeen and a half?'

'Call it eighteen. Heck of a long dive, Mark.'

'Yes . . .'

Thinking about it. The arithmetic – so many hours for this, so many for that – had been easy, hadn't stirred the imagination in any personal, envisageable way. But seventeen or eighteen hours, in a seven-foot sphere three miles down: he wasn't *trying* to imagine how it might feel, imagination was self-activating, one tried if anything to suppress it. Remembering having asked his uncle years ago about claustrophobia, whether it hadn't affected him at all in his submarining days, and his uncle assuring him that it hadn't, ever, hadn't affected any of them: and Mark thinking to himself that it would have affected *him*, all right . . .

'I suppose –' he cleared his throat – 'suppose the obvious question is: what's the duration of life-support?'

'Twenty hours, normal.'

He nodded. 'Which for a *ten*-hour dive—'

'Yes.' Skaug nodded. 'I spoke of this with Huard.'

'Safety-margin of two-and-a-half hours.' Looking from Lofthouse to Skaug. 'Would that be more or less normal – acceptable?'

'Well – barring—'

Skaug had checked himself. He'd probably been going to say 'barring accidents' . . . He substituted, after a fractional pause, 'If all goes smoothly.' Not wanting to mention accidents, since there'd been some: and Bairan having backed out in consequence.

So who *wasn't* superstitious?

Skaug lifted a large forefinger: 'A point Huard made is that while your first load is being brought up, you could sleep for perhaps three or four of the five hours.'

Lofthouse cut in, explaining to Mark, '*Good* point. Asleep – anyway resting, relaxing completely – you use less oxygen and emit less carbon dioxide. So you extend the life-support time.'

Back to Skaug: 'That's if they find they *can* sleep. Can't count on it, there might be more work to do than that video suggests. I agree it looks straightforward enough, easily accessible, but—'

'Until they're down there, we can't know. And I must say, before you decide either way –' Skaug's big hands clasped each other – 'you volunteered for this – "to save our bacon" was Mr Kinsman's expression, on the telephone half an hour ago – but you can change your mind too, if you so wish. It would be perfectly acceptable – right, Pete?' Back to Mark: 'Nobody would have grounds to criticize. Also – I must say this again, I should not have left Dundee without two other pilots. That is the real cause of this situation, I take full responsibility.'

'You were under a lot of pressure –' Lofthouse cut in with this – 'and what's more, I should have backed you. Trouble was, Kinsman being my boss—'

'Any case, I *want* to do it.' Mark nodded. 'And shifting to one dive of seventeen hours instead of two of ten or twelve each – especially if Huard's in favour—'

'Oh, he is. I didn't mention it, not to influence your own decision, but – yes—'

'Fine, then. I was going to say – at first sight, a dive that long sounds a bit arduous, but in fact—'

'Less so.' Lofthouse agreed. 'Definitely.'

'Good.' Skaug was pushing himself up. 'By the way – Mr Kinsman bringing some young woman, he said?'

'His Personal Assistant. Name of Lucy Greenstreet. Did he have anything to say about the longer dive?'

'Oh, yes. He – well, you can imagine—'

Lofthouse murmured, 'Can indeed.'

Wanting every ounce of gold that he could get. Not having his outlay covered yet, even. One certainly *could* imagine.

'I told him the decision would be made by you, Mr Jaeger.

Mark. As obviously it had to be. But it's surprising he hasn't joined us yet.'

'Don't have to wait for him, do we?'

'Well – no, I suppose we don't. In fact as soon as the hoist's OK—'

'Great. I'll nip down, see Huard.'

'Mark –' Lofthouse stopped him. 'Need to double-up on rations, won't you? I'll tell the galley.'

The Crab, still in its cradle, had been moved right aft, close under the massive A-frame that towered over the ship's stern and by which it would be lifted, swung out over the boil and heave of the sea and lowered into it. The cable was already hooked on: from the lift-hook at the rear end of the sail it ran up and through sheaves in the apex of the 'A', thence back overhead to a capstan-winch at this end of the helicopter deck. When the time came the Crab would be lifted out of its cradle, the hydraulically-operated A-frame would tilt out over the sea and the submersible would be inched down towards it. Divers with a Gemini inflatable would be standing by to unhook first the lift and then the towline – which was already hooked on, too. Not that there'd be much towing involved, with the *Eventyrer* navigationally static, held in position by the Dynamic Positioning system; the towline would only hold the submersible in close until the moment came for her to start her long free-fall to the bottom.

That was Bairan climbing out of the sail now. Spiderish, in his brown overalls. Huard, on deck and looking up, waiting for him, had changed into a padded waterproof jacket and trousers similar to Mark's; there was a white stripe down the side of the pants and the French flag across his back and shoulders. He'd worked for some French state outfit for a long time, he'd mentioned: it might have been that lot's uniform.

Bairan had something white between his teeth. Paper-work of some kind. Removing it as he came off the ladder, handing it to the Frenchman now. The pre-launch check-list, Mark realized – having been shown one some days ago by Lofthouse, as part of a lecture on the workings of submers-ibles. Lofthouse knew it all, and had often been down in submersibles, but only as an observer and in comparatively shallow water. What he knew most about was the general administration of underwater work, and the control sys-tems and so forth. Huard was scanning the check-list, Mark saw as he moved up closer: running a finger down the list of items that had been marked off – ballpoint ticks, or in some places figures. Bairan's work, just completed. It would be multi-lingual, presumably, certainly annotated in French as well as Russian. The one Mark had seen had been printed in Russian with notes added in Norwegian, some of which Lofthouse had been able to translate; the figures had been readings of battery voltages and oxygen cylinder pressures, but altogether there must have been about fifty different items, all of which had to be verified before each dive.

Huard had a hand on Bairan's shoulder, holding the card where they could both see it, Huard's lips pursed as his eyes ran down the list.

Finally: 'OK.' A pat on the Ukrainian's shoulder. Mark turning away too – hearing at that moment the racket of Kinsman's helicopter. He went over to the side, saw it levitating away from the yacht. Huard came over too; behind him a diver by name of McAlastair, one of those whom Monteix had recruited in Aberdeen. And another diver, name of – Wilson, or Williams. Both in wet-suits. Huard showed Mark the check-list: 'All OK. This time, no problem.'

'Bairan agree, no problem?'

A shrug, and a French sound of contempt, a sort of 'Pfui . . .' Mark pressed the question: 'Does he?'

The shrug again. 'He – fonny man.'

'Makes you laugh, you mean?'

'*Quoi?*'

It wasn't worth going on with. He'd only wondered whether the Ukrainian might have tried to explain himself at all. The helicopter's racket was deafening as it swept in and hovered, then began lowering itself towards the pad. Mark thinking that he might go up and see them, in a minute. Would have to go up anyway, for a last-minute visit to the heads. But see *her*, anyway; to hobnob with Kinsman was *not* a priority. In any case there wasn't going to be much time for conversation: Kinsman might have delayed his departure from the yacht with precisely that in mind.

Huard shouted in his ear, 'Long dive – eighteen hour?'

'Yeah. But listen – when we finish – quand c'est fini – *you* –' pointing at the manipulators – '*you* take the pinger and the guide-wire off the wreck – right?'

He hadn't got it: but he caught on at the second attempt, with some miming and evidently comprehensible bilingualism.

'Oui.' A pat on Mark's arm. '*I* do zis. Pas de problème.'

'Otherwise – wire-cutter on that one?'

Pointing at the Crab's stern, the rear manipulator. 'Pour couper?' Moving fingers like scissors. 'If you had to *cut* wires?'

Shake of the head. 'Is not necessary.'

'OK.' He'd thought he'd suggest it, just in case. 'But one other thing – your rations?'

'Uh?'

'Food.' He made motions of eating. 'Et café – for eighteen heures?'

'*Sure*, all fix!'

'Right. Bon . . . Look, I'll be back . . .'

Figures for the dive's expected duration were running

through his head again as he made his way forward –
and the helicopter's noise cut off. Dead silence suddenly:
ship-sound and sea-sound growing through it then, as his
ears retuned. Skaug would take Kinsman and Lucy to his
day-cabin, he guessed. Or to the van, maybe. Show them
the videos: Kinsman would like the shots of the gold coming
up, even though the amount recovered so far *wouldn't* quite
have covered his overheads. Seventy bars, value roughly
seven and a half million, whereas costs had been estimated
at eight million. But this dive now – it was going to take the
Crab three hours to get down to the wreck, and five hours to
get back up again; two work-periods of say two hours each
– eight plus four, twelve. With a five-and-a-half- or six-hour
waiting period in between, while the basket was hauled up,
emptied and sent down again: calling it six, there was your
total of eighteen. The figures repeated themselves – the
way they tended to sometimes – most often in half-sleep,
of course – overwrought brain doing its best to come up
with a better answer, in this case perhaps find an error to
reduce the figure by an hour or two, increase the margin of
safety. If they could winch the basket up faster, for instance
. . . Presumably they couldn't. But eighteen hours, and
life-support only twenty – depending on – as remembered
from Lofthouse's dissertations – not only oxygen but some
other chemical. He'd got there – soda-lime crystals. There
was a gadget they called a scrubber, an electric-powered
fan arrangement, which drove the air through a canister
of the soda-lime, which absorbed the poisonous carbon
dioxide, thus cleaning the air and in the process lowering
the atmospheric pressure, allowing for the release of more
oxygen.

On one of Huard's and Bairan's dives the life-support
system had failed, and by the time they'd got to grips
with it they'd come close to suffocating. That was when
Lofthouse had explained the workings of it in some detail

– swearing he'd never heard of any such breakdown before, and assuring Mark that repairs and replacements made subsequently guaranteed it couldn't happen again.

Touch wood . . .

But the safety-margin – back to *that* again – he guessed that if one had life-support for only twenty hours, and near the end of an eighteen-hour dive something or other went badly wrong, delaying you on the ocean floor when you didn't have the reserves to keep you alive for more than say an hour or two—

But – what Skaug and Lofthouse had been saying – if you slept after sending the first load up – two or three or four hours, say – the life-support period *would* be extended.

Which made prospects a little better.

Still fairly perplexing that he had volunteered for this . . .

He'd passed up the side of the workshop – in which amongst other things they kept the towfish – and then the length of the control van, and as he'd rounded that corner there she was – emerging from the van in a canary-yellow jump-suit, her cropped black hair like a glossy helmet.

'Hi!'

'Mark, *hello!*'

In recent thinking, she'd been Lucy II. Now, this moment, he was looking at Lucy I: that vision, breathtaking silhouette with arms lifted, fingers smoothing back damp, dark hair, sunlit esplanade and seafront for a background . . .

Illusion?

'In doubt whether it's me?'

Laughing, and reaching to him: the steel door of the control van had been pulled shut behind her. Kinsman would be in there, for sure, talking to Lofthouse and Skaug, perhaps looking at videos. The hell with him: he was an afterthought and an anachronism, Lucy was *here*, her arms tight round his neck. He told her – wanting the illusion, to get back to it and to have it last – 'Looking wonderful . . .'

'After being sick all night? Not so good now either, tell you the truth . . . But listen – d'you *have* to go through with this?'

'Yes, I do. Leave it at that, can we?'

'But *why*?'

'Get my fifteen percent of another fifteen million's worth?'

'You don't *need* it!'

'*Lucy!* Don't tell me *need* comes into your business ethos now?'

'Tell me honestly – why?'

'Well – one thing – on what we've recovered so far, several other people get damn-all – Monteix, for one, but the man I'm diving with too – *and* others.'

'So it's just – altruism?'

'No. It's for several good reasons. Number one, my uncle?'

'Well – I realize – I mean I guessed—'

'Mostly.' He nodded. 'And the French, though. If I wasn't doing this we'd be drawing stumps and going home, what's still down there'd be left for them to pick up – which in all the circumstances . . .' Shaking his head: 'No. No way . . . The one snag, I might say, is that in the process I'll be helping to enrich Kinsman – which incidentally you should approve of – shouldn't you?'

'Mark—'

'You *are* still – getting on with him?'

'Of course! If I wasn't, I'd—'

'Not put off at all by the fact he tried to get away with not coughing up the million?'

'He *would* have paid it. It was simply that at that time—'

'He hadn't the least intention – bastard was counting on me being under such pressure here—'

'Mark, I'm not informed or consulted—'

'I'd have thought you *would* have been. Quite a personal issue – I'd have thought – *our* relationship, and yours with him – wouldn't have been *only* a matter of the money – would it?' He changed the subject: 'His daughter's with you, of course. You were flying out to Vigo with her, you said.'

'She's in the yacht, with a stewardess looking after her. She and I share a cabin, incidentally.'

'You and the stewardess?'

'Monica. The child. I mention it because I know how your mind works, Mark – or how it *has been* working – and I assure you, just this once and never again—'

'Special occasion? Don't go down the mine, Daddy?'

'Oh, God . . .'

'Frankly, I'd much rather *not* be going down—'

'So don't! Let them find someone else!'

'There *is* no-one else. Just happens I can do the job – after a fashion—'

'What about Pete Lofthouse?'

'He's never worked a manipulator. Obviously if he *had*—'

'Literally *no-one* else?'

'We sailed two pilots short because your boss was insisting we shouldn't wait even another hour – remember?'

'Are you saying it's *his* fault?'

'To that extent, yes. OK, so the French were looking dangerous – and God knows how long it might have taken to get hold of replacement pilots—'

'Not the way *I* heard it!'

'Oh, I believe you. But – plain fact is –' checking the time – 'Lucy, it's water under the bridge, I'm not out to prove anything—'

'No – nor am I—'

'Situation is as it is, that's all.'

'You're starting as soon as something or other's mended?'

'Salvage-winch. Thing that hauls the gold up. And it

must be fixed by now. I'd better see what's cooking.' A nod towards the door of the van, and a hand out to her: 'Coming?'

As he'd guessed they might, they were showing Kinsman the video of an earlier dive. There were six or seven others in there, including the second mate, Rolf Friedlund, at the driver's console – with nothing much to do, only watch the computer doing it all, holding the ship *in situ* with constant adjustment of revs on her screws and thrusters. Varying shades of light and dark in here, illumination coming from the video screen at the far end, a few other monitors here and there and a shaded strip-light over the automatic plot at the nav. centre. Navigator Knut Messel presiding there: with at this stage even less to do than Friedlund had – except take a close interest in Lucy as she passed him, following Mark towards the starboard after corner where the video was showing. Kinsman diminutive beside Skaug, and Lofthouse providing a commentary, using a foot-rule as a pointer, its tip at this moment outlining the area of torpedo damage – which was becoming gradually more clearly defined and in better focus as the submersible closed in towards it.'

Mark murmured in Lucy's ear, 'Where the torpedo hit. This was the first sight of the wreck we had.' It was a video brought up from the Crab's first, exploratory dive: exciting enough at that time, but the thrill of it tempered by there being no certainty of gold still inside, or reachable, recoverable. Since then that area of mangled wreckage had been further opened up, first by explosive charges, then with cutting-gear, but Lofthouse was giving Kinsman the story from its beginning, presumably to demonstrate to him that although the yield in gold bars hadn't as yet been all that great, no stone had been left unturned, everything that could have been done *had* been. Kinsman, Mark guessed, might have expressed dissatisfaction, to have given rise to this. The bastard probably *would* have done, in fact . . . Lofthouse at this moment explaining that the initial surprise to *him* had been that, despite having been practically blown apart, the submarine had remained in one piece not only at the time of the torpedo hit but also throughout its three-mile dive to the sea-bed – which would have been rapid, rate of dive constantly accelerating, terminating in what must have been a fairly shattering impact.

'Why rate of dive accelerating?'

Kinsman's question. Lofthouse told him, 'Principle of Archimedes. Deeper a body goes, heavier it gets. Because it's being compressed, therefore displacing less water. Vicious circle – cause of quite a few submarine disasters in years gone by. But when this one hit the bottom, the impact must have been cushioned by silt. It's surprisingly deep. As you can see – or will in a minute. See here – looks like fog, doesn't it – that's a cloud of it, disturbance from the Crab's approach. Maddening for the pilots – every move they make, poke in with a manipulator for instance, it rises in a cloud and they're blinded.'

Wreckage coming into close-up now. Steel girders intact but out of shape, diseased-looking. Like a corpse's decomposition, Mark thought. Marine growth all over: barnacles, weed, even anemones. Steel plates scabrous with rust bent inward and upward into darkness, fringed with tassle-like growths to which Lofthouse referred as 'rusticles'. At moments the glare of the Crab's lights was reflected back dazzlingly at the viewers, bounced back off silt-cloud like a car's headlights in fog.

Lofthouse, suddenly: 'Now watch *this* . . .'

Movement – slow at first but gathering speed, and the camera pulling back – well, the Crab itself had been pulling back, backing away from what looked like the start of an avalanche, a mass of unidentifiable wreckage for no visible reason suddenly on the move – sliding, falling into an immediate upsurge of the silt-fog. Picture obscured again . . . Lofthouse telling Kinsman, 'First time I saw that I thought for a moment it was the gun-shield. The right shape, and size, roughly, and falling externally because the boat's leaning quite hard this way – angle of thirty degrees or so, leaning *up*hill, you see. From our point of view, the wrong way entirely. She's on a slope – see, pointing almost but not quite straight down it? Hence the larger build-up of silt on this slightly higher side. She probably slid on downhill after impact, stopped only when her bow was well and truly dug in, and since then the muck's accumulated not only against her but right *inside* that great hole in her. Right up to its own outside level. D'you see?'

'Not really. But—'

'I could re-wind, start from the longer view again—'

'Don't bother. I don't need to follow every detail.'

'Right. What I was saying – fact is, my mind must have been wandering – I.67 carried no gun, therefore no gun-mounting or -shield either. They got rid of all the heavy gear they felt they could dispense with, to maximize cargo-carrying capacity. On reflection I'd say that what we saw collapsing was a large part of the bridge – upper part of the conning-tower, that is, close to where the gun-mounting *would* have been. And as you *can* see—'

He'd checked himself. '*Damn* . . .' Clouding up again. 'Sorry about this.' Skaug meanwhile looking round – probably wondering what the hell was happening with the salvage-hoist – seeing Mark and Lucy in the flickering half-light and lifting a hand, acknowledging their presence. Lofthouse telling Kinsman, 'I'll fast-forward. Something the pilots can't do, of course, just have to possess their souls in patience . . . But – clearer now – OK? Right. You see, this was the obvious point of access for us, for more than one reason. To explain that – well, as I say – no gun, but this boat was laid down as one of a class that certainly did have guns, and only at a latish stage was she taken over and completed as a cargo-carrier. So internally her construction would have been the same as for the rest of that class. The gun – a 4.7-inch, very large calibre for a submarine – would've been just forward of the conning-tower, and the magazine – ammunition stowage, in other words – would have been directly under it and two decks down. Main deck providing living and working accommodation, you see, so one deck below that. It seemed to me a racing certainty that they'd have stowed the gold in there. As it happens, Mark Jaeger's uncle told *him* the same thing, from his own knowledge and experience – plus common sense. Reasons being – one, it's a secure stowage, lock-and-key secure, as good as a safe. A fair size, too – for shells as large as 4.7s it had to be. For security again, it's right under the captain's and officers' quarters – wardroom – which itself must have direct, fast access to the control room, so it can't be anywhere else. One could imagine that once the gold was loaded, the skipper'd most likely have kept the only key; after all, they were calling at other ports *en route* – Singapore, Penang . . . And one other factor, by the way, is that it's just about dead amidships, which from a trimming point of view is obviously the best place by far to put a small-dimension but extremely heavy weight.'

He took a breath, and went on, 'So – we had no doubt, if the gold was anywhere, *that* was where. And as it happened, Mark's uncle had done us a great favour by scoring his hit right amidships here. The strength in any submarine is its pressure-hull: if he hadn't done it for us, we'd have had to blast our own way in, using much bigger explosive charges than we *have* used here, but internally. Internal structure – bulkheads, decks, tanks, subdivisions generally – are made of lighter steel than the pressure-hull. Same with the casing – which is built *on* the pressure-hull –

and the bridge, which as I said is where I think that collapse came from – rusted plating dislodged by the Crab's motors' thrust. Anyway – the really hard part had been done for us. What we had to do was clear a way through this mess of wreckage – you'll see in a later video what a truly cavernous hole it left – then cut away part of an internal bulkhead right at its junction with what was actually deck-plating, the floor of the magazine. We could do that because the boat's lying so far over on her side. But I should have said – because it was leaning so hard this way – which was the bugbear we faced initially – a preliminary to all that was to excavate – dig away the mountain of silt alongside, then a few more tons of it out of that torpedo-damaged area.'

'How did you do that?'

'Water-jet. The Crab has a high-powered mud-pump – *very* high-powered, has to be, to work at that depth – and an armoured hose with a special nozzle on it. Nozzle's held and moved around in the grip of a manipulator. It's used mostly for sea-bed pipe and cable-laying – digging trenches in which to bury cable out of reach of fishermen's deep trawls, for instance.'

Camera swinging left, giving a different view of the tangle of wreckage. Lucy had slid her arm inside Mark's, was holding herself close against him: he disengaged that arm, put it round her. Closeness justified by the fact there wasn't all that much room for both of them to have a clear view of the screen. Cosy, anyway – a lot cosier than he'd be for the next eighteen hours . . . Lofthouse pointing at the screen again: 'Internal bulkhead – a transverse one – reasonably intact, at first sight, but actually flaking away with rust. We weren't on the level that the camera was at this time, though; after the excavations, we were well below the level of the main deck – which at this point had been blasted upwards, the torpedo striking well below what would have been the waterline – that's to say, the waterline when the boat was on the surface in a reasonably calm sea. When Commander Jaeger made his snap attack – brilliantly executed, incidentally, in what must have been extremely tricky conditions – the Jap was neither surfaced nor fully dived, he'd just started on his way down. And it was a rough sea. Jaeger would normally have had a depth-setting on his torpedoes of something like eight or ten feet, but I'd guess that at the moment of impact his target must have been rolling to starboard – he was attacking from the port side – so his torpedo would have hit well below the belt, so to speak. Hence the upward blast, through a main ballast tank and God knows what else – leaving us with an assortment of scrap-iron mostly buried under the bloody silt.'

'The blast *all* upward?'

'Oh, no. Right through the boat. I said "upward" only in respect of its results as you see them on the screen. No, it would have slammed through the whole boat from end to end, killed all hands instantly. There was no reason watertight doors between compartments should have been shut – and they weren't. If they had been, there'd have been compartments shut off and airtight, watertight, and when the boat sank below its designed maximum diving depth, the pressure would have imploded them, like cracking nuts. She'd quite likely have ended up on the sea-bed in *several* pieces. The fact that didn't happen makes it certain she was completely flooded right away, went down full of water.'

'Bodies?'

'No bodies. None we've seen, anyway. We didn't expect to – if you remember. When we were discussing the possibility of any War Grave objections?'

'Crabs. White ones, someone said.'

'Yes. Highly effective disposal agents. Worms too, though. Remember one of Ballard's *Titanic* photographs, that pair of shoes?'

'I – think I do . . .'

One pair of shoes, lying on the sea-bed in such a position that the wearer might still have been in them. But *nothing* in them; not even a scrap of bone.

Lofthouse was saying, 'I'm told the crabs are white because they spend their whole lives in the dark. But – here we are – end of Reel One. If you can stand any more, we might skip to the first sight of gold, rather than—'

'Kaptein!'

Friedlund, swinging round on his swivel seat with a telephone in his hand. After a quick exchange of Norwegian, Skaug announced in English, 'We can start now – at last. The hoist is OK, they are sending it down.'

Friedlund was using a broadcast system to summon the diving control team. Knut Messel had flicked some lights on, and Lucy had separated herself from Mark.

Almost *jumped* away . . . Before Kinsman saw that arm around her – the huddle they'd been in?

Mark was looking at her: she knew it, was *not* looking back at him. He asked her, 'Wouldn't he approve?'

'Mr Jaeger.' Skaug, dropping a hand on his shoulder. 'I wish you a successful dive.'

'Thanks, Captain. I'll – get going.'

As priority, a final visit to the heads – the last for minimally eighteen hours. Then collect spare sweater et cetera from the cabin. And check the rations had been sent down to the Crab. Safe keys – better leave those behind. A tight feeling in the gut was recognizable as a symptom of fright. But also, Lucy and that give-away reaction of hers a minute ago still nagged. He looked back at her: 'Wouldn't have wanted to embarrass you. I did tell the little shit we were lovers – remember?'

'Ah – Mark . . .'

Little shit himself – in jeans and a suede jacket. He might well have heard that: but if so, must have decided he'd sooner not have. Smiling – and with his hand out. Politician-fashion, Mark thought. Hearing the man purr, 'It's splendid, that you're doing this. We've had our differences – misunderstandings – but—'

'Pete!' Ignoring him, beckoning to Lofthouse. 'Give you my safe keys, shall I? The strong-room key's inside it, you'll need it. Other stuff too – you know what's there.'

'Yes. Right—'

'Did you fix my sandwiches and stuff?'

'I told them to double the quantities of whatever you'd ordered.'

'Thanks.' He looked down at Kinsman. 'You say something?'

A shake of the head: tight-lipped, angry-looking, and moving to go on past, but Mark caught him by an arm.

'What the *fuck*—'

'Understand one thing. I'm not doing this for *you*.' He let him go. 'Lucy—'

She came back to him. A glance over her shoulder, *en route*. Then: 'Wish you weren't doing it at all.' Kinsman, on his way out – there was a lot of coming and going now – could *not* have heard that murmur. 'How long will you be down?'

'Eighteen hours, roughly.'

'*Eighteen*—'

'Plan is to stay down until we've sent two loads up. Weather's not going to last, it's the only way to handle it. Ask Pete, he'll explain. He'll also tell you it's OK, dead safe – et cetera. Listen – think we dare kiss goodbye?'

7

—————⟫•⟪—————

You could make a joke of it, but it wasn't all that rollickingly funny – her reluctance to allow that bastard to see the two of them in close physical contact. Why should it embarrass her – unless she was in a similarly close relationship with *him*?

Huard lent over from the Crab's sail and took the bag containing four thermos flasks of coffee from him. Cartons of milk and bags of sandwiches, apples and bananas were already on board. Also extra urine bottles and polythene bags, and sticky tape for sealing the bags when full. Or half-full. You'd hardly fill one: or re-open one that had already been in use.

He got off the ladder on to the Crab's casing, and from there into the sail. Looking down into the hatch, getting a bird's-eye view of Huard moving around inside. A thought fleetingly in mind that he could still draw back, *not* join him down there . . . Looking around then – an excuse for delay? – seeing Carl Qvist, the stocky, pot-bellied diving superintendent, on the lip of the helicopter deck with a microphone in one hand and a loud-hailer in the other, overseeing the team of winchmen and others who were taking up their positions for the launch. Crewmen who'd handle the restraining-wires, for instance, waiting on both sides near the A-frame's feet, the wires already snap-hooked to eyebolts in the Crab's sides, their purpose being to prevent it swinging around, crashing against the frame's massive uprights instead of passing midway between them as they swung back over the sea astern. And the Gemini inflatable already launched, with the divers in it – two divers, one driver, all three in wet-suits and needing them too, the grey rubber boat plunging and bucking over the swells down there on the support ship's quarter.

There'd be spectators too. Further aft on this deck, probably. Or up where Qvist was. Lucy and Kinsman with the skipper and Lofthouse – maybe others. Lucy, anyway. Skaug and Lofthouse might be in the van with the control team. Maybe just her and bloody Kinsman. He'd already said goodbye to her – getting his face wet from hers in the process, hadn't realized until that moment that she was crying – and Kinsman he didn't want to see. Certainly not within a mile of *her*. Therefore didn't now even glance that way.

Too late *not* to go through with it now, anyway. Didn't have the guts to back out, might be another way of putting it. He crouched inside the sail, took his weight on his hands on the rim of the hatch and let himself down, dropping the last foot or so on to the sphere's slatted wooden floor, then folding himself down on Huard's left, the Frenchman mock-saluting with a forefinger: 'Welcome on board, M'sieur!'

The sea was virtually in close-up down here. The viewports being low down in the sphere, from this position on the *Eventyrer's* stern you were looking straight down at it. Blue-black, white-whorled, heaving. He took his eyes off it, glanced around the sphere, which was even more cramped than he remembered. He had known perfectly well how small it was, but when you got in – well, you *felt* it. Remembering his uncle telling him that claustrophobia in most people was only a state of mind, that unless you were chronically prone to it you didn't have to let yourself succumb. And – all right, nothing acute, no screaming panic, only – a certain discomfort, one might call it. Having forgotten in the month or five weeks since Odessa how it felt to be shut in an extremely small, globular space packed with instrumentation – electrics, life-support, gauges for this, that and the other, sonar, echo-sounder, underwater telephone, VHF radio, trimming systems, pump and motor controls and several dozen other switches – in the pilot's console, and everywhere else around the sphere's curved sides – and of course the rather obtrusive black manipulator controls grouped around the left-hand viewport. Three of them: two side by side, and the one for the manipulator at the submersible's rear end above the other two, under its own down-slanted TV monitor.

'OK, Mister?'

'Mark – s'il vous plaît. But – oui, va bien.'

Huard's slightly evil grin. He'd been fiddling with the radio, and turned back to it now. The telephone could only be used underwater, of course, pre-dive communications with the van and the Gemini would be by VHF radio. To give himself something to do Mark was shifting plastic bags of sandwiches and thermos flasks back out of the way, clear of the vicinity of the viewports and the pilot's console. There wasn't really space for any of it: the only loose gear that belonged here were two stools – padded, and no more than four inches high – because of the low viewports, you wouldn't want to sit higher – and bench-type cushions enabling two men to lie sardine-like side by side with the stools as head-rests. You couldn't have stood upright, quite; the sphere's internal diameter was six feet ten inches, but the wooden flooring raised you about a foot, the space under it packed with yet more plumbing and electrics.

Home – for the next eighteen hours . . .

The radio crackled, then burst loudly into voice – that of a Norwegian whom the *Eventyrer*'s owners had flown from Oslo to Hamburg to replace one of those who'd deserted the original diving control team. He was the underwater telephone man too.

'Control to Crab – how do you hear me? Over.'

Huard turned the volume down a bit. He said into the hand-held microphone, 'Hear you good, Control.'

'Did you shut your hatch yet?'

'I do now.' On his feet then, using a stool as a step and reaching up. Thump of the hatch banging down shut, and a clang as the locking-ring engaged. Crouching then, picking up the mike: 'Hatch I have shut.'

'About to lift you off, Crab.'

'Roger.'

Mark was remembering Lofthouse having warned him it might be 'a bit bouncy', this launch. Launching and recovery, he knew, could be tricky in anything like rough weather. Not that it looked all that rough now, but it wasn't a flat calm either, and the swells might be bigger than they looked from up here. Seasickness on the cards again, therefore. How instant might it be? He *hoped* the dive would start as soon as they were launched. By the time you were down to about forty feet – which would take roughly thirty seconds – the Crab would be rock-steady, Lofthouse had assured him, its only dynamic the downward drift.

Lofthouse was great with his assurances. And there might be time to get sick *before* you dived. Then – well, in this very small, airtight space, with eighteen hours to go – that *stink* . . .

Lift-off. A small lurch, and you were airborne, the Crab plucked smoothly out of its cradle. Swinging a little: but the restraining wires would be taking up any slack, Qvist bawling at the seamen handling them to see to it she didn't get *any* lateral movement on her, at least before she'd passed through that big gate-like structure. Mark crouching at his viewport, fingers locked into the slatted timber decking, seeing it all in his mind's eye, his spectator's view of earlier proceedings. The submersible rocking around a little on its cable, and the sea astern of the *Eventyrer* a rolling, dark-blue swirl which almost immediately seemed to be coming up to meet them. *Did* look rougher, too – especially with the Gemini in sight again suddenly – off to the right, to port, to the right as one looked astern – and tossing and bouncing over the undulations. Flash of the sun's reflection from a diver's upturned face-mask. The thought persisting that it was weird, unreal, to be doing this himself: astonishing that they'd accepted his offer, even considered it for a moment . . . He saw a diver slide over the Gemini's nearside blister only maybe ten or twelve yards away: and that was his *last* sight of the ocean's surface: within a couple of seconds without noticeable impact it was suddenly all violent motion – the Crab's weight off the cable, in the sea's power, and the viewports already submerged, swirling kaleidoscopes of fizzing colours – blues, greens, whites. That jerk would have been the towing-wire jumping up bar-taut, wrenching the submersible's bow around to hold her like a big fish on a line, plunging over and through the swells.

Which certainly *were* bigger than they'd looked from the support ship.

And seasickness *could* be instant. Not helped by the need *not* to be. *Feel* it – OK: but to vomit, at this stage . . . *Don't think about it. Think about – oh, Christ—*

Radio crackling again.

'Diver is boarding you to disengage the lift-hook. OK? Over.'

Tell him *No, lift us back on board?*

If there'd been something wrong, Huard could have, obviously. All he *had* said was 'Roger'. You could hear the diver up there, his fins plonking along the casing to the sail. The lift-hook was above it, of course. Surrounding noise meanwhile turned up high – racket of the sea and the Crab butting through it, swells thumping hard and regular and some on top, impacting against the sail. Seasickness by now bloody awful and made worse by the sense of tight enclosure, barely having space to move. In Odessa it hadn't felt *this* small.

Because in Odessa you'd been in flat-calm water and not about to go down three miles?

'Crab. Lift-hook has been disengaged.'

'Roger . . .'

Diver leaving? No – climbing forward, there were non-weather sounds from that side of the sail now. To disengage the tow, of course, sever one's last link to the support ship.

Sooner the bloody better . . .

'Crab – diver's on your stem to cast off the tow-wire. All right with you? Over.'

Different voice, that one. Scotsman. Driver of the Gemini, he guessed. At close quarters, where he could see exactly what was happening. Huard told him, 'Yes – OK.'

Meaning go ahead, cast off. Then we can start the dive – please God. Illness approaching crisis point, the urge to surrender to it almost uncontainable: he had a plastic bag in his hand, ready for it. Starting a silent count-down, both in anticipation of release and to distance his thoughts from vomit, plastic bags and the prospect of eighteen hours cooped up with a Frog who'd hate your guts for it. Starting at twenty. Nineteen. Eighteen—

'Tow gone!

He'd have known it – the Gemini driver would – through having seen the diver's hand-signal. Diver by now having jumped over the side, doubtless swimming back to the cavorting rubber boat. Crouching in the sphere, you felt the bow swinging away, the submersible flinging round across the direction of wind and sea, tipping over on the shoulder of a swell; down into a trough – *thump* – and rolling back the other way. Christ . . . A problem was that when you needed to grab for support there was only gear you daren't lay a finger on. The deck was safest. Crouching, white-faced, sweating, teeth clenched: promising himself – fifteen, fourteen – *Only a minute now . . .*

'Crab, you receiving me? Over.'

'Loud, clear—'

'Clear your vent!'

'Clear vent. Roger. Out.'

Huard didn't bother much with procedural 'over's or 'out's. Reaching in a quick stabbing motion to some switch or other while his gaze travelled swiftly over other dials. A brief dark-faced, white-eyed glance round at Mark, then an explanatory mutter of, 'Vent air out, see.' He *did* see, as it happened – actually remembered it being explained to him: air being vented from the top of the ballast tank allowed sea-water up into it from the bottom, creating what Lofthouse had referred to as 'negative buoyancy'.

Vision of Lucy watching, seeing the red sail disappear, black ridges of ocean rolling unbroken where it *had* been.

She scared, too?

He could feel the heaviness, the sluggish beginning of descent.

Time – 1054.

Huard had finished with the radio, had pushed that mike back into its slot. Glancing at Mark again, amused at seeing him still clinging to the deck although the motion had virtually ceased, was already only a gentle rocking. Not even *that*, now. The Frenchman pointing downwards with a forefinger, raising his eyebrows, querying his passenger's comprehension of the dive having now commenced. The whites of his eyes bright in contrast with a swarthy complexion darkened further by a day's growth of stubble. (Lucy's snuffly protest in very recent memory: 'You haven't shaved!' He'd told her, 'Nothing to *cry* about, is that?') He'd got Huard's message anyway: unlatching his fingers and shifting into a sitting position, hugging his drawn-up knees. Reaching behind him then to stuff the plastic bag back where it had come from. Huard didn't know what he'd missed – or how narrowly. The Crab was well under now, sinking on an even keel. In the viewports, shimmery blue-green water sliding upward was still patched and streaked in shifting shades of colour, but the differences were fading towards a deepening blue. Illumination in the sphere now was from small lights in its dome. But – all as smooth as silk now – after that horrendous start. He was recalling Lofthouse's further assurance that since just about everything that could have gone wrong had done so in the earlier dives and subsequently been put right, and everything else checked over half a dozen times, there was really nothing left for anyone to worry about. And you could begin to *believe* it, now – especially in the light of Huard's calm self-assurance, obvious competence. And the peace and quiet, with no motion at all other than the swift descent. Maybe *too* swift? Judging by the movement of the needle in the depth-gauge, knowing the rate of dive should be about a hundred feet per minute, suspecting it might be significantly faster than that . . . Approaching eighty feet – after only half a minute. But Huard knew what he was doing: and if he'd decided they were falling too fast he could have shed water-ballast from that tank with a guff of high-pressure air from the external air-bottle. Lofthouse had explained this too; including the fact that you could only blow the tank with HP air when you were still fairly near the surface. At depths such as they were heading for now, he'd pointed out, ambient sea pressure would be at least equal to that of the bottled air – so what use, et cetera . . .

Mark had asked him, 'Is that what went wrong when they found they couldn't get off the bottom?'

'No. Nothing to do with it.' The submariner had looked surprised. 'Didn't I explain all that?'

'You did. But I didn't take it all in, I'm afraid.'

Because (a) technicalities weren't his forte, he had really to exert himself to cope with them, and (b) Bairan hadn't at that stage opted out, so he, Mark, hadn't even for one crazy second ever contemplated going down in the Crab himself. The detail hadn't much concerned him, therefore; those two had darned near come to grief but finally *had* made it to the surface – that was all that really mattered. But this time he'd listened carefully to the explanation. First of all, that a trimming system that *could* be used when the Crab was in very deep water involved pumping oil into rubber-membrane external bags: this increased the Crab's displacement and thus made it lighter in the water.

'Principle of Archimedes.' Lofthouse had quoted, 'A body immersed in water experiences an upthrust equal to the weight of water which it displaces. Greater volume, greater upthrust, i.e. buoyancy. Get it?'

'She gets lighter in the water?'

'Right. Gets lighter, starts upward. Because on the bottom the principle's to be in virtually neutral buoyancy, so a small change makes a lot of difference. Expand her a little, up she goes.'

'And the oil-pump didn't work – right?'

'Wouldn't start. They've fixed it since, of course.'

'Didn't some other system fail as well?'

'Yes.' He'd grimaced. Pushing blunt fingers through his short, gingery hair. 'Which is a bit much – when you're three miles down. Their own bloody fault though, this was. There's a drop-weight – right? Under the bottom of the sphere, and it's released by cranking a spindle – from inside, of course, actually under the wooden deck. You with me?'

He'd nodded. 'Couldn't do it, for some reason.'

'The wrench wasn't on board. That's why I say it was their fault. It's an item on the check-list – bottom-weight wrench on board. They'd both assumed it was, didn't physically check it, just ticked it off. Won't make *that* bloomer again, I don't suppose!'

'Tell me again how they did get up?'

'Huard – well, look, there's another trimming system. Mercury trim-line, tanks at both ends and a pump. Purely for the submersible's angle in the water, doesn't affect the overall weight, only corrects any bow-down or bow-up angle.'

'Right.'

'Huard pumped all the mercury to the stern reservoir, to give her bow-up angle, and went full-ahead on the motors. Luckily there was enough juice left in the batteries – *just* – they were damn near flat by the time he'd done it. Up-angle plus forward impetus, you see. And the fact is – Archimedes again – once you start coming up, all other things being equal it's a continuing process. Bloody lucky, though.'

Lofthouse truly believed there was nothing *now* that could go wrong. After Bairan had backed out and Mark had offered to take his place he'd arrived at that conclusion, and asked Mark later, 'I suppose you'd thought it through that far yourself?'

He hadn't, though. Hadn't known enough about it to 'think it through'. He'd prevaricated – 'Well – you know. I mean – more or less, I suppose, but—'

'It's a cert. Believe me. I admire you for taking it on – we all do – but the plain fact is – as I say . . .'

Now, passing a hundred and fifty feet, Huard was giving the ballast tank that blast of air. Checking first that the vent was shut – a pinpoint of light glowed above the switch when it was open – then reaching to a valve without having to look for it. Hiss of air clearly audible. Eyes on the depth-gauge: hundred and sixty feet, time 1055. So they'd been dived barely one minute. He had a stopwatch in his hand, and he'd stopped blowing, touched the switch again to shut the vent. Eyes still on the gauge. It was the shallow-water one: Mark remembered this from Odessa, when he and Bairan had dived inside the outer harbour – *an* outer harbour – in no more than forty feet of water. At greater depths, they'd explained, the procedure was to shut off the clock-faced gauge and concentrate on the digital one.

Hundred and ninety feet. 1055 and a half: ninety seconds since they'd started down. They were about fifty feet deeper than they should have been, if they'd been going by the book; anyway the needle was moving more slowly now, and Huard looked content as he reached for a different microphone – the underwater telephone's – and thumbed its switch.

'Crab calling Control – test telephone.'

Black now, outside there. Had been blue-black, like blue ink, was now completely dark.

'– loud and clear, Crab. You likewise?'

'Loud, clear.' A shrug, apologetic glance in Mark's direction. It had been loud enough, but not all that clear. 'Two hund'ed-twenny feet. You call, intervals thirty minute?'

'Roger. And depending how it goes we'll give you your direction of drift. Out.'

Huard hung up the mike, asked Mark, 'Unnerstan' – drift?'

'So you'll know which way to go to get to the wreck, when we're on the bottom.'

Approving nod. Passenger not a *total* idiot, maybe. Huard had reached for his pilot's log and was making some pencil notes in it. Time and depth, whatever. But the passenger, Mark thought, was in reasonably good shape – was more or less reconciled to the lack of space, had not as yet felt much in the way of panic or claustrophobic stress. Touch wood . . . The 'drift' business, though: Pete Lofthouse had explained that underwater currents tended to be unpredictable after periods of bad weather. And in the *Eventyrer*'s control van they'd have the Crab as well as the I.67's wreck – or rather the transponder which Messrs Huard and Bairan had anchored close to the wreck – on their screens. When Huard touched down on the sea-bed they'd give him a bearing and distance from the wreck anyway, but if on the way down there was a lot of drift – especially drift towards danger, meaning the salvage-hoist wire and the guide-wire, or at the point of landing on the sea-bed the salvage basket itself, the chance of landing on top of it – if there were any such hazard, getting due warning from the surface Huard could keep himself out of trouble by using the submersible's motors to distance himself from it. He wouldn't if he didn't have to: it wasn't the motors' intended purpose, and battery-power was best conserved for when you got down there. Especially when facing a dive of this duration. You'd need all you had, over that length of time, for propulsion on the sea-bed, lights, all the electrically operated control systems – and for the underwater telephone, for instance. *And* the manipulators. Their machinery was hydraulic, but the control of it from inside the sphere was electrical.

Three hundred feet. In the viewport, only blackness. Even putting his face as close as possible to its lower rim, trying to look upwards, there wasn't a glimmer. Then he realized: wouldn't have been anyway – the Crab's casing projected forward above the viewports, would have blanked off any upward view.

He sat back, feeling stupid. Glancing at Huard: the

Frenchman reached to a switch – again without having to pre-locate it. 'Voyez!'

The Crab's lights bored out to a range of about twenty or thirty feet, through dark, empty sea. Not a fish, not a bubble, nothing but black water. Space without stars.

He reached again, switched off.

'Save – for later.'

Save the amps, he'd meant. Five hundred feet. Time – 1058 and a half. Well – 1059 . . . But five hundred feet: Jack Jaeger's WWII submarine, he remembered the old man telling him, had had a maximum tested diving depth of *three* hundred feet. He'd been to five hundred in her, he'd said, but only inadvertently; near some coast in the Far East, where *Tigress* had motored into what he'd called a fresh-water patch, probably a river's outflow, suddenly 'started down like a lift', and within seconds had been in imminent danger of being crushed in a sea-pressure she hadn't been built to stand.

'But –' his own voice, in memory – 'you got away with it . . .'

Jack Jaeger had shrugged. 'Devil looks after his own, eh?'

And maybe that same evening – tongue somewhat loosened – talking about Lucy: *She's no Sally, is she* . . .

Generation-gap, and a different viewpoint: most of all, not knowing Lucy, as he *had* known Sally. In other words more pro-Sally than anti-Lucy: to which one could hardly have taken exception . . . Here and now, anyway – eleven o'clock, depth six hundred – six hundred and twenty – he wished to God old Jack had been alive so he'd have been looking forward to describing this deep dive to him. Knowing how enthralled he'd have been. *And* happy – knowing Edith was going to be taken care of, no matter what.

In the event of his own demise, for instance. All in Sammy Moed's hands, then.

Six hundred and fifty feet. By this depth that old submarine *would* have imploded, he guessed.

'OK, Mark?'

'Yup.' Nodding to Huard. 'Fine.'

'Why you not sleep?'

Why not, indeed . . . Saving oxygen et cetera in the
process. 'Maybe I will.' Nodding again. 'You've been a
pilot – aquanaut – quite some years, have you?'

'Me?' Grimacing: compression of the wide, thin lips, eyes
rolling upward. 'Fifteen year, pilot.'

'Worked for some state outfit, didn't you?'

'IFREMER, is call. *Institut Français de Recherche pour l'Exploration des Mers.*'

'Sounds – big stuff.'

'Sure. Big stuff.' He muttered it again as if to memorize
it: 'Beeg stoff . . .'

'Why did you leave it? Better job *autre part*?'

A snort: he slapped one hand with the other. 'Bad boy!'

'Uh?'

Heavy shrug – holding the hunched-shoulders position
for some moments before relaxing. Shake of the narrow
head, then. 'The wife of my chief. *Very* beautiful. Also too
young for *him* . . .' He slapped that hand again, repeated
'*Bad* boy . . .'

He'd snoozed, woke hearing the Norwegian telling Huard
over the underwater phone that the Crab's drift so far had
been on a bearing of one-seven-zero at approximately a
quarter of a knot. Not a lot: if they'd been bottoming now,
the distance to the wreck's pinger would have been about
three hundred yards.

'OK.'

'So far, so good – eh?'

'No problème.'

At least they weren't heading for any entanglement in

those wires. Their drift in fact had been in the opposite direction.

'Talk again midday, then.'

They'd signed off. Mark saw that Huard had the digital depth-meter in use now. Depth three thousand seven hundred, time 1132. There was a faint humming noise, somewhere close. But what *wasn't* close . . . Following his own instincts as well as his late uncle's advice, he was holding his imagination in check, excluding from his consciousness (for any longer than it took to dismiss it) any visualization of the vast, crushing weight of black water through which the Crab was still free-falling – at the rate of – checking depth-change against the second hand of his watch – as near as damnit one hundred feet per minute.

Difficult *not* to let the picture leak in, though. Especially the Crab being such a peculiar-looking object, as well as so minute in the ocean's surrounding hugeness.

The humming sound, he realized, was coming from the scrubber motor. He put a hand on it, felt the slight vibration. It was about the size of a tin of humbugs; while the canister that was fitted on top of it was larger, about fifteen inches long and five or six in diameter. Air was being sucked through that tin, leaving its poison in the crystals. There were spare canisters in clips lower down.

'Not sleep more?'

'Maybe later. Thanks.' He felt muzzy. Nodding towards the scrubber: 'Every thirty minutes, you scrub for ten – right?'

'Thirty, forty-five. How it goes.' A shrug. 'Finish now.'

Leaning over, he touched a switch and the faint noise ceased. He was checking the reading of a thermometer-like gauge mounted in a square metal fitting labelled RINGROSE CO_2 INDICATOR. Ringrose being the manufacturer's or inventor's name, presumably either British or American. Huard's long fingers wrapping themselves around a valve on top of the nearer oxygen cylinder, opening it a little: eyes on a gauge showing the sphere's own atmospheric pressure, oxygen – a thin, faint hiss of it – now replacing the CO_2 that had been extracted.

A nod. 'OK.' He shut it off; told Mark, rapping on the scrubber cylinder with a knuckle: 'Soda-lime OK, but better is lithium hydroxide.'

'So why don't we have that?'

'Cost more. Also only from USA.'

'But this stuff's all right? Does the job?' He shook his head. 'Silly question. Sorry. But tell me – life-support system went wrong somehow, with you and Bairan the other day?'

Staring at the depth-metre . . . The figures flicking over were three nine eight zero: three nine nine zero . . .

'Four t'ousand feet. More deep you ever was, eh?'

'You could have said that when we were at *fifty* feet. How did this scrubber gear go wrong, Emile?'

'Ah.' Gazing at it: probably getting the English words together, some way that he could tell it. Nodding, then . . . 'Oleg Bairan switch on, say to me OK – like this –' a thumb raised – 'but – *not* start, see. Motor is not run, but Bairan –' Huard touched his ear – 'not hear. So –' waving a hand around, indicating the atmosphere surrounding them – 'breathing not good, and here –' pointing at the Ringrose indicator – 'is not go down, is go *up* – and pressure is not fall, so not yet oxygen. Is *his* work, I sleep a little – gone *back* to sleep, huh? – and I wake up, I'm—' hand to his face, and panting. 'How long for, I don' know, I sink maybe *he* sleep also . . .'

'Might even not have woken at all? Either of you?'

'Is possible. But –' shaking his head, and the panting bit again – 'I'm sick, too, and – Bairan like *this*.' Miming it: the Ukrainian slumped, head hanging . . . 'Scrubber motor ne marche pas. Is *not* run – runn*ing*. I feel it – *not* going.'

A nod towards the Ringrose: 'See also *that*. CO_2 up, up. I think: Jesus, man, what's *doing*? But some minutes, I find – loose connecting wire – *there*, huh? So switch is on, also *not* on. OK, pas difficile, mais—'

'You fixed it.'

A nod. 'But some more minutes only – alors, c'est finis, je crois!'

'You'd 've been dead.'

Imagining it. The breakdown had occurred during the long haul to the surface. You could visualize recovery of the Crab, that hatch shut and having to be opened – somehow – from the outside, then finding the two men's bodies *in*side . . . Huard muttering, 'What for the wire is not fixed like it should – why, *how* this happen—'

'Bairan had passed out, had he?'

A nod. Phlegmatic expression, gesture with the hands . . .

'So if you had too—'

'Sure. Sure.'

'I thought he was a very experienced pilot.'

A few seconds' silence, taking that in. Then: 'Sure. Very much experience.'

'Around *this* submersible especially.'

Thinking *that* out: then getting it. 'Spécialement – oui. C'est vrai.'

'So how the hell . . .'

'Fonny man, he.'

He'd said that of him before. Mark asked him, 'Were the other accidents his fault too?'

Pause. Huard's eyes on the flickering depth-metre. Four thousand six hundred: four six twenty . . . A sideways glance, frowning: 'Huh?'

'Les autres accidents – aussi sa faute?'

'Non. Du tout. Mais—' A pause, and a heavy sigh. Then: 'Bairan is – il a grand peur. How to say – is lose his nerve?'

'Because of the accidents – that something *else* might—'

'Sure. Not dive again, I think. Jamais.'

'But *you* know now it's all dead to rights?'

'Dead – right?'

'Vous – Emile – vous savez – you know all the systems are – comme il faut?'

'We talk French, eh?'

Grinning at him . . . Mark wanting that reassurance – and not getting it. He didn't like to push it, though, appear any more wimpish than he had to.

Midday call from the surface. He'd been slumbering again, and again woke up to that disembodied voice. Depth six thousand five hundred, he saw: a third of the way down. There'd been virtually no lateral drift since the check half an hour ago, he heard. So it was *still* a case of 'so far, so good'. Huard finished his brief exchange with the Norwegian, and hung up.

Leaning over to this viewport, then: peering closely at the ring of hexagonal nuts encircling it. Touching a smear of wetness – fastidious touch, tip of one middle finger: and tasting it.

Mark asked him, 'Anything wrong?'

The Frenchman shrugged as he edged back to his own console, the other viewport. Even then they were shoulder to shoulder. The cramped space still didn't bear thinking about, you had to take it for granted, *not* think about it . . . Huard's dark gaze moving around *that* lot of penetrators now.

'I was remember – small weeping there – five day since. Engineers take out, change two penetrator. Now is only – what you say – condensation.' Waving a hand around again: 'Everywhere, condensation. Not worry, eh?'

'Were you tasting it for salt?'

'Sure. But *not* salt, so—'

'If it *had* been – might have been a leak?'

'Little, little . . . Not leak. You say – seepage?'

'There was one a few days ago – right?'

'Maybe. Engineers only to make sure – take out two penetrator, grease them, so forth.'

'Threaded bolts, are they?'

'Shape *so*.'

'I don't follow, quite . . .'

'See.' He made a quick pencil sketch on a back page in his log. 'Like – *so*.'

'Cone-shaped. Tapered. Yes – I see.'

Pressure would tighten it, force it in, even if on the surface it had been loose. At least, one would expect so . . . But if the engineers had gone to the trouble of extracting some of these – and Huard had felt he had reason to check by tasting that dampness . . .

You wouldn't do either for no reason, surely?

These weren't by any means the only penetrators. Others carried electrical conduits through the titanium hull wherever such leads or connections were essential. Around the manipulator controls, for instance. And if one of them did blow – the threading give way, for instance, or the bolt crack right across – in a split second this sphere would be cracked wide open.

Huard watching him, guessing at his thoughts. Mark glancing up at the depth-metre – fast-flickering figures approaching zero seven five zero zero – then back at the Frenchman.

'Where did you work after you left your job with – what d'you call it, IFREMER?'

'Oh . . .' Blinking, maybe surprised at the abrupt change of subject. 'Plusieurs choses. Your North Sea oilfields, several year. Aberdeen, eh? Monsieur Monteix I know well. Also Americains – when I work for IFREMER. Marianas Trench, that – *very* deep. They call me up –' he held his nose, spoke with a nasal twang – '"Hey, Emile, want job, top pay?"' A shrug. 'French sub then – *Nautile*, is call. Like this Crab, *very* like, also twenny t'ousan' feet. I guess is for this Monteix is call me up – huh?'

'You've been around, anyway.'

'Huh?'

'Rolling stone . . . Monteix called you when we got back from Odessa, did he?'

A nod. 'Ask me, "How soon you get Hamburg?" And from Hamburg, Dundee – meeting you . . . How come *you* gone Odessa?'

'Went with Monteix. You know about my uncle, who sank the Jap, knew where we'd find the wreck?'

'Also some person kill him. I am sad. *All* were sad.'

'I'm going to find the bastard too. When this is over.'

'You think – possible?' Quick, sharp stare: and wiping his nose on the back of his hand. 'Vraiment?'

'Vraiment. *Got* to.'

Slow nod. 'Oui. Je comprends.' The stare continued: as if he might have had something more to say or ask, but no words for it: or didn't *like* to ask . . . A shake of the head then as he glanced away.

'Anyway, my uncle told me about the wreck, I went to Robert Kinsman and he agreed to back a salvage operation.' He saw a look of non-comprehension, added, 'The money man? Came this morning in the helicopter?'

'Ah. Yes.'

'He gets most of whatever profits there may be, of course.'

'You also?'

'Get some. Got some already, I sold Kinsman the information. You know, when—'

'I know. Yes . . .'

'Wasn't exactly flavour of the month, was I?'

'Huh?'

'Never mind . . . You get a percentage too, don't you?'

A hand on the region of his heart: 'I 'ope. Also my wife an' children, *they* 'ope. Uh?'

'So you're married, with—'

'You not?'

'My wife died – a while ago. I have a son . . . Emile – get two full loads up now, you *will* be in the money. But I was saying – Kinsman sent Monteix to Hamburg with another man, one of his own people, but that guy couldn't go to Odessa so *I* went.'

'Huh.' Nodding, but looking as if he hadn't understood it all. Glancing up at the depth-metre: they'd passed ten thousand feet without noticing; ten thousand nine hundred now: at 1243. Mark said, 'You're still wondering why he'd send me, when I know damn-all about this business.'

'*Then*, damn-all.'

'Even less, then. Damn little *now*. But you see, Kinsman wanted someone there to – well, mainly it was about finance.'

'Ah, finance, sure . . .'

That one word seemed to explain it all to him. Just as well; you couldn't hope to fill in the background at all comprehensibly, in any detail, with the linguistic handicaps. And wouldn't even have wanted to explain his suspicion that at least a part of Kinsman's motive in jumping at that proposal of Monteix's might have been to get him out of the way – out of his and Lucy's way.

Paranoid? He thought: what *she'd* say . . . Then finished answering Huard's last question: 'And they let me play with *these* things.'

Touching one of the manipulator controls. Black, plastic-covered, jointed to the same extent that a human arm is jointed – wrist, elbow, shoulder-joint. The manipulators themselves had the same joints in them, could be moved in any direction – bend, twist, reach, double-up, travel up, down or sideways. Whatever you did with one of these was copy-catted instantly by the full-size robot arm outside. Also on each of the controls was a trigger-like device, bare metal, which operated the pincer-like grabs. Which themselves – the grabs – could be detached for other tools to be fitted in their place; for instance, when Huard and Bairan had been cutting their way in, after the blasting operations, on the business-ends of the two forward manipulators had been abrasive cutting-disks, hydraulically powered like the manipulators themselves. Alternatively you could fit a clipper that would cut light wires and heavy rope, or a guillotine-type cutter to cope with heavier stuff, or various types of drill.

'You guess –' Huard's eyes on the depth-metre again, with the Crab approaching twelve thousand feet – 'what pressure, here?'

'Two tons to the inch?'

'Two and half.' Nodding grimly. '*More.*' Eyes going to Mark's viewport again, the ring of penetrators and the sheen of condensation. You could see little rivulets of it actually trickling down. Mark glanced from that to Huard, about to comment on it, but the Frenchman got in first: 'They show you good time, Odessa?'

8

He'd told Emile yes, the Ukrainians had been hospitable enough. Even an answer as simple as that had taken a bit of paraphrasing, with his limited command of French. In fact the question had come as a surprise – as either small-talk, hardly typical of Huard, or suggesting that word might have got out as to how the Ukrainians certainly had tried to show Monteix a 'good time'.

That almost surely *was* the answer. Source of the leak – obviously – Oleg bloody Bairan!

Huard had the scrubber running again; he'd set a timer to ring every forty-five minutes, scrubbing for ten minutes each time and then bringing the sphere's atmospheric pressure back up to par with a fresh release of oxygen, in between whiles also checking the reading on the CO_2 indicator – the Ringrose. And every half-hour answering a routine telephone call from the surface, telling the Norwegians sure, no problem, depth – twelve thousand, a minute ago, twelve thousand one-fifty now.

One hour to go, therefore. Mark wondering what might have been in Huard's mind when he'd asked that question about Odessa. Having previously asked why he, Mark Jaeger, had gone there in the first place – in other words why they'd sent *him*, when he'd known damn-all about the business. Maybe Huard and Bairan had discussed it, puzzled over it. It was a fair question too, although with the linguistic difficulties it would have been impossible to answer in any detail. *He*'d been surprised when the proposal had been made – by Monteix, as it happened, and then to his even greater surprise supported by bloody Kinsman – in Kinsman's sumptuous private office, and incidentally at a meeting to which Mark hadn't even been invited.

The background to it – untranslatable even if one had wanted to satisfy the Frenchman's curiosity – was that Monteix and the man Kinsman had sent with him came back from Hamburg with a deal more or less sewn up, but subject to confirmation after the projected Ukrainian visit. Monteix had been in favour of taking a chance on it, chartering the *Eventyrer* there and then, but Kinsman's man – name of Vernon Price – had vetoed this.

Monteix clearly hadn't liked Price at all. He'd already told Mark he couldn't stand him, and it had been very obvious at this meeting – with Kinsman presiding, those two back from Hamburg the day before, and Mark gate-crashing. Monteix warning them, 'Could lose it, see. *Still* could. Be up the creek then, all right, you won't find another *Eventyrer* goin' beggin' this time o' year. The guy from Oslo told me straight—'

'Bulldozing you.' Price had a pinkish, flabby face on which at this moment was an expression of contempt. Telling Kinsman, 'All he wanted was a signature on the charter-party and he'd have run home happy.'

'And why shouldn't he?' Monteix blinking at him . . . 'I'd 've been happy, too!'

'Not if it turns out the Ukrainian submersible's unsuitable, you wouldn't. Nor would I or Mr Kinsman. Your Norwegian friend would be laughing his head off, wouldn't

give a *damn* if we were stuck with an expensive charter and
no way to make use of it!'

Kinsman cut in: 'How soon can the pair of you get to
Odessa?'

Mark had only been present at this meeting – on August
1st – because Monteix had rung him the night before
about it, from his London hotel. He and Price had been
at loggerheads from the start, he'd said, and he thought
the bugger 'd probably try to persuade Kinsman to ditch
him. So please – be there, help Monteix fight his corner?

In fact, no-one had told Mark there was to be a meeting; it
was a week since he and Kinsman had almost parted brass
rags over the Amelia Hutt business, and they hadn't seen
each other since. But he'd promised Monteix he'd be there,
then rung Lucy and asked her to tell her boss the same thing.
She'd clearly been embarrassed, had waffled uncertainly
that she thought Kinsman must have *intended* to invite him
– he hadn't actually discussed it with *her*, but—

'Lucy, tell him I'll be there, and if he doesn't like it we
can drop the whole thing, I'll find a backer Monteix and I
can get along with. No, look – I'll tell him myself. If you'd
have me put through—'

'Actually he's not in the building. I'll tell him as soon
as he gets in. But truly, Mark, you weren't deliberately
excluded . . .'

He'd been almost surprised when the ground-floor security staff hadn't tried to keep him out, and again when
having ascended to the holy of holies Kinsman himself
had greeted him quite pleasantly.

Vernon Price had answered the question 'How soon
can the pair of you get to Odessa' with a shake of his
balding head. 'Have to count me out, Bob. Toronto –
Tuesday – remember? Unless you'd take that on yourself – which I should think they'd *very* much appreciate—'

'Not possible.' Kinsman drummed fingers on the glass-topped desk. 'No, that's very much your pigeon, Vernon. So – I don't know, let's think . . .'

'I'm due back in Aberdeen tonight.' Monteix looked hung-over. 'And tomorrow it'll be dawn to dusk. Next day too – Saturday though it is. Sunday – no, that's not so good. Monday – make it Monday. Two days travelling, maybe two days there'd be all I'd need – back Friday?'

'You're suggesting going on your own?'

He started at Kinsman for a moment. Then: 'I'm a big lad now, Robert.'

Lucy had come in, shutting the door behind her very quietly. She passed behind Mark and Monteix, slid a plastic file on to the desk at her boss's elbow, and Mark saw Kinsman's hand move to cover hers for a moment before she'd had time to withdraw it. It was the point on which his memory of that meeting primarily hinged: that, and the glance she'd flashed towards him as she turned away – concerned, obviously, that he'd have seen it. Kinsman meanwhile telling Monteix, 'I do think it's as well to provide back-up, on this kind of exercise. No reflection on you at all, Dick – just the way we work here. OK?'

Price put in stiffly, 'I wouldn't want to be sitting here now if we'd agreed to an extremely expensive charter of a ship for which we may well find we have no practical use at all!'

Monteix growled – with his flat bull-nose up – 'Wanna bet on it?'

'I *beg* your pardon?'

'All right, Vernon. Let's not back-track.' Kinsman nodded to Monteix. 'Proof of that pudding's in Odessa. You know the ins and outs of all this, and unfortunately we don't; I dare say the chance *might* have been worth taking. Vernon's right too, though – we *wouldn't* want to find ourselves stuck with it, paying through the nose for something we couldn't use. So – let's just move as fast as we can, from here on. You say you'd be free to fly to Odessa on Monday, that's the – fifth.' He looked over at Price. 'We're spread a bit thin at the moment, aren't we? I'm not sure *who*—'

'How about Mark here?'

Kinsman stared at Monteix. Then transferred his attention to Mark: who wasn't taking it as a serious suggestion at all. Jokingly: 'Love to go on a jaunt with you, Dick, but I hardly think—'

'You know – that's not a bad idea at all . . . Mark – would you – help us out? Could your own business spare you for a few days?'

'I can't really see—'

'We'd pay all your expenses, naturally.'

'– that I'd be much use. How you do things, you were saying – I've no idea. Frankly I wouldn't care, all that much. You and I haven't exactly seen eye to eye—'

'Exactly, Mark. If I may suggest this, mightn't it be a chance for a whole new start? However much our personalities may conflict – or let's say *have* conflicted – my interests and yours coincide, surely. We both want to get the show on the road as quickly as we can – we know it's going to cost a bomb but also that there's a good chance of a commensurately large return – and we're agreed that we're lucky in having Dick here as our technical consultant, and the two of you obviously hit it off – it was you who *found* him, heaven's sake. All right, I agree, forget about our *modus operandi* – let's work *together*, Mark! What the hell, you're a businessman, you know the score, and I think the pair of you'd make a great team! Vernon, don't you agree?'

Who gave a damn, Mark remembered thinking, whether 'Vernon' agreed or didn't. He'd say he did, if that was what this little shit wanted. Little shit's main motive, he guessed, being awareness that without him, Mark Jaeger, he wasn't going anywhere at all, certainly not anywhere near fifty million quids' worth of gold bullion. They'd almost come to blows a week ago, and when he'd rung Lucy about this meeting he'd again threatened to back out. So now Kinsman wanted him locked *in*.

Monteix had growled something like, 'Give it a go, Mark, why don't you?' Price meanwhile expressing agreement with his boss, and Lucy standing well back – behind Kinsman, on his right – looking at Mark smilingly, letting him know *she* thought it was a brilliant idea.

Well – she *would*.

Remembering – vividly – that brief contact of the hands. Demonstration – takeover bid? Which she was going along with – even if it had embarrassed her a little to have him – Mark – see it?

What the hell. If that's how it is . . . An Elizabethan couplet jumped into his head out of ancient memory: *If she be not fair to me, What care I how fair she be?*

If he'd got it right. Probably hadn't, but it made sense anyway – in principle, and if one could face up to it – as one might *have* to . . . He'd glanced at Monteix: 'All right, Dick. I'll go along with you.'

Full-scale display of the teeth: 'Man, that's *great*!'

'Thank you very much, Mark. I really am most grateful. Hopeful, too. We'll work as a team hereon, huh? Lucy – perhaps you'd take care of the detail. They'd fly via Moscow, I imagine – or Kiev. Dick, you'd be ready to leave on Monday, you said – that suit you, Mark?'

'Suppose we'll meet out there.' Monteix added, 'Me starting from Edinburgh – however flights go, like?'

Lucy murmured, 'I'll get some research going.' To Kinsman: 'If you'd excuse me . . .'

Lucy exit left.

Kinsman: 'Dick – what about advance notice to the Ukrainians? Ukrainian Navy, is it?'

'Guy by name of Gonchar – submariner, Russian or

Ukrainian Navy captain – could be ex-captain, he dodges the question, sort of – he's the king pin. I'll call him when we know about flights.' Droopy eyes on Mark: 'There'll be red carpet treatment, likely. They want that sub off their hands.' A nod to Kinsman: 'I'll get you a good deal, don't worry.'

'I'm sure you will.'

Price cut in, 'Bob – you have all the facts and figures there.' Nodding towards the paperwork Lucy had brought in. 'Would you excuse me if I ran off? With the Canada trip coming up—'

'Go ahead. Of course.'

'– *and* having been away, you see—'

'Let's put our heads together before you take off. Monday, perhaps. Fix it with Lucy?'

'I will.' He was on his feet. 'Mr Jaeger. Dick . . .'

Monteix smiled, winked at Mark as the door clicked shut. Kinsman sliding papers out of the file, flipping over a few pages. 'Here we are . . . The nitty-gritty of it. Don't want to be here all day, do we. Ah – *here*. Charter of the m.v. *Eventyrer*, crewed and staffed, with a full diving control team and towfish using sidescan sonar – whatever the hell that means, but don't tell me now, Dick – all-in charter price seventeen and a half thousand pounds per diem. Well. I remember your rough verbal estimate was twenty thousand. On the right side, therefore.'

Monteix shrugged. 'Could've been a lot worse. She's a fine ship in good nick, with a tip-top crew.'

'But – other notes here – modifications required – and – additional personnel required?'

'Right. We'd need to replace two diving-team engineers who took off when the charter fell through an' left 'em stuck, and an underwater telephone guy. The owners' rep told me he reckoned they could find us replacements – which is fine, although it'll cost us, seeing as they won't be on

existing contracts. Can't be positive on that either until the
charter's definite, of course – one reason I'd have jumped
the gun, see.'

'Yes—'

'Like you gotta break eggs to make your omelette – uh?'

'Yes – well – Dick, I'd like to cover this rather quickly –
simply get a general view of it as it stands, assuming it *will*
all tie up. All right?'

'Sure. And – on personnel, weren't we – pilots for the
submersible, we'll need, but that'll be clearer later – see
what's offering from the Ukrainian end, maybe. Need four
pilots – two pairs, see, work alternate dives. And that about
does for the high-earners.'

'Modifications and equipment, then?'

'Mainly wires – steel wire rope – as specified there. Two
of 'em, one heavy and one lightish, each not less 'n twenty
thousand feet. That's a *hell* of a lot of wire.'

'The submersible's lowered on a wire, is it?'

'Christ, no . . . The submersible free-falls. Main wire's for
the cargo-hoist, other's a guide-wire. Cargo basket too, but
that's no problem – I hope. Modifications – well, we'll need
to change the cargo winch, and fit cable-holding drums
to back it up like, hold all that wire. Could be done in
Hamburg – or some of it could – and the rest *this* side.'

'Aberdeen?'

'Or Peterhead. See how it works out – where the gear'll be
coming from and who'll install it. Once we know it's *on*—'

'And the cost of all this?'

'Mr Kinsman –' shaking his shaggy head – 'seeing as it's
still all bloody question-marks—'

'Inside say half a million?'

'Oh, Christ, yes . . .'

Lucy told them later, in her own office, 'Neither Moscow
nor Kiev, apparently. Our travel section says the best

way is by Austrian Airlines via Vienna. Nine-thirty from Heathrow, you'll be on the ground in Vienna for about forty-five minutes and arrive Odessa 1635. Local time, that is.'

'How about me then, from Edinburgh?'

'Heathrow for you too, I'm afraid. You'll have to be up early.'

'Spend Sunday night at Heathrow, maybe.'

'If you like. Fly down that evening, you mean. Yes, why not.' She went on, 'As for accommodation – I'm advised that the best place is the Hotel Odessa – nineteenth-century but completely renovated quite recently. This is all on the Kinsman Group, naturally – but I just wonder: is it possible your Ukrainian hosts might want to put you up?'

'Dunno. Might, I suppose. They're keen, *that*'s a fact. Look, what if I give Gonchar a buzz . . .'

'Gonchar?'

'He's the gaffer. Have to call him anyroad, tell him we're coming. Do it from here, shall I – give him a chance to offer?'

She cocked an eye at a clock. 'Odessa must be on GMT plus either two or three, I'd guess. They *should* be out of bed.' She reached to a phone. 'Have you got his number with you?'

That had been a Thursday. On the Friday evening Mark went down to Hampshire to spend the night and bring his uncle up to date on the subject of the Norwegian support ship in Hamburg and the submersible in Odessa. Fascinating stuff for the old submariner to hear about; not that Mark could answer many of his queries about it, other than the facts that it was crewed by two 'pilots' and could go down three miles, using robot arms to extract and recover the gold bullion.

'*If* there's any there, mind you – and it can get at it.' Warning him, scared of potential damage to the old boy's morale if this thing fell flat. 'Best not count *all* our chickens. Until Monteix sees the thing we can't be sure it's suitable, technically speaking. If it turns out it's not, we'll be wasting Kinsman's money and our own time, and Monteix 'd have to cast around then for something else. And – well, the French are still there in the wings, apparently.'

'Yes—'

'What I'm saying is we aren't anything *like* home and dry yet.'

'All right. I've been warned . . .'

'But money – contractual details of – well, it's more or less agreed, between my lawyer and Kinsman's. I really don't want to raise your hopes too high—'

'Don't, then. I'll keep my fingers crossed. But tell me—'

'Tell you this. *If* it works out and goes ahead, you'll have no financial worries whatsoever. For now, can we leave it at that?'

'My dear boy—'

'As you say – fingers crossed.'

'What I was about to ask – what's your function to be, exactly, in Odessa?'

'You may well ask. Short answer is Kinsman wants Monteix to have someone with him, on the face of it to consult with, but really to keep an eye on him. Odd, isn't it – in a sense, representing Kinsman – whom I don't like at all—'

'Your girl's still with him, is she?'

'Lucy. Yes. But that's not strictly relevant.'

'You surprise me.'

'I meant, in this context. The fact is, Kinsman's a sharp little sod – he'd have to be, wouldn't he? – keeps a close eye on whatever's going on around him. Well – your redhead for instance?'

'The lovely Amelia. If you happen to run into her, tell her any time she cares to drop in for another half-dozen double gins—'

'If I ever meet her – I will. Without fail. Might get to be rather expensive, mind you, if she took you up on it?'

'Might, mightn't it . . . Tell you what – ask her to bring her own bottle, will you?'

'Now that's the sort of invitation *any* girl 'd jump at. But – what I was saying, Kinsman has most likely had them check on Monteix, as he does on everyone, apparently, and he may consider he has reason not to allow him too much rope. Booze is one problem – and not the only one. I like him, and I've no doubt his professional judgement's sound – which is what matters. In other areas he may be – slightly less sound.'

'So you'll be nursemaid.'

'Try to see he's sober when he makes his judgements, doesn't get soused and start buying pigs in pokes. Should have a good story for you when we get back, anyway.'

'And if he decides the submersible's right for the job, things 'll *really* start moving, eh?'

'Hope so. Air 'll go thick with faxes, no doubt. Part of the deal with the Ukrainians will be to deliver it on board the *Eventyrer* in Hamburg. That's Monteix's expectation, anyway. Don't get me wrong about him – he's got his head screwed on all right, despite his – eccentricities.'

'Such as? Apart from the booze?'

'Mainly booze. Bit of skirt-chasing on the side.'

'*Will* have your hands full, then. Speaking of booze, though – that glass is empty. So's mine . . . Ah, Edith, what *perfect* timing!'

'What's that, dear?'

She'd just come in from the garden, had some mint sprigs in her hand. Supper was to be lamb chops. Her husband asked her, 'Your usual tipple?'

'Oh, lovely . . .'

Mark fetched the drinks, and his uncle said when he came back with them, 'I've been telling Edith about your forthcoming visit to Odessa.'

'Odessa!' She was surprised: as if he *hadn't* just told her . . . 'Well. I thought you said . . .' Pausing, smiling, as he put her glass of vermouth and tonic down beside her. 'Thank you, Mark . . . Jack, I don't know *what* I thought you said. But wasn't Odessa where those dreadful things happened – where your father was?'

'You're absolutely right.' The old man nodded to her approvingly. He told Mark. 'My father, your great-uncle, was there in '19, when the French were pulling out. The most ghastly scenes. Bolshies closing in on the town, refugees in thousands, a lot of 'em with – cholera, or typhoid – and damn-all the French could do, wouldn't have had room in their ships for more than a small fraction of them, had to defend the ships in fact against being over-run, swamped with 'em, I mean they had to use machine-guns. And worst of all – *imagine* it – whole families committing suicide right there on the jetties. Bang, bang, bang – and the last bullet for oneself. *Can* you imagine it? I hardly can, but it was happening. Because of what they knew was coming. Unspeakably awful. Mind you, we'd had to do much the same in Novorossisk a month or two earlier . . . But Mark – see what a good memory my dear wife has, when she tries?'

'Hardly *good* memories—'

'But you *do* have good ones, don't you? So do I. Work on *them*, shall we?'

'Well – one *does* . . .'

'Yes. Yes, I suppose . . . Anyway, here's to your trip, Mark. Wish I was going with you.'

'I wish you were, too.'

'And *I'm* very glad you're *not*!'

She'd seemed brighter than she'd been of late. Infected perhaps by her husband's new-found hope and optimism, and probably understanding at least some of the reason for it. At any rate she'd seemed to, at times. In the morning, for instance, when Mark had been leaving – early, wanting to put in a day's work in the office, make sure Amanda had things under control, also talk over several rather pressing matters with his partner Tony Brooks – the old girl had hugged him: '*Dear* Mark – you're doing so *much* for us . . .'

He'd had this picture in his mind a lot, since then. Over her head, the sight of his uncle emerging from the cottage, coming to see him off. In frayed cords and a checked summer shirt with an old cardigan over it: it was a lovely morning and would soon be warming up, but at this stage it had still been cool, with a heavy dew soaking everything. Mark protesting to his aunt, 'No, it's nothing. I mean, no effort—'

'Good luck, lad!'

'Thanks.' He'd let go of Edith, shaken his uncle's hand. 'For everything. I'll call you – about the end of the week, we're due back on the eighth.'

'Jack – isn't that the day I'm going to Elsie?'

'You're right. See, Mark? On the ball!'

'Absolutely . . .'

'She's going down there eighth, back tenth. Piddletrenthide, if you please.'

'The tenth's a Saturday. Today week. All things being equal—'

'Come on down, tell us all about it?'

'Bring vodka, shall I?'

Edith pointed at him: '*And* caviar!'

'Well, naturally—'

Jack patted his shoulder. 'Better be off, old boy.'

For the last time ever, in normal circumstances. Edith

already walking back towards the house, but the old man standing motionless, one hand up and blue eyes slitted against the low sun's dazzle. A snapshot printed indelibly on his memory.

Not that he had been aware of it at the time. It had lain dormant, to flash up vividly on the mental screen a week later when he'd had Edith on the phone telling him, *He's dead, Mark. Dead. Jack – yes, Jack, my darling, precious Jack* . . .

He'd wondered in retrospect, had Jack had fingers crossed, on that raised hand?

Huard had seemed not to have caught on to what Mark had told him in answer to his question about Odessa, so he tried it another way: 'They did their best. OK?'

'Did – best?'

Twelve thousand nine hundred feet. Free-falling still at one hundred feet a minute almost exactly. Time – five minutes to one – lunchtime, and it felt like it too: having had hardly any breakfast. Glancing back rather impatiently at Huard: 'In Odessa. You asked me, did they give us a good time . . . But listen – less than an hour, we'll be working. Might eat now? Manger sandwich?'

'Manger, bien sûr—'

'Crab. Control. *Eventyrer* calling. You hear me, Crab?'

Huard reaching for the mike . . .

'Hello, Control. Crab OK. Depth t'irteen t'ousan' feet. We goin' eat now. One hour more – how's drift look?'

Thinking of them up there, hearing Huard's voice booming from the loudspeaker in the van. Lucy there, perhaps? Or sitting down to lunch with bloody Kinsman – either in the Norwegians' saloon or back on the yacht. Maybe that was the most likely, since Kinsman's daughter was on her own there. Unless they sent the chopper back for her, of course. He was thinking then of the warmth of

Lucy's greeting earlier on – the mutual warmth of their greeting of each other, and how it contrasted with his own reaction at that pre-Odessa meeting in Kinsman's office, when he'd thought – more or less – 'Fuck it, let them *have* each other!'

Habit died hard. Habit or – whatever you'd call it. There'd been a word for it, but it hardly seemed appropriate now. Not usable, anyway: except in wishful thinking.

'OK. Forty, forty-five minute, I try find bottom then call. OK?'

Huard switched off the mike, glanced round for his lunch.

Cheese and chutney sandwich first, then a ham and egg. Both delicious. They'd each given the *Eventyrer's* chef their personal preferences, and he'd come up trumps. Huard had a lot of tomato and onion in his, and what smelt like salami.

The coffee was good too. Mark drank his black, and sparingly – conscious of having fourteen or fifteen hours to go yet.

Approaching fourteen thousand feet. Viewports like black sightless eyes: eyes of some insect sinking through darkness with live creatures in its belly.

Monteix, on the Odessan trip, had drunk lager from Heathrow to Vienna, and whisky throughout the Vienna–Odessa stage. Mark had slept some of the way, and thought a lot about Lucy, also about his son Timothy, to whom he'd sent a postcard from Vienna. He'd spoken to him on the telephone on both the Saturday and the Sunday evening; the boy was in Yorkshire with Mark's sister and her children and their ponies now, but in about a week's time would be off again, this time to stay with a school-friend's family in Perthshire, where he'd been before and spent practically every day persecuting salmon, often quite successfully.

Mark was only too well aware, though, of not having seen much of him lately. And that after Scotland there'd be only about a week before he went back to school. The fact they hadn't spent enough time together wasn't attributable to any lack of inclination, it just happened to have worked out that way. The property market had been warming up, and one development project that was very much his own baby had surprisingly come back to life, after having shown earlier signs of dying stillborn. Consequently he'd been extremely busy, and it wouldn't have been so great for young Timothy to have been left hanging around in Brighton mostly on his own.

Might give up that business, he thought. Watching Huard noisily suck down a second mug of coffee. Why *not* sell out? Being a great deal richer than he had been even ten days ago. Timothy didn't know anything about that, yet. No-one did, except Lucy, Kinsman and Sammy Moed, who'd finally made Kinsman pay up. Have to be careful how he broke the news to Timothy, incidentally, having always made his views clear on the subject of obsessive interest in money. But with a million in the bank now, even if it took about half of it to support old Edith in some comfortable and caring retirement home . . . Besides – touching wood, the slatted deck – that million was only the start of it. Getting two more loads up now, there'd be a lot more to come.

Work it out. One and a half tons, say. Actually more than that – or should be. Skaug's people were stipulating three-quarter-ton loads as maximum, but that would be sixty bars, and there'd been seventy in the Bairan/Huard hoist. But one and a half, say: value roughly fifteen million pounds. Kinsman's outlay was already *almost* covered: but to be on the safe side call it twelve million rather than fifteen. There'd be VAT to be allowed for, anyway. All right, say *ten* million. His own fifteen percent therefore one million, five hundred thousand – on top of the million already banked.

Who'd want to go on selling houses?

Except that things *were* going pretty damn well now . . .

Priorities, anyway, would be: one, look after Edith; two, use some as reward money, to nobble whoever had shocked Uncle Jack to death; and three, set up a trust for Timothy. Then see how much was left, and decide what to do next.

One thing for sure would be to spend a lot more time with that boy.

Fifteen thousand feet. Time, 1322. Huard still eating. Mark folded down the top of his sandwich bag and pushed it back with the other stuff. Fifteen thousand one hundred feet. Remembering Monteix asking Gonchar through his girl interpreter, 'When did she last go down as deep as eighteen thousand feet?' Meaning the Crab, not the girl interpreter – who was dark, moon-faced, with Mongolian-type eyes. She'd told him, after a brief exchange with her boss, 'He say not long.'

'But how long?'

'Maybe – six months? *Maybe* . . .'

'And where would that have been?'

'Please?'

'Nowhere in the Black Sea even half that depth, is there? That's why I ask. Out in the middle there, what've you got – seven thousand feet, maximum? And your sub's been here quite some time, eh, having the third manipulator fitted?'

'Not so long. Is come overland, from Murmansk – on train, flat-bed truck.'

'So the certificate's in date, is it?'

'In date?'

A spread of Gonchar's short, thick arms, and an expression of surprise. Irritation in it too: jabbering away at the girl now . . . He was a short, thick man, with a wide head of close-cropped greying hair, blunt features and a blunt, aggressive manner. He spoke no English except for the phrase 'How do you do?' – which he'd made the most of, in the first minute of their first meeting with him, here in the Odessan naval dockyard. From then on, though, he'd relied entirely on the interpreter, whose name – Mark had scribbled it in his notebook – was Masha Veronskaya. They'd met her last evening at the airport, which was about twelve kilometres out of town, where she'd come with a youngish man who'd introduced himself as *Leitnant* Nikolai Petrovich Kobilchak and begged them to accept Captain Gonchar's apologies for not having been able to meet them personally. Kobilchak had proposed fetching them from their hotel at nine a.m., if that would be convenient, to take them to the captain's office.

The Hotel Odessa, for which Kinsman was paying, and to which the lieutenant drove them from the airport, had turned out to be an attractive low-rise building of early nineteenth-century origin, facing on to a rather pretty street called Primorski Bulvar. There was a tree-lined promenade, the trees throwing long shadows in the soft evening light, and the famous Potemkin Steps leading down towards the passenger port. Despite having been modernized in recent years, the hotel retained a lot of its 150-year-old elegance: a grand staircase, big rooms, wide corridors. The food wasn't bad either, and the bar was all right, except for the prices.

Gonchar had seemed to be answering Monteix's question about the Crab's certification at great length, but the girl had interpreted it all with a nod and a curt, 'Sure. In date.'

'May we see it, please?'

There were some more asides in Russian; then she informed Monteix, 'Is coming in post, from Moscow. We hope tomorrow coming.'

'Any way you could make sure of that? I'll have to see it, you realize, before we could – hell, even negotiate on this!'

Gonchar shrugged, muttered some answer, and the girl told them, 'Kapitan Gonchar say he will telephone to Moscow, make sure it coming.' She added – off her own bat, it seemed, pointing at her boss's desk, 'All other papers there for you to see. The work as has been done, so forth.'

'The certificate 'll be in class as well as in date, will it?'

There was argument about this. First the answer 'In class – yes', but Monteix then queried whether the work done in this dockyard, especially the addition of the third manipulator, might not have called for re-classification. And was the certification by Lloyd's of London, or Norwegian – Norsk Veritas – or the American, ABS?

He murmured to Mark while the interpretation of that into Russian was in progress, 'Has to be one of them three. I'd guess Lloyd's, most likely.'

The girl told him, 'Is Lloyd's, London. In date, in class, not worry. Coming tomorrow, or day after. You still here, day after?'

Mark said, 'Thursday the eighth, that'll be. We fly home that day.'

'Is plenty time, I think. You like see Crab?'

'Well – yeah . . .'

'But you like some coffee before?'

They'd had coffee, largely because Gonchar had wanted some. Mark had used the time in questioning the girl, Masha, about the Russian-Ukrainian dispute over ownership of former Soviet Navy warships. Since the break-up of the USSR the Ukrainians had been claiming a share of them, especially Odessa-based ships, as their own. Some degree of compromise had been agreed, he knew – probably read it in a newspaper, some time ago; but how did it affect the ownership of this submersible?

'Belong Ukraine.'

'Although you've no water anything like that deep?'

'Our vessels not confined to Black Sea. *Blue*-water fleet we have – you know?'

'All right.' He thought that was probably bullshit, but didn't know enough to argue. 'But we were given to understand it had been sent here solely to have the third manipulator added – because the engineers who devised it were Ukrainians who had been up north with the Soviet Navy but were now out of it and working here, and the Russians made some deal with you to fit up the Crab. Isn't that what you were told, Dick?'

'Yeah. But the way it comes over the grapevine – well . . .'

He'd winked, on the side the others couldn't see. Mark left it, therefore, for discussion later. In any case it seemed to him that the legality of ownership under Ukrainian or Russian law was hardly his own concern. As long as (a) the Crab turned out to be what they wanted, and (b) the charter – which would be vetted by Kinsman's lawyers – could be legally watertight, internationally.

The certification business would be sorted out too, presumably. Although – locked in his own thoughts, while Monteix seemed to be chatting up the girl and Gonchar was busy on a telephone – although if this was a Ukrainian dodge to get the Crab out on a lucrative charter of their own before the Russian Navy could reclaim it – possession being nine-tenths of the law, allegedly – and if the Russians held the certification – maybe there *would* be a problem, getting hold of that piece of paper.

Gonchar would be aware of it, too. Therefore wasn't being all that honest. But maybe one could by-pass the problem anyway, agree a charter *without* the certification and have the Crab certified by Lloyd's when one had it over there.

As long as it was certifiable, of course . . .

Gonchar had finished his telephone conversation, and was gulping down his coffee. Monteix had an arm draped over the back of the interpreter girl's upright wooden chair;

he was asking her in honeyed tones, 'Floor show every night? Mid-week, even – like tomorrow night? If you was to book a table for us – for tonight, even – what I mean is, would *you*—'

Gonchar banged his mug down, pushed himself up out of his heavy oak chair. 'Po-idyom!'

'We go.' The girl got up too. Looking at Mark, not at Monteix. 'If you please . . .'

Whirring sound. And cold. Opening his eyes, taking in first the depth-metre – reading seventeen thousand two hundred feet – then the time by his own watch – 1342 – and then focusing on Huard, who was leaning over to a small rectangular screen set in a cream-coloured metal box, adjusting knobs below the screen. The light in it flickering, and the speed and volume of the whirring increasing or decreasing as he made adjustments.

A glance round at Mark then, quick shake of the narrow head: he reached for the microphone.

'Control. Crab call *Eventyrer* Control.'

'Hello, Crab!'

'Hello . . . Depth, seventeen-five. Sounder running, not find bottom. Seventeen-six . . .'

Eight hundred feet to fall, still. Eight minutes. Except he'd slow the descent, he'd said, through the last few hundred feet. Mark wondered how it would feel to hit the bottom when falling at this present rate.

Rather not find out.

Four tons to the square inch out there now – as near as damnit.

'Crab? Still no bottom?'

'No. How's drift?'

'You'll be off-base by about five hundred yards. Give you a course when you're down. Roughly northwest.'

Condensation was heavy on and around this viewport.

Everywhere, in fact. If a penetrator had been weeping it wouldn't have been easy to detect visually. In fact that huge pressure would be driving the penetrators in harder than ever, effectively re-sealing any such defect.

As long as it didn't crack one. Thinking of Huard's interest in them. *Some* reason . . .

Huard began, 'Control – depth is eighteen t'ousan' . . .' Then: '*Hah!*' He'd given the echo-sounder a pat. 'Bottom at t'ree-fifty! Control, you hear?'

'Roger, Crab . . .'

Now he was pumping oil. The pump's noise a high whine, from the machinery sphere which was at the submersible's rear end, while the oil it was pumping into the ballast envelopes would be coming from the smallest sphere of the three – amidships, somewhere.

Hell of a powerful pump, to be able to inflate those bags against such an ambient pressure. This was the pump that had failed, caused one of Bairan's and Huard's accidents. It was working now, though, and having the desired effect, the rate of descent definitely slowing. Huard was watching the depth-metre and keeping one hand on the switch controlling the pump, to stop it when he reckoned he had it exactly right, buoyancy just sufficiently negative to take them on down but a lot more slowly.

Because you *didn't* want a crash-landing.

'Mark – start scrubber?'

'Right.'

There was satisfaction in doing anything at all – even as little as touching a switch. Had to be the right one, though – Christ's sake . . . There was a switch for it on Huard's console too, but he'd had his hands full, at that moment. Mark put his palm on the scrubber motor, felt it running. Forty-five minutes since they'd run it last, of course: but what with this and the oil-pump and the echo-sounder there was a considerable machinery-hum now.

'OK. OK . . .' Huard muttering to himself. Descent had become less a fall than a slow drift downward. He stopped the pump, picked up the mike again: 'Two hun'ed feet more. Depth eighteen one-eighty.' Still holding the microphone in hand, and the echo-sounder still whirring. Left hand moving to his console, to the switches at this end of it; the Crab's external floodlights clicked on, burning out into surrounding darkness. A pool of suddenly bright water: like a fire's glow, hazy at the edges. Eighteen thousand two hundred feet. Mark leant closer to the viewport, looking downward: then used his sleeve to wipe away condensation. Remembering the absorbent paper then and grabbing a few sheets, using that instead, much more effectively.

'Only hun'ed feet now.'

He'd started the pump again.

There!

Grey-black mud-scape, the lower reaches of the headlights exposing that black-edged contrast, an elliptical patch of dull grey expanding slowly into the dark surround. Flat grey sea-bed becoming less seemingly flat as the Crab sank down to it. Undulations were becoming visible: and what looked like a generally upward slope – to the right. Whichever direction *that* was . . .

Huard again: 'Eighteen t'ousan' four hun'ed.' He'd stopped the pump. 'Fifty now. Maybe—'

A lurch, and a slithering but virtually soundless impact. A fog of silt swirling up. Huard's mutter again, 'OK, OK . . .' Reassuring *whom*? Himself? He'd switched off the echo-sounder but had the oil-pump running again – just for seconds, then off. 'OK, Mark?'

'Sure . . .'

'Control – *Eventyrer*?'

'Receiving you, Crab!'

'On bottom. Eighteen four-forty feet.'

'Bravo, Crab!'

'Huh.' Left hand reaching up to the short-wave sonar: in the monitor above his console the beam lit up and began to circle. Pale orange, otherwise like a little toy lighthouse beam, continually sweeping round. Huard was asking Control for his course and distance to the wreck; outside, the silt-cloud was beginning to subside. There couldn't be any bottom current: the fog had risen, hung there, was now settling with no sign of any lateral movement.

'Crab – your course to the wreck is three-four-zero degrees, distance about four-fifty yards.'

'Three-four-zero . . .'

He put the mike down, and flipped switches to start the motors. There was one each side, and no rudder, you steered with the propellers, using little joysticks which were close enough to be worked one-handed – as one, when the motors were being used in concert. At this moment he had the right-hand stick right forward, the starboard motor pushing the Crab around to port, to that course of roughly north-northwest.

Downhill, that would be.

Silt clouding up again. Motors loud in this tiny, drum-like space.

'How long, Emile?'

'Half-hour. Twenny, twenny-five minute maybe . . . Hey – finish scrubber?'

Five minutes to two. Huard attended to the slow release of oxygen.

Plastic bottle time, Mark thought, in fifteen minutes – to leave it as late as possible before getting down to work. Over the sound of the motors he heard the scrape of the Crab's skids over the ground, and felt the vibration; Huard was peering forward into the last remnants of the silt-cloud, which from now on would be streaming out astern. The last vestiges of its previous disturbance swimming up like

sleet and vanishing past the viewports' outer rims. Slight
list to port: the slope, of course, the up-gradient was behind
them to the right. It was hard to tell how far he was seeing
– the reach of the headlights – but it might have been
about thirty yards. Nothing in sight or visibly alive, no
glowing eyes, movement or flash of colour. The albino
crabs would have to be somewhere around, he supposed.
Might bury themselves in the mud, perhaps. Others hiding
in the wreck. They'd have been scared off by Huard's and
Bairan's blasting, for sure – some might well have been
killed by it, in which case the survivors would have eaten
them. In general, he'd been told, they fed on whatever died
and came floating down to them – fish, men . . .

Huard had moved suddenly: arm up, stubby finger pointing: 'Voyez?'

Sonar screen: to the left of top centre. Each time the
circling beam passed through that bearing it painted and
then left behind a small, elongated smudge of light which
immediately began to fade, had almost gone by the time
the beam got round and lit it up again.

'That *it*?'

Whites of the Frenchman's eyes this way for a moment,
and a nod. The mike back up to his mouth then: 'Crab call
Control. Sonar contact . . .'

9

⊲━━●━━⊳

Wasn't always so easy, going by what Lofthouse had said. The sonar often gave false contacts or distorted bearings – bearings being bent, by variations of sea-bed temperature. Or it failed to pick up objects that demonstrably were there, or magnified an oil-drum into something the size of the *Titanic*.

None of that today – touch wood. No getting lost . . .

Eerie, though. Whine of the motors, and the skids' scraping. The ground under them had to be more solid than quick-rise clouds of silt suggested. Lights blazing from a few feet above the viewports bathed a cricket-pitch length of grey, empty, flat-looking mudscape, carved out this slow-moving cavern of brilliance through an enclosing mass as black as pitch: the threatening wall of darkness on the periphery of the lights' reach and spread looked as if it was only waiting to close in again, reclaim territory temporarily lost.

How long then before the *next* intrusion? Hundred years? A thousand?

Progress seemed *very* slow. Needing that pee now, too. Fine thing to be occupying one's mind, he thought, when you were experiencing something that practically no living person had seen or ever would.

Wouldn't want to see it again, either.

'OK?'

Huard – half-turning, dark skin and whites of eyes lit mostly by the reflection of light from outside. Mark grunted, gave him a thumbs-up: the Frenchman already turning back though, hunching back over his console, concentrating on the gyro course-indicator, the circling orange sonar beam above and his own viewport's slow-moving mix of greys and blacks. All familiar to him, of course. Eyes narrowed into the brightness flooding down the glass, left hand on the twin joysticks holding the Crab on course, countering the influence of the sea-bed's dips and slants.

Mark leant to his left for a view of the CO_2 indicator. OK – less than five percent poison in the atmosphere. That apparently was the crucial level. And the oxygen cylinders' gauges: one cylinder in use, one in reserve, each with a capacity of sixty-three cubic feet. Average oxygen consumption per man, according to Lofthouse, being one and three-quarter pints per minute, but only half that amount if they were resting.

As in theory they would be later, for a period of several hours. But also – again, according to Pete Lofthouse – in the event of a serious mishap, for instance an accident of the kind Huard and Bairan had run into when the high-pressure oil-pump had failed and they hadn't been able to release the drop-weight – standard procedure if you were immobilized on the sea-bed would be to relax totally and thus eke out the life-support system. In theory you should be able to stay alive for about three days, if you were totally inactive – except for running the scrubber, et cetera – and that was the length of time the submarine rescue organization based at Renfrew near Glasgow and on permanent twelve-hour stand-by were entitled to *expect* you to survive.

Although in present circumstances and at this depth,

Lofthouse had been about to admit – but then shrugged, left it unsaid . . .

Lurching – over a rise that hadn't been visible until the skids rode over it. Sudden lift, then toppling slightly nose-down, nose – or rather, bow – falling off to the left. Huard's spread right hand edging the left-hand joystick forward and the other back, to bring her back on course.

Two-fifteen. Bottle time. Empty, wide-necked bottle in its plastic bag: he got it out, uncapped it, unzipped himself. Fearful of another lurch that might cause spillage. All well, though, thanks to great care and concentration. Extreme relief, too. He screwed the cap on tightly, replaced it in the bag and parcelled that around it.

In Odessa, the water in the harbour basin hadn't been clear like this. More like soup: and the bottom littered with rubbish of all kinds. The longest of his dives with Bairan had been two hours. They'd launched the Crab from a crane on the quayside, and Ukrainian sailors in a chugging diesel motorboat had come alongside to disengage the lift-hook and then tow them out into the middle of the basin. But when he and Monteix had first set eyes on it, it had been on the quayside – in its cradle – close to tramlines on which the crane moved. Monteix had climbed the ladder and then into the sail – gingerly, because of his injured back – then slowly and probably painfully manoeuvred himself down inside, but remained right under the open hatch, with the interpreter girl crouching in the sail above him. On the jetty with Gonchar, Mark hadn't realized until he heard a new voice from inside that there'd been this Ukrainian on board already, who'd no doubt have assisted in Monteix's descent from the hatch to the wooden deck. Oleg Bairan, of course – then the Crab's one and only pilot.

Monteix had had himself helped out after a few minutes, the girl had come down the ladder, turning to give him a hand as he stepped off it, and with him was this long, thin

Ukrainian in oil-stained overalls. Pale, heavily moustached, peculiar-looking: could have been modelled, Mark had thought, on that character in the Moulin Rouge paintings of Toulouse-Lautrec.

Shaking Mark's hand: 'Zdrastye. Oleg Bairan.'

Masha told them, interpreting for Gonchar, 'Engineer-pilot Bairan can go with Crab, if you desire.'

Monteix, still massaging the small of his back, stared at him . . . 'Worked on her all the time, has he?'

'All time here in Odessa. Fitting this . . .'

Stumped for the word, shaking her head. Monteix prompted, 'Manipulator?'

'Yes. He is – knowing *very* well, is – how you say—'

'Expert.' Mark's suggestion – which she accepted. 'Thank you. Yes, is expert. Engineer, also pilot, much experience.'

'Could have his uses, then.' Monteix nodded. '*If* we go ahead. You might cost him in as part of the deal, even.' To Bairan then: 'Speak English?'

'Little. Not good – little . . .'

'Other languages? Norwegian?'

Shake of the narrow head. 'Nyet.'

'French?'

'Français un peu.'

'Right.' A nod to the girl and to Gonchar. 'Due course, we'll talk about it.'

He'd explained to Mark later that the Ukrainian having some French could be useful too; he'd already had in mind a Frog by name of Huard, an experienced submersible pilot with whom he'd had dealings before and who he'd heard was currently kicking his heels in Rotterdam, who might team up with this guy. Especially as he'd been a pilot in a French submersible, the *Nautile*, which was damn near a twin to the Crab.

If, he'd added, the bugger hadn't by now been recruited by the Franco-Kraut lot. Which unfortunately he might well have been.

On the jetty, Gonchar had asked Monteix through the interpreter, 'With your disability, you don't want make dive, huh?'

'No. Like to, but – no. Unfortunately . . . Look, though – Mark here – Mr Jaeger—'

She'd turned to him. 'Make dive, with Engineer Bairan?'

'Why don't you, chum? Wouldn't hurt, see what it's like. See –' waving a hand in the direction of Gonchar's office – 'going to take me all the time we've got, working through that bumph. Whole shittin' lot in Russian, this kid and I'll have our work cut out. Bore you rigid, wouldn't it?'

'Well. I suppose—'

'Good man.' Monteix had laughed, clapped him on the shoulder. 'Come back up, least we'll know it's watertight . . .'

Monteix had wanted to have the girl to himself, of course. In retrospect, even quite soon afterwards, Mark had realized this. Gonchar must have too, and had evidently had his own proprietorial (or, giving him the benefit of the doubt, paternal) interest in her, but had also seen the inadvisability of punching a potentially valuable customer on the nose; which would account for his having sent *Leitnant* Kobilchak out later on to hire one of the local whores for him.

They'd obviously been *very* keen to get the Crab out on charter. Ahead of some imminent Russian claim on it, almost certainly. And Gonchar, former Soviet Navy officer but a Ukrainian – in civilian clothes although keeping his rank and authority – probably making a damn good thing out of it on his own account. So Monteix had guessed. Mightn't have been wide of the mark, at that.

Half-two now. Huard still crouching at his viewport, the Crab's motors' output of sound fluctuating as he manipulated the joystick; sonar beam still circling. Mark with his eyes close to the glass and its sheen of condensation. Cold: something like sitting in a fridge. He remembered that on Lofthouse's advice he'd brought an extra sweater.

Thank God. Glancing round: glad he'd thought of it now and not later when he'd be busy.

Sitting back, reaching for it, then unzipping the padded jacket. Eyes resting for a moment on the manipulator controls. It was the left-hand one – port-side one, beg its pardon – that he'd be using. The other front one's claw had been clamped on to the nozzle of the mud-hose, in case in recent days there'd been any mud-slide or silting-up that might need clearing. Huard would handle that one, if it was necessary.

Sweater on, jacket on and zipped. Wool hat on too: he'd last worn it skiing in Italy with young Timothy. He'd survive the cold now – touch wood – but was aching here and there from the cramped positions he'd adopted in the past few hours. Looking at the manipulator controls again: hoping he hadn't lost the knack he'd acquired in such a short space of time in Odessa. On the second afternoon, with the Crab up on dry land, Bairan – who'd been impressed by his performance the day before – had challenged him in his strangely accented English to build a wall, using bricks which he then brought along in a barrow from some demolished wharfside building. Mark had got the hang of it much more quickly than he'd expected – even to the extent of cleaning some bricks of encrusted mortar by using the robot arm to tap them on the cobbles, before laying them; and after a lot more practice he'd managed to lay a few with the rear manipulator, using the TV monitor.

That had *not* been easy.

Be ready for the noise, he reminded himself. It was a hellish row the hydraulics made, unnerving until you got used to it – like an alarm hooter, which was what he'd thought it was, at first. To Bairan's great amusement, he remembered.

Bairan who'd lost *his* nerve . . .

Two thirty-five. The transit taking longer than Huard had thought it would. The uneven terrain back there, maybe, having had to keep the speed down. Not that you'd call it *speed* . . . Mark was looking over the Frenchman's head, trying to make out what was happening on the sonar screen, when he saw him stiffen, peer intently out of the viewport.

'Là, là!'

'Uh?'

Pointing with his chin: and reaching for the mike, thumbing the switch on. 'Crab to Control. I have visual – salvage basket. So OK . . .'

The phrase *I have visual* learnt from his time with Americans, no doubt. Mark was on it too, though – a splash of whiteness where the Crab's lights barely reached. Wouldn't have known what it was if it hadn't been for Huard's report: would have now, though, only seconds later, as the image clarified. There was a sense of remoteness: the scene out there dream-like, more likely to have been created on a computer than to be real. Maybe seeing it through the thickness of the viewport contributed to this: and the certainty that out there, *in* it, one would have been crushed instantly to death. Huard had changed course slightly, steering directly for the basket; Mark looking for the wreck, for the kind of profile he'd seen on the videos, and in the same context recalling Lofthouse's description of the cargo-hoist arrangement – guide-wire anchored forty feet from the access-point, the torpedo-damage area, and the linking 'messenger' thirty feet in length; the cargo-hoist plumbed the access-point, so the weighted basket should in theory touch-down exactly there, couldn't in any case come down on top of the wreck – if for instance there'd been excessive drift or the cable had developed a swing, through tidal action or any other influence – because the 'messenger' would restrict its movement.

They were passing *across* the silt slope now, he realized. Ground sloping down from right to left, salvage-basket right ahead: approaching the wreck on its port bow, therefore. Should have it in sight by now, surely . . . Catching his breath then – a streaky flash up close and to the right, right-hand sector of the viewport . . .

'Guide-wire – voyez?'

Silvery and vertical as the lights had caught it and now held it. Not what taut nerves had suggested – his instant impression in that second of a splintery crack right across the glass from top to bottom. If it had been, you wouldn't have had even a *fraction* of a second in which to register it . . . Now, he was staring at the low, murky outline of the wreck. Lowest at this left-hand end, and the lumpy, higher profile of the conning-tower rising mostly behind the white of the salvage-basket. Which therefore *was* more or less where one needed it.

Glancing round at Huard: 'Voyez – le sousmarin?'

'Bien sûr.' Tight smile: none of this being in the least new to him, let alone as purely weird as it was to Mark. Weird *was* the word. Huard had slowed the motors, the timer he'd set began to bleep, and he silenced it and switched on the scrubber in virtually one swift movement. Telling Control then that he had the wreck in sight and was about to inspect the access-point. That was the first thing, to establish whether or not they'd need to do any preliminary clearance with the mud-hose. Mark hoping they would *not* have to – from the point of view of losing time – on the clearance itself, however long that might take, then having to wait for the silt to settle before you could do much more. Even without raising any silt-clouds it was rather like looking through – well, clear soup, say. Guessing at distances: knowing (from Lofthouse's research) that the submarine had been three hundred and thirty-two feet long and that the conning-tower – and the access-point to the gold-stowage, therefore – was at about two-thirds of the submarine's length from its bow – in other words about two hundred feet from that low, left-hand extremity down-slope, where it had nosed into the sea-bed at the end of its three-mile dive more than fifty years ago, churning a deep furrow as it ploughed in, until the mud's resistance stopped it. Mud and sand might have been scooped into that wound in its side in the course of the ploughing impact, he guessed. Might have increased the list this way, the way the whole length of it was leaning – most noticeable there in the middle, the overhang of the conning-tower. Close enough to see that now: and the dark cavity below it.

But – two hundred feet from bow to conning-tower, then *one* hundred from there aft. The knowledge provided a good yardstick, in judging any other distances.

Huard stopped the motors. Nothing audible then except for the scrubber's hum and his own and Huard's breathing. To the right, about fifty feet away, the silver vertical of the guide-wire. The messenger wire would be lying along the bottom, laid out in a straight line to the salvage-basket. The hoist being plumbed directly over the enlarged torpedo-hole, that was how it *had* to be. Huard was peering concentratedly at the wreck: dark-stubbled face close to the viewport, right hand mopping away condensation and the other at rest beside the joystick.

Moving that one to pick up the microphone. 'Crab to Control. Looking like no change, should be OK.' Switching off, glancing at Mark: 'Huh?'

'Not – far as *I* can see.'

Didn't have the Frenchman's eyes – or for that matter his familiarity with the scene, any point of comparison, except for as much as he remembered of the videos. They'd been taken from a different angle anyway.

The Norwegian in the *Eventyrer*'s van had acknowledged, and added they were all glad to hear it.

As they should have been: with time passing, life-support time ticking away. The need for further clearance had been a possibility, not a probability; there'd been general agreement that not even the worst of storms would be likely to affect anything at this depth. Having the mud-hose ready had been only a precaution: if you needed a tool and hadn't brought it, you couldn't just nip back and get it – not when it took you three hours to get down here and five to get back up.

The port-side motor started up as Huard touched its switch, revved as he slid the joystick forward. Swivelling the Crab right: to get to the guide-wire now, unclip the messenger wire from it. Mark's job: although he'd never done anything quite that fiddly in Odessa. If he didn't manage it straight away, he thought, Huard could do it. Not to waste time was what mattered now.

Huard stopped the Crab a few feet short of the guide-wire and its heavy clump-weight anchor. From close-up it looked as much like a vertical steel rod as a wire. The silt-disturbance which had come with them on this short transit was settling, within a minute of the motors stopping: you could see the messenger-wire's snap-hook where it had caught – as it was intended to – on a wide joining-shackle four feet above the guide-wire's anchor. Otherwise it would have slid down into the silt, making this job more difficult than it had to be.

The shackle was something he or Huard was going to have to deal with later, too – when it was all finished and they were packing up.

When. From here, now, it felt like looking into eternity. 'OK?'

He nodded – hand already on the switch – and power on, for the left-hand manipulator control. Aware that Huard would be watching his every move pretty closely, ready to step in if he started doing anything really stupid. Both hands on the jointed control unit, then – unfolding it – wincing at the hydraulics' sudden racket – like an alarm signal, a hoot of protest startlingly loud even though he had known it was coming – and seeing the steel robot arm outside there unfold as well, to exactly the same extent. He'd made it move out as it were from the shoulder-joint, at the same time bending up at the elbow, bringing the grab into close view in the lights' full glare, and seeing the giant pincer open when he moved the bare-metal lever on the side of the control arm. Shut – open again: shrieks and hoots of hydraulic protest at each move. Then straighten the whole arm a little. He did still have the hang of it, the trick of thinking only about the full-sized robot arm outside, manipulating this little replica but thinking of it as the full-sized one whose joints he was opening or closing, bending up or down or twisting, tilting this way or that. Like your own arm, wrist, hand, but you watched the big one, not this little fellow. Turning the wrist-joint so as to settle the open grab around the vertical wire: and lowering it – elbow straightening and simultaneously pulling back closer to the viewport – sliding it down the wire into contact with the snap-hook – which was broad, a metal collar encircling the wire like a loose bracelet two or three inches wide, the hook about nine inches long overall. Partly closing the jaws of the grab now: at the same time moving it along the hook to get a grip on the spring tongue section. Turning it – wrist-joint turning – so the gap when you opened it would be *this* way. Right – tightening now, squeezing the hook open.

It *was* open. So now the final move – extend the arm so as to remove the hook from the wire.

Done it. Having thought for a moment he'd got it stuck . . .

Huard nodding: 'Bien fait, Mark!'

'Well – for a beginner . . .'

'Huh?'

The hook and the messenger wire had to be brought to the salvage basket now, to go up with it. Easy enough to take it over there: the manipulator held on to the hook – holding it out well clear so nothing got caught up – and the wire dragged along behind. He'd considered as an alternative towing it from the stern manipulator, but that would have meant dropping the hook and Huard then manoeuvring the Crab into a position from which it could be picked up again – finding it, to start with, in the mud, using that rear camera and very likely making a hash of it – and wasting time. Better this way. But the thing was – as had been explained to him in the *Eventyrer*'s saloon last night – that on its way *up* the basket didn't need the other wire's guidance. With three-quarters of a ton of gold weighting it, it could pass through even heavy weather near the surface without any swing developing. And while the gold was being unloaded on the support ship's deck, they'd snap the hook back on to the guide-wire for its next trip down.

The salvage basket was lying half over a mud-bank on the edge of the excavations. The bulk of the submarine loomed over it, over the Crab too as it drove up close – slowly, then stopping, Huard waiting first for the silt-cloud to dissipate and then for Mark, when he could see what he was doing, to clamp the snap-hook on to the basket close to the hook that was already on it. When it was loaded and they winched it up there'd be a fifteen-foot loop of wire dangling: unseamanlike, Lofthouse had regretted, but unavoidable. As long as the bight of it – 'bight' was the word he'd used – was out on its own when the lift started, couldn't take anything else up with it. Like the Crab, for instance. That had been a joke – last night in the saloon, Huard staring at Lofthouse with obviously no idea what he was talking about, but managing a chuckle when Lofthouse himself did, and Mark had got as far as smiling . . . Meanwhile – here and now – there was a heavy few yards' surplus of black hoist-wire lying across the basket, also the collapsed 'wigwam' of white-painted chain cable: it had to be so disposed that when they began to lift, and the hoist-wire was dragging the three chains up before it took the loaded basket's weight, it wouldn't be scattering gold bars out into the mud.

He'd done it as well as he could.

'OK?'

Leaning aside, to let Huard put his face at this viewport and inspect what he'd done.

A nod, pulling back to his own side. 'Bien. When you load – take care, huh?'

'Right.' Care that the chain didn't get buried under the bullion, presumably. He was settling the manipulator's jaws over the basket's rim: then taking a grip on it. Huard with the mike ready: switching on. 'Control – you receive me?'

Murky water, sediment still swirling . . . Cheerful Norwegian voice crackling from the speaker: 'Loud and clear, Crab!'

'Please to drop salvage-basket weights?'

'Roger. One moment . . .'

Background noises: there'd been music playing, rock and roll, but that had cut off now. A mélange of voices including one that was female. Not Lucy's, presumably the navigator girl's. Then: 'Crab – releasing anchor-weights – *now.*'

Mark saw it happen; the basket rocked as the weights fell away from under it, triggered by sonar impulse from the support ship. Not a hope of coming anywhere near understanding it, it simply happened, that was all. As miraculously as the way they'd triggered the explosive charges after Bairan and Huard had placed them and then withdrawn to a few hundred yards' distance before passing up a similar request. But without its weights, the salvage-basket was now easy to move around; he'd raised a thumb, and Huard said into the mike, 'OK. Sank you.'

'Our pleasure!' Snort of amusement. 'Go to it, Crab!'

Jocular: maybe rather pleased with himself. Or with his command of English. Performing for an audience, maybe? Lucy *might* be there in the van?

Five past three now. Huard was moving the Crab astern – the basket following, coming easily off the bank of mud and raising a cloud of silt. Still visible, though – at close range, and being white, a ghostly, wavery image – and the Crab turning, with the port motor ahead, starboard astern. Entry – or rather approach – had to be slantwise, from the edge of the torpedo-damage area looking towards the stern, towards where the ammunition store had been, amongst a tangle of girders, holed and rusted plating, pipes, et cetera. The Crab at rest now, on the threshold. This was the video-view in the film of the last Bairan/Huard dive; they were in the position now from which they'd extracted that first – and so far *only* – load of bullion. He was bringing the salvage basket up closer: raising the manipulator's elbow-joint then swinging the whole arm right a little. Glancing at Huard, and getting a nod – and a pointing finger then: 'Voyez?'

The gold – as visibility improved. Having had this view of it on video it was recognizable as such although silt-covered, nondescript among the wreckage. What all this was about – what the old man had died for. Mark testing the reach of the manipulator in relation both to the gold and the salvage-basket: taking hold of the basket's edge again and pulling it forward by about a yard. That was about as good as you could get it, the basket hard-up against a skeletal mass of wreckage, while ahead of the Crab's lights and viewports was where explosives had considerably enlarged the torpedo-damaged area, and manipulator-mounted hydraulic cutters had then been applied more scientifically – as decreed by Lofthouse, presumably – who certainly did seem to know his business. What they'd done with the cutters, essentially – well, right ahead of the Crab now, in the lights' brilliance was what was left of a bulkhead that had had its lower part cut away – the thin, rust-scabbed plating's edges still contrastingly bright-edged from that operation – just above what had been the floor of the magazine; the bullion had come from there, sliding or maybe cascading through into this nearer space, where it was now in reach. Had perhaps been induced to pour through by Bairan ferreting with a manipulator – or with both forward manipulators together. Bairan was extremely adept with them – as he'd demonstrated in Odessa.

'OK?'

'Yup.' Trying it, at full stretch. With the thought that to have poked a manipulator into that inner space the Crab must have been in further than it was now. A scary thought, rather – as it looked and felt at this moment, anyway. He was aware also, though, of the time – three twelve – and the fact that more than an hour had been used up between landing on the sea-bed and being in position now to start work, and that no such hour had been allowed for in the estimate of a seventeen-or eighteen-hour duration.

The gold-heap was well in reach; he was trying out the movements necessary for shifting bars one at a time from there to the basket.

'Uh?'

Huard: he'd been readying the video, the recorder which was low down below his console. Its camera was external,

on a pan-and-tilt unit behind the lights. The Frenchman's
look demanding now: *What are we waiting for?*

"m. OK. Just – trying it . . .'

He had the manipulator back at the gold: silt rising as
the grab nuzzled at it and then took a grip on the first bar.
It would go faster when he got into the swing of it. Up,
now: the steel elbow up a little, and the arm then retracting
as it circled left, taking with it one gold bar weighing
twenty-eight pounds. If you dropped it, the mud wouldn't
support it, bloody Kinsman could kiss it goodbye.

Kiss your own fifteen percent of it goodbye too. Safely
over, though. And down, into the middle of the basket.
He re-opened the jaws while lifting and swinging back to
the heap.

Might do it in one hour instead of the two they'd allowed
for, make up the hour that had been lost? He had the
second bar on its way to the basket, and Huard was
telling the team up top, 'Loading gold now.' Second bar
down neatly beside the first. The load which Huard and
Bairan had recovered had looked a lot more like gold
than this did by the time the hoist had dumped it on
the *Eventyrer's* welldeck, after having three miles of sea
sluiced through it, and soap, water and scrubbing brushes
had done it a further power of good. Three bars in the
basket now. About fifty-seven to go. Eighty to the ton.
Huard was watching the mud-floor and the surrounding
debris: if he saw movement, like a slide developing or the
scenery shifting, he'd back off. Not *out* – the Crab wasn't
in the wreck, just in the edge of it – but the possibility of
having to move quickly to avoid getting snagged or stuck
was one of the reasons he wouldn't have been allowed to
make this dive alone. He might have handled it perfectly
well solo, but situations *could* arise in which one man
on his own might find it hard to cope. Lofthouse had
told Mark this when he'd asked; Mark had shrugged,

said, 'Won't be all that much use, I'm afraid . . . Just do what Huard tells me – right?' Lofthouse had nodded: '*Exactly*, Mark.'

Bar number six on its way to the basket. Taking about two minutes to pick up and transfer each one, he guessed. In which case, since he'd started at three twelve, it should now be three twenty-four.

Three twenty-six. But it was going better than it had with the first two or three. So – minimally sixty bars at two minutes each – one hour twenty. Saving only forty minutes – *if* he managed it in that time.

Another hour and a half of this *bloody* racket!

He'd dropped one. Hadn't had the jaws on it squarely. It was slithering down the heap now . . .

Caught it. At least, stopped it. Holding it pinned while settling the grab over it. Telling himself *no* – not one hour twenty, *damn* it – two whole hours . . .

Four p.m.: twenty bars in the basket. He was having to shift some of the chain back up to the top rim: but it was still taking as near as damnit two minutes to the bar. He told Huard, 'Twenty bars in. One-third of a ton.'

'Ce n'est pas mal.'

It was the first thing he'd said since the start of this, except that there'd been half-hourly checks of the underwater telephone link; he'd been wisely leaving Mark to concentrate on the job. Which he'd resumed now, bar twenty-one on its way over. One of the aims was to lift each bar from the heap with minimal disturbance of its surroundings; the water was permanently cloudy from the movement in any case, and one didn't want it any worse than it had to be. If Huard had had the video running at all, the film wouldn't be up to much.

Well – none of them had been. Bar twenty-two now.

Bedlam, this hooting. Hoots or groans, very loud, at

every move: and the movements were continuous, had to be. Twenty-three . . .

At five o'clock he was able to tell Huard, 'That's fifty bars.' Having loaded exactly thirty in the past hour. The basket was already well laden, and several times he'd had to move chain around. But ten more bars, and you'd have the three-quarter ton. By five twenty, that should be. Maybe continue loading until half-past?

Huard broke silence for the first time in an hour: 'Seventy bar – uh?'

It would be five-forty, then, before the whistle blew. He would have been at it for two and a half hours – not two, as allowed for. But – Huard's decision . . . He nodded, without taking his eyes off the job; bar fifty-two, this was – *in* the basket, allowing him to glance at the Frenchman: 'Seventy. OK.'

Bar sixty-nine was in the basket. Time, five thirty-nine. Bringing the manipulator back for number seventy. The jaws closed on it – hoot – the elbow-joint echoed that as it bent upward and moaned its way round to the now heavily loaded basket.

Down . . .

'Seventy. That's it – eh?'

'C'est bien accompli.'

Folding the robot arm down, hooting, to the basket's top rail, in preparation for towing it clear. That was if Huard was intending to back out. Alternatively he might turn on the spot and move out frontward, in which case he might use the rear manipulator. Mark saw him stop the video camera. He'd most likely only had it running for a few minutes. He made a note in his log now, then reached for the mike: Mark stretching, easing cramped muscles: he felt almost as if he'd had to lift all that gold himself.

'Crab to Control. Basket is full, seventy bar. We pull him clear now. Wait, please.'

'Great work, Crab!'

'Wait, uh?' He switched the mike off. Seemingly in deep thought for a few moments: decision, then, and looking at Mark – a dumb-show of turning the Crab, and jerking a thumb to indicate the rear manipulator. That hand to the camera switches then, and flicking on the rear closed-circuit TV. Light flickered and then glowed in the monitor above Mark's viewport: but no picture yet. Huard grunted, turned on the single rear light.

'OK – *you* do, Mark? For tow astern?'

He nodded. Surprisingly, he'd understood him. 'OK.'

Well – why not? At least, try. If he looked like bungling it, Huard could take over. Except he'd have his hands full anyway, manoeuvring the Crab with that weight in tow . . .

So *don't* bungle it!

Huard was still thinking about it, though. Gazing out into the flood of the lights, the graveyard litter, disentegrating steel, haze of floating silt.

'Non.' Jerk of the black head. 'No – don' like.' A hand up to the control unit of the starboard manipulator, the one on his own side, which at the moment was clamped to the nozzle of the mud-hose. Nodding to Mark: '*I* do this.' Using his hands to indicate a turn-around and that starboard grab going out to the basket: meaning he'd drag it along on that side instead of towing it from the rear one.

'OK?'

'Fine. And I won't need *this*—'

'Finish, that.'

In other words, switch off the stern light and the closed-circuit telly. Mark did it: half-sorry, half-relieved that he wasn't to be allowed to display his skill via the small screen and the back-to-front imaging. Huard meanwhile had the port motor running ahead, starboard astern, manoeuvring the Crab around, varying the motors' power as necessary to keep the turn on this spot, with the scenery in the viewports shifting jerkily right to left. Mark with nothing to do, a passenger in all respects: seeing Huard move a hand to the lever on the side of the manipulator control and pull it back – releasing the mud-hose nozzle – which he might or might not be able to get hold of again, if they needed it at some later stage. Mark didn't know. The nozzle in its out-of-use stowage wasn't in sight, he thought, even from *that* viewport. In Odessa as far as he remembered there'd been no mud-hose fitted.

Stopped, motors' whine cutting out. Ahead, grey vista of mudscape: in the immediate foreground the up-gradient from this excavated level. Clearly an up-gradient: and probably the reason Huard hadn't wanted to come out astern, dragging the basket in this port-side manipulator; because when running astern the motors could deliver only about half the power they developed in forward gear – so he'd been told – and shifting the basket with close-on two thousand pounds' weight of gold in it would call for no small effort.

Huard had the basket on that side now. Face close to the viewport for a sight of it, and both hands up on the manipulator control, unfolding it. There was a lot of silt hanging, from the mud-stirring effect of the turn. Hydraulics' sound-effects startlingly loud as he made his adjustments.

Pushing that lever up, to close the grab – on the basket's rim, obviously. Had got to that stage that quickly . . . Now both motors slow ahead. The hoist being plumbed here vertically from the head of the *Eventyrer*'s crane, he wouldn't take the basket any further than he had to, Mark supposed. The manoeuvre nearing completion was to ensure that the basket didn't snag in the wreck when the hoist took it off the mud, but if you dragged it too far out, lift-off might start it swinging – which with the wreck so close might be disastrous.

Stopping again. Huard releasing the clamp: not all at once but gradually, watching intently, doubtless to ensure the basket stayed where it was, didn't slide away down-slope. Although it wouldn't, surely – *that* much weight? Now he was folding the control unit upward to lift the manipulator clear: and retracting it. Motors ahead again, up-slope and angling left – distancing the Crab and its skids from both the basket and the trailing loop of messenger-wire: none of it was visible from *this* viewport.

Soon would be, though: he was already turning again – right-handed, starboard motor stopped, the silver streak of the guide-wire gliding from right to left across the viewport – and out of it, as it were off the screen. Huard would be taking them out of the messenger's thirty-foot radius, so that when the basket came back in five or six hours' time it couldn't land on top of them.

At least five and a half hours, Mark realized. By the time they'd unloaded the gold, checked the mechanism and fitted a new set of anchor-weights. Eight minutes past six now. Starboard motor still stopped, the other one working hard to push the Crab around: at any moment they'd have the salvage-basket in sight again.

As now: and Huard had stopped that motor. Reaching for the microphone.

'Crab to Control. You receive?'

'Loud and clear, Crab!'

'Basket is clear. Take it away!'

'Roger . . .'

He glanced round at Mark – smirking, repeating 'Take it away – eh?' Pleased by his own use of the catch-phrase. They were watching the load go then: seeing first the taking-up of the slack in the black hoist-wire, then the white

chains levitating up into their wigwam shape and finally
the basket itself stirring, turning a little on the cable as it left
the mud, silt-cloud rising around and under it like smoke.
The dangling messenger wire was visible only momentarily
before the basket rose out of the viewports' sight.

Just like that: gone. Silt-haze slowly dissipating between
the Crab and the illuminated section of the wreck. Huard
was shutting down the video camera; evidently he'd filmed
that load's departure.

'We eat – huh?'

Yawning and stretching. Infectious yawn . . . Mark agreeing: 'You bet.' He reached for the sandwich-bags and coffee
flasks; thoughts returning meanwhile to the likely timing of
events from here on. It had been vaguely worrying at the
back of his mind for some while that the schedule wasn't
panning out quite as had been predicted. Time now, for
instance – well, call it 1815. Minimally five hours' wait for
the basket's return – 2315. Then half an hour to get back
to the coalface, and – say two hours' work: 0145. Half an
hour then getting the basket clear for hoisting – as they'd
just done – 0215. And this time there'd be the guide-wire to
detach from its anchor, also recovery of the pinger – which
was on the wreck's other side, near its stern; best part of an
hour for that? 0315. Or say 0300. Five hours then for getting
back up to the surface – roughly, say 0800.

And the dive had started just before 1100. Not seventeen
or eighteen hours, therefore, but twenty-one hours. With
the life-support period supposedly twenty?

But the sleep-period would make it OK, he guessed.

Huard was on salami and onions again, had already
demolished the first one. Mark had selected ham and egg,
but had put it down while unscrewing the cap of a thermos
flask. Asking Huard, 'Won't finish down here until about
0300 – right?'

'Quoi?'

Gust of salami-and-onion breath. But there were worse things. Were likely to be more of them too, before much longer. He passed the Frenchman his mug of coffee. 'Finisserons ici peut-être vers trois heures?'

Becoming positively bilingual . . . Huard took the mug from him. Dark-brown eyes blinking as he made his own calculations. Then he'd frowned, as some other thought occurred: turning back towards his console, cramming the last of the second sandwich into his mouth and extending the other hand to switch off the outside lights. Saving amps: the frown would have been because he should have done it two minutes ago. Only the small interior dome lights burned now; outside, the eternal darkness had regained possession.

10

———◦———

Tired, but not much inclined to sleep yet. The repetitive action of loading the gold, transferring bar after bar through the same sequence of movements over and over, hung in his mind like something you could have put to music. The atmosphere wasn't all that pleasant either, since Huard had defecated into a plastic bag and might have been quicker in sealing it up.

Do his own level best to hang on until after the magic hour of 0800, he'd decided.

September 18th, tomorrow would be: three days short of Lucy's twenty-ninth birthday. He wondered if she'd be there when they surfaced. You could bet Kinsman would be – waiting to count his gold – but Lucy might have gone back to the yacht. To look after the child, maybe.

But they'd probably both have gone back. And Kinsman would return in the morning – with or without her. Might in fact have stayed – or be coming back in the chopper around nine p.m. – for a sight of the load that was now on its way up. While Lucy would do whatever she was told, no doubt.

Drop out of her life, now – or rather, drop her out of his?

On his back, head on the stool, eyes on the hatch above him and the three dome lights surrounding it: trying to analyze his feelings, even come to a decision. At least decide what he *wanted* to do. Cut his losses – or hang on, fight to get her away from Kinsman?

But what if you managed that and then wished you hadn't?

'You did good, Mark.'

The small brown eyes on his, at about twelve inches' range. Like being watched at very close quarters by some sort of animal.

'Took longer than it should have, I'm afraid.'

'Non. Done good. More quick *next* time, maybe.'

He'd switched off the scrubber only a few minutes ago – to Mark's disappointment; he'd had hopes of it clearing the atmosphere of more than just CO_2. The timer was set for one-hour intervals, but they might be extended further, according to how much less scrubbing and oxygenation proved necessary while they were sleeping or at any rate not working. When Huard had been switching off just now Mark had kept his eyes shut, simulating sleep; thoughts about Lucy had re-opened them, and the little dark-faced Frog had noticed. Asking Mark now, 'Bairan teach you because Monteix tell him?'

'Not exactly. Monteix was busy – paperwork – and I couldn't have helped, so – just happened.'

Blank stare . . .

'Better sleep, hadn't we?' He shut his eyes. Mind going back to Odessa now . . . Exactly what had gone on between Monteix and Gonchar – well, he wasn't sure. At the start, what had seemed to matter most was the Crab's certification, and to everyone's relief that did arrive on the Wednesday, by hand of a courier who'd flown down from Moscow. It turned out to be only a photostat of the original Lloyd's certificate, but it was 'in date' and what Monteix had called 'in class', and he'd accepted Gonchar's assurance that the original would be forwarded to London as soon as he could lay his hands on it. An Engineer Rear-Admiral, without whose say-so it couldn't be released, happened to be away in Vladivostok at that time – about as far away as he could have got, in fact – and it had been as a personal favour to Gonchar that another former colleague had not only provided the photocopy but sent it down by courier.

Monteix had commented to Mark, in the hotel at lunchtime, 'Got pull in high places, that guy. Don't let up easy, neither. Wants the sub out on charter, seeing it fucking *gets* out on charter!'

'Which suits us too.'

'Say that again. Only doubt was the certificate – and OK, this is a copy, but we know it exists – Lloyd's, at that – and it's in order—'

'So we go ahead. You call Kinsman, or shall I?'

A hand on his shoulder: 'Calling him this afternoon, from Yak's office.'

'Yak?'

'Gonchar. Yakov Aleksandrovich Gonchar. Yak for short. Well, you'd need one. He's booked the call for me – five o'clock here, three o'clock there. D'you want a word with him, while we're on?'

'No – thanks. Any case the decision's a technical one, isn't it – you can expand on it, I couldn't. Apart from that – charter costs are in line with expectations – better than you'd expected. *And* including Oleg Bairan?'

A nod. 'He'll come with the sub, wages paid here, into his bank. Mind you, *he's* still got to agree to that.'

'He's keen to stay with the Crab.'

'And his wife's left him, and Yak's keen to *have* him stay.' One droopy eye closed, opened again. 'Got it made, has our Yak. And OK – suits *us*, you're right. But listen, change of subject . . .'

He wouldn't be with him, he'd said, on this last night. Nick Kobilchak had got him tied up with some young lady, and

he'd had to agree to take her to dinner and a floor-show at
the Hotel Krasnaya – about four blocks south of the Odessa.
But she'd be coming here first, so if Mark would care to join
them for a jar—

'No – thanks all the same—'

'Not what you think, chum.' Shake of the head, pursed
lips. 'Definitely not. Couldn't 've got out of it without
appearing rude, that's the truth. Yak's layin' on the cor-
porate hospitality like, that's all.'

'Not trying to bribe you?'

'Well, what's the difference?' He dropped his voice,
though. 'What if that *is* in the bugger's mind? This sub's
what we *want*. We got the support ship – least, I *hope* we
have, that's a thing Kinsman better get on to damn quick
– well, with this Crab, we're home an' dry. OK, so Yak's
on some fiddle. Kiev versus Moscow, who owns what. And
what I reckon – reading between the lines, this is – he's on
his way out, no future where he is – Christ, they're not
even paying their fuckin' sailors, they got families usin'
state-'o-the-art warships like fuckin' mobile homes! So he's
lookin' around – might wind up running charters off his own
bat – eh?'

'Where from?'

'Timbuktu – who cares? Look, I'll tell you about it – all
I *know* – on the flight tomorrow. OK?'

'In plain language, Gonchar's out to line his own pockets.'

'It could be. *Could*. But is that our business? Fact is,
we'd be bloody stuck without this sub. Long as we got
the *Eventyrer*, an' all. Kinsman better make sure he's got
both before he signs up either one – that's what I'll tell
him – and do it quick or the Frogs'll be out there first.
What I was saying – we *want* it, and if Yak's so kind
as to offer me the company of this young lady – show
me round the town, like – don't want to offend him *or*
her, do I?'

Mark had run into them that evening, in the wide corridor outside their rooms, Monteix rather more flushed than usual, and this fleshy, hard-faced blonde coming out of his room with him. She'd been delayed, Monteix explained, he'd told them he'd wait up here till she arrived, and since all the telephones down there had been in use she'd got the number of his room from a porter and come up to fetch him. They were off to the Krasnaya now, only hoped they hadn't missed the start of the floor-show.

'Sure you don't want to come along, Mark?'

'Thanks all the same. Really.'

A wink at the girl. 'Got plans of his own, dare say.'

Bovine stare: no comprehension whatever . . .

He'd had a meal and then gone for a stroll, along Primorski Bulvar and down the Potemkin Steps to Morskoy Vokzal, the passenger port. During the day, pleasure boats ran from there to the various local beaches, which he'd heard were crammed with people who had to pay for about a square yard of sand to sit on. The boats had stopped by this time; otherwise he might have taken a trip. It was a very warm evening, and the pavements were crowded with holiday-makers in shirtsleeves and cotton dresses; near his hotel, music boomed from an open-air disco. No alcohol was served in it, the Odessa's porter had told them, only ice-cream and *zakuski*. It wasn't really his sort of town, Mark thought; he went back into the hotel, finished an Elmore Leonard paperback he'd bought at Heathrow, and slept right through to the seven a.m. alarm call he'd asked for. Then having showered, shaved and packed, he thought Monteix might either be sleeping it off and need waking, or be ready to come down for breakfast: Kobilchak had said he'd be along at about eight to drive them to the airport. But the telephone wasn't answered, and a chambermaid who came by when he was knocking on the door refused to let him in – or she couldn't, didn't have a key or wasn't allowed to

– whatever. He went down, therefore, and alerted the hall porter, who also tried the telephone without result, then said he'd go up and see: he did have a master-key. Mark went in to breakfast, and had about finished when the porter came to inform him that his friend had just arrived back in the hotel and gone up for a shave and to pack his bag; and hard on the heels of this came Kobilchak and Masha Veronskaya, Kobilchak apologising for being late. Mark tried to delay things by offering them coffee – which they declined – and was at the desk settling his and Monteix's accounts when the man himself came shambling down, saying he'd overslept. 'Sorry – must be the sea air.' Nodding to Masha, then: 'What puts the roses in *your* cheeks, I dare say!'

In the car, she was polite and friendly enough to Mark, but ignored Monteix. Nobody said anything about the evening before, or mentioned the blonde. Then at the airport, a few minutes before they were supposed to go through to Departures, Gonchar had turned up – pumping their hands and talking voluble Russian, some of which the girl interpreted. He was delighted and honoured to have met them, she said, and happy that their business had gone so well: as soon as the charter terms were agreed in London, the Crab would be on its way to Hamburg, accompanied by Oleg Bairan. Captain Gonchar wished them every success in whatever their salvage project might be, and hoped to see Monteix again.

'Come to Aberdeen, you *will*.' He'd shown his teeth at the girl then. 'Come with him, will you, my dear?'

She hadn't answered, only pursed her lips and turned her back. Kobilchak had winked at Mark.

In the plane, Monteix had ordered beer with a vodka chaser and expanded on his own understanding of Gonchar's situation and ambitions. In a nutshell, that his intention was to move West, either to Britain or the USA, and that he had several financial irons in the fire, the Crab for the moment being number one. As Monteix put it, either the Russians or the Ukrainians were going to fail in claiming possession, and Gonchar thought it might be possible to see they both did.

'Unique situation, like – as he sees it. Get him started, wouldn't it? I mean – charters at ten thou' a day?'

'Big overheads, though? Maintenance, skilled men's wages? And a lot of the time *not* out on charter?'

A shrug. 'Have Bairan there working for him, won't he? Suit us down to the ground too. Mark, listen – no reason to mention the young lady – eh? Didn't influence the deal one iota, did it. Truth o' the matter, I'd 've said "No thank you" – if he'd asked me first.'

'Of course you would.'

Remembering that seriously sincere expression: and Monteix's droopy, pinkish eyes . . . 'No need for Kinsman to hear of it, is what I'm saying. But one thing I've changed my mind on, Mark, old lad. Just sort of thinking it through, like. Reckoning on using Aberdeen, wasn't I – or maybe Peterhead – when we shift the *Eventyrer* from Hamburg?'

'Not going to, now?'

'See – the oily ports, as we call 'em – folk all want to know each other's business, don't they. Who's doing what, an' where. It's a small world, Mark – like I was wanting to know where'd I find a support ship or an ROV, and so forth, I'd only to put my ear to the ground like. And seeing as we've got this Frog lot treadin' on our heels – huh?'

'Still don't know what's going on with them, do we?'

'Kinsman was reckoning to find out. Keeps *his* ear to the ground, I reckon . . . But what I'm saying – we don't want 'em knowin' what's going on with *us*, do we? Yak swore to me there'll be no leaks *his* end – and you can believe it – so if we stay away from the oily ports—'

'Where instead?'

'Well – keep it under your hat, but Dundee 'd be as good as anywhere. Just between ourselves – right? Talking o' Frogs, though, I'll get on to this pilot I mentioned . . .'

Huard had been up on his knees, checking the reading of the CO_2 indicator, and noting the time and reading in his log. Folding himself down again now. Mark asked him. 'You know about the French salvage team that's waiting in Brest? Equipage Français, au port de Brest?'

'I hear, sure. Know some people, too.'

'You do?'

Surprised look: as if Mark's surprise surprised *him*. A shrug: 'Sure. Long time in this business, me.'

As Monteix had said, of course – small world . . . Mark nodded. 'But what I'm asking – when Monteix suggested you join *us* – well, these people must have been recruiting before that, so—'

'Huh?'

He paused, and put it simply: 'Why had *they* not taken you on?'

Brown eyes staring – trying to make sense of it . . .

'Look . . . You are – very experienced pilot. And French. In Rotterdam, with no work?'

'Work in Rotterdam finish. I am home, Toulon. With my wife, three chil'en. Very moch *need* work – need *money*—'

'But why hadn't these people in Brest taken you on?'

Still puzzled . . . Then light dawning . . .

'Mark – not *man* submersible, they have ROV. You know – ROV?'

'Oh . . .'

The French team would be using an ROV – Remotely Operated Vehicle, or vehicles – *un*manned submersibles, robots, such as Monteix would have gone for if there'd been any available for charter. As he'd explained in Aberdeen that first evening. Mark could hear him saying it now: *Does as much as a manned submersible can, and there's no lives in danger, see . . .*

New train of thought: *were* lives in danger here and now? Even to ask the question, he realized, he must to some extent have become acclimatized. Lying here in a bubble of air under three miles' depth of ocean, for God's sake . . .

You stopped *thinking* about it, was the answer. Starting again now, though. In particular, remembering Huard's earlier inspections of the penetrators: how he'd tasted the condensation, thus tacitly admitting at least a possibility of some influx of salt.

Which there had *not* been. Well – obviously . . .

'Emile. When you –' he pointed at the black, sightless viewport, then mimed it, extending a forefinger and tasting it – 'the penetrators?'

'Eh bien?'

'You think – pensez vous – il y a quelque danger, là?'

Shake of the head. 'Du tout. Only – engineers think – maybe, so take out, make all good, put back. Uh?'

'Wasn't any need to?'

Less a shake of the head than a single jerk of it, dismissive . . .

'But you were still checking.'

'Engineers do this – because Bairan, *he* is frighten.'

'Why – what of?'

'Ask *why*? Ask *me* why?'

'Well – he's an engineer as well as pilot, and he was with this Crab in Odessa. Fitting the new manipulator, for one thing. Knew it *all*, so – that's why *you* were wondering what had got into him – right?'

'I – sorry . . .'

'Emile – how would penetrators become defective?'

Blinking steadily, working that out. Mark guessing that even a skilled and experienced engineer *might* be scared of it – if he had any imagination – for no other reason than that the penetrators were the only piercings of the immensely strong titanium hull. A sphere being the shape most resistant to outside pressure – plain common sense told one that – and titanium – info by courtesy of Lofthouse, as always – titanium being forty percent stronger than steel, weight for weight.

'Is possible –' hands up above him, a fist hammering into the other palm – 'hard, like so?'

'Hard knock. But in what circumstances?' Blank stare again. He tried, 'En quelles circonstances?'

'Launch – not hold on wires – hit A-frame?'

'Oh. Did happen, didn't it?'

'One time.' Pointing upward with his chin, eyes on a spot somewhere above the viewports. 'Break light?'

It had happened during the only launch Mark hadn't been on deck to see. Qvist had been deeply mortified. They'd aborted the launch, put the Crab back in its cradle, refitted the broken light and checked for any other damage, but found none and started the dive again several hours later.

'So you think that might have – damaged penetrators, or—'

'Mais *non* . . .' Frowning, then: and waving a hand towards the stern – 'this manipulator – *maybe* . . .'

The new one. Its controls and its TV monitor were above the port-side viewport, but the wiring ran somehow around inside the sphere – under the deck maybe, he had no idea, could only guess – to penetrators which would be as close as possible to the relevant gear – that manipulator's hydraulics and the camera on its pan-and-tilt mounting, not immediately under the sphere but further aft.

'You saying there might be some weakness – danger?'

'No.' Staring . . . Then, '*Not* say.' He shrugged: with a movement of the eyes upward, thoughts of the surface – and maybe of Bairan's fears. In connection primarily with the rear manipulator? Which could be why Huard had

changed his mind, decided against using it? There'd been
some reason – which he hadn't given or even tried to give.
Muttering now as if to himself, '*Bairan* . . .' Brown eyes on
Mark's again, then: 'Why?' Another shrug. 'Not knowing.
He – Bairan – maybe not knowing. I tell you, he—'

'Lost his nerve.'

'Sure. *Sure* . . .'

'Doesn't scare *you*, though?'

'Me.' Eyes narrowed at the dome lights: then a sideways
glance. 'What for, scare?'

'Well – good question, but—'

'I tell you. Be scare – OK, stay in Toulon. Do what – clean
roads? What my chil'en eat, how my wife have – vestments?'

'Clothes.'

'Ah. Clothes. What I *do*? Be scare, cost money – uh?'

'Well – yes, I suppose . . . I was thinking just now, Emile –
when you said they'd be using an ROV, wouldn't need a submersible pilot. If that's the trend – not good for *you*, huh?'

Shake of the head: 'Plenny work, *man* submersibles. Not
eighteen t'ousan' feet, gold, big money – pas souvent,
savez—'

'Oilfield work, though.'

'Sure. Also cables, pipe-lines . . .'

'That's OK, then.'

'Not pay so good, however. Not profit-percent pay.'

'Right . . . I thought when you said you were in Toulon
with no job—'

'I am happy – see my wife, my chil'en—'

'And this trip you'll make good money.'

'You say?' Eyes on him again. A terrier's small brown eyes.
'I *need*, but – you say so?'

'Well – I don't know, what percentage—'

'Monteix say five tons gold. For me maybe twenny-five
t'ousan' livres. Pound, sterling, twenny-five t'ousan'. Two
hun'ed t'ousan' francs – uh? But – see – five ton is four

hun'ed bar. Now –' he held up three fingers – 'chaque fois seventy bar, profit is maybe two load – hun'ed-forty bar. So how much, me?'

'I don't know.'

It didn't sound so good, though. Not for *this* chap. By the sound of it he was in for a small fraction of one percent. If percentage shares were to be based on a ton and a half instead of maybe four tons, the Huard family weren't going to be exactly rolling in it, this Christmas. Smallish return on getting scared and shutting your mind to it for the money's sake. That was what he'd been saying, effectively – that he couldn't afford to be scared, which in itself was an admission that he *was* scared. And the source of it not the ring of penetrators around that viewport, but somewhere below the wooden deck and in the sector facing toward the Odessan-fitted manipulator.

Which Monteix had queried, at that first meeting with Gonchar, when he'd challenged the Ukrainian's assertion that the Crab's certification was 'in class' as well as 'in date'; whether the addition of the third manipulator wouldn't have changed the classification. And, come to think of it, Pete Lofthouse had raised the same point – with Monteix. Lofthouse had joined the team on board the *Eventyrer* just before she'd sailed from the Elbe for Dundee. Monteix had been on board at that time – he'd made the short trip in her – and Lofthouse had afterwards told Mark that when he'd asked him how the Lloyd's certificate could have covered what was by all accounts a very recent structural alteration, Monteix had only swiped the photostat of the certificate with the back of the other hand and told him, '*Here*'s how. Bloody *certified* – and in date – see? OK, only a copy, but it's kosher – right? See *there*, that signature?' He'd held it out, stabbing a nicotine-stained forefinger at the bottom line, the signature over the printed words *Surveyor to Lloyd's Register* . . . 'OK – Commander?'

Lofthouse had been fishing for further information when he'd told Mark about it, and of course Mark hadn't been able to help. This had been on the day they'd sailed from Dundee, when there'd been other things to worry about as well – first and foremost, leaving without a second team of pilots. The harassed submariner had concluded – effectively giving up on the problem – 'Must have fitted the third manipulator *before* that date.'

'Possible, I suppose.'

'The answer, isn't it? I'm sure it *is* kosher – as your chum put it. I'd only wondered whether the Ukrainians might have conned him. Would have double-checked, if there'd been time. Mind you, if we'd gone to Aberdeen or Peterhead – as Monteix had originally intended, hadn't he? – well, wouldn't have had to, they'd have been checking on us right, left and centre, minute we docked. Always like that, in the oily ports.'

After Odessa, it had been all rush. To start with Mark and Monteix had reported back to Kinsman, who'd already confirmed the *Eventyrer* charter – after the call to him from Gonchar's office – and it was decided that Monteix would fly to Hamburg next morning. The terms of the Crab's charter had been agreed, and it was to be shipped immediately from the Black Sea to Hamburg, Oleg Bairan travelling with it. Monteix would meanwhile be organizing the necessary modifications on board the *Eventyrer* – cargo-hoist winch and drums, et cetera. The wires were to be obtained and delivered on board in Scotland; Monteix was still playing his cards close to his chest, intending to be no more specific even with Captain Skaug than 'Scottish east coast port'. Since this was now a race with the French, he'd insisted to Kinsman, better not go public on anything before one had to: Kinsman had told him OK, it was up to him, *he* didn't give a damn which port they used as long as they got out of it again bloody quick. Meanwhile essential personnel were being taken on; Huard was on his way up from Toulon, and had told Monteix that two experienced Canadian submersible pilots with whom he'd worked before were at that moment on their way back to either Aberdeen or Lerwick from holidaying in Canada and probably didn't have jobs lined up yet – so Monteix was chasing *them* – while the *Eventyrer's* owners in Oslo had jumped the gun in replacing absentee diving-control team members, had signed up two engineers and an underwater telephone technician, and a diving superintendent – Qvist – had already arrived on board the ship in Hamburg. So it was all go. Kinsman had even had reassurance to offer on the subject of the French competition: their support ship had developed engine trouble and hadn't even reached Brest, was under repair in Cherbourg. How long it was going to take wasn't immediately ascertainable, but for the time being the Frogs were stopped in their tracks.

Monteix had asked him, 'Will we get updates on this?'

'You can leave it to me, Dick. Just don't waste a minute.'

Little sod playing his cards close to *his* chest, Mark had thought. As likely as not getting his information from Frank Gillard and Amelia Hutt: whose report might have been more reassuring than he was letting on. He was, after all, putting a lot of money on the line now, must feel sure the French were up against it. Otherwise he'd have been more anxious than he was. Aiming to avoid any complacency in the ranks, probably.

That meeting took place on the Friday morning, and Mark got away from it early – telling Lucy he'd phone her when he could – to get down to Brighton, where he was relieved to find that his office had been and still was extremely busy, and that Amanda had not only been coping remarkably well but had received good support from his partner Tony Brooks. The continuing improvement in the property market seemed to have given Brooks a shot in the arm.

A fair-weather partner, one might say. But – OK, the

business climate did seem to be set fair, so – make the most of it. Especially as Mark's own potentially lucrative development project was still on the rails and picking up speed. If he went to sea on board the *Eventyrer* in a couple of weeks' time – which seemed to be the likely timing, at this juncture, and he'd more or less agreed with Kinsman that he *should* go, as representative of his and his uncle's and the Kinsman Group's interests – well, Brooks would have to continue to take the strain, that was all.

The other partner, Swanton, was proving as useless as ever. Lucy had been right, he *should* have found some way to squeeze him out. Talk to Brooks about it – when there's time . . . Another conclusion though was that Amanda's usefulness might have been rather taken for granted lately; he called her into his office, thanked her for the good work she'd done, awarded her the title of Office Manager and gave her a salary increase to match it. She was delirious with happiness, and wept.

He rang Timothy, in Yorkshire, and they had a long talk. Tim was off to friends in Scotland in a day or two, and was excited at the prospect. Mark promised to ring him again before he went. He had no idea then, of course, what dreadful news he'd have to impart when he did make that call. There and then, in fact, the next call he'd had to make was to his uncle Jack – who sounded in excellent health and spirits, even more so at the news that everything was now going full speed ahead.

'My dear boy, that's *splendid!*'

'Yes. But—'

'I do congratulate you. When you think – only a month since I brought it up!'

'Best save the rest for when I see you, Uncle. Don't you think?'

'Ah. Of course . . .'

He'd arranged to go down there for lunch on the Sunday.

Saturday, he'd be working all day at the office – this was
Friday evening, when he called him – and Edith would be
coming back from Dorset some time tomorrow too. She was
being brought back by the old chum with whom she'd been
staying at Piddletrenthide. Elsie Scrimgeour, aged ninety-
one.

'Still driving?'

'Heavens, yes. That old Morris Minor, too! I'm sure *she*'ll
be here for lunch on Sunday – stay a night or two, probably
– but at some appropriate moment you and I can sneak off
to a quiet corner – eh?'

The last conversation they'd ever have. On the Saturday
afternoon Amanda buzzed through and told him there was
a Mrs Scrimgeour on the line; it took him a moment to
place her. Then he had the phone at his ear, asking 'Not
Elsie Scrimgeour?' – he didn't think he'd seen her since his
school days – and heard her ask Edith, 'Do you want to talk
to Mark, or shall I tell him—'

'No – *I* will. Please . . .' Edith took over, then. 'Mark.'

'*Yes*. Aunt!'

'He's dead, Mark.'

'Who – what—'

'Dead. Jack—'

'No – *no*—'

'I'm sorry, Mark, but – *yes*. My darling, precious Jack . . .'

Crying . . . Then: 'Mark, this is Elsie. Can you come down?
I'm afraid we need you. Police, doctors – Edith's being
wonderful, absolute brick, but—'

'What was it? I mean how—'

'Heart-attack – so they're saying—'

'I'm on my way.'

Edith had only really succumbed to shock at about the
time Mark got there. The family doctor had still been there;
the police doctor had left – as had Jack's body, in an ambu-
lance – and there were a lot of police around. They included

a Detective Chief Inspector Henderson, who after Mark had identified himself – in the sitting-room, which looked as if it had been systematically wrecked; he'd stopped in the doorway near the foot of the stairs, shocked by the sight and the realization that it couldn't have been a heart-attack pure and simple – the policeman's raised tone getting through to him then, saying he'd like to ask him a few questions.

'All right. I'll see my aunt first.'

'Well, sir, her doctor's up there with her—'

'Yes. Excuse me.'

Elsie Scrimgeour had been getting Edith to bed. Muttering something about a hospital being the right place for her; the doctor, emerging from the bathroom, quietly agreed, but added, 'Not immediately, though. For tonight, she's better here. Mrs Scrimgeour, I know it's a strain on you, but—'

'Nonsense—'

What he remembered was the sense of chaos and disaster, loss, helplessness. And the doctor's deeply lined, troubled face as they shook hands. 'Heard a lot about you, Mark. Glad you could get here so quickly. It was thought you were abroad somewhere.'

'Back since Thursday. I'll – just see her.' To him and to Elsie too: 'If that's all right?'

'Yes. But—'

He whispered to Elsie, 'Heart attack? With all that mess downstairs? *Someone* must have—'

'Heart-failure's what they're calling it. I don't know. Frankly, it's Edith I'm concerned for now. Mark – hang on.' Head round the bedroom door. 'Edith, dear, here's Mark . . .'

She was ice-cold, teeth chattering – despite blankets and a hot-water bottle and the warmth of this August evening. He kissed her, held her hands, hugged her while she broke down entirely, wailing, streaming tears. He was guessing there'd been a break-in – burglars, whatever: the word in *his* mind then had been 'murder', and in keeping with that was Elsie Scrimgeour's *what they're calling it* . . . And the policeman who wanted to question him had murmured something like, 'If we can establish what they might have been looking for'; at the time his only thought had been to get up here to Edith, but it came back to him now, and with it the realization that he knew damn well what they'd been looking for.

Whoever 'they' might be . . .

Downstairs, eventually – the doctor was giving Edith an injection – he told Henderson – who was fair, freckled, looked young for his rank – 'I can tell you what they were looking for. Also that they didn't find it. My guess is they'd have pushed him around, hurt him or at the very least threatened him. He wouldn't have told them where this thing was, you see – definitely would not have. But tell me first – when did it happen – and what's *your* view of it?'

'At this stage our doctor's opinion's worth more than mine, sir. His off-the-cuff view is that death was due to heart-failure and occurred some time last night, probably before midnight. When did you last see him, Mr Jaeger?'

'A week ago. Roughly. But I rang him yesterday evening at about seven – seven-thirty it could have been – and he was fine then. We arranged I'd come down for lunch tomorrow.'

'From Brighton, I believe.'

He nodded.

'You say you know what they were looking for?'

'Don't know about *they*. More than one person, was it?'

'We don't know – yet. Forensic—'

'What happened to my uncle? Was he – hurt, I mean wounded, or—'

'The doctor mentioned contusions which could have been caused by the fall itself. He was on the floor – in there. On the other hand he *could* have been knocked down: we'll know more when we have the full medical report. No wounds as such, no – not that we know of *yet* . . . Your uncle was – eighty-seven?'

'Yes. But if a heart-attack's brought on by violence or a threat of violence – that's murder, isn't it? At least manslaughter?'

'It could be – the latter, yes . . . Mr Jaeger – sit down, shall we?'

'He didn't just drop dead of heart-failure, did he? Whoever did all *this*—'

'Yes. Well.' Sitting: he and Mark and another policeman, also in plain clothes. Henderson shrugging: 'As yet, that's – hard to say. But – tell us what you think they'd have been looking for?'

It had taken a lot of explaining. This second man, a sergeant, had been taking notes, occasionally putting in a question of his own to clarify this point or that. They also exchanged glances from time to time, as if having difficulty understanding or believing all of it. Henderson eventually summarized: 'A navigational position in latitude and longitude, then, which was in a notebook that's now in *your* possession – which this person or persons could not have known. Well –' glancing round – 'obviously they didn't.'

'But they wouldn't necessarily have needed the notebook – the original. My uncle might have jotted the figures down – on the back of a cheque-book, or – *anywhere*.'

'Needle in a haystack, in fact. Mr Jaeger – is it likely that people other than yourselves or colleagues actively involved in it could have known of the salvage project?'

'It's possible. People in London, and Aberdeen, and – oh, Hamburg, now. Incidentally, were those reporters I saw outside?

'There were a couple, sir, yes. But don't worry—'

'Nothing I tell you is for the Press, please. Not only for my aunt's sake, but – there's a lot at stake here—'

'In connection with the salvage project?'

'In particular, there's a rival salvage team – French, or Franco-German – going after the same wreck. They don't have its right position, only one that's – well, a very long way out. The fact is that except for my uncle – all right, *me*, now—'

'Could this rival party have been aware that your uncle had the information – and this address?'

'Yes. The fact that he sank the ship – submarine, actually, in 1944 – is on public record – with a position that's wildly wrong. That's the point. And anyone can dig out an address, can't they? Voters' rolls, Council Tax records, Directory Enquiries—'

'Yes . . . Mr Jaeger – is there anything else you can tell us that may be relevant? In particular any other – outsiders, if you like, or interested parties – we ought to know about?'

'Not outsiders exactly – that I know of. But the man backing the enterprise is Robert Kinsman.'

'*The* Robert Kinsman?'

He nodded. 'And *he'd* like to have that information. He'd give a lot for it. In fact he sent a private investigator down here, about a fortnight ago, to try to worm it out of my uncle. Unsuccessfully, I'm glad to say – and I'm *not* suggesting she'd have had anything to do with – *this*. Just happens to be a fact – which as you say, you should know about.'

'You said "she".'

'Name Amelia Hutt. She has a partner – or boss, maybe – called Frank Gillard. They do a lot of work for Kinsman.'

'But – forgive me if I'm being obtuse, sir – why would he – if he's financing the project—'

'Yes, I'll tell you.' He waited for the sergeant to finish whatever he was scribbling. 'OK?'

A nod . . .

'Well – Kinsman secretly enquires into the backgrounds of all employees or potential employees. I suppose over and above a certain level of responsibility or salary. He uses Gillard and Amelia Hutt for that. Maybe for other things as well – I don't know. Why he'd want the latitude and longitude figures – simple. Because he could then cut my uncle and me out of it. As it is he's contracted to pay for the information – a large cash sum in advance of the start of diving. He could save himself a million on that, for starters. All right, we have a contract, but—'

'Mr Kinsman's not by all accounts a *poor* man.'

'He's a multimillionaire.'

'Exactly, sir.'

'He didn't get to be one by accident.'

'Ah. Well . . . May I ask – the approximate value of the gold?'

'Something like fifty million sterling.'

'*Christ* . . .'

The sergeant. Apologizing: 'Sorry—'

'As much as *that*.' Henderson shaking his head. 'Great heavens . . . Well, no *wonder* . . .'

'What?'

'Only – thinking aloud, sir . . . But now, these private investigators you've mentioned—'

'Amelia Hutt – and Frank Gillard.' The sergeant had flipped back a few pages. 'Trading under what name – would you know, sir?'

'No. If you like, get on to Robert Kinsman's office – in Docklands – and ask for his PA, Lucy Greenstreet. She could tell you – if she's allowed to. Otherwise Kinsman himself.'

'Lucy – Greenstreet . . . Would that be Ms, or—'

'Miss.'

Trying to convince himself: old Jack, dead . . .

And Edith like some old cat that's been run over.

Some shit. Some total *shit*.

Henderson was saying, '– lot you've given us, sir, to be going on with.' Glancing at the sergeant. 'One tycoon, fifty

million in gold, Franco-German competitors . . .' He sighed.
'We'd better have a word with Mr Gillard and Miss Hutt,
anyway.'

'But – for the record, Chief Inspector – I'd bet against
their being involved in – *this*. I raised strong objections
to Kinsman after he sent her down here, and his defence
was that it was justified – being invited to lay out several
million, why shouldn't he check on all our *bona fides*. Which
may be arguable – except she wasn't just verifying, she was
after that particular information and it could only have been
on his instructions. But that's – something else. This rough
stuff – could be he'd have nastier elements to call on.'

'In your view Mr Kinsman might have instigated this, but
probably not through either of those two individuals.'

'I wouldn't put anything past him. Although – whether
he'd have stuck his neck out a second time – no, I *don't* know
. . . Sorry if I'm sounding – muddled. I *am*, I suppose.'

'Understandably. But you're being extremely helpful.'

'Incidentally, the girl was pretending to be a TV researcher.
My uncle saw through that – told me about it quite soon
after, and he was laughing about it – he'd rather liked her.
She was doing what she's paid for, obviously, but – well,
this sort of thing wouldn't be in her repertoire, I'm sure.'

'That's your own opinion—'

'More my uncle's. I *'ve* never set eyes on her, it's the view
he'd have given you. He was a good judge of character,
too, so—'

'I appreciate your – forthrightness, sir.' Henderson was
gazing at the sergeant's moving ballpoint. 'Although –' deep
breath – 'just where our investigation should start is –
somewhat problematical . . .'

He'd said *something* like that – expression of doubt or
uncertainty – and Mark remembered suggesting – on edge
by then to get back upstairs, see how Edith was, what
old Elsie's and the doctor's plans for her were, what if

anything *he* could contribute – he'd advised Henderson, 'I'd start with the French. Deepwater salvage team mustering in Brest, delayed by their ship having broken down in Cherbourg. Can't give you any names or more detail than that, but Frog police might investigate for you? Whether the people running it have links over here, for instance?'

'You'd leave Mr Kinsman out of your calculations, then?'

'I think – probably. Because – well, he's a bastard, but that doesn't make him stupid. And he's been caught at it once. I'm sorry, I'm probably a bit over-sensitive on the subject of Mr Kinsman. Anyway – if you'd excuse me . . .'

The scrubber was running.

Aware of it as if he'd been listening to it for a long time: but also of having dozed – and deeply enough not to have been woken by Huard's timer, which must have gone off. Otherwise *he* wouldn't have been awake, to have switched the thing on again . . . Memory had side-slipped into dream, he guessed: or just faded into sleep. Back now, though, to that awful Saturday night and Sunday. Getting Edith into hospital – a private bed, old Jack had kept up her medical insurance although he'd allowed his own to lapse – and routing the family solicitor out of his Sabbath rest – because he knew he *had* to get back to work, in Brighton, on the Monday. The solicitor had come round, anyway, when he and Elsie had been clearing up the mess in the cottage. There'd also been visiting-hours in the hospital, sitting and holding Edith's hand: with a phrase in mind, *naught for your comfort* – the frustration of having no real way of helping or ameliorating: only silence and holding hands, for once hoping her mind *was* wandering . . .

Then, on the telephone at the cottage, trying to track down Lucy and failing, getting – as he'd feared might happen – only Dizzie, who'd been amused by his tone of urgency. 'My dear Mark, if I said I hadn't a clue I wouldn't strictly be telling the truth. But I'm sure your guesses must be at *least* as good as mine . . .'

He'd let Dizzie down, of course. Hadn't been back for more.

He'd rung his sister, told her what had happened and promised to keep her informed, given her the hospital ward's telephone number and the doctor's, agreed with her six or seven times that it was the most shocking, *foulest* thing – et cetera – and asked her if she'd break the news to Timothy. Kicking himself then for being a coward: but the telephone was such a cold and merciless instrument, whereas his sister and Tim could at least hug each other: he'd said before ringing off, 'Give him my love, tell him I'll write him a long letter very soon.'

He'd got Lucy on the Monday morning, calling her from Brighton.

'Mark – how are you? Look – could we talk later? I'm so dreadfully rushed, everything's happening at once—'

'Just give your boss a message for me, will you?'

'Of course.'

'Tell him my uncle's dead?'

A gasp: 'Mark – *no*—'

'I tried to get you during the weekend. No joy. Not even Dizzie knew where you'd gone.'

'I had to shoot down to Devon. Mummy's having her hip operation, and – Mark, I'm so *sorry*! What did he die of, I mean *how*, when—'

'Allegedly a heart-attack, but provoked by someone who broke in at the cottage and practically tore it apart. Looking for something. We know *what*, don't we?' He'd heard her gasp. 'So do the police – they may be contacting you, they want to talk to Amelia Hutt and her partner. I suggested they ask either you or your – Kinsman. But – I'm very busy too, Lucy, so—'

'Is Edith—'

'In hospital. Shock. An old friend's there with her. I'll be commuting between here and there from now on. Anything urgent, best thing 'd be either fax to this office or leave a message with Amanda. OK?'

He'd rung Sammy Moed then, in case of any legal complication with the Kinsman contract. Sammy assured him there wouldn't be, but said he'd have a word with Edith's solicitor – whose name and address he already had.

'Just as a matter of form. In fact I'll be representing your own and the estate's interests – effectively your aunt's, now. Would have been simpler, d'you see, if we hadn't formally brought them into it. I can't really see you'd have let them down!'

'But if I fell under a bus between now and the golden harvest?'

'Ah, yes. That was your thinking, wasn't it? Yes, of course . . . Mark, I'm damn sorry. You and he were very close, I know.'

'Were. Yes.'

'Is the old girl holding up all right?'

'By and large. In hospital at the moment – shock, et cetera – and an old friend of hers is standing by. I'll be more or less commuting between here and there, I expect. If I'm hard to get hold of and you need to, leave a message with Amanda here?'

'I *will* need you up here, to sign a few things – if it's going ahead now, as I gather from Kinsman's man it is. But take it easy, Mark. Give buses a wide berth, eh?'

The timer had bleeped, and Huard had switched off the scrubber. In the silence, the thin sound of oxygen hissing from the cylinder into the sphere's atmosphere was clearly audible. And had now ceased: Mark saw Huard screwing down the valve.

The reserve cylinder, they were on now.

He shut his eyes: escaping back to the image of Sammy Moed. Toad-like, grim-faced; a forbidding character, at first sight. He *could* be, too – as Kinsman must have discovered when he'd been trying to avoid payment of the million – as late as when the *Eventyrer* had been two hundred miles west of Cape Finisterre, and Mark Jaeger the least popular man on board. Sammy had yelled at him over the telephone, 'Don't tell 'em! Let 'em crucify you, if necessary!'

Then, a few hours later: 'Immovable object's shifted – touch wood. And I've become a blackmailer. City rumours our boy wouldn't want to see in headlines? Anyway – when the banks open in the morning, should have good news for you. Haven't been keel-hauled yet, I hope?'

Eyes open, smiling: remembering the huge relief next morning, Sammy's voice fairly booming over about a thousand miles of sea. 'Mark – we've got it. Certified cheque. Putting it in the account in approximately ten minutes. You can tell 'em where to start looking now!'

'Right. And you can tell Edith's solicitor – anything she needs?'

'I'll do that, Mark. You look after *yourself*, now.'

And a few minutes later, Skaug's quiet smile. 'Thank you, Mr Jaeger . . .'

'Hah.' Huard: bearded face up close, small brown eyes glinting. *Some* kind of animal . . . 'You wake, Mark!'

'Seems so. Haven't really slept. Least, don't *think* . . .'

Must have, though. Must have been telephone checks, surely, and he hadn't heard any. Or maybe there had *not* been: the object being to sleep as much as possible, could have discontinued that routine.

Shivering – inside three sweaters, a thick shirt and a thermal vest. Partly because he *had* been more or less asleep off and on, he guessed. Coffee might be a good idea. Warming. Needing a pee anyway. But *move*, let blood circulate . . . He sat up, working his shoulders, asked the Frenchman, 'CO_2 level OK?'

'*Now*, OK.' A nod. Glancing at the indicator. Maybe it had *not* been . . . Tapping his wristwatch: 'Know what time?'

Five past nine. For a moment he wondered *so what*? Then caught on: the salvage-basket ought to be just about surfacing. The lift had started at six-fifteen, and had been supposed to take three hours.

'Tell us, will they? When it's up there?'

'Uh-huh.' A nod, then. 'I will ask.' Reaching for the mike, and switching on, free hand rubbing his hairy face. Small ape, perhaps. 'Crab call *Eventyrer*. You receive, Control?'

Crackling, booming . . . Then: '– clear enough . . . You OK?'

'Sure – OK . . .'

More interference than there'd been before. Caused sometimes by fish, Lofthouse had said.

'Can't sleep, Crab?'

'*Plenny* sleep. Basket up – huh?'

'Soon will be . . . *Something* – crew's on deck. Call you back shortly, OK?'

'Yeah. Call back.'

Recovery crew, the missed word would have been. Huard had put the mike aside: twisting towards the coffee and food . . . 'Uh?'

'OK.' Mark took over – he was better placed for it. 'How many children d'you have, Emile?'

'Two girl, one boy. Girl both very pretty – like Mama!'

'And the boy like you?'

'Hah! He *better*!' Eyebrows hooping: 'You have boy – and wife who die?'

''m. Few years back, now.'

'Find new wife, eh?'

He shrugged. 'Maybe.' Passing food: adding to himself, *Thought I had* . . .

11

———◆◇◆———

Sitting cross-legged, sipping coffee, hands clasping the mug to get some benefit from its warmth externally as well as internally. This was from a hitherto unopened vacuum flask, and the coffee was good and very hot. Huard, crouched over his own mug of it, was also munching one of his salami sandwiches. Cement-mixer action, solids and liquid all in together. He looked like something out of *The Muppet Show*, Mark thought – not critically by any means, rather liking him for it. Jet-black stubble as wiry as a pot-scraper; while his own – he ran a hand around his jaw – was as thick but softer. Luxuriant might be the word for it. Remembering Lucy's small-fingered hand stroking it, on a weekend in pre-Kinsman days when for some reason he hadn't shaved the day before; her murmur suggesting – warm breath on that ear – 'Might be fun if you let it grow. Like a teddy bear.' Her hand passing over his chest and belly then: 'Like all this is. I love this. And as for *this* – oh, *golly* . . .'

He'd uttered some sound: a grunt, or groan. Clearing his throat then, to cover it – and shifting position, covering *all* involuntary reactions to that memory while reaching to put the mug out of the way behind him, but with Lucy still in his mind.

Might be like that with Kinsman?

Self-punishment. But there was no doubting she'd lied in respect of the Australian weekend. Or that there could have been any other reason to have done so.

So what about Dizzie?

He shook his head. Nothing to do with it. Absolutely *nothing*.

Time now – 2110. Visualizing that loaded steel framework rising through the last few hundred feet of water, surface movement beginning to swirl and fizz around and through it, the recovery crew on the ship's welldeck waiting for it, and the team in the van also waiting, probably with a tape playing on the stereo. Skaug's choice was usually Mozart, Eriksen's country or rock and roll, Frieda Stenberg's Mahler. Frieda might be outside on deck snatching a quick smoke.

Lucy?

Kinsman would probably be there, anyway. Most likely up forward, waiting for the gold. But Lucy probably not. They'd have gone back to the yacht for supper and for Kinsman to kiss his child goodnight, and she'd have stayed – to keep an eye on the brat, wash her hair, whatever – while her employer flew back to see his gold brought on board and counted.

Putting himself in personal profit to the tune of about five million. With another seven or eight to come. He certainly wouldn't be getting anything like the fifty million that had dazzled him to start with.

Loudspeaker crackling: time nine-thirteen. Huard put his mug down, performed a sideways roll to grab the mike: looking up at the speaker then, as if that would help him to hear it . . .

'Crab? Control calling. Receive –' bubbling noises – 'Crab – you hear me?'

'Hear but –' glancing round at Mark, whites of eyes

wild-looking in that moment – 'not good. Say again?'

'Crab –' louder, but now a lot more interference too – 'Your –' whatever, the bubble-blowers at it again – '-ing aboard now . . . OK? Over . . .'

'Say gold on board? Over.'

'Crab?' A new gush of aquapherics: it cut off as abruptly as if someone had touched a switch. The Norwegian voice came through normal-toned and clearly then: 'Two hours more for sleep now, Crab. Sleep – OK?'

'Crab to Control. OK. Going sleep, sure. Merci. Out.'

He'd switched off. Squirming back to the position he'd been in before. There was a character in *The Muppet Show* called 'Animal', Mark remembered, who played drums and had that wild look – which he hadn't really noticed, until now. Share a seven-foot-diameter hole in the ocean with someone else for more than a few hours, you began to *see* him. Huard commenting, apropos of his recent garbled exchanges with the surface, 'Not good. Better before, eh?' Passing him his empty mug to dispose of. 'Sleep now, Mark.' He jerked a thumb upward: '*He* say sleep – huh?' Shrugging that off, that evident concern for them, but on his knees then, checking the CO_2 indicator – which of course the talk of sleep was all about. Another shrug: the reading presumably OK. Mark in any case still preoccupied with thoughts of Lucy: thinking maybe she *would* be there, holding the little sod's hand?

In fact she was with Kinsman and his daughter Monica and Pete Lofthouse, in the open port wing of the *Eventyrer's* bridge, looking down on the floodlit welldeck and, a few yards clear of the ship's side, the salvage-hoist's black wire glistening as it rose – a shimmery, quivering effect, the tension in it scattering spray like silver sparks, the wire as it were flowing to the head of the crane jutting from the deck below them, snaking through sheaves there before slanting down inboard to another sheave at the crane's foot, thence horizontally to the winch. From there it passed round a drum and then went to ground – via a pipe which Lofthouse, explaining the set-up to Monica, had called a navel-pipe – to storage drums two decks lower down, in what might have been called the ship's hold.

Lucy had asked Lofthouse a few minutes ago, 'When the submersible itself comes up, does the same wire pull *it* up?'

'Oh, no. Just floats itself up. Independent – like it went down, free-falling.'

'Ah. Of course.'

There was a gusty breeze now, and a lively-looking sea. Not much movement on the ship, only this slight rise and fall, with frequently changing sound and vibration as propellers and side-thrusters held her static, head to wind and sea. Dynamic Positioning: Lofthouse had explained that too, and to Lucy's surprise the child had seemed to understand it.

She herself had said something about the weather – that the wind seemed fresher than it had been before they'd gone back to the yacht for supper – and he'd told her, 'It's how it'll be when they surface that counts. You don't feel it, at any depth – even a hundred feet. And where they are now it's absolutely still, dead quiet.'

'Must be creepy.'

'Right. I've never been anything like that deep, mind you. Well – as I told you.'

'And you a submariner. Then Mark comes along and—'

'Shaming, isn't it?' A smile: 'He's a great guy, though. As I'm sure I don't have to tell *you*. You knew each other a long time before all this started, he mentioned.'

She'd glanced away: avoiding Kinsman's stare too, as he turned – by which time she was looking at the wire and the patterns on the sea's floodlit, shifting surface.

Asking Lofthouse then, 'They'll be surfacing at – five or six o'clock, you said?'

'No – we were a bit optimistic, with that prediction. It'll be more like eight o'clock. Depends, rather. Apart from the loading job they have various tasks with the wires and—'

Monica screeched, '*Look!*'

There'd been a shout from the deck too. The white lift-chains rising swiftly out of the broken waves, the rim of the basket cutting a circle then – all surprisingly fast-moving, a white foam-spilling mass, saucer-shaped, heaving up for a moment like a chunk of sea and foam itself being wrenched up out of the rest of it. Already right up and clear of it though, foam sluicing down, and the rate of lift suddenly slowing.

Stopped: and swinging, a swing imparted to it by the otherwise barely noticeable rolling of the ship. Monica pointing: 'That all *gold*?' Lofthouse told her, 'It better be', and laughed. Monica bright-faced, thrilled, well-wrapped against the night breeze. A tubby child, tubbier still in her brightly patterned outfit. Kinsman behind her with his hands on her shoulders, watching the crane swivelling to bring the load in over the welldeck, with a salt rain scattering down over the heads of the recovery-crew. They'd got hold of a loop of wire that was trailing from it, though, were now able to stand back in the dry and use that as a steadying line.

'Commander?'

The junior officer on watch in the bridge had pushed a side-window open. 'Message from the van, Commander. Crab was on the telephone asking has this load surfaced, and it has now been confirmed to them. They are OK, no problems.'

'Fine. Thank you.' He turned back, looking pleased about it. '*That's* good.'

Kinsman asked him, 'Were you expecting problems?'

'No – certainly not. But we've had a few – as you know.' Lofthouse sounded surprised – and defensive. 'Good news always welcome, that's all.'

The load was on deck, its weight off the hoist-wire, and the three legs of white chain beginning to sag. The winch stopped lowering; crewmen moved in to detach two of the three chains. All standing back then: a signal to the winchman: *up* . . . Hauling up on only one chain, tipping the basket. Rumbling sound as the angle increased and the bars began to tumble out: only a few at first, then an avalanche. Tipping on up, then stopping with the basket standing more or less on its rim, sailors moving in again to lift out the remaining few bars. Lofthouse said, 'Hot water, soap and scrubbing-brushes next – to clean off the salt, mostly. Meanwhile they'll be getting the basket ready to go down again. If your father wants to take you down there now, Monica—'

'Oh, please!'

Kinsman patted his daughter's head. 'You can help count it.' He asked Lucy, 'Will you stay here? Or – wait in the saloon?'

'Yes – don't worry—'

Lofthouse suggested to him, 'You'd like to see it into the strong-room, I imagine. I've got the key – out of Mark's safe – so when they've finished the washing-up—'

'Yes. Fine. Come on, Monkey!'

She asked Lofthouse, 'Mark said you'd explain why it had to be such a long dive. Actually the captain explained it to us. And it's going to be even longer now, of course . . . What I *don't* know – what you and Bob were saying about problems – meaning accidents?'

He nodded. 'In the early stages – as you must have heard—'

'And the Ukrainian backed out. Rather – frightening. It *has* all been put right now, though?'

'Yes. It has.' He nodded. 'Nothing to worry about now at all.'

'The point Bob was making, though – the message saying they're OK – did seem to suggest they might *not* have been.'

'As I think I said – more or less – good news is better than no news. That's all. Normally we're in touch via the underwater telephone every half-hour, you see, but as they're supposed to be getting a few hours' kip we aren't doing that, so this was the first contact in – oh, three hours.' He smiled at her. 'So it *is* good news. All right?'

'Makes sense.' She nodded.

'Doesn't alter the fact we're sure there *are* no problems now. Believe me, everything that's checkable *has* been.'

'I believe you.'

'Great.'

He'd turned back to the rail, looking down at the floodlit scene below them, where 'washing-up' was in progress. Monica was taking part: with a gold bar all to herself, and proud father watching. Doubtless counting, too. While clear of all that, two men in white overalls were working on the salvage basket. The submariner explained to Lucy, 'The basket has anchor weights attached so it'll sink reasonably fast. When it's down there – anyway, before it's hauled up again – the weights are dropped off, triggered by a sonar impulse from up here.'

She rolled her eyes. 'Weird and wonderful world, we live in!'

'*Pretty* weird . . .'

'Does Mark understand all that stuff? Sonar impulses?'

'Not – intimately, I don't suppose.'

On the welldeck, those technicians were standing back from the basket now, making way for crewmen to re-attach the other two legs of the chain-harness, also hook on one end of the loose wire that had come up with it. Lofthouse was checking the time . . . 'Schedule allows them thirty minutes, to get it back over the side and on its way down – to where our heroes are awaiting it.'

She smiled: murmured it to herself: 'Our heroes . . .' Seeing the crane being swung over and the wire being re-attached to the basket's chain-lift. That small, rotund Norwegian – Qvist, his name was, Captain Skaug had introduced him to her and Bob, earlier on – signalling to the winchman, and the black cable beginning at once to straighten: taking the slack out of the chains and probably some of the weight, then pausing, Qvist having held up one of his rather short, thick arms to call a halt while he quickly checked all the attachments – or whatever . . . He stood back then, repeated the 'hoist away' signal.

Lifting . . .

She was thinking about the Ukrainian, Bairan: and all the reassurances, everything checked, all that. If it was so damn safe, why wasn't *he* in it now?'

'Pete—'

'Twenty-eight minutes. Not bad.' He pointed: 'Washing-up's about finished too, by the looks of it.'

'Somewhat perfunctory wash!'

'Well – never mind . . .' He was peering over, saying something about having to leave her now, and Kinsman picked the same moment to look up, with a hand up shielding his eyes against the lights. Lofthouse cupped his own hands to his mouth, yelled, 'On my way!' Asking Lucy then whether she could find *her* way to the saloon: 'So we'll know where to find you. They'll give you coffee, or whatever . . . Look, I'll show you – only a skip and a jump—'

'Tell me one thing?'

'Sure. In here – after you . . .'

'If the engineers have checked everything there is to check – doesn't the Ukrainian know it? And if he *does*, why—'

'That I can't tell you. We go down here, now. Well – no, I *can*. He's lost his nerve. Those *were* potentially deadly accidents – two of them were, anyway – and he's funked out. Another thing is he's not paid by us, so – nothing to lose, maybe. Look, mind this step . . .'

There'd been an engineer eating ham-and-eggs, and a girl radio officer reading a magazine and smoking, until just minutes ago; but she had the saloon to herself now, sipping coffee and nibbling a biscuit, thinking of Mark three miles down on the ocean floor while Bob K. was in this ship's strong-room counting his bars of gold.

You could have spoken that thought aloud in a certain tone of voice and made it sound fairly damning. *Could* have – if you were politicizing the issue, trying to compare one individual adversely with the other. But as so often with that kind of innuendo it wouldn't have stood up to logical analysis. Mark was down there entirely by his own choice, and Pete Lofthouse had given his opinion only minutes ago that whatever defects had existed in the Crab had since been put right. While Bob would have been a damn fool *not* to count the gold into its secure stowage. It would have been counted on deck while they were washing it and presumably was now being carried bar by bar down into the bowels of the ship; it would only take one or perhaps two larcenously inclined sailors for a bar to vanish into some dark nook or cranny, if it wasn't counted again on arrival down there.

No reflection on Scandinavian sailors, either. How many dark-suited, highly paid executives in the Kinsman Group wouldn't dump one into the boot of a company-owned BMW if they thought they could get away with it?

Just on ten o'clock. The salvage-basket would be back on the sea-bed at about eleven-fifteen, Pete Lofthouse had said. Then it might take 'our heroes' half an hour to get it and the submersible into position to start loading again. Two and a half hours, loading had taken them this last time: in which case they'd finish at about two-fifteen. Then three hours' hoisting: basket back on deck around five or six, and the submersible following it up two or three hours later.

Please God.

Thinking about 'our hero'. *Seeing* him down there . . .

How much might it change him, she wondered, being rich? He wouldn't have less than a couple of million in the bank. *And* his business, she knew, was going pretty well now. In his shoes, she thought, she'd sell out – sell on a good and still improving market. It wasn't after all a business to which he was in any way devoted. But – he wouldn't ask *her* advice, and she wouldn't be so silly as to offer it. She remembered disagreements they'd had – in the days when everything had been fine between them – had been marvellous, in fact – on the subjects of business and money. She could hear him now, riding that hobby-horse of his: 'Money's the one and only yardstick, isn't it? Not only in business – everyday life – everyone's scratching for it . . . Man can be a total shit, but if he's somehow got rich—'

Now *he* had.

'Excuse me – Miss Greenstreet . . .'

The steward who'd brought her the coffee . . . 'Telephone from shore for Mr Kinsman, Captain Skaug send me to him but Mr Kinsman say please *you* take it?'

'All right. Where—'

'I show you. Please – this way. Captain Skaug's day-cabin, he say you can use.'

'That's very kind of him.'

'He's kind man, the captain.' Joke, she gathered, and laughed too. They'd come up a ladderway – were at the back of the bridge again, she'd realized – he opened a door, switched on a light and ushered her into a surprisingly attractive room. 'On this line, should be . . .'

A wall-telephone: he held the receiver to his ear. 'Hello?'
Nodding: 'Yes, sir. Miss Greenstreet is here. Please . . .
Handing it to her: 'Mr – Gillard?'

'Oh . . .'

Because Bob always took his or Amelia Hutt's calls . . .
'Frank – Lucy here. Bob said I should take this, he's tied
up.'

'It's him I need to talk to. Hi, Lucy . . . But if he says so –
call's already costing a bloody fortune—'

'He *told* me to take it. So please – go ahead?'

'Well – OK. First, d'you know what I'm here for?'

'Where is "here"?'

'Oh, Christ . . . Lucy, listen. I'm in Odessa. Investigating
Monteix's deal with a character who's disappeared. Just
relay the essentials of this to Bob K. – right? I'm flying back
tomorrow, I'll call him again from there. Listen. Not speaking the language, I hired an ex-cop turned investigator, and
he came up with this girl Masha – she's an interpreter, ready
to tell anyone *anything* about either Monteix or her former
boss, Ukrainian naval captain by name Gonchar – from
whom you have the charter for the submersible. Thirty-day
charter at ten thou' a day pre-paid into the Narodnii Bank
in the City – right?'

'Right.'

'Well, Bob had reason to guess some of it might be going
to Monteix – seems there *has* been a fiddle elsewhere – and
he wanted to know (a) was this so, and if so how much,
(b) what might it have been for. Now Gonchar's taken off,
vanished, run out on the girl – who was expecting to go
with him – didn't know where, only they were going to live
happily ever after. Hence, woman scorned, talking freely. So
– the answer to (a) is Monteix's getting – or has got – forty
thousand quid. Most likely been moved out of the Narodnii
London account – which is in the name of Y.A. Gonchar –
to someplace else. Ditto the remaining two-sixty thousand,

likely as not. Bob K. paid three hundred thousand into that account two or three days after Monteix and Mark Jaeger got back, didn't he? Incidentally, Jaeger didn't know about any of this, Masha says they deliberately kept him busy around the sub. You getting this, Lucy?'

'And taking notes. Go on.'

'Question (b) now. Masha *thinks* the sub's certification isn't valid. She was doing the interpreting, but not everything was being said as explicitly as it might have been. For instance, fixing that forty thousand they'd jotted down pencil figures, Monteix scribbled fifty, Gonchar put a line through it and wrote twenty-five – and so forth. Ended as forty – she saw the doodles later. And Monteix'd tap the certificate or some item on it and shake his head: what about *this*, then? What about the work they'd done *here*? She's not well informed technically but she *thinks* it means work that was done wasn't covered by that certification. But she won't swear to it, says it could just as well have been because Gonchar didn't have any right to charter the sub out, Monteix realized this and without that inducement mightn't have risked getting Bob K. involved in an international dispute. She *thinks* the sub actually belongs to the Russian Academy of Sciences who'd given an operating licence to the Soviet Navy. Which barely exists now, I gather, it's a bloody shambles. And where there's blood there's vultures, right? But anyway – my own guess is the answer may be both those things – certification invalid, *and* no Ukrainian right of ownership.'

'It's incredible . . .'

Also frightening.

'Well, you can believe it.'

'I know. Just *seems* – unreal. Frank – even though this girl's uncertain – *and* with a grudge to settle – you think the certificate *is* invalid?'

'On the basis of everything else I've heard – yeah. But

first thing I'll do in London is check with Lloyd's Register. Nobody thought of doing that, did they?'

'Not as far as I know.'

'Can't imagine why not. Even an enquiry over the tele-phone—'

'They went by what Monteix told them. No-one would have seen any reason to check anything. He was the expert we all relied on – and he hung on to that certificate too, the copy—'

'I bet he did. Where's the sub now?'

She hesitated before she told him.

'Three miles down. On the sea-bed under us here. With Mark Jaeger in it.'

'Jaeger – why? Christ's sake, he's not—'

'Long story, Frank. Look, I'll tell Bob K.—'

The cabin door had jerked open. Speak of the devil . . . He had his hand out for the phone as he crossed the room. 'Tell Bob K. *what?*'

Scrubber running again. Time, ten twenty-five. Mark sur-facing from a snooze, focusing on Huard who was curled on his side making an entry in his log. Glancing round at Mark stirring out of slumber . . .

'Va bien.' A jerk of the head towards the life-support gear. 'But – like *you* saying – better we sleep, eh?'

Meaning, Mark guessed, that it was OK but not all that deliriously OK. Not to worry – because worrying consumed oxygen too – but—

But.

Remembering that there'd been a call from *Eventyrer*'s van, presumably just before he'd dropped off, telling them that the salvage-basket's lowering had commenced at nine forty-eight. ETA on the sea-bed thus eleven-twenty. Just a bit less than an hour to wait now, therefore.

He'd nodded agreement. 'OK.'

Meaning OK to the 'better sleep' suggestion – although it involved restraint. He'd been thinking earlier, in regard to Huard having said he knew some of the rival French salvage-team – and did know quite a bit about them, for instance that they'd be using an ROV, not a manned submersible – that he might conceivably know whether they had any connections in the UK. If he did, it might at least provide a starting-point, somewhere for either Henderson or the French police to put their noses to the ground.

Or to initiate his own enquiries, if Henderson wasn't keen.

He'd turned up at the funeral – Henderson had – looking more like an undertaker than a policeman. Dark suit, rigidly solemn face, hands folded together in front of him as if on guard against anyone kicking him in the balls.

Occupational hazard?

He'd snorted, stifling appreciation of his own joke. Unfair anyway: it had been decent of him to have attended the funeral at all. Huard glancing sideways, then folding his pencil-stub into the log and moving for another look at the CO_2 indicator. Perhaps keeping himself busy because he'd have to stay awake for a while anyway, in order to switch off the scrubber and let some more oxygen into the atmosphere. He was checking battery voltages now.

Finally, back to the log and jotting down figures.

Should have been making his own notes of all this, Mark thought. You always thought you'd remember everything – like now, for instance, memories crowding in thick and fast, often treading on each other's heels – but detail could become confused, and it would have been worth having some of the essentials down on paper. For Timothy, especially. For Uncle Jack, would have been even *more* 'especially'. He'd found he was thinking of the old boy quite a lot. 'Gilt-edged' had been Amelia Hutt's description of him: and in total contrast slightly later she'd referred to

Bob Kinsman as a prick. In both cases astute observations, he'd thought. This had been at the funeral. He'd known immediately who she was – even before his aunt had murmured, 'There's that charming girl who wanted Jack to appear on television!' And as he'd been more or less supporting Edith at the time it hadn't required great powers of intuition for the ace detective to identify *him*. On top of which Henderson had then introduced them. At the small village church there'd been only a smallish band of mourners, nearly all well into middle-age or long past it. A few younger local people, and Mark and his sister and her husband, Amelia and the policeman; otherwise grey, white or bald heads, among them some ancient former naval cronies. Mark's sister didn't bring her children; she'd parked them with friends, largely because Mark had insisted that Jack Jaeger would have preferred Timothy to be fishing for salmon on the Tweed than crouching in a damp church listening to a load of mumbo-jumbo. He'd told Tim over the telephone, 'Spare him a thought or two while you're fishing. Catch a good one for him – that's what he'd have liked.'

It was, too. He'd never been a man for ritual, formality, conformity. 'Mumbo-jumbo' was an expression he'd used quite often.

A grunt, beside him. *Not* – as fancy suggested for about half a second – his uncle conceding that point, but Emile Huard as he moved to switch off the scrubber.

Ten-forty: must have had it running since ten past. Hiss of oxygen now. It was a small valve, designed to leak the stuff out slowly, giving the user assured control, no risk of a sudden gush that might waste it.

Like wasting blood. Except that a body made new blood – somehow or other. When that cylinder was empty, it *stayed* empty.

But – a thought that had occurred before, notably when Sally had died – a long, *long* time ago now, but it had been more than just a thought then, actually a strong feeling which even returned now, sometimes – if there was an after-life of any kind, mightn't the recently deceased continue at least for some while to take an interest in the surroundings and people they'd left? Or was that only wishful-thinking by those deserted: who found it difficult to accept the permanence, irrevocability of her (or his) departure?

Edith had been impressive, at the funeral. White as a sheet and trembly – which he'd actually felt, being in physical contact with her much of the time – but replying levelly to old friends' condolences, mustering small smiles. Then when her husband had been in the ground and the last prayers said, she'd murmured 'Home now – can we?' Facing *that* – the going home alone . . . Her weight on his arm, Elsie Scrimgeour on her other side; he'd assisted them into the back of the car and was getting in himself when she'd piped up with 'Oh, that nice red-haired girl – Mark, has she been asked?'

Amelia: smart in a pale-grey linen suit and a small hat perched forward on all that coppery-red hair. The old friends had been invited to come to the cottage for a farewell drink, which Mark was in fact providing, but Amelia of course hadn't been expected or even thought of.

'Ask her, shall I?'

'Oh do, please . . .'

He'd gone over to her – having had only a brief word or two when Henderson had lugubriously performed the introduction, and told her that his aunt would love it if she'd join them.

'How extraordinarily – forgiving.'

Old Jack had been darned right; she was strikingly attractive. In low heels – which he'd noticed – he and she were about eye to eye. An adjective that came to mind was 'elegant'; but there were others too. He'd said, 'There's nothing to forgive. Except for you to forgive me for telling the rozzers about your visit. Actually you made a great impression on my uncle – he talked about asking you back.'

'Well. How – *very* sweet of him. Thank your aunt for me? I'd love to.'

'Good. Should warn you, she still thinks you wanted to put him on the box. I'd let that ride, if I were you. She gets a bit – confused . . .'

Huard cut into the daydream: 'Before work, Mark – eat, drink coffee?'

Checking the time: the recollection running on, though – at the cottage Amelia said she'd have a glass of wine and he'd challenged that, mentioned his uncle's exaggerations about her consumption of gin and tonic, and that he thought the old boy would have been disappointed if she'd had anything else. She'd laughed, commented 'Gilt-edged, that man!' and agreed: 'But just one. And not strong, please. I've a long drive . . .'

He nodded to Huard: 'About eleven? Onze heures, manger?'

'OK.' A shrug. 'And after –' pointing upward – 'going up, eat *all*, uh?'

'Look forward to *that*!'

'En effet.' Nodding, agreeing profoundly. 'En effet . . .'

Meaning *he'd* be glad to have it over, too.

Well – because it was a boringly long dive, that was all.

'Emile, I was wondering – you said you know some of the French salvage team that's in Brest?'

Hunching his shoulders: 'Eh bien?'

'D'you know if they have friends – colleagues, or an agent – anybody – in this country? I mean en Royaume-Uni?'

'Sure. Pas *résident*, je crois, mais—'

'*Not* based in UK?'

Shake of the head, and a long sigh . . . 'Mark – somesing I tell you. I am going Aberdeen, you know – when we come Dundee? I visit – two days, two nights, one very good old friend. You know?'

'Go on?'

'*Eventyrer* arrive Dundee – what day . . . August twenny-five. You come next day, huh?'

'Day after that. The Monday.'

The funeral had been on the 24th, a Saturday. The *Eventyrer* had been due to dock in Dundee on the 25th and sail on the 27th, probably late that evening. Mark had driven from Hampshire to Brighton latish on the Saturday evening, spent Sunday clearing things up in his office, and flown up on the Monday, 26th. It had seemed like cutting it a bit fine – in Kinsman's view it had, anyway – but not all that much. Kinsman had been fretting because he'd had news that the French support-ship had left Cherbourg on its way to Brest. He'd been on the phone to Mark in near-panic: what if the ship had only to call in at Brest, embark the team and its gear and push straight on out?

'Then they're out there ahead of us – but they won't be looking in the right place, will they? As far as we're concerned, the Canadian pilots won't be with us until Monday, so what's *my* rush? Especially with Monteix there – and this ex-submariner you've found. What's his name – Lofthouse?'

At that stage he'd only known of Lofthouse's existence from telephone conversations he'd had with Lucy. He'd been fully occupied with his own business and with old Edith and her solicitor and so forth; he'd been informed of the progress of events around the *Eventyrer* but not involved in them. Whereas Lucy had been, very much so – head-hunting Lofthouse, for one thing – and too busy generally to have been able to get away for the funeral, even on a Saturday.

But – Huard had pushed off from Dundee as soon as the *Eventyrer* docked, to visit this old chum of his in Aberdeen. Lofthouse hadn't been too pleased, apparently, but the Frenchman had sworn to be back on board by noon 27th, and in any case would have had no work to do on board

during the weekend. All they'd been in Dundee for, apart
from victualling, fuelling and topping up fresh water, had
been to embark and stow several miles of wire cable.

Mark remembered that Monday night very well. Mainly
because the Canadians hadn't shown up and there was no
way they could be contacted. They'd been in Paris with
some girls they'd picked up somewhere, had told Monteix
they'd be in Edinburgh on the Sunday and come up either
that night or at the latest by noon on Monday; but by
midnight there was still no word from them. Kinsman
had been whining about it over the lines from London –
mainly at Monteix, who was doggedly following up leads
to other pilots – and drawing a blank, time after time – but
also at Lofthouse and – as soon as he got there – Mark. As if
he could have done anything about it.

Anyway, Huard had returned on time. Small mercies.
They had *one* team of pilots at least, him and the Ukrainian.
Then on the Tuesday morning one of the Canadians telephoned from Edinburgh, where he said they'd just landed,
having been delayed by circumstances beyond their control,
which of course would be explained. They were hiring a
car and would be there shortly. Relief had been enormous,
sailing time fixed for 1700. Then postponed twice, each time
for one hour, and finally put off to the Wednesday morning, and at about midnight a police car had come slowly
along the quayside and stopped at the *Eventyrer's* gangway,
bringing the news that following a car smash somewhere
near Perth the two men were in hospital concussed and
suffering from multiple injuries.

Mark had put a call through to Kinsman's flat, the place
he'd repossessed from his estranged wife, to break this
news to him. Waiting for the ringing to be answered he'd
wondered whose voice might come on the line; but all
he'd got was an answering machine. The tycoon himself
had rung back at about five a.m. insisting furiously that

they sail immediately, make do with the one team they had. In fact they stayed put; Monteix apparently still had hopes of finding other pilots, and Skaug had backed him up; Lofthouse, as it had seemed to Mark, had been rather sitting on the fence – yes-sir, no-sir to Kinsman while agreeing with Skaug that they *had* to have a reserve team. Eventually, under almost demonic pressure from Kinsman – who'd persuaded the ship's owners to lean on Skaug too – they'd sailed a day and a half late.

Mark asked Huard, 'So what happened in Aberdeen?'

'I say it was – Sunday?' Nodding to himself. 'Yeah. Sunday, l'heure du déjeuner. Me an' my frien' are in the boozer, huh? Guy there also – I see him, he don' know I see him – name Colley—'

'Colley.'

'He seeing me, goes telephone. Then come over, say hi, Emile, have drink? He is – like Monteix, set up deal – this, that. Saying have drink, I know is something he want – uh? We *don'* want, we got plenny talk about – like – long time no see, old frien's?'

'Right.'

'Coming soon then this Irish, name O'Connor. He's diver but getting old now. Has been in IFREMER when I also. Irish but mother is French, wife also, I think most time he's live in France . . . So, he also sitting down. I guess Colley has telephone him – uh? So how it is, O'Connor asking me, "You dive for some English crew now, Emile? Norwegian ship *Eventyrer*, old Dick Monteix setting it up, got a submersible from Russia?"'

'Knew it *all*.'

'But is surprise, seeing me. He's asking where *Eventyrer* now? Coming here, Aberdeen, is why *I* am here? Many question – but most is *when*, *where*. I don't tell him Dundee or sailing – when it was – Tuesday – but I'm thinking *he's* work for those others, uh?'

'Did he say why he was in Aberdeen?'

'I don' ask *him* questions. Don' want from him nothing, only fuck off!'

It might add up, he thought. Recalling Kinsman's anxieties over the support ship having left Cherbourg for Brest: they – the French – would have been as worried by hearing that *Eventyrer* was on the move. Then seeing Huard, whom they'd have known was part of the UK team, O'Connor might have thought that after all they *didn't* have to worry – he'd check on that, and report back to the other side.

Something like that. Not that it got one any distance.

'Either of them say anything else of interest?'

Avoiding eye-contact now . . . 'Don' like to tell this, Mark.'

'Tell what?'

'O'Connor say it's going roun' some old Navy guy been tellin' Monteix the gold wreck is not where they been look before? Some place else – where *you* going, in *Eventyrer*? I say don' know – he tell me bullshit, Emile! Which way from that place, how many mile?' Huard spread his hands. 'I say – tell me dive, I dive. I *don'* know where . . .'

'Why didn't you want to tell me this?'

'No – what I don' like – O'Connor ask also, "You hear the ol' Navy guy drop dead?"'

Mark watching, listening tautly . . .

'First *I* hear this. Before, nobody tell me. I think in *Eventyrer* nobody knowing? So I am surprise – O'Connor *see* I'm surprise.'

There was no obvious way anyone on board the support ship *would* have known, Mark thought. Not even Monteix – who'd been either in Hamburg or on his way there when it had happened. There'd been nothing in the national Press, as far as he knew. Kinsman had known – after Lucy had passed that message to him – and he'd have been in touch with Monteix on day-to-day issues, but they weren't on what you might call chatty terms. Lofthouse had known – from either Kinsman or Lucy, presumably, in his briefing before he'd left to join the ship in Hamburg, but he'd been a stranger to everyone else on board and there'd been a rush on, he'd have been getting on with the job, not yarning.

So in Aberdeen – this was what mattered – how could *anyone* have known?

Monteix – if he *had* known – might have passed the news out. With all his connections there, the oily-world grape-vine. Possible – but not likely. He had a stake in the success of this expedition, after all, why spread bad news about it – or *any* news . . . ? Another source *might* have been police enquiries; but Henderson hadn't mentioned any – and would have, probably, to show he was doing *something*.

He'd have a place to start now, anyway. Two names: Colley and O'Connor.

Huard shaking his head: '– then I meet you, I don't *like* to say – what he's telling me.' Shrugging again: 'Also, I think – not important?'

'Could be, though.'

Anything, better than damn-all.

Cheese and chutney again. The sandwiches had been well wrapped, seemed as fresh as they'd been twelve hours earlier. That was the length of time they'd been dived. Five past eleven now, and they'd started down just before eleven in the morning.

Huard had mayonnaise in his beard.

'Emile. You said O'Connor lives in France. D'you know where?'

Cheeks bulging: shaking his head.

'Know his first name?'

He'd swallowed. 'Frank, is call.'

'And Colley?'

A nod, as he bit into another sandwich. 'Jim.' He was back on salami and salad now. 'Jim Colley.' Touching his own head. 'He is – how you say – bald?'

'And Frank O'Connor?'

'Plenny hair, he, but gris.'

'Grey.'

'Grey, si. Small man – like me, small.'

'Right . . .'

'Tough guy.' Flash of white teeth and chomped-up sandwich. '*Also* like me – uh?'

The loudspeaker came to life. Buzzing and crackling: but interference faded as the Norwegian's voice came through. 'Crab, wakey-wakey! You receiving me, Crab?'

'Loud 'n clear, Control!'

'Better than it was – thank God. You OK, Crab?'

'Sure, sure.'

'No problems at all? Life-support, battery – OK for the next nine, ten hours?'

'I have say – all OK. What more you want?'

'Making sure, that's all . . . Crab – the salvage-basket is passing eighteen thousand feet, they're letting it down slower now. Eighteen thousand one hundred – slowed now to one hundred feet per minute. Eighteen one-fifty. OK, Crab?'

'Three minute to go. Switching lights, so . . .'

He'd touched the switch. And while he was at it, started the scrubber too. Mark with his mouth full of the last of his supper glancing at the suddenly floodlit scene outside, then quickly down again: he was having a pee, having saved it for the last minute before starting work. Taking great care, *not* looking at the viewport again, the lit and empty mudscape which for the past five hours had been left in its millennia-old total darkness. Any albino crabs one might have caught a sight of would have scuttled back into cover by this time. Cap back on the bottle and screwed tight:

bottle into plastic bag. Bottle just about full, next time start another. Fly zipped. *Now*, look . . .

The Norwegian was telling them, 'Eighteen thousand two-fifty feet. Are your lights OK, Crab?'

'*Everything* OK!'

Glancing round at Mark, eyebrows hooped in surprise at all these enquiries: like some nursemaid up there, consumed with anxiety for them, for some reason. Mark checking the gauge, reminding himself of the depth here: eighteen four-forty. At the viewport then, close up to it, seeing the wreck's sombre grey-black profile. The deepest black was inside the area of damage, where the lights from this distance and angle didn't penetrate. Off to the right, perhaps forty yards away, the silver streak of guide-wire was only partially, flickeringly illuminated.

Back in weirdland, anyway.

'Basket's at eighteen four hundred feet, Crab!'

'*There.*' Pointing, finger stabbing at the cold, wet glass. Ghostly whitish saucer-shape floating down into the upper reaches of the light. Right *in* the lights then – a clearer, harder whiteness that was going to land about midway between the guide-wire and the wreck. So OK, no problem . . . Huard had told Control, 'Visual on basket' and added now, 'Basket landing . . . OK, is down. Start work now – bye-bye . . .'

12

⎯⎯➤◆◄⎯⎯

Silt still hung like smoke-haze around the basket, its pale image fading and sliding towards the viewport's left edge as the Crab's port motor drove her round. There'd been a few seconds' anxiety when increasing battery-power had imparted no movement other than vibration: the skids mud-bound, he supposed, after five hours' immobility, and the power of only one engine at low revs insufficient to break them free. Turning now, anyway – into the direction of the guide-wire, salvage-basket out of sight and that vertical streak bright silver in the flood of light. Huard put the other motor ahead – arresting the turn, driving forward.

'Mark.' Forefinger raised: 'Unclip messenger hook.' Middle-finger up beside it: 'Puis, take pin from shackle. We do it now – OK?'

'Oh. Yeah – OK . . .'

Try, anyway. Huard's probably unintentional 'up you' sign folding . . . The point being that when discussing procedures before this dive – the clearing-up operation, collecting the pinger and releasing the guide-wire from its anchor, they'd made this one of the last things they'd do, *after* sending up the refilled basket. But this new idea of

Huard's made sense: was obvious, in fact. With the basket delivered, there was no further use for that wire, and if you freed it now (a) there'd be no need to pay it a second visit – so you'd save maybe half an hour, overall – and (b) up top they could start hauling it in right away, probably have it all up and stowed below decks before work down here finished.

Coming up close to the silver wire again. Slowing, whine of the motors fading as Huard eased his joysticks back.

Stopped. Mark switched on the port-side manipulator control. Unfolding the control unit itself then, and seeing the movements followed precisely outside there. Wincing – mentally anyway – at the onset of the hydraulics' hooting: like the creature itself groaning as it stretched that limb. Amazing, though: the sense of control one had. And the shackle, which he could see more clearly as the silt-cloud they'd brought with them dissipated, wasn't going to present much difficulty either.

Touch wood . . .

'Spring-hook le premier, uh?'

He grunted, didn't look at Huard. The shackle was actually supporting the spring-hook, which having slid down the three miles of wire had snagged on it, as it was supposed to do, four feet up from the bottom mud. Manipulator-head up and poised, in the lights' downward glare. He moved his left hand to the bare copper-coloured lever which operated the pincer-like grab. Wondering whether Huard had the video camera running: a fleeting thought that, if so, he'd get himself a copy of the film – if only to be able to convince himself in years ahead that he'd actually *done* this. He had the pincer grip open against the silver wire: sliding it down, closing the jaws a bit, and – *now* – moving it over the spring-hook. Huard's voice on his right: 'Control. Taking messenger from guide-wire. Then to break shackle – not need guide-wire no more – OK?'

'Crab – wait, before you do that?'

'OK. But quick . . .'

Referring Huard's intention to higher authority. Loft-house, presumably. Mark wasn't going to wait for it, once this part was done he'd go ahead. It made sense – and what did bloody Lofthouse know about it? Well – a lot more than *he* did. Fuck him, anyway. He had the jaws over the spring. Danger of them slipping off at this point, if you didn't have it exactly centred. But – getting there . . .

OK!

'Crab – go ahead, cast off the guide-wire.'

'Roger. Mark, you hear?'

'Yeah.' The hook was off the wire. He moved the manipulator-head to the left, about eighteen inches, opened the jaws and noted where the hook fell. Small silt-plume rising. Folding the control back in then, the robot arm mantis-like, in preparation for this next trick. Absorbed in it: like moving his own arm and hand, whichever way he wanted it, no more needing to know how or why it worked than you did when it *was* your own arm, hand, fingers. He had the grab poised close to the shackle from which the pin had now to be removed. Closing the jaws to almost shut: and edging the head forward to slide the pincer-grip over the pin's flat, two-inch-wide head. Like – so . . .

Tightening them now, getting a grip. Now, it was – should be – only a matter of turning. The wrist-joint being capable of making turn after turn in the same direction – revolving, in this case anti-clockwise, to unscrew.

'Doing good, Mark.'

Wrist-joint still turning, unscrewing the pin, and the hydraulics moaning away. This robot arm could lift two hundred pounds, so starting a possibly salted-up screw hadn't caused it any problems. Pausing for a moment: checking the grip was still tight, wouldn't slip off when there was only a thread or two left and the pin might have a tendency to wobble . . .

Pin *out*!

The shackle fell apart. The upside-down U-shape from which he'd removed the pin hung loose from the eye in the guide-wire, while the lower part fell away, a four-foot wire strop collapsing into the mud in which the clump-weight anchor had buried itself during the past nine or ten days. He loosened the pincer grab, let the pin fall: archaeological treasure for some searcher in a thousand years' time – oceans dried up, transformed into deserts. Roamed by giant snow-white man-eating crabs? Picking up the snap-hook of the messenger wire now, from where he'd dropped it a few minutes earlier, and extending the whole arm out to the side, well clear. Huard's voice grating into the microphone: diminutive, black-bearded figure hunched with the mike cupped in both hands to shield it from the hydraulics' groans – although in fact the noise had abruptly ceased, with the robot arm stuck out and static.

'Take up guide-wire. All gone. Moving to wreck now.'

'Bravo, Crab!'

'Yeah. He good, this guy.'

A flash of white teeth to show he didn't mean it. He had the port motor running astern for about ten seconds before putting the other one ahead: turning virtually on the spot, silt smoking up but carried away in the motors' slipstreams. He was turning the Crab short of the discarded anchor and its gear while Mark kept the messenger-wire well clear to port. Huard had also switched off the scrubber: now, his right hand hovered over the joystick while he leant to the left with the nearer one, reaching to the valve on the reserve O_2 cylinder. Exuding an odour of onion and salami through clenched teeth. Mark meanwhile mentally rehearsing the procedure from there on, which would be the same as it had been eight or nine hours ago – felt more like a week, but – nine hours. Couple of minutes short of midnight now, and it had been about three p.m. when they'd been at this stage before. Anyway – next thing would be to stop at the basket – which was in sight dead ahead, with the black cavern in the wreck's side beyond and to the right of it – and on arrival there snap this wire on it, while Huard would call Control and ask them to trigger the release of the bottom weights.

At slow speed, about halfway to it. Huard back at his console; he'd turned off the oxygen.

Giving the motors more power . . .

'OK, Mark?'

'Fine.' He pointed with his chin towards the gauge on that cylinder, and the CO_2 indicator – that section of the whole mass of gear which from the depths of his own ignorance was best left entirely to Huard's sharp comprehension: '*That* OK?'

Sideways glance: then what had looked like a headshake but must have been a shrug: expression of slight annoyance . . .

'Sure. *Sure.*'

Sensitive, to that kind of question?

Twelve-twenty: in position to start loading, on about the same spot they'd occupied last time – ditto the salvage-basket, in manipulator-reach on the left and slightly further back. Not wanting it any closer in than that, since you were going to have to drag it out again when it was a lot heavier. Huard had told the man in the *Eventyrer's* control van, 'Commencing to load', and the Norwegian had acknowledged with 'OK Crab, OK!' Actually, his jolly tone of voice could become irritating – if you let it. Mark judging his manipulator-distances to the gold and to the basket, finding that Huard *had* stopped on the same spot exactly. Lifting the first bar now carefully, silt floating away in a tail-stream behind it as he swung it left – bringing the

robotic forearm up while the shoulder did the turning. Stop
– down – release – into the middle of the basket. OK. But
speed it up, make this more like a one-hour job. Back for
the second bar: aware of Huard scribbling in his log, and
the crazy hooting. Wondering whether hydraulics *had* to
make such a racket, whether it would be the same in other
submersibles. Not that he personally gave a damn, he'd
never be in another . . . Bar two on its way, through the
bright light flooding the interior of the I.67's gutted carcass.
Leprous-looking steel, rust-scabbed girders, marine growth
slimy-looking. Couldn't see upward, from this close in, but
from more distant views of it one was aware of the massive
overhang of the conning-tower et cetera. Remembering also
the huge sheet of rusty steel that had slithered down, partly
disintegrating as it fell, in that video. Eventually wouldn't
the whole wreck disintegrate? It should: like any other
carcass. But more of that weight up there *could* fall . . .
Fourth bar in the basket: back for the next. He didn't think
it was taking as long as two minutes per bar, this time.
Confidence improving performance, maybe. If it could be
completed in one hour: by one-thirty, say . . . Then half an
hour to see it on its way up, maybe that again for retrieving
the pinger – two-thirty. Surface at seven-thirty?

Any advances on 0730?

Five bars loaded, sixth on its way. Time now, twelve
thirty-one.

'Doing good, Mark.'

'Too slow.' Back for the next. 'Number seven, this is
now.'

'No need for count. Fill basket – finish.'

'Reckon what we can see there *will* fill it?'

The blank look. He tried: 'Assez ici, pensez vous, pour
remplir—'

'Sais pas. Don' know . . .'

'Emile – autre question. Is it possible – est-ce possible –

to go up quicker than in five hours? Possible ascender plus vite que cinq—'

'Non. Pas possible.'

'Why not?'

'Crab must de-compress. Means slow, for go up. Also batteries then gassing.'

'Ah.' Bar number eight. Thinking, out of total non-comprehension, *Why bother to bloody ask?*

'Quarant-quatre.'

Forty-four. Huard had said there was no need to count, but he was doing it himself now – calling the score out loud, leaving Mark to concentrate on the action, just shift the stuff as fast as possible. Robot arm following the same path and the same adjustments of its joints each time, complaining stridently while its dark shadow swept time after time across the floodlit background of mud, wreckage and marine detritus. He was managing one bar every ninety to one hundred seconds. Time now 0128: and concern at not having achieved his own target – filling the basket by half-past – had been overtaken in recent minutes by a new one – a suspicion which was becoming near-certainty as the silt-covered pile diminished.

'Quarant-cinq.'

Forty-fifth bar in. He'd have paused to rearrange the white chains if it hadn't been for the probability that you weren't going to make it fifty, wouldn't need more room than you'd got.

Huard said it, then: 'Presque fini, uh?'

'Not sure yet.' He could see the outlines of only three more bars – including the one he'd just clamped on to – but when he'd loaded them it was possible that probing with the grab might turn up a few more.

'Quarant-six. N'est pas mal, Mark. Encore deux – two more?'

Shouldn't have let him count in French. Using it all the time now. Like a tiger that's tasted blood. But he was right that forty-eight bars wouldn't be too bad. Well over half a ton, on top of the amount brought up already. Not much wrong with the idea of knocking off, either. In a matter of just minutes – up, up and away?

He had the manipulator back at the heap, closing its jaws on number forty-seven. It did look like only one more. But – see what happened when you spooned into that muck.

Up – and left. Honking protest . . .

'Quarant-sept.'

Down. Release. Up: robot arm and its black shadow traversing right. Last bar, now – probably. Last ever – in one's life.

Got it. And on second thoughts, with the grab clamped on it, shifting it about in the surrounding mud. Silt rising, and mud sliding. Broken ends of piping in view before the mud flowed back around and over them.

OK. *Up.* Out of the mud and into the light. Huard intoning, 'Quarant-huit . . . Et c'est tout. Bien fait, Mark.'

This time he rearranged the chains before bringing the manipulator back. Time – 0140.

'Mark.' Huard was pointing, a forefinger touching the glass. 'Voyez – à gauche de – left side, where the gold is come *from*?'

'Left side . . .'

'*Below* where it has been – and more back?'

'*Oh*. Yes . . .'

That *was* more gold, he thought. Guessing that when it had burst out through the hole they'd cut, some of it must have been diverted that way – towards the submarine's centre-line, the very back of this devastated area. Diverted by the main rush of it as it poured out, he guessed.

'See if I can reach.'

Manipulator-head extending, elbow-joint straightening,

the whole arm rigid then and pointing into the narrower inner reaches which had been opened up by the explosive charges – not by cutting-disks on the manipulators, since they couldn't have reached.

He had the arm lowered now, and it didn't come *near* reaching.

'No good.'

'So.' Huard shrugged. 'OK. Finish.'

'Unless we could get in closer?'

He was considering that: studying in particular the slope downward between here and there. Decisive shake of the head, then. 'No. I am sorry—'

'No, I'm sure you're right. But listen – can you – est-ce possible – get hold of the mud-hose again?'

'But for what?'

'Well – if you directed it –' pointing at the out-of-reach gold bars – '*behind* that lot—'

'Quoi?'

Explaining it with his hands. The gold here: directing the hose *there*, above and behind it, so the backwash would dislodge it, wash it into the manipulator's reach?

He'd caught on, but wasn't noticeably keen. Considering alternatives, maybe – the obvious one being to call it a day. Which did certainly have its attractions. With nearly fifty bars in the basket and seventy in the last load they wouldn't have done badly. Leaving *some* for the French – if they got down here and could get at it – but damn little. And packing up now, at 0145, the prospect of being clear and ready to start the long haul to the surface by perhaps 0230 – which was the best hope one had had . . .

'Emile—'

'Oui.' Huard nodded. 'OK.'

'What—'

'We try this.'

Unexpected decision followed by immediate action: moving one hand to switch on his own manipulator control, also checking the time – 0145 – with a glance towards the scrubber – but the half-hour since he'd last run it wouldn't be up for another five minutes. Glancing at Mark again – on his knees at the starboard control-unit, unfolding it, and the manipulator doing the same outside there – 'Try only one time – uh?'

'Right. In fact—'

'OK.' He already had the manipulator-head low down to starboard, close in below the sphere, where the mud-hose and projecting nozzle would be. Peering out of the bottom corner of the viewport: a few small adjusting movements, with accompanying hoots of protest from the machinery: then his left hand was on the lever, closing the grab's jaws. Demonstration of how deftly and quickly it *could* be done. Straightening the robot arm out ahead then: nozzle secure in the grab, hose extended to what was probably its full length. Aiming the nozzle, then leaving it while he switched on the mud-pump – which would be in what they called the machinery sphere. There were three – this one, that one right aft, and the third somewhere between them containing oil. Pump running now: initial hum rising to a throbbing whine, and a sensation of jarring impact as the jet powered out. Blasting through ambient sea pressure of four tons to the inch, the system had to involve using that pressure to boost its own, Mark guessed. Reminding himself, *But don't ask* . . . Now, with both hands on the manipulator control again, Huard was adjusting the nozzle's aim: silt already swirling, rising more thickly than one had seen it up to now.

That heap was breaking up. Gold bars separating, slipping away to the left. Down into deep mud – irretrievable – between smashed, blast-compressed machinery and internal structure. Silt pouring up and outward like an atomic mushroom-cloud. Huard had switched off the pump. Which way the water-jet might be deflected hadn't been predictable, Mark realized. They'd both envisaged it washing back *this* way. This new sound wasn't the pump: as that whined down to nothing this replaced it – both motors running astern, at full revs – and the Crab shifting, lurching round to starboard but also sliding forward, *into* the wreck: not the motors' doing, the motors were supposed to be countering it, regain control, Huard having seen this coming – a mud-slide from behind, started by the jet-stream's backwash: mud *rush*, into the virtual crevasse below the wreck. He'd put the motors astern but without – as yet – any good effect. A clang – double-clang, overhead – and a loud, harsh scraping from astern on this port side. Mark had folded his manipulator in: intinctively, realizing suddenly he'd left it stuck out there.

All silt, now: blinding – a total blindfold. The motors had stopped, he realized. Crab listing to port, and at rest; no motion of any kind, no sound either.

Huard switched on the scrubber. Time, 0150. For the scrubber and life-support, exactly right. The phrase came to mind, perhaps incongruously, *First things first*. First things like staying alive. Which you couldn't do if you couldn't breathe. And if you were stuck here, how long—

'Wait for – this.' Huard gestured towards the viewports: for the silt to clear, he meant. Mark moving up close up against his, looking out into what might have been dense, sand-coloured smoke. As taut as a wire, body and mind clenched tight and the thought: Staying alive *if possible* . . .

Making himself relax, then: or trying to. Seeing Huard checking the CO_2 indicator: and now the battery voltages.

'Sorry, Emile.'

'Huh?'

'Not a good idea.'

A gesture, dismissing that. Looking again at the view-ports, the Crab's blinded eyes.

Silt-fog beginning to thin a little: the brightness of the headlights was more of an element in it than it had been a minute ago. A minute that could have been half an hour.

Huard was checking the CO_2 level again, how well the scrubber was or wasn't doing. Mark appreciating – if that was the word – that if you were stuck for any length of time the life-support factor – its endurance, the length of time you had left – became somewhat crucial.

Meanwhile, waiting for *what*?

Godot?

OK, he told himself, *make* your pointless jokes . . .

Huard murmured, 'Getting better . . .'

The visibility. If you could call it that, when there wasn't any.

Just wait. Remembering Uncle Jack's remarks and remi-niscences about control of the imagination, concentration on the practicalities of the situation you were faced with. Fine setting for such a memory – a wreck of his creation. He'd said once, 'Might've been shit-scared but they didn't show it. Truly didn't. Jokes nowadays about stiff upper lips and so on, but – I never saw one twitch. And you all got quieter. Always *was* quiet, mind you.'

'See now.' Huard broke *this* silence. Watching misty outlines of the submarine's mangled innards developing in the viewports. Very much like a photographic print developing, growing out of the thinning silt. Mark's face against cold, wet glass – not actually glass, some composite, ultra-strong – searching to the Crab's left for the white-ness of the salvage-basket. Not there, though. That way, also more directly ahead, the mud surface sloped down-ward, earlier mud-hose excavations by Messrs Huard and Bairan having left virtually a crevasse – depression, anyway – under this port side of the submarine and below its waterline, to take advantage of the pre-existing torpedo damage. The mud-slide from outside had flowed into this but by no means filled it.

On its far side, he remembered, the salvage-basket had been up against wreckage. That must have held it, and the Crab had been carried on past it. So now it had to be astern, somewhere. So if Huard put his motors astern again – and if they could cope with the up-gradient – which was by no means certain – it would be in the way. Not as heavy as it might have been, but still a fairly solid obstruction. Forty-eight bars each weighing twenty-eight pounds: call it fifty bars, for simplicity – fourteen hundred pounds. In soft mud, and uphill, and with the motors running astern – i.e. at about half-power . . .

He leant back, making way for Huard, who was also looking for the basket. Only spending a couple of seconds on it, then shifting back to his own viewport. 'Basket *here*.' Pointing astern. Hand flat then, and inclining upwards: 'Also . . .'

'Uphill.'

'I show you.' Reaching for his log and pencil, flipping to a blank page at the end, starting on a sketch. 'Here, Crab. *Here* – wreck. Pieces – pieces of wreck. Huh?' Grimace – frustration at his inadequate command of the language: but showing the Crab's port bow (or left-hand front corner) up against that wreckage. Mark nodded – guessing it would have been what had stopped the Crab in her slide. Otherwise they'd have been even further in. Visualizing it: the Crab nose-down in that hole, *completely* jammed in, viewports with nothing outside them except mud – the solid kind. So – count your blessings . . .

Peering over Huard's arm, seeing him put in an outline of the basket astern of them. Also that there was a slight shake in the pencil hand when it lifted off the paper.

Better *not* see that. Any more than he would want to display his own – anxiety. Jack Jaeger again: *Might've been shit-scared* . . .

'Un'erstan'?'

'Well—'

What he wanted wasn't a review of the situation, but a way out of it.

'Motors astern, not good.' Sign-language again, showing the up-slope behind them. 'But to turn – pas possible.' Shaking his head. So obvious it hadn't needed saying. Pencil-point on the wreckage they were up against at *this* end. 'Pas simple, Mark. Also possible more slide.'

'So – *back* out?'

'See now –' putting the log aside – 'where is basket.' Nodding towards the monitor of the closed-circuit TV, then flipping switches: the TV first, then the stern light: rapid flickering filling the screen before any picture formed. Mark suggested – it had been in his mind a minute ago – 'Tell them in the *Eventyrer* what's happened?'

'Sure . . .'

But not yet – apparently. And come to think of it, *they* should have been calling, by this time . . .

But – what the hell. Inborn reaction, nothing else: *Daddy, help me* . . . You were on your own: even if they *had* known what had happened there was damn-all they could have done about it. Huard's teeth showing for an instant in a grimace like a snarl – concentrating on the monitor as the picture formed. Surprise, surprise – close-up of the basket. It *was* up against wreckage: as it had been before, both times, the far side of it when he'd positioned it for loading – and on the level, the top of the slope. Most prominent amongst the wreckage that had held it was a bent-back, jagged sheet of plating – detail of Jack Jaeger's artistry and distinctive enough to recognize. The basket hadn't moved at all, therefore; only the Crab had been carried on past it, down-slope and turning that hind-quarter to it.

'See.' Huard's log again: adding to the sketch. Showing a manipulator extended, its grab clamped on the basket's rim: then he was changing that, scoring it out with a wiggly line, re-positioning the manipulator with its grab clamped to the nearer wreckage.

More obviously in reach. Basket too far and too high. Huard was breathing hard, Mark noticed; as he'd found he was himself. Nothing to do with CO_2, he guessed: just taut nerves, quickened heartbeat . . . The Frenchman explained, 'Puis – motors. *Here*' – pencil-tip indicating the manipulator in his sketch – 'hold here so not slide.'

'But – hold on, while –' demonstrating it, Mark's own arm out, trunk turning at the waist – 'moving her backwards – astern – or any way at *all*—'

'Si.' Jerk of the head towards the control unit. 'You working *this*.'

'OK. *If* it can reach—'

Although he saw the point: latching on so that if the Crab's movements started another mud-slide she wouldn't go with it. Huard was shaking his head, though – pointing: '*That* one not reach. *This*.'

The stern manipulator's control unit, he'd pointed at.

'See.' Flipping open the log again and starting a new sketch. Crab, wreckage, basket. The Odessan manipulator with its grab where he'd said – on that wreckage. 'Motors astern. You *hold*, but also – see . . .' The manipulator elbow depressing, shortening its reach. Pulling – exerting pull to assist the motors.

If that was possible. Even with the forward manipulators – which of course didn't come into this, but which one might at least have trusted.

'Strong enough? Assez fort, celui?'

Round, dark eyes on his: shoulders hunching. Wordless

reaction readable as *Damn-fool question, isn't it?* Also the *obvious* question, though – which Huard, not being an idiot, must have had just as clearly in mind. Mark's nod and gesture – apology, of a sort – acknowledged it: the simple fact being that the Odessan manipulator would reach, and the others wouldn't.

No evidence that there was any weakness in it, anyway. Only Bairan's fear of it. Well – no, not *only*: whatever Huard had *said*, he hadn't wanted to use it.

He was taking another look at the CO_2 reading. Scrubber still running. Couple more minutes, Mark guessed. Checking the time then: dead right – two minutes to two.

'When we get far enough back – astern – switch to this one?'

The starboard front manipulator – *if* you got that far back: and *if* the Odessan one had stood the strain . . .

Huard shrugging: using his sketch-pad again. Showing the Crab back in what had been her position during loading: pencil-tip circling, then . . . 'Here, turn. See?'

Where he'd turned her before – outside there, in the clear, where there was room to. But to get there meant getting her up-slope *beside* the basket. Loading, you'd had it close on the Crab's left. The mud-slope had brought you down: but to get back up, stern-first, on a slope that looked steeper now than it had before – and with barely an inch to spare laterally . . .

But what else? He nodded. 'If we *can*.'

Because his own job as he'd agreed it with Lofthouse was simply to do what he was told. Two heads might be better than one, but Huard was the professional. Thoughts returning then, via Lofthouse, to the team in the *Eventyrer's* van . . . 'Control haven't called us for a long time. Don't you think – call *them*?'

'Here, waste time.'

'Why?'

Because – as he'd told himself just now, having them know how things were wouldn't make any difference?

No. *Not* what he was saying: even if that had been in his mind too. Hand above his head, horizontal. 'Acier. Like say roof?'

Acier . . .

Steel.

The submarine's: because you were under some of it. Communication blanked off, therefore. Huard shaking his head: definitely short of breath. Pointing astern: 'Out, *then* call. Not so far – two, three yard? Listen – I pump now a little, make not so heavy. Little, *little* – don't want –' more sign language – 'float up, uh?'

Wouldn't be room to. If it hadn't been for the excavated sea-bed she wouldn't have got in at all, would have slid up against the overhead and stopped there. Or jammed – whatever. Still might – clearance measurable in quarter-inches, he guessed – over the sail, for sure. And there *had* been some banging around overhead . . . But theoretically – as far as he understood it – she'd been in neutral buoyancy, or as near so as damnit, since landing on the sea-bed thirteen hours earlier. Neutral buoyancy meaning weightlessness in the water – like weightlessness in space, only in reverse, the hostile element being pressure instead of vacuum. Lightening her more would give the motors an easier time, he supposed, also put less strain on the manipulator when – if – she was more or less hanging on it.

If that was Huard's intention. *As far as one understood it* was very much the operative phrase. Time now, 0201. Lucy all tucked up, oblivious, in dreamland – up there in that other world. Immensely distant world: and from here, now, barely material at all, more of a concept than reality. Here, Huard had switched off the scrubber, and let oxygen into the sphere to bring the internal pressure back up to atmospheric. Glum look at the reserve cylinder's contents-gauge as he screwed down the valve. *Now* adjusting the trim: running the pump for no more than a few seconds. Pointing with his head at the Odessan manipulator's control-unit, then: 'You like *I* do it?'

The job with the manipulator. And why not – he *was* the professional – and for the moment had his hands free . . .

'Please. Show me how.'

'Huh.' Token smile, as they changed places, Mark positioning himself to watch over the Frenchman's shoulder – a back-to-front picture, manipulator unfolding itself astern while you were looking forward, so that a move to the left here actually resulted in one to starboard. The expert demonstrating swiftly that the robot arm wouldn't reach the basket: he'd started by trying that, now had it poised over the mess of wreckage. Hydraulic moans, and the grab's jaws opening as it reached out as if of its own accord – one of this creature's arms. Contact: jaws closing over a jagged edge.

Quick and very deft. 'Merveilleusement fait, Emile.'

'Pas difficile.' Twitch of the head. Pleased, though. He was shifting back to his console. 'Starting now starboard motor. Port side too close.' Too close to wreckage on that side, that must have meant. 'You –' a wave towards the Odessan control-unit – 'you see how she goes, OK?'

Some briefing, that had been. He nodded. 'OK.' But really, *some* briefing . . . Starboard motor already running astern: sound, and slight vibration. Huard had the joystick right back, fingers of his left hand crooked round it and his dark, chimp-like, white-eyed face close up to his viewport, watching avidly for results. And she *was* moving – stern pulling over towards the point of rigid tether so that the grab was trying to twist: you could hardly have blamed it if it *had* found that strain excessive. Mark began reducing it by retracting the manipulator very slightly: and turning it at the 'shoulder'. Less exerting any force than going with it.

Scared of doing more than that?

But pulling with it wouldn't have helped. The Crab had to be manoeuvred up *beside* the basket, not below it and up against it.

Mutter from Huard: 'Bon. Bon . . .'

Nothing one could see to be all that pleased about . . .

Except that the list had been corrected; she seemed to be standing more or less squarely on her skids. *Something*, he supposed. But otherwise – Huard trying to keep spirits up, nothing much else . . . Pulling the arm back another six inches now. The Crab edging around slightly, edging her forepart out. Running the port-side motor, when Huard felt it was safe to do so, would reduce *that* problem. Meanwhile she *was* still creeping astern – on a fairly gentle slope here, steeper bit yet to come.

Yet to be *attempted*. Even with both motors . . .

Retracting the arm some more. Also loosening the grab – to allow the angle of that grip to shift – before re-tightening it. Trial and error: learning what worked and what didn't. In poor lighting, and a haze of silt that would have been worse if the wash from the motor hadn't been carrying it away.

'Mark.'

'Yeah?'

'Starting port motor now. Be ready, maybe let go?'

'That what I should do?'

'Don' know for sure. Depend – how it is, eh?'

He guessed – interpreting this, after a fashion – that under increased power, moving faster, it might become (a) impossible, (b) unnecessary, to hold on. Best way to cope might perhaps be to open the grab now: still be hooked on but not *holding* on, only have to swing the arm up, to free it.

'OK, then.'

Sudden clattering, and huge vibration . . .

The port motor: shaking itself and everything else to bits . . .

Stopped now. Switched off, clattering to a halt. Immediate relief at the cessation of the noise and shaking overwhelmed by a sense of mounting catastrophe. He remembered that metallic impact during the slide, and the long, harsh scraping. The propellers were in protective cages, but – not protective *enough*, evidently. The cage itself crushed in, fouling the blades?

All right – so you could understand *how* it had happened. Might have been useful knowledge – if you could have got out and fixed it . . . Huard had taken a quick look at the monitor – checking that the manipulator was still holding them, Mark guessed – and now back at his console, stopping the starboard motor. Shaking his head.

Net gain, maybe two feet, two and a half at most. Net loss, one motor.

And any real hope of getting out of this?

'Mark – possible now reach basket?'

'I'll try.'

But *then* what?

Lack of comment on this latest mishap might be due to linguistic limitations. That, plus the fact it was so obviously – or say *potentially* – disastrous, that there wasn't any practical solution to the fresh or worsened problems which it created. As far as he could see or guess. Or by the look and sound of him, as far as Huard could envisage either. But – continuing present efforts, meanwhile: at this moment, loosening the grab, thinking it *might* reach the basket. The Crab had been shifted backwards by less than a yard, but the single motor's slight turning effect had closed the distance to the basket by maybe another foot. And as her stern had risen to the beginnings of the steepening slope, she was now angled slightly stern-up – which might help, since the basket was on a higher level. He was starting cautiously, raising the grab from its present anchorage by just a few inches: could have latched on again if there'd been any slide. But the slope here although steepening wasn't as loose, as soft, as it was where they'd started from; danger of re-starting a mud-slide might therefore be remote now. Against that, the up-gradient astern – up to where the basket was sitting on a comparatively level mud surface – well, to get up there, stern-first and on only one motor . . .

Concentrate on what one *could* do.

Such as – now – lifting the manipulator and swinging it to the left. Hydraulics as raucous on this one as on the others. Down: the open-jawed grab passed just short of the basket's rim, the top rail, but only by a whisker; so try for the *second* rail. And he could still straighten the arm a little. Doing so: and at maximum reach then, pushing in under the top rail – and sliding over the second.

'OK.' He tightened the jaws. 'What next?'

'Try pull more close?'

If this Odessan device held together.

But even then – if it did . . .

Lucy 'd stay with Kinsman, he guessed. Might even marry him. She'd be all right, anyway – by *her* lights, she would be. Edith would be OK too, and so would Timothy; Sammy Moed with power of attorney and a million in that account would see to it all. He'd get another million or so out of Kinsman too, on the contractual percentage deal. Thank God for old Sammy. And for some degree of foresight, for which he could reasonably be thankful. Small, cold comfort . . . Retracting the robot arm a bit – mostly by drawing the elbow-joint back – and aware of the starboard motor running again, backing up this effort – as far as it could. As well as burning up precious amps. But what alternative – even if the effort wasn't as doomed as he couldn't help feeling it was – other than sit, do nothing, conserve power, wait for the O_2 cylinder to run dry?

From that point, it wouldn't take long, he guessed. At

any rate you'd soon be unconscious, wouldn't know much about it. Maybe nausea first, before coma?

She *was* edging up closer, though – inch by slow inch . . .

'Doing *good*, Mark.'

Realistically, in the past half-minute he didn't think they'd made any useful progress. Only got jammed in closer to the basket. You'd need to shift her two or three yards – uphill and well to that side of the basket – before you'd be back more or less where you'd been during the loading process, where in theory there'd be *room* to turn, but with only one motor surely no way of doing so. That was the dead-end, the ultimate helplessness. Last time, by working the motors cleverly, Huard had turned her on the spot – he'd had to because that was all the room there'd been. You didn't need to be any kind of seaman to realize that you couldn't perform tricks of that sort on *one* motor.

The starboard motor stopped.

Looking quickly to his right – and quick relief, seeing Huard had *switched* it off – that it hadn't stopped of its own accord.

'Mark – what we do now – I show . . .'

Another sketch. Mark was to shift his grab to a point on the left side of the basket's rim – for guidance as well as pulling purposes – and with the motor running astern, Huard would use the port forward manipulator to push and/or pull her up-slope. Pushing against whatever wreckage was in reach.

'Will that work?'

'Why *not* work?'

Staring at him, trying to envisage it. But recognizing – with a degree of shock – the Frenchman's desperation: the tone of it, and the look almost of anger . . .

Chances would be pretty slim, he thought. With the steepest part of the up-slope coming now. You'd have to make it work first time, too, because of the draining away of battery-power – voltages, going by Huard's reactions when taking readings, not being all that encouraging. If you ran the batteries flat – well, next stage would be the limits of life-support. No possibility of further movement: just a few hours – sitting or lying – until you suffocated. Nausea first, then . . .

Here, now, a long intake of breath. Eye to eye with Huard: who was still holding the log-book open at the sketch and angled so they could both see it. But having no contribution to make that would be of any value, none at all, having in fact only Huard's expertise to go by – well, the little guy shouldn't be asking for one's own reactions or have any interest in them, ought simply to be telling him *Here's what we do* . . .

As he had. One shouldn't have questioned it. Should have just agreed, *OK* . . . Equally, Huard should have just brushed off his question and got on with it – this plan of his that *might* work and to which anyway there was probably no alternative.

Opening his mouth to say something like, 'OK, Emile, let's try it', when eye-contact – mind-contact, even – possibly – was severed, Huard glancing away to switch on the scrubber. After – how long, that frozen, wordless consultation? A few seconds? Few minutes?

The mind played tricks. Before long, might play *worse* ones.

Wasn't the scrubber motor's hum, though. Could hear that now – *just* – but—

Huard moved suddenly, swiftly – a chimp rolling across its cage – grabbing at the mike of the underwater telephone. Chimp's companion slower on the uptake but awake to it now: loudspeaker hum getting louder, and a crackle of interference. Having come far enough out from underneath for the transponder to break through? Warning himself quickly against any euphoric reaction: what difference, after all, except that up there they'd know how and why? Which would be a good thing anyway – for some reason: his reasoning wasn't exactly rock-steady, thoughts weren't all that logical or cohesive, in these moments. Huard with one hand on the telephone's panel of controls, turning the volume up to maximum – other adjustments too. Loud clicking and whistling, the hum expanding into a gale of sound with the Norwegian voice croaking and crackling through it: 'Crab!' Gone faint again. 'Crab, do you receive? Control calling Crab . . .' Despondent Norwegian fading then: and background music, for God's sake . . . Huard cutting in: 'Control – Crab – receiving you! Not good, mais – you hear *me*, Control?'

'Crab!' A scream, almost. 'Receiving you, *jo*! Where you *been*, you bastards? You OK?'

'Inside the wreck. Was mud-slide. Stuck here now. *Near* out – why we hear you now, but—' Panting like a dog . . . 'Control – wait, Mark Jaeger explain better—'

Eighteen minutes to three. Taking a while to get their act together, up there. Well – three minutes, so far, since the end of his talk with Lofthouse, but it could have been – Christ, three *hours*. Mark was waiting now with the microphone in his hand, Huard at the TV monitor, which still showed the salvage-basket and its hoist-wire like a black snake disappearing over the far side, the white chains draped over the gold and the basket's rim at that point, and a few more yards of black wire dimly visible behind, curving away up and vanishing into outer darkness.

He – Mark – had drawn the sketches this time, for Huard's clear understanding of what had been discussed and agreed, since he hadn't been able to follow it all that well. Beating the interference hadn't been easy anyway – getting the essentials of this situation over, telling the submariner through three miles of ocean, 'Port motor's

finished – propeller smashed – we're arse-end outward'
– he'd had to repeat that several times – 'and can't turn
– well, obviously – and the mud-slope's steeper than it
was before we crashed down it. *If* we can get out past the
basket – which is still on the outside – that's to say, at the
point of access, where I was loading it – so it's partially
blocking our way out. Fifty bars in it – heavy . . . Other
thing is—'

'Crab – d'you hear me—'

Interference at some points had to be given its head. You
could only wait for it.

'Pete – we have our stern manipulator clamped on the
basket's rim. Also near-flat batteries, Huard says, and
reserve oxygen's low—'

'Mark – *wait* . . . You said *stern* manipulator. Could you
get one of the forward ones on it instead? Over.'

'No. Told you, arse-end out – and can't turn, so—'

'Roger. Have you been using the stern manipulator?
Over.'

The answer of course had been yes, using it a lot, seems
perfectly OK. But they knew something up there, he'd
guessed, which they hadn't known when the dive had
started yesterday forenoon.

Bairan let his hair down, maybe, spilt beans of some
kind?

In which case the bloody thing *was* unsafe?

Too bad. To all intents and purposes, it was all they'd
got.

Anyway – despite acoustic problems they'd evolved
this plan. Explaining it to Huard, Mark's first sketch had
shown the situation here in profile: the slope between
the basket and the Crab, and the hoist-wire trailing away
to the point over which it was plumbed from the crane
on the support ship. The Crab with its stern manipulator clamped to the basket's rim. Then, second sketch.

Same scene, but the cable pulled taut – almost but not quite vertically. Not quite, because where it was now was about twenty feet closer to the wreck than where the crane had it plumbed. So when it was lifted off the sea-bed from where it lay now it was going to swing – *some* distance towards its naturally suspended position, out there clear of the wreck. And the Crab, holding on, would go with it.

Huard had stopped the scrubber and boosted the sphere's atmosphere with the prescribed dose of oxygen. Back beside Mark then, watching the closed-circuit monitor. Struck by a new thought, though . . .

'Don' need forward lights, eh?'

'Suppose not. No.' He wasn't taking his eyes off the screen, although Lofthouse would be on the telephone again before they started winching. This waiting now – it was thirteen minutes to three – would be due to their having to get the winch-crew out of their bunks and up on deck, get power on the winch and clarify – with Carl Qvist, presumably – how this job was to be handled. Instant communication between welldeck and van, for instance.

Huard had switched off the forward exterior lights. Saving *ampères*. Viewports blind again: the single light at the stern did nothing to lighten *that* darkness. Made it darker inside the sphere as well, so that by contrast the monitor screen seemed brighter.

One snag to be coped with when this started was that the Crab wasn't directly below the basket: until now they hadn't wanted to be, the aim and most of the problem had been to get her up beside it. It meant that when the first pull came they were going to have to be lightning-quick adjusting the angle of the manipulator.

That or lose it, snap it like a matchstick.

Huard's job, thank God. The expert's.

Not that there was any certainty of this working. Better

to have the professional than the amateur on it, that was all. That and – that same old plea, *please God get us out of this . . .*

'Emile.' Mark demonstrated, using his left fist to represent the basket, right hand as Crab, and Huard's pencil as the manipulator. Left fist jerking away, danger of the pencil breaking or the Crab – well, Christ knew *what . . .*

'You telling *me*?'

'No – not telling. Only thought—'

A laugh, hand on his shoulder: 'Don' *worry*!'

Old morale-booster Huard . . .

'Crab – Control calling Crab. D'you receive me? Over.'

Jerk of Huard's head: Mark had hesitated, allowing him the prerogative – although it had been Lofthouse's voice again.

'Pete – receiving you. Over.'

'We're about to take up the slack. You ready? Over.'

'Go ahead!'

'Stand by, then. Out.'

It was already happening. Snake of wire lifting beyond the basket, only a few yards of it visible but the curve coming out of it as it rose. The white chains stirring too – lifting above the basket's contents: and now stopping: the hoist-wire *appearing* to be ruler-straight above the chains' apex.

'Crab – how does it look? Over.'

'Chains are up, wire looks – taut. *I* call the shots now – right?'

Silence. He added, 'Over.'

'Mark – Qvist tells me six inches at a time is minimal. Each time you tell us "hoist" that's what the winchman will do. Ready now, we're standing by. Good luck. Out.'

Huard was kneeling, hands ready on the control unit. Mark squatted where he could see the monitor past that noticeably outstanding right ear. 'OK, Emile?'

'Sure.'

'Here we go, then.' He put the mike up, thumbed its switch. 'Control – *hoist*!'

The chains jerked upward: the basket seemed to shiver, silt stirring around its base. Here, they'd felt the jar of it, transmitted through the manipulator, but there'd been no actual shift. A final taking up of slack was all that had amounted to.

'Ready, Emile.' Into the mike again: 'Control – *hoist*!'

On the screen he saw the basket jerked upward: then an impression of a bounce as lifting stopped and the swing began. Realizing this just afterwards: no swing detectable from this angle, only about a second later the Crab's stern as it was snatched at and dragged violently up and across the slope: Huard not only operating the control unit but clinging to it, and Mark who'd been in a crouch with his fingers hooked into the deck's slats being thrown back against the oxygen cylinders. After the first wrench the Crab was still moving astern up the incline: with nothing on the monitor except, at the bottom of the screen, the narrowing upper part of the pyramid of white chain. Because the camera at the Crab's stern was pointing up at that steep angle, of course. And silt filling the screen now. Huard, Mark realized, had coped with that sudden partly-sideways wrench somehow or other: must have swung the manipulator left in virtually instantaneous reaction – *and* lowered the grab-end . . . The grab *might* also have shifted on the basket's rail, wrenching either itself or the rail somehow, but the unit as a whole seemed to have survived intact. Essential – because they weren't there yet, weren't there by a long chalk yet, and *needed* the manipulator, trust it or not, they couldn't have done without it.

In the aftermath of those few seconds of frighteningly violent motion there'd been a rocking movement. Basket rocking – gold bars maybe settling into some more natural disposition, following the shake-up, maybe. Gradually diminishing – and finished now: all still again.

'Moment – s'il vous plaît . . .'

'Huh?'

'Trim – make better, fix up a little . . .'

Huard was adjusting the trim, for some reason: pumping oil out of the external bags, thus making her heavier, but then also shifting weight from forward to the stern. That was a separate system, using not oil but mercury, had its own small pump, also a spirit-level above the pump's switches to show the fore-and-aft level, bubble this way or that.

'For when pull is *up*.' Hand-gestures then: none of it comprehensible. Shaking his head . . . 'Crab stern up – not on hill, un'erstan'—'

'Non – comprends pas. Mais n'importe.'

Didn't *need* to understand. Fortunately. Watching the monitor again, the wigwam of chain which was still all you could see – being on the slope, stern pointing up above the basket itself; the camera at the Crab's tail-end could have been tilted downward, but Huard wasn't bothering. He knew anyway that the basket would have grounded again, in the course of its pendulum-like swing, might be about halfway to its plumb-point now. The principle behind all this being lift again, swing again. One more lift, possibly two, would – *should* – be enough to get the Crab up on to the level.

'Crab – are you all right? Over.'

'Control – Pete . . . Yeah – OK. Huard's adjusting trim. We're on the incline – stern pointing up, not much view.' He saw that Huard had finished those other jobs and was back at the monitor, hands ready on the control unit again. 'OK, Pete – ready now. Tell 'em stand by? Over.'

'Roger, Crab. Whenever you say. Over.'

'OK, Emile?'

'Sure, OK . . .'

He thought, *Get it over* . . . Thumbed the mike's switch again. 'Control – *hoist!*'

Flinging up – as if *projected* upward. Impressions were of Huard wrestling with the control unit, the Crab for some moments stern-up at an angle of something like forty-five or even fifty degrees, and in the next second toppling – stern *falling* – as he imagined it, over the ridge of the slope, the weighted bow ending its down-swing as violently as if it had hit concrete. He'd been thrown back against the cylinders again, and in that second *before* the stern crashed down had had in the monitor an extraordinary view of the basket vertically overhead and this time *really* bouncing, two of the three chains' lower ends – the hooks on them – flying free, the basket then falling this-edge down, chains flying like white ribbons and the dark mass of the bullion tipping out. The Crab's stern on its way down by then – picture lost from the screen – stern hitting – that pulverizing crash – and a recollection of Huard telling him hard knocks could crack or split penetrators. Nothing on the screen then except mud-coloured silt, and her forepart crashing down less hard than the stern had, but still no *soft* landing. Crab lurching and rocking on its skids, while he cowered, tensed against what he'd seen coming a split half-second ago, that shower of twenty-eight-pound gold bars falling from a height he couldn't guess at. Huard was on the deck too, sprawling – no loss, there'd have been no more either of them could have done than if they'd been in a tin drum going over Niagara. Bombardment starting then: a dozen or maybe twenty very loudly impacting missiles.

Then silence. They could stop cringing. The rest of it must have gone into the mud – where these others would have finished up too, bouncing off. Never to be seen again . . . And nothing on the screen except a heavy swirl of silt. Huard wriggling around checking gauges here and there, taking readings. Pausing to tell Mark in a tone of astonishment, 'Grab was – tear – torn *off* . . .'

He was rather gingerly folding the control unit. Mark watching – waiting – feeling some degree of relief at getting the customary hooting sounds, possibly indicative of compliance from the manipulator itself. And the sphere intact – apparently. He was waiting, he realized – still slightly dazed – for *bad* news . . .

Maybe they'd had their ration?

Crossing his fingers: 'Try the forward lights, d'you think?'

'*Ah* . . .'

'Crab – Control calling. What's going on? You OK? Over.'

'That last hoist. I said six inches – must've been six fucking *feet*!'

'We know. Winchman slipped up. Sorry. Qvist is going spare. Are you *OK*? Over.'

'Tell you in a minute. Emile's checking. Listen, tell Kinsman—'

The lights blazed out. So there still was power. Blazing out into hanging silt, that mud-coloured fog.

'Crab? Mark? Last word received was "Kinsman". Over.'

'Yeah. Tell him he's just lost half a ton of gold.'

Finale

—————◆—————

In his last exchange with Lofthouse over the underwater telephone he'd said – to save Huard having to say it – 'Sorry about the pinger. Only one motor, can't steer, just have to leave it.'

For the Frogs – if they were coming. It was about all they'd get. One 'pinger', a.k.a. 'transponder', moored to the sea-bed with a clump-weight anchor and a flotation-buoy to keep it upright. If the French did *not* come, might still be there when that archaeologist came trekking across the White Crab Desert?

State-of-the-art now, but by that time it might be like finding a Stone Age axe-head.

Dozing. Leaving it all to Huard now. 'It all' meaning continuance of the life-support routines, adjustments of trim – maintaining an ascent-rate of one foot per second, sixty feet per minute, eighteen thousand feet in five hours – and every half-hour responding to a brief communications-check from the surface.

They'd eaten all the sandwiches and drunk nearly all the coffee. Next meal would be in the *Norsk Eventyrer*'s saloon. Eggs, bacon, fried bread, et cetera. Or steak, maybe. With onion and fried spuds.

Beer?

Lucy present?

Amelia Hutt had stated baldly, 'Bob Kinsman's a prick.'

At the funeral: actually, after it, at the cottage, where she'd joined them for a gin and tonic but only one, since she'd had to drive back to London right away. Mark had walked out to her car with her; partly because he'd wanted to ask her whether later on she'd advise him on the subject of tracking down whoever had done this to his uncle. But he'd mentioned Kinsman and she'd made that comment, so matter-of-factly that he'd answered in much the same tone: 'Oh – you've noticed.'

'Noticing's my line, really. Trained observer, all that?'

'How did you get into your racket?'

'Well – rather a *long* story, Mark . . .'

'Another time, then.'

'All right. If there *is* another.' Wave of a hand to show him which car was hers. She was a very elegant-looking woman, he thought. As well as curvaceous. He'd said, 'I'd very much like there to be. Apart from anything else, when I get back from – well, I'm off now – few weeks, probably—'

'I know about it.'

'Ah.' He'd linked this to Kinsman getting reports of the goings-on in Brest and Cherbourg. 'Been across the Channel recently?'

'Uh-huh. My partner Frank Gillard does the foreign jobs. But we know what each other's up to, most of the time.'

'I see. Anyway – when I'm back, if the police aren't getting anywhere with this, I thought perhaps—'

'You'd like help. Of course. Any way I can. I'm no Miss Marple, mind you.'

'I'd like to see you again anyway. But tell me one thing – using your own name, even when you're pretending to be someone you aren't?'

'I *am* sorry about that.'

'Don't be. He very definitely did enjoy meeting you. Goes for me too. But the name thing?'

'Own name avoids complications. If I run into some-one later who says, "Ah, Miss Jones!" – and I'm *not* Miss Jones—'

'Not in television research either?'

'Sadly, no longer. Got fired, maybe . . .'

Huard – squatting, hugging his drawn-up knees – watching him . . .

'You dream fonny, eh?'

'Uh?'

Depth a bit less than eleven thousand. Figures clicking over in tens, therefore one click every ten seconds. At inter-vals Huard was having to lighten her, pump oil out of the expansion bags, back into the oil-sphere. Otherwise, he'd explained when they'd been leaving the mudscape, she'd soon have been going up a lot too fast.

Mark guessed he might have sniggered in his half-sleep at the memory of Amelia's comment on the character of her employer. He nodded to the Frenchman: 'Funny dream, yeah. Une rêverie assez amusante.'

'Tell of it, please?'

'Oh – difficult. Vocabulaire, tu sais . . .'

Agreeing, empathizing – it was the same for him. A spouting of fast French, telling him this. Something they had in common now, maybe to be cherished – inability to con-verse, except in the most mundane and basic fashion. But in fact there *was* a bond between them – the shared experience, what they'd been through together. One acquired – mutual respect . . . He shut his eyes again, thinking about that. Then remembered Huard telling him that his expectation of reward as formulated by Monteix had been of something like twenty-five thousand pounds, for this job. So, since with a far smaller amount of gold recovered it couldn't come to more than about half that, might ask Sammy Moed to find out from the accountants what his cut actually turned out to be, and make up the balance. With a Christmas card perhaps: *joyeux Noël* to Emile, wife an' chil'n . . .

Owed him something, anyway, for the names of Colley and O'Connor. To which if Detective Chief Inspector Henderson did not positively react – well, in any case, talk to Amelia about it. And in Aberdeen, pick Monteix's brains? He'd know those characters, for sure. Might even have conclusions of his own to offer. And from Monteix, or through him, find out where O'Connor lived in France, and talk to the French police about him. How to make contact in the right area there – well, try through either Henderson or Amelia Hutt and Gillard.

Expedition to France, then? Taking Amelia?

Eyes re-opening, at this brainwave . . .

Depth nine thousand four hundred. Roughly halfway up. Pressure out there in the darkness only a couple of tons to the square inch – or thereabouts. Kids' stuff. Nine three-eighty. Three-seventy . . .

The scrubber was running. Emerging from another period of sleep, he could hear it. Huard must have changed the soda-lime canister again too, there was another empty in the rack where there'd been a full one. Life-support system holding up at least partly through his own contribution – to wit, doing absolutely damn-all; but not making it by much either, he saw suddenly in a double-take – that was the *last* canister they were on . . . Depth-metre flicking past four thousand two hundred. At sixty feet per minute, or three thousand six hundred and sixty feet per hour. Not much more than an hour to go, therefore: and the time now – 0712.

On board the *Eventyrer* by – 0830?

Huard was on the move again, switching off the scrubber. Mark with his eyes shut, ears alert for the hiss of escaping oxygen. (To be referred to hereafter, in aquanaut's laconic phraseology, as O_2.)

Hearing the hiss now. *Just* hearing it. Couldn't be a lot left. Couldn't be anyway, by this time, but through half-open eyes he could read it in Huard's taut expression too – and the speed with which he screwed the valve down shut, not wasting any.

Leave the worrying to him. No way you could help, or change anything. Just – fingers crossed . . .

It was going to make a great yarn for young Timothy, all this.

Get a video or two out of Lofthouse, he thought – or from Huard, a tape from *this* dive – by way of evidence. Small boys tended to be cynics, smelt bullshit a mile off. Tim did, anyway. Once convinced, though, he'd love it.

'My father's an aquanaut, you know . . .'

Hell of a lot better than 'The old man's an estate agent.'

Take Tim skiing this winter. Definitely.

Or at any rate – touch wood. All things being equal – et cetera.

O_2 shut off. Huard expelling a gust of salami breath as he flopped back on the adjoining cushion. Extraordinary, when you thought about it: two men as diverse as they were, total strangers in just about every way imaginable, shut up for twenty-one hours in a tin drum three miles down and at one stage damn near finished . . .

Ending up as friends for life?

Well. Retrospectively – in memory – yes. And some lessons learnt. But in practice, amounting to what – exchanges of Christmas cards?

The money business, of course – do that. Then better *not* even Christmas cards, better to leave it at that . . . Quite another lesson learnt, though, had been in those minutes when survival prospects had seemed remote and in a review of the likely effects of his own non-continuance one had thought of Timothy and of old Edith, and of Lucy, and in her case the solution had seemed quite clearly and naturally to rest on her relationship with bloody Kinsman.

With no pain in that at all.

Three thousand five hundred . . .

He'd known surfacing might be bad, but not how bad. Descent of Niagara in a barrel couldn't have been *much* worse. The control team had asked Huard to reduce the rate of ascent, from five hundred feet upwards, giving the support-ship time to shift to within a couple of hundred yards of where they were going to surface; they had the Crab on their sonar screen, of course, but they'd been disconnecting from the Dynamic Positioning system's computer control, partly because the submersible's drift had been greater than usual so that there was distance as well as worsening weather to be coped with. In any case they'd had no reason to stay put over Jack Jaeger's kill, by then. When the Crab did surface, the Norwegian on the telephone told them, there'd be two Gemini inflatables close to them, divers ready to board immediately with (a) towline, (b) lift-line, (c) restraining wires, and the Crab would be lifted on board with the two of them still in it, rather than opening the hatch in what were now, it seemed, turbulent surface conditions and transferring them by Gemini, hoisting the Crab empty. So they were committed to this slow float-up into initially alarming and then – on the surface – unbelievably violent action. Worse than the launch had been. With the threat of a three-mile fall into black oblivion if anything more went wrong – having by this time no HP air left, Huard had said, virtually no more oxygen and the only power from an emergency-use 12-volt battery which he'd connected during that pause at five hundred feet. It was *much* worse than the launch had been. Trying to cling on, not at all successfully – and with one oxygen cylinder torn out of its stowage too, which for a minute or two wasn't funny. But then – quite suddenly – all over: they were out of it, sucked up and airborne in the new day's early, reddish sun, swinging low sweet chariot – well, hardly *sweet*, by this time – but miraculously not having been seriously or permanently crippled. The abrupt cessation of the violence *did* seem almost miraculous. In its place, smooth motion and a dramatic slow-turning motion-picture view from the ports – of the support-ship in a boil of white sea and with a lot of activity on her decks, upturned faces – and the helicopter on its pad, he saw. Restraining wires imparting solid jolts then, as they checked the swing . . . Huard grinning and shouting reassurance, crazy ape-like, ignoring blood trickling from a damaged area of his forehead, yelling, 'OK, Mark! *OK!*'

Like a half-pint, half-mad Tarzan . . .

Lofthouse told him – on the *Eventyrer's* stern deck a bit later – 'There was a call from the private eye – Frank Gillard – last night. Miss Greenstreet – Lucy – took it. He was in Odessa—'

'Gillard was?'

'Yep. Discovered the Crab's certification was up to maggots. Forged – neither in date nor in class. Monteix knew it, made sure you didn't get a whiff of it, took a back-hander of – I think she said forty thousand quid.'

'Christ!'

Quick vision – on top of all the rest of this – of saggy, pink-rimmed eyes, and those bark-stripping teeth . . .

'But technically speaking, you see, Mark – with no certification—'

We shouldn't have been down there.' He nodded. 'Right. And crikey – Bairan – he must have known—'

'Knew *something*, didn't he. High pay from Odessa not astronomic enough to combat eventual blue funk, is my guess . . . But since you *were* down there, and we were damn sure the problems had all been sorted out . . . Well,

Kinsman and Miss G had quite a dust-up. She wanted us to bring you up.'

'And he didn't. Sooner have his gold up – right?'

'Well – for the record, I have to tell you – *I* helped convince her the Crab was sound – is *now*, I mean – therefore to let you get on with it.'

'OK. But then why did she and Kinsman—'

'Couldn't tell you. Only that she's resigned, may be coming back with us instead of cruising to the Azores with him and Monica. If she does stay she'll bunk with Frieda Stenberg and Kari Damm – there's a third berth in their cabin.'

'But – hasn't made her mind up?'

'I honestly don't know. Only she wanted *you* to know – well, about the row they had, and my own persuasive efforts. Which I've now told you about – right?'

'Right.'

'Only other thing that's new is we'll be calling in at St Peter Port, Guernsey, to land the gold. Some accountancy advantage – to do with VAT, I think – delaying payment, or something.'

'Tell you what *I* can't delay much longer, Pete . . .'

He'd envisaged being able to proceed directly from the stern deck to the heads. Instead, first a surprise reception – all hands on deck clapping and cheering him and Huard as they'd climbed out of the sail and then stood with their arms round each other's shoulders, receiving applause – for having stayed alive, made it back up, presumably. Mark looking around in a state of some bemusement, recalling a time when if he'd had anything from this bunch it would have been catcalls and rotten eggs: first when he'd been refusing to reveal the wreck's position, and then for a day and three-quarters while the *Eventyrer* had been dragging her towfish up and down and not finding anything. That had been a *very* bad time, because he'd begun to have his own doubts of the accuracy of Jack Jaeger's calculations: whereas in fact the reason had been simply that the wreck was on that slope, the ridge to the northeast of it screening it from the slant of the side-scan sonar.

No rotten eggs or abuse in this reception, anyway. Only what had looked and sounded like a genuinely enthusiastic welcome. Followed by a rather odd few minutes face to face with Robert Kinsman. Lucy hovering in the background in that bright yellow outfit of hers, but her employer taking precedence, excluding all others, shaking Mark's hand and telling him, 'Want you to know I accept it wasn't your fault you lost that load. It was – believe me – a very, *very* anxious business for us up here too. Some time I'd like to hear from you how it was at your end . . . Mark, I'm going on south to Ponta Delgada now – promised my daughter, can't back out of it. But later on – when it suits you and we're all back – get in touch?'

'Well – maybe. But in any case my lawyer will—'

'Leave all that to *them*, can't we? Mark, Lucy's wanting a word with you, I know. I'll – leave you to it.'

Looking after him, wondering *So what's got into you, you—*

Amelia had put it accurately as well as succinctly, he thought. *Whatever* the sod was after . . . It was Pete Lofthouse's turn then, anyway. Lucy walking with Kinsman towards the ladderway that led up to the helicopter deck, and Lofthouse intercepting Mark before he could make a run for it – heads, shower, shave . . .

There'd been five gold bars lodged in the Crab's sail. Small bonus: on its way down to the strongroom now. Leaving him, having said his piece on matters which Kinsman had *not* seen fit to mention, Lofthouse had been on his way down there to open up. While Kinsman had gone on up that ladder to the chopper deck, and Lucy was coming back.

Pale, distressed . . . 'Mark. Mark, darling—'

'I'm in a foul state, I'm afraid.'

'You're *here*, that's what matters.' Her arms round him, hugging. He hugged her too. Her voice below his ear: 'Never in my life prayed so hard!'

'Probably what did the trick. Thanks. But Lucy—'

'Pete's told you, I know. I saw. He said he would. I asked him to – I mean, rather than me trying to say it all, protest too much—'

'He said you've resigned your job. I don't get that. After all, Pete was in favour of letting us get on with it – and Skaug must have been, too? So why the fuss and bother?'

'Wasn't *only* that. Those were – professional opinions, my view was – all right, emotional—'

'No reason to give up your job, surely?'

Thinking he might have to continue this discussion later, meanwhile make a dash for it; but she was rattling on, intimating that her row with Bob had been much more broadly based than the issue which had sparked it off. All sorts of things – personal things . . .

'Personal issues coming to a head because I was down there maybe for keeps?'

'Well – I was a touch hysterical, I suppose, but—'

The helicopter had started up. Both of them looking up that way. An expression almost of panic on *her* face . . . He raised his voice: 'Personal issues which I've – might say I've been aware of as the way things *might* have been going – or at least *seemed*—'

'That's the right word, Mark – *seemed*, to *you!*'

'Anyway it hasn't been as happy as it used to be, has it? So now I'm no longer in any danger of sudden death – or lingering death either—'

'Mark, *please*—'

'I don't think you *should* resign. Or – break off with him. If that's a good way of putting it. You're having second or third thoughts, obviously – but a blazing row in the middle of the night in extraordinary circumstances – does that describe it?'

'Well—'

'Plus a touch of hysteria. You'd be *crazy*—'

The helicopter was taking off.

'Lucy?'

'He said he'd send it back, if—' Shaking her head. 'Said it had to be my decision.'

'So *make* it.' Looking up, as the thing clattered up and away over the jumpy sea. Glancing up quickly like that had made him dizzy, for a moment: he put a hand out to the rail. Seeing Huard beside the Crab's cradle, and Bairan: Huard waving his arms around, telling the Ukrainian – and Qvist, who was joining them now – all about it . . . But – *her* decision, *his* decision . . . Looking down into the wide blue eyes again, recognizing that it was actually *the* decision, the *only* one. What was more, she knew it, Kinsman had known it, this was simply a performance. He told her, 'Call him up, tell him to send it back for you.'

Hesitation, now. A hint of dilemma. In truth it wasn't a bad act. 'If you're—' Stumbling over it: tongue-tip in sight, moistening her lips. No doubt about it, never had been, she truly was – sensational . . . 'Mark – *darling* Mark—'

He stooped, touched her cheek lightly with his stubble. 'I'm filthy – probably stink . . . Use the R/T from the van, will you?'

'The what?'

'Radio telephone, to the yacht?'

'Oh – yes. Yes . . .' Twitch of her dark head then, as if another part of her was saying 'no'. Her surprise – which she was trying *not* to show – at least that was genuine, he thought. Well – it *would* be.

'Mark –' Her hand tight on his arm: '– still love you—'

'Yup. Have to run, though. And look, *you*'d better—'

'See you *very* soon?'

'You bet. When we're home. But—'

Hang around too long, he thought – somewhat distract-edly, standing there watching her go – at last – but now she'd stopped to look back, blowing him a kiss – leave it too long, he was thinking, Kinsman might change *his* mind.